Praise for Cherrie Lynn's
Leave Me Breathless

"Lynn's third Ross Siblings novel is a blazing-hot success that blends touching romance with sinful sensuality."
~ *RT Book Reviews*

"*Leave Me Breathless* is an emotional journey of self discovery for two very different people who simply wind up together on the same path. It's beautiful, it's crazy, it's wonderful....it's life."
~ *Guilty Pleasures Book Reviews*

"For readers looking for a hot and steamy story that actually says something...*Leave Me Breathless* is one you won't want to miss."
~ *Long and Short Reviews*

"...brash and raw and completely addictive."
~ *Fiction Vixen*

Look for these titles by
Cherrie Lynn

Now Available:

Unleashed
Rock Me
Sweet Disgrace
Far From Heaven

Leave Me Breathless

Cherrie Lynn

SAMHAIN
PUBLISHING

Samhain Publishing, Ltd.
11821 Mason Montgomery Road, 4B
Cincinnati, OH 45249
www.samhainpublishing.com

Leave Me Breathless
Copyright © 2013 by Cherrie Lynn
Print ISBN: 978-1-61921-502-3
Digital ISBN: 978-1-61921-379-1

Editing by Linda Ingmanson
Cover by Angela Waters

First Samhain Publishing, Ltd. electronic publication: November 2012
First Samhain Publishing, Ltd. print publication: October 2013

Dedication

To everyone who read *Rock Me* and asked me for this story. Without your encouragement, it wouldn't have been written. Every single word of this is for you.

Chapter One

Being single on Valentine's Day sucked.

Macy Rodgers sipped her Dos Equis and mused that plenty of people would argue with that statement. People happy in their carefree singlehood. And that was fine. She could remember when she'd been one of them.

Her two best friends, Candace and Samantha, cackled over the noise in the too loud, too warm bar. Apparently, some joke had passed between them while Macy had been pondering bolting for the door to spend the night at her apartment in blessed solitude watching *Bridesmaids* for the five hundredth time.

It wasn't so much that she lamented the fact she had no one to send her flowers or give her chocolate or take her out to a candlelit dinner before tumbling her into bed. That was partly it, but no...the worst part about being a single girl on Valentine's Day was well-meaning, relationship-entrenched friends who decided you were a pity case and took it upon themselves to distract you from the oh-so-obvious tragedy your sexless life had become.

She did enjoy seeing the girls, though. Lately, it didn't happen often enough.

"So what is this surprise you said you have for me?" she asked Candace when she could get a word in edgewise. Candace and Sam had been all aflutter about something when they dragged Macy out of work earlier, and now not a word about whatever was in store had been mentioned since.

Her friends exchanged glances and furtive grins. Great. They were about to embarrass the crap out of her somehow. Candace checked her cell phone, tapped out a text and then slipped it back into her purse. Macy didn't like the self-satisfied look on her face. "Patience, my dear."

"Is this...a good surprise, or an I-get-to-maim-you-later surprise?"

"I honestly can't answer that," Samantha said, and Candace nodded her agreement.

Macy slapped her hands on the tabletop. "That's it, I'm out—"

"No!" Each girl grabbed a shoulder to keep her seated. "It's okay, Mace," Candace soothed. "Relax."

Macy swept her gaze around, frowning. What the hell could it be? A male stripper? Surely not in here. And surely her friends knew better than to cook anything up between her and Jared.

Yeah, to put the nail in the coffin of her Valentine's night, her ex-boyfriend was here. They'd remained on good terms, and she even gave Jared's twin daughters horse riding lessons twice a week, but that didn't mean she wanted him to see her in here practically wearing a big sign over her head that flashed *Still Single After All These Years!* in neon letters. So far, she'd mostly managed to keep the entire bar between them. But he was divorced from the woman who'd come along after Macy sent him running, and he didn't appear to be with anyone now, so that was a bonus.

Maybe they bought me a male escort. Ha! Sure. The girls might have grown as tired of her aching dry spell as she was. As much as she wanted a relationship, there just wasn't time to seek one out—or even a little oasis in the drought. Between managing her parents' outdoor retail store and riding lessons at their ranch and seeing her friends whenever her schedule and theirs would allow, she felt stretched too thin. Wound too tight. A man thrown into the mix might very well cause her to snap.

Then there were days like these that made her look around and feel like a colossal failure for not having achieved what her best friends had: true happiness.

She tried not to dwell on it. Mostly she didn't, but tonight was different. Dammit, twenty-five wasn't old, but when she considered the fact that she'd like to have kids before thirty, she didn't have a whole lot of time.

"Brian wants to pierce my nipples," Candace announced.

Or...maybe she was doing pretty well on her own, if that's what true happiness entailed.

"*Awesome.*"

"Oh my God! You're not going to let him do it, are you?"

Candace looked back and forth between Sam and Macy and shook her head. "See, I played this conversation out in my head before we got here. So far it's going exactly as I had envisioned."

"You know us so well," Macy said wryly, taking a swig of her beer to chase down the swallow she'd nearly choked on. She should've grown accustomed to Candace's little Brian-related bombshells by now, but she hadn't. In Macy's mind, he belonged with Ghost in a far-off universe she would never understand, and there they would both remain.

Ghost. Given the funk she was in, the last thing she needed was to start thinking about *him.*

"That is so freaking hot," Sam said, still shouting to be heard over the blaring country music. "But you get a hands-on demonstration of Brian's hotness every night, right? Lucky girl."

"He's hot because he wants to drive a needle through her nipples?" Macy asked.

"Well, I brought it up to him," Candace said. "He doesn't push anything on me, and if I told him no, he'd back off. But I'm having fun letting him try to convince me." An impish smile curled her lips, an expression Macy never would have imagined seeing on her sweet friend a year ago. Hell, a year ago, she'd have laughed riotously at the thought of even having this discussion. With *Candace*, of all people.

But her once straight-and-narrow best friend now sported three tattoos, a belly ring, hot pink streaks in her blonde hair and who knew what else. All thanks to her tattoo-parlor-owning boyfriend, Brian Ross. Why Brian and Candace weren't together on their first Valentine's Day as a couple was a mystery Macy hadn't quite put together and didn't really want to ask about. But if they were talking piercings, then everything must be hunky-dory in their world.

11

Sam gave a quasi-orgasmic little shudder. "You'll have to tell me what it's like. I might think about doing it too."

Sam was another story. This kind of talk from her didn't come as any surprise.

"He says it really heightens sensitivity."

"It can also eradicate it altogether," Macy muttered, knowing she was whistling in the wind. "It can do permanent nerve damage. Not to mention—"

"That's what I've heard," Sam said to Candace, but it wasn't in response to Macy's warning.

"Yeah, it drives him crazy when I play with his rings."

"There's also rejection, infection—"

"Brian knows what he's doing, Mace."

Macy subsided, pulling her lips between her teeth to contain the retort. Of course. Brian knew everything. The sun came up in the morning because Brian said it should. Forget simple *facts*.

"But he might get so excited because it's *you* he's piercing that all the blood will drain south from his brain, and he could really mess up." It was one of the more sensible things Sam had said.

Candace laughed. "Maybe I'll spring it on him out of the blue one day when we're just hanging out at the studio. He won't have time to think about it much."

"And neither will you," Sam said. "That's the only way I'd have the nerve to do it. If I had too much time to think about it, I'd chicken out."

"You guys really are crazy. Why even do something if it scares you so much?"

Candace shook her head. "It's not that it's *scary*, Macy. But it's...intense. It's a rush."

"Why do people bungee jump? Or skydive?" Sam said.

"Freaking adrenaline junkies," Macy muttered. "All the piercing and tattoo stuff, you say it's all about your 'self-expression', but in the end I think it's simple addiction."

"For some people, maybe. And it's fun. We're not depraved or something because we like it. My thrill is simply different

12

than your thrill."

"That stuff you did on a horse, Mace? See, that's crazy to me," Sam said. "You were a little kamikaze. When I would watch you barrel race, I could hardly pry my fingers apart to peek through them."

"Agreed," Candace said.

Macy shot a glare at Sam. "Bad analogy. We all know how that ended."

Both the other girls clamped their mouths shut, and Macy instantly wished she could take the words back. She covered her face with her hands. "I'm sorry. I'm just...I don't know. I love you guys. But maybe this was a bad idea."

"No, I'm sorry," Sam said quickly, her rueful expression making Macy feel worse. "It's not you. That was a totally insensitive thing for me to say."

"But you know I'm usually not so sensitive about it," Macy said. "At least not with you guys. Like I said, I don't know what's wrong with me."

"You need to get laid." Candace declared this as if it should be obvious to everyone.

Macy rolled her eyes and laughed. "That's never been a cure-all for me, and you know it."

"Maybe because you haven't found someone yet who can do it right." Candace twirled her barely touched beer bottle between her hands. "It's too bad Ghost left, huh?"

She hadn't wanted to think about him, and she damn sure could've done without the mention. Ghost was Brian Ross's best friend and employee who had somehow managed to short-circuit Macy's brain. It was the only explanation for the way she'd behaved with him that one night all those months ago...

Now was the time to choose her words very, very carefully with her friends.

"It wouldn't have mattered. I was...intrigued by him. But I'm just being realistic here. He and I have absolutely nothing in common. I mean, it's not that I need to have my perfect match or anything, but we have to mesh in at least *some* areas." She took a breath. "Besides, it's a moot point. Who knows when he'll be back?"

"But what if he did come back?" Sam asked, twirling her dark blonde hair around her finger and grinning. "I mean...what if he walked in the door *right now*?"

Macy shrugged. "I've made up my mind."

"You're saying you didn't mesh in *any* areas? You admitted you had a lot of fun when you hung out with him. That's a start. A good start."

"He's not my type. A more not-my-type guy never existed."

"Oh, throw the types out the window," Sam said. "He's hilarious—"

"He's *wrong*."

"That's what's so great about him, though. Plus he's sexy as hell. I love bald guys. I love their shiny heads. Just makes me want to rub 'em. And rub some more. And rub and rub and rub..."

Candace and Macy dissolved into laughter as Sam carried on with her imaginary rubbing. "What would he need me for?" Macy asked Candace. She jabbed a thumb in Sam's direction. "Send this one over to him. For all his head-rubbing needs."

"No, no," Sam said, sobering. "I've got Michael. Not that he'd ever shave his head. But I think when Ghost gets back, you need to give the guy a break."

She'd given him one. But her friends did *not* know that, and did not *need* to know that, because they would be insufferable. Oh yes, she'd given him a hell of a break. And then she'd run scared because of how good it had been. And then, just like that, he was gone, off to Oklahoma to deal with a family crisis. Months had gone by. She knew he still kept in close touch with Brian, but Macy hadn't heard a word.

So it was crazy to think anything could come of it now. She'd messed up too bad, too soon—but that was okay, because like she'd told her friends, their pairing didn't make sense. At all.

Even if the thought of giving him another "break" sent a shiver all the way to her toes and had warmth curling in decidedly more interesting places on her body. The beer she'd imbibed wasn't helping, but she should have known better than to think it would take the edge off. It only made it sharper. That didn't stop her from taking another swig.

"His dick is probably pierced," Sam said thoughtfully.

Macy barely forced the swallow of beer down her throat before erupting in a groan. How in the hell was she going to play *this*? "Oh God."

"You don't know what you're missing," Candace said with a singsong tone, leaning over to pinch Macy's arm.

"Wait a minute. Does he...is it... I mean, do you *know*?" Sam asked Candace. "Did you guys have some ménage action going on over there?"

"No! It's not like I've *seen* it, jeez. I'm only speaking from experience with Brian. But it's a pretty good guess."

Candace had guessed right. He had some kind of piercing going on down there. Macy hadn't seen it herself—it had been too dark in the car for that—but she'd felt it. God, had she ever felt it. "You guys have got to let up on me. I'm...going to be traumatized."

"Macy, just give the guy a shot."

"There's just one problem with that. He's. Not. *Here*."

Sam's brown eyes flickered over Macy's right shoulder, in the direction of the entrance. Her face brightened in a big grin. "Are you so sure about that?"

"Huh?"

Candace followed Sam's gaze and squealed in delight, jumping from her seat and darting off behind Macy's seat.

All of a sudden, she was terrified to turn around and see what was coming her way.

Oh. Surprise, surprise.

She leaned toward Sam, knowing murder was in her eyes. "You did not."

Sam's eyes twinkled. "Oh, honey, we did. We're tired of you moping around. I don't know what happened with you and him, but clean the slate. Here's your chance." Her words ran so close together at the end, Macy knew he was almost at their table. What was she going to do now? Her heart halfway up her throat, she was forced to glance up when it seemed a shadow fell across her.

Yes, she was absolutely going to maim her friends later.

Chapter Two

Ghost. Where the hell had he gotten a name like that? He wasn't particularly pale. Well, maybe a little. But not what she'd call ghastly or anything. There was nothing...*wraith*like about him at all; he was a very solidly built six-two or so, judging by how tall he stood next to her five-six.

Tattooed. Pierced. Shaved head, though right now he wore a black baseball cap pulled low over his eyes with the hood of his black sweatshirt over it.

The very antithesis to everything she wanted, or thought she wanted.

He was looking right at her, shit-eating grin in place, one dark eyebrow arched. That stare was like a vacuum. Or a black hole. Nothing could escape it.

"Hi!" she managed to squeak—she even managed a smile. When his own grin widened, she pushed herself up from her seat to give him a hug. Unfortunately, her legs were Jell-O, and his tight squeeze kept her from getting up close and personal with the floor even more than those shaking appendages did.

He felt good. Warm, despite the chill of the night air still clinging to his hoodie. Familiar, even if she'd only been in those arms once.

And then he had to speak, the rumble of his voice raising the hair at her nape. "Hey, killjoy."

Everyone laughed, delighted at the return of the nickname he'd pinned on her not long after they'd met. She only then realized Brian had joined them too, and was snuggling into the booth next to his girlfriend.

"I have a question," Ghost announced as Macy reclaimed her seat and he slid in beside her, practically cramming her against the wall. His denim-clad thigh was rock hard against her bare one. Sam claimed what was left of the seat on his other side, so she was well and truly trapped. A shiver worked through her. "What in the actual fuck are we doing in a *honky-tonk*?" He motioned around at the plethora of cowboys and cowgirls dancing to the twang of country music.

"It's Macy's night," Candace said as Brian nuzzled her neck. "She got to pick."

"Ah, that figures. Just don't get Brian and me into a brawl with any rednecks. I'm not too stoked to spend the night in jail when I just hit town." Ghost winked at her. God, those eyes. If she hadn't been so close to him she'd have sworn he lined them. But no, his bottom lashes were just that thick. If he had hair on his head, she figured it would be the same chocolate brown as his goatee—and maybe he did have hair on his head now for all she knew. She couldn't tell. But he was one of those guys who definitely rocked the look—his features were strong enough. He stretched out both arms, one behind Macy and one behind Sam, and tilted his chin up at Brian. "I've got double your fun, dude."

Brian, who was mid-smooch with Candace, broke away and laughed. "Good for you. I've got all the fun I can handle right here." Candace blushed and beamed.

Macy nearly jumped out of her skin when Ghost leaned over and put his lips mere inches from her ear. "Am I crashing your party, babe?"

Her face flamed. Did he know about her Valentine's pity party? "Crashing *my* party?" she echoed lamely. "No, not at all—I mean, it's not a *party*. Nor is it mine."

He chuckled. "All right." Her friends were sending her knowing little smirks.

Yes, maim them.

But she couldn't deny that it was good to see him, that a part of her had missed him and she hadn't completely realized it until now. "Are you back for good?" she asked.

He shrugged, pulling his arms back and resting them on the table. "Nana's doing...okay, considering. She's settled in the nursing home and my sister lives near there, so I figured I might as well come home and try to get back to normal, at least for a while. I'll be going up there to visit a lot, though."

His grandmother, who'd raised him from the time his parents were killed in a car accident when he was six, was in failing health. Macy didn't know much beyond what Candace had told her about the reason for his absence, but she couldn't help noticing the set of his mouth seemed a little grimmer than it ever had before. He must've been through a lot in the past few months.

"I'm sorry," she said softly.

He shrugged again, but she wasn't fooled by his feigned nonchalance. "She's hanging in there. So how've you been?"

"Oh, fine. Great. Working a lot, you know."

A waitress came by and placed beers in front of him and Brian. Macy's pulse hadn't slowed a bit. What was up with that? He was pressed in so tight against her she wondered if he could feel her racing heart, prayed that he couldn't.

Ghost leaned across the table toward Candace and Brian. "Candace," he said, and for a moment Macy thought he might actually say something sincere. No such luck. "I really advise against leaving him alone with me again. Two hours away from you and he was coming on to *me.*" Everyone else at the table broke up in laughter. It only egged him on. "I mean, I know he wants me. He's made it clear. And I'm growing weak, I tell you. I *missed* him. If he does it again, I'm gonna give it to him."

Brian was shaking his head. "God, we missed you," Candace said.

"Did we?" Brian asked.

Ghost reached over and placed his hand on Candace's. "Don't worry, though. We're not going to shut you out. You're welcome in our house anytime, sweetheart. I might even share him with you. As long as, you know, I can watch."

"This is actually pretty hot," Samantha observed, and Macy could just imagine the sparkle of interest in her eyes.

"You can come too," Ghost said, earning Sam's flattered laughter.

"Fuck you, man." Brian punctuated the words with the

corresponding hand gesture, but Macy could tell from his grin he was probably the happiest person at the table to have his friend back.

"I'm trying *so hard* to resist that, Brian. You damn moody Capricorns. You would only hurt me in the end." Ghost drew a shaky breath. "But I think...I'm ready to take the chance."

"You're gonna have a hell of a fight on your hands," Candace told him, running her hand over Brian's shoulders. "This one belongs to me."

"Yeah. Stake your claim, baby. Save me from him."

As the banter continued to fly and Macy slowly began to realize it seemed to be just business as usual here, she found herself relaxing. She took a deep breath, distancing herself from the memories of what she'd allowed to happen between her and the guy sitting next to her not long before he left town.

That's it, get a grip. So what, you were confronted with him when you least expected it. That would throw anyone.

But it shouldn't. Not her, no way. He was part of a world so separate from her own it would be impossible to bridge the chasm between them. He was heavy metal. She was all country, all the time. He wouldn't belong at a rodeo, and she wouldn't belong at one of his wild concerts where they probably sacrificed live chickens or bit the heads off bats onstage.

That was that. Since the accident that had damn near killed her, sensibleness had ruled her world, not impulsiveness. And certainly not her heart or hormones. She was the one in control here, and she liked it that way. If she messed up, she could at least mess up knowing she'd weighed all her options and made the best decision possible.

Even being miserably single on Valentine's Day wasn't enough for her to give up that position.

Ghost's thigh pressing more firmly against hers was cause enough for her to do a quick reassessment.

Sam's boyfriend joined them soon afterward, and the party was in full swing. Despite everything, she marveled that she had friends who were willing to do this for her—take her out, buy her drinks, try their damnedest to hook her up—at the expense of their own plans. Surely Candace and Brian had way better things to do on their first Valentine's night than babysit her. Same with Samantha and Mike, even though those two had been together for years.

"It's damn good to be back with you guys," Ghost announced, holding up his beer. Bottles clinked as they toasted.

"I'm just damn glad to have you back at the parlor." Brian grinned, sporting two dimples that belied the image conveyed by all the ink and piercings and longish, unkempt black hair. Unkempt mainly because Candace couldn't keep her fingers out of it.

"Oh, is that all I am to you? Your fuckin' workhorse?"

"Whatever else you are, the fact remains that we've been busting ass since you left. And now Connor is gone, so it's not going to get much easier, but at least it won't get any worse."

"I can't wait to get back at it. But I can't help you out Saturday."

Brian's bottle thunked down. "What?"

"Can't do it. I need to practice with the guys."

"But dude. *Saturday.*"

"I'm picking up what you're puttin' down, honey bunch, but they've been panicking, and they're going to end up kicking me out of the band if I can't make the next gig."

Macy grinned at the endearment he tossed in. Brian shook his head wearily, sitting back in his booth. "You son of a bitch."

"Look at him pout. Don't pout, dude. Ross the boss will get the job done."

"A helluva lot easier if I had the Ghost with the most at my side."

"Aw. Is that a proposal? See how he loves me? Candace, you don't stand a chance."

"Oh, will you stop? Macy's going to get jealous." Candace winked and jumped in her seat as Macy kicked her in the shin.

But Ghost didn't miss a beat in his exchange with his friend, shaking out his right hand. "I might be a little rusty, Bri. Can I practice on you?"

"*Hell* no."

He leaned his shoulder into Macy. "How 'bout you, sweetness?"

"Um, no. No ink for me."

"Yeah, good luck with that," Candace said. "She would shriek and run if that needle came anywhere near her."

"It's not the needle. It's the thought of being permanently...marked." The very idea gave her the heebie-jeebies.

She nearly leaped out of her skin when Ghost's pinky finger traced the edge of her denim mini under the table, coming dangerously close to her flesh. "Maybe it's all about who's doing the marking."

"No, it's definitely..." His fingertip grazed the top of her thigh. She tugged the collar of her shirt. "Ahem. Definitely not something I'd be interested in, no matter who's doing it."

"But I do it so well."

Macy narrowed her eyes at him, pouring all the will she had left into her gaze. He did a lot of things well. That didn't mean she had to let him do them to *her*. "I know you do. But it's still not happening."

His hand left her leg, and he faced forward again, his grin as infuriating as she'd ever seen it. "All right."

Dammit! When she realized her words hadn't held a double meaning like his, she hated herself. She hadn't meant for him to stop touching her.

His long fingers curled around his beer bottle, when they could've been on her. She watched in helpless fascination as he lifted it to his mouth...one of the best mouths she'd ever seen. Full, sensuous and defined, yet devastatingly masculine. She could apply that description to every part of him, really.

"Macy!" A familiar voice yanked her from her greedy perusal. Her heart sank as she looked up and saw Jared passing by their table, a big grin on his handsome face that clearly said he'd had a few too many.

Forcing a smile, she gave him a wave she hoped was a good balance between friendly and dismissive. "Oh, hey. Good seeing you."

"You'd better dance with me before you leave here, girl!" And the crowd swallowed him back up.

Brian and Candace exchanged a glance and although Ghost didn't comment, she could sense the tension that seeped into his body.

Really, though, what did he care if she danced with someone else? They'd had sex in his car once. Very, very good sex, but still. Big freaking whoop.

She drained her beer and waved for another.

Somewhere in the steady stream of alcohol the waitress— God bless her—kept bringing Macy, she found Ghost's hand back on her upper thigh. She might have even grabbed it and put it there herself. Who knew? All she cared about was that his palm was big and warm and possessive, and she liked it being on her skin. But damn if she was going to let him get between her legs—

Oh. Crap. He was going there. And she was letting him. The heat coming from her sex wouldn't allow for anything less. She squirmed in her seat, the tiny motion making her skirt ride up more. His fingertips followed, feathering higher up her leg. He was almost to the edge of her panties, which had gone incredibly damp since—

"Are you all right, Macy? You look a little flushed."

Just as Macy began to nod quickly, Ghost swigged his beer and jerked his head in her direction. "She looks that way because I have my hand up her skirt."

He did not just say that. She went ramrod straight and snapped her legs closed as everyone at the table laughed. Candace said, "Oh, you wish."

All Macy had succeeded in doing was trapping his hand between her thighs.

His thumb stroked across her skin, coaxing her to open to him again. She wanted to. But if he was only going to embarrass her in front of everyone...

She gave the back of his wrist a little warning smack. Beside her, his lip quirked, and he gave her a *see what I did there?* wink.

For the hundredth time, she thought about how she should stop this. She should. But his fingers curled into her flesh and pulled her leg against the side of his and dammit, she didn't stop him, couldn't stop him. Once he had a little room to work with, he slid his hand up, bunching her skirt again.

She killed her drink and ordered another. His pinky finger grazed the silk of her panties, silk he'd find wet and little barrier to the throbbing flesh beneath. Thankfully, the waitress plunked her refreshed drink in front of her, so she had something to hold on to instead of clenching her fists on the tabletop. With the side of his finger, he was drawing tantalizing circles around her aching clit through the damp fabric.

The conversation still went on among her friends. Ghost even took part, laughing and wisecracking while her freaking toes curled and she resisted the urge to...*bite* him. Or grab his head and kiss him wildly. Or fling herself back in the booth and have a heaving orgasm. Or at least help him pull her panties aside so he could sink his fingers into her.

But she knew he couldn't. Crammed together in the booth, he didn't have the range of mobility for such a feat without giving them away. She couldn't let him make her come or—

"I think you should slow down," Candace said, and it took a moment for Macy to realize she was talking to her.

"What?" she asked, cursing the husky breathlessness of her own voice.

Candace chuckled. "Don't you think you've had enough?" Enough...no, not nearly enough. Her gaze alighted on her empty drink. Shit. She meant alcohol. How many had she had, trying to squelch the heat and keep her hands busy so she didn't yank Ghost on top of her right in front of everyone?

"Damn, Mace, you do look shitfaced," Brian observed.

Her brain took stock of her situation. She was breathing erratically and half leaning on Ghost. A trickle of sweat tickled at her hairline. Her lips felt swollen and...numb, and she swept her tongue across them. Not that her friends could tell, but her nipples were hard as pebbles and rasping against the cups of her bra. "I—I need some air." She turned pleading eyes on her accomplice beside her. His fingers disappeared from between her legs, and it was all she could do not to go after his hand. Return it to where it belonged. She wasn't drunk; she was in the wildest sexual heat she could remember since...oh, hell. Since the last time he had her this hot.

"I got her," Ghost said, sliding from the booth and helping her across after him. She tried to fix her skirt and could only hope she did a passable job as she stood up beside him. For a moment, she feared her shaking knees wouldn't support her, and she leaned against him as the only stable thing in her world.

"Are you all right?" Sam asked, sounded genuinely concerned as she reclaimed her seat. Michael scooted around to sit beside her now that there was free space.

"She's straight," Ghost said. "We'll go outside for a few."

"Take care of her," Candace called after them as he led her away from the safety of their booth.

"Oh, I intend to," he said, for Macy's ears only.

Chapter Three

The rush of cold air outside snapped her out of her lust- and alcohol-infused funk. Somewhat. She was still aware of the slippery pool of need he'd inspired between her legs. That heat wasn't dissipating any time soon, at least not due to any external climate change.

Macy expected to stop outside the door so she could catch her breath, but Ghost kept a hand on her arm and steered her into the parking lot.

"Where are we going?"

"I'm parked out here. Thank *God* I brought my car." The last few words were muttered under his breath. He still hadn't answered her question, but her mind hadn't stopped functioning so much that she couldn't figure out the answer.

Ghost drove a shiny black '69 GTO convertible he'd restored to mint condition. Her heart rate tripled when it came into view. She hadn't been in that car since—

He wasted no time unlocking the door and ushering her into the backseat...*oh, the backseat.*

And then the door closed and they were alone and it was dark and he was in her arms, his mouth hot on her neck.

"I can't do this here," she managed to pant. But her traitorous body made no move to shove him off. She only pulled him closer, shoving off his cap—yes, still shaved—and absorbing his body heat.

"Just like you couldn't before? Just like you couldn't let me get under your skirt in there?"

"I should have stopped you."

"Mmm. But you didn't. And you're not going to now, are you?"

It was the million-dollar question, and she couldn't think

about it right now while he was nibbling her earlobe, his big body pressing her down into the seat. She had to spread her legs to accommodate him in the cramped space. Her skirt bunched around her hips again, leaving only her panties as a barrier. One thrust of his groin against her throbbing clit would probably have her coming. Despite her protests, she needed this orgasm like she needed the next beat of her heart.

"We have a penchant for backseats, don't we? What's it gonna take for me to get you in a bed?" She couldn't answer him, and she didn't think he expected her to. His mouth trailed a hot path down to her breast; she could feel the gust of his breath through her T-shirt. He didn't spend time there, though his hand came up to knead her as he continued his journey downward. She stiffened when he lifted the hem of her shirt and licked a circle around her belly button.

"Fuck, Macy." His tongue darted into the indentation. "You smell so fucking sweet. You were perfuming up the place in there. I couldn't wait to get you alone."

Heat roared in her cheeks until it almost matched that being generated below. She turned her face into the back of the seat, the upholstery cold against her dewy forehead.

She shouldn't be doing this. She didn't *do* this. Not again. But she was deluding herself if she thought she wanted it to end.

Satisfied with his exploration of her belly button, he pushed the denim of her skirt up farther, and his fingers slipped into the waistband of her panties. She whimpered as he pulled them down, knowing she was bared to him now, though she still refused to look at him. He folded her knees to her chest to divest her of her panties.

"Aw, I did get you primed, didn't I?" His fingertips slid though her swollen, slippery folds, sending an electric jolt through her. She arched against his touch, trying to get those fingers on her clit where she needed them. So gently she wanted to scream, he breached her, only stoking her need as he slid deep and swirled. Her mouth opened in a silent moan. Her nails bit crescents into her spread thighs so that she didn't grab his head and shove it down to the maelstrom of fiery desperation he'd created between her legs.

"Look at me." With his free hand he moved one of her thighs to his shoulder and then stroked it from knee to hip, exerting just enough pressure with his short fingernails to leave tingling trails in their wake. The soothing caress gave her the courage to turn her face to him.

Once she obeyed his request, she couldn't look anywhere else. There was just enough light filtering in to cast his face half in shadow and put a wicked glint in his eyes.

"You want me here?" he asked. Her internal muscles gripped his slowly thrusting finger.

She sighed as he slid in another, cried out as he pushed them deep and brushed her clit with his thumb. "Yes! Soon." It was all she could think about. He squeezed a third finger in, and it effectively stilled all her restless movements. "Oh...God." She held motionless, whimpering, as he worked his fingers deeper.

"Christ," he whispered. "You feel good. I can't wait to fuck you."

"Why don't you?"

"I will, baby. Long and hard and deep, just like you need it." To punctuate his words, he dragged his fingers out to their tips, teased her and thrust them back in. "But not in the car this time."

She moaned, grinding her hips on his hand. Dammit, they'd done it before. "Why not?"

"We just can't. Not here. Not the way I want to do it, we can't."

Everything she'd been thinking in the club, everything she'd been thinking for the past few months without him, was effectively negated with everything she was feeling right now. "I *need* it. Please, I need it so much..."

With a curse, he shifted and dropped lower. How he was folding himself down to get on her level, she didn't know, nor did she care. A burst of his breath tickled across her mound, then his thumb was gone, replaced by something warmer and far, far wetter—

"Oh God, yes!" she cried. It inflamed him. His free hand grasped her thigh and yanked it wider, an animalistic sound tearing from his throat. She grabbed whatever she could to anchor herself to the earth as he licked devastating patterns over her clit, hooking his thrusting fingers to find the spot on her upper wall that had her hips wrenching off the seat. Suddenly she couldn't open wide enough, couldn't get close enough. Her staccato whimpers dissolved into one long unending plea.

His mouth covered her clit, and he sucked, wrapping his arm across her stomach and holding her steady as she convulsed against him. The incredible tension she'd been carrying around for so long inside her broke in waves and waves of ecstasy. She didn't care if anyone outside heard her keening cry, or his answering groan that vibrated against her pussy. Her thigh muscles locked, she shuddered, she writhed, she fell back on the seat and contemplated passing out as he wrung the last vestiges of her orgasm from her.

Gently, he relinquished his suction on her, giving her several long, slow licks to bring her down. His fingers pulled out, and he lowered his kisses to her opening, tasting the remnants of her pleasure.

Macy wanted to stretch and purr like a cat. She couldn't stop undulating against him, and dismay set in as she realized she wasn't done yet. He'd only taken the edge off. She needed more. Needed him inside her, filling her.

He lifted his head, and she grimaced at the emptiness he left behind. Little aftershocks skittered under her skin, making her shiver. But he was trying to get up, and she had to move to let him. She backed into the corner of the seat, and he slid onto his, blowing out a breath and rolling his head on his shoulders.

His expression was unreadable, but the firm set of his jawline hinted at the same level of pressure that had been holding her captive until he set her free. He unzipped and stripped out of his hooded sweatshirt, but he wasn't moving to unfasten his pants—didn't he expect to get his after giving her hers? Apparently not. She didn't know what to say or do, so she leaned down and began the slightly mortifying task of trying to locate her panties on the floor.

"Missing these?" he asked, and she glanced up to see the scrap of silk dangling from his index finger.

"Um, yeah." When she tugged them, he hooked his finger, a slight smile turning up one corner of his mouth. Macy giggled when he didn't give them up without a brief tug-of-war, but finally she claimed them.

He'd made her feel so good. It had been exactly what she needed.

"You know, I don't have to put these back on yet." She reached between his legs and ran her hand over the bulging ridge in his jeans. He had to be hurting. It looked like pain that crossed his face when she touched him.

But he seriously must not have meant to go any further. He caught her wrist and pulled her until she was straddling him. His hand smoothed down the outside of her right thigh. "Thank you for wearing a skirt tonight. From the bottom of my heart, thank you."

"You're welcome." Macy shivered as his fingers' journey back up her leg took them under the hem. He must've thought she was cold; he grabbed his discarded hoodie and wrapped it around her shoulders. She pushed her arms through the sleeves, inhaling deeply as his scent engulfed her.

"Now that that's out of the way, talk to me. What have you been doing since I left?"

"Nothing." She snuggled down onto his chest.

"No other guy's been in the picture?"

She grinned into his neck at the surliness that entered his tone at that question. "Jealous?"

"Not when I was the one with my mouth on your pussy two minutes ago, no."

Macy didn't know if she'd ever get used to the way he talked to her. If it had been anyone else, she'd have been appalled, but with him...she loved it. Part of it was knowing he didn't give a damn what anyone thought, not even her. She would love to be that way. It just wasn't in her nature.

"You seem different," he said.

Now that gave her pause and a little surge of unease. She leaned back to look at him. "How so?"

He trailed a finger down her cheek. His gaze held hers, seeing way too much. "Are you sad?"

"I—" What did she say to that? In a scant few minutes, he'd pinpointed something she'd been hiding from everyone for months. Something her best friends hadn't even picked up on...any more than usual, at least. But she couldn't confirm his suspicions. He might think it had something to do with him. "No."

That too-knowing gaze narrowed. "Then are you always a mopey drunk? Because that would suck."

She scoffed. "I'm not drunk. Not *that* drunk. And I don't know why you think I'm...mopey."

He shrugged. "Well, let's recap. I seem to remember us hooking up in this very backseat in the parking lot of Dermamania. I remember us talking almost until the sun came up, laughing our asses off at stupid shit. You amazed me with how funny you were. I wasn't expecting that. The 'killjoy' thing was a private joke because we both knew I saw a different side of you than anyone else. And then suddenly, you pulled a disappearing act. Then I had to cut out of town. From what I've seen of you tonight, I wonder if you've laughed much since then."

As he spoke, she'd busied herself by absently tracing the collar of his T-shirt, not meeting his eyes. "You know what's crazy? Despite all that, I don't even know your real name."

He sighed at her diversion. "Seth."

"Seth," she echoed, needing to feel it on her tongue. "That's nice. Why didn't you ever tell me before?"

He suddenly became very interested in picking at something invisible on her shirt. "You never asked."

Her bottom lip trembled. Great, so he thought she was a stuck-up bitch on top of a depressed drunk. "But I did wonder. What's your last name?"

"Warren. Why?" He smirked. "Gonna run a background check on me? Need my date of birth too?"

His question gave her a split second of panic. She really didn't know much about this guy. Her brain ran through its usual gamut of worst-case scenario. *Does he have a record? Is it bad? What if he's done time or something? Some of those tattoos look kind of suspect—*

He sat back, exasperated. "Jesus, Macy. No, I'm not a convicted felon."

"I wasn't thinking—"

He put a hand pensively to his chin. "Except for that one bank robbery that went terribly awry..."

"Quit making fun of me."

"Hey, it's cool. I didn't mean anything. You okay?"

She only nodded. Considering how tiny her voice had just sounded, it would be nonexistent now, so she didn't even try to use it. He must have noticed her distress, because he reached up and rubbed her shoulder.

Macy couldn't help it; her eyes closed, and she knew he didn't miss her intake of breath. All at once, she wished she could feel the warmth of his skin on hers. She'd been denied it even before. Bare flesh to bare flesh...his hard, hot and intricately marked, hers soft and yielding and...

The images swirling through her mind had her temperature rising again. He smelled unbelievably good. Something darkly sweet and almost lemony. She didn't want to talk; she just wanted to bury her face in his neck and breathe him in, knowing he tasted as delicious as he smelled.

"So what's the story?" he asked.

The question pulled her back to reality hard and fast, and the truth came tumbling from her mouth before her brain gave it permission. "I don't belong."

She didn't have to see his reaction. His surprise was palpable. "Don't belong where?"

"Here. With you. With...them." She lifted her head and nodded in the direction of the club.

"Says who?"

"Me."

"Well, then...what are you doing here?" Genuine curiosity laced the words.

She shrugged.

"So...what? Are you thinking about turning your back on everyone, just going your own way?"

"No, I don't want that. At all."

"Look," he said, "I don't know what happened to you to make you go from the cool, confident woman who always made me feel a million times better when we hung out to the wad of misery I'm seeing right now, but it can't be that bad. Let it go. That's my philosophy: learn to not give a fuck, at least about petty shit. Life will be much simpler."

Her eyes burned as she looked at him. She rarely cried, and when she did, it damn sure wasn't in front of guys she hardly knew. "I'm glad I made you feel better."

"Well, now I'm trying to return the favor. So talk to me."

"I just can't relate to them anymore. Ever since Candace and Brian got together... I mean, I'm happy for her, all right? Don't get me wrong. But things are different, and I guess I don't take change well. Like, at all."

"I hear you. It was the same around the parlor before I left. We like her, but sometimes it's a pain in the ass knowing the boss's girlfriend is hovering around. So you're not alone. We've all had to adjust."

"But she's been my best friend since we were kids."

"Yeah, and Brian and I have been tight for a long time too. I think you're letting it get to you too much."

"We just seem so distant now. And hard as I try, I can't be...one of you."

"Okay... Macy, what exactly are *we*?"

She scoffed at him. "Come on. Look at me, and look at you, and then tell me the difference. I'm not implying anything bad. I'm only saying... The things you guys are into just aren't for me, and vice versa, and that's the way it is."

"I honestly think any distance between you and your friends is a figment of your imagination, or was put there by you, because you're so hung up on all this 'us and them' stuff. You should, you know...lighten up a little, killjoy. That's all."

Macy couldn't help but smile at his playful ribbing. "I try to. It just never works out and we always end up arguing. We were on the verge before you guys showed up."

"There's no reason you can't simply live and let live, you know."

"I know. It just sometimes makes me think I'm not interesting enough for... Never mind." She snapped her mouth closed. Alcohol had loosened her tongue enough tonight. Here she was spilling her guts to a guy who was extremely adept at scrambling her brain, not to mention other parts of her anatomy. Their conversation had done little to mitigate the need still pooled between her thighs—his voice only exacerbated it.

"Not interesting? What the hell are you talking about?"

"I don't know. Maybe I am drunk."

"Naw, you've been pretty damn coherent, so don't cop out now."

Her mind was going in a hundred weird directions, and she decided to follow one of them to see where it would lead. "I tried to talk Candace out of getting with Brian in the first place. I could've caused her to miss out on her happiness. What if she had listened to me?"

"She didn't. So it's a moot point."

"But sometimes I feel like I'm talking myself out of happiness too. I can't seem to make myself...shut up."

She caught the flash of his white teeth even in the dimness. "Do you need someone to shut you up?"

"Honestly? I really think I do."

"I might be useful in that capacity." His voice positively dripped with suggestion. There was no question what he meant. His big hands rested casually on her thighs now, and oh, how she wanted to feel them move up higher. She couldn't deny this thing between them. She'd never been able to.

The excitement she needed in her life, the spice she was craving, was sitting underneath her. Something to get her through this slump, or whatever it was. A bridge across the gap to where her friends stood waiting for her to catch up. She didn't want to get left in the dust—she loved them too much.

Mere inches separated their lips, and she knew he could feel her breath gusting against his mouth. She felt his. Still slow and easy, it tickled her lips. He hadn't kissed her on the mouth since they'd slid in the car. He'd *never* kissed her, even before, a fact that had kept her awake at night. But that encounter had been like this one: sudden, rushed, scalding hot. Now, she craved more of a connection, needed it so much it eclipsed everything else.

Gently, she took his face in her hands, looking over him. Outside the car, someone shouted and a few vague, colorful shapes moved past the fogged back windshield toward the club, but she didn't worry anyone could see them.

She closed her eyes. Leaned toward him. Covered his mouth with hers.

A shudder went through him, and his hands—*finally*, at last—moved up her thighs. His lips were as delectable as they looked, and he let her tease them apart so she could lick her way inside and taste him. A whimper escaped her; his fingers dented her flesh. His tongue slid past her teeth, flickering against hers in a sinuous dance that had her moving shamelessly on his lap. Sliding her hand behind his neck, she pulled him closer, needing more, fantasizing about what else he could do with his tongue, what he'd just done to her. A groan slipped from her throat.

Macy wanted to weep with relief when his hands moved around to her ass. Surely he would touch her again in all the places her body was going wild. Instead, he let her go, then gently cupped her face until her clinging lips were forced to relinquish their claim on his. She gazed at him reproachfully.

"Damn, girl," he breathed. He sounded as ragged as she felt. "I think I can handle 'mopey drunk' if you're also 'incredibly horny drunk'."

She tried to lean toward him again, but he evaded her, and she resisted the urge to pout at him. "What are you doing?"

"What are *you* doing?" he returned, his voice a low, sexy

murmur that went straight to all the neediest parts of her body and resonated.

"Isn't it obvious?"

His answering chuckle was dark. "With you? Babe, nothing with you is obvious. Tomorrow, are you gonna just pretend tonight never happened, like you did before?"

"What does it... I didn't really think you..."

"Didn't think I cared? Thought I was only after the score?"

It had crossed her mind. Her guilt-ridden mind. It had helped her sleep at night, that was, after she'd tortured herself over the fact he hadn't kissed her.

Her cheeks burned, and she was glad he couldn't see her well enough to detect the color that must be raging in her face. Even now, she didn't like to think about how she'd lost control of herself with him. She was in serious danger of doing it again.

"I know you can't forget it," he went on. "I remember how many times you came. I felt it each time, how tight you squeezed me and how wet you were. I remember your breathing in my ear, your begging, your nails clawing my back."

His words and the way his dark eyes held hers, frightening and feral, were quickly turning mortification into something far hotter. He couldn't leave her like this, so unfulfilled. Judging from the thick ridge in his pants, which she'd been brazenly rubbing against, she wasn't the only frustrated one.

Fine. He won.

"Go home with me?" she asked softly.

Seth's eyes closed, and his head met the back of the seat. She wanted to attack his throat with her lips. She settled for tracing a fingernail down the line of one of the tattoos peeking above the neckline of his shirt. "I told Brian I'd help out at the parlor so he could have the night off with Candace. That's why I hardly drank anything tonight. I need to get over there."

"Brian won't...?"

"Let me off the hook to get laid while they work their asses off? I wouldn't ask." He raised his head to look at her. "I imagine you'll be passed out by the time I'm done."

His mouth was back in close proximity to hers—too close.

She brushed it with her own. Gave his bottom lip a tiny lick.

"Fuck," he said in a whispered rush, though he still didn't move. "Macy...you're gonna get me fired before I even get started back." He captured her lips with his, once, twice, again. She ached and throbbed and pressed as close as she physically could. His hand disappeared under her shirt, sliding along her bare skin until his fingers covered her breast in the lacy cup of her bra. The pleasure centers in her brain positively purred. Her nipple pebbled against his palm, chafing against the fabric. He must have felt it; he circled the tight peak with his thumb.

"Yes," she whispered, arching into the much-needed contact. He leaned forward to kiss and lick at the base of her throat.

It was crazy, and it was everything she'd tried to convince herself she didn't want, but God, it felt too good. His thumb slipped under the lace of her bra, and she nearly lost her mind. In one swift movement, he shoved her baby tee up over her breasts and growled a string of curses, lowering his head to nip and lick the swells above her bra cups. She stroked his smooth head and almost grinned at the memory of Sam talking about bald guys. It was different, but she liked it.

Oh, she liked everything about what he was doing. If only he would do it a little faster...

"Please," she whimpered, shifting in an attempt to bring his decadent mouth in contact with her puckered nipple. Even through her bra, she didn't care; she just needed the contact. He kept deliberately avoiding it, teasing her without mercy. She'd never ached so much as when she was with him, but surely this time it had to do with the wrongness of this situation, almost shirtless in his backseat in a bar parking lot. With a guy she shouldn't be with.

And last time?

Well, last time had almost been the same circumstances, save for the location. It had been dark and isolated, not in clear view of everyone in a busy parking lot. Whatever the reason, she couldn't stop moving against him, and those little moans coming from her throat that sounded like some other far more

Cherrie Lynn

wanton woman than she—surely it was some alternate universe she'd fallen into affecting her actions. Her reactions.

Seth pulled his head back. It was all she could do not to hold it in place. "I gotta stop, babe," he said, bringing her world to an end. "I'm sorry, but if I don't now, I won't be able to later. And we'll get caught." Carefully, he slid her shirt back in place. Then his dark eyes flickered up to hers.

She could only imagine how she must look. The vast majority of her hair hung in her face. Her lips felt swollen, her eyes heavy-lidded. Tremors shook her hands and pretty much the rest of her body.

"Beautiful," he whispered, as if he'd read her thoughts. He reached up to smooth her hair back. "Hey. I can't go with you now, but if you really want to continue this later, you know…my number's still good."

Pulling her bottom lip between her teeth, she tugged his hoodie closed over her chest. He expected *her* to initiate the booty call the next time she got horny? "You have my number too," she pointed out.

He flicked the end of her nose. "The major problem there is you quit answering."

Maybe I will now. Oh yes, I will. "I'm turning over a new leaf."

He chuckled. The tip of his finger caught her under her chin, and it was enough to still all her movements. "Tell you what. If you need help with that, if you need someone to shut you up, or even if you just need to walk on the wild side every now and then…I'm your guy. I'll show you the ropes, killjoy." The way he winked at her made her think he meant that idiom way more literally than most people. "I don't know what kind of identity crisis you're having, but I think you're all right."

You're all right. It didn't sound like much, but for some reason it meant a lot coming from him. It made her want to kiss him again—and again and again—but that time seemed to have passed.

"Thank you," she said softly. "Just one thing, though…"

"Yeah?"

38

"Can I call you Seth?"

A grin broke over his face. "I think I can live with that." And then a fist battered against the window.

Chapter Four

"Oh my God. Were you getting it on?" Candace's eyes were big as saucers as Seth pushed the door open.

"Well, not anymore, thank you. Jesus, what kind of friend are you?"

Macy shoved her face into his shoulder, trying in vain to squelch laughter she didn't understand given the awkwardness of their situation. At least they'd stopped when they did. Except...dammit! She'd never put her panties back on. At least his hoodie was big enough to hide anything that might still be on display.

"Is it safe?" Brian asked from an area near the back of the car.

"Yes, they're clothed, at least."

He appeared next to his girlfriend. "Hey, man, we're ready to jet. But Candace's car has a dead battery. Do you have cables?"

"Do I have cables. You know what's pathetic? That you *don't* have cables. Have I not taught you anything?"

Macy didn't miss Candace's little grin as she extricated herself from the car so Seth could get out. Immediately, she staggered on her weak knees, which she knew had very little to do with the beer she'd imbibed and everything to do with what he'd just done to her. Seth reached out to steady her, his knowing gaze holding hers for a moment longer than necessary. Cold air tickled the bare heat between her legs, and she shuddered.

"You straight?" he asked. She nodded, suddenly feeling shy under the scrutiny of their friends. As she was about to glance away, she noticed the white writing on his black T-shirt, visible now that he wasn't wearing his hoodie. It read *Why can't you all die and leave me alone?*

Macy frowned. Jesus. Couldn't take him anywhere. But then, public appearances probably wouldn't be part of this deal, anyway.

Any relationship between them would be founded on nothing but sex. Raw, hotter-than-hell sex. It was all they had, really—this blazing chemistry that turned all her once coherent thoughts into grainy mush.

Was there anything really wrong with that, though? All her life she'd prepared herself for The One, and subsequently examined each potential relationship only for its capacity to become something enduring. It didn't have to be that way. Seth was a guy she wouldn't want to be with long-term, and it was probably a good thing because he didn't strike her as the relationship type anyway. But damn, he made her hormones growl.

Even now, her gaze clung to him. Maybe that had always been the case, but it was ten times worse at the moment. She was fidgety, empty, unsatisfied. Still aching, still trembling deep inside. She should've asked him what time he would get off, and if she could get him off soon after.

He and Brian set about their task of jumping Candace's car, and Macy found herself laughing with the other girls at their banter, especially when Ghost made the crack about Brian and Candace being so into each other even their vehicles were copulating. They had her car up and running in no time. Then Brian and Candace spent a good five minutes saying their overly affectionate farewells, even though they were only parting for the few minutes it would take to drive back to their apartment in separate vehicles.

Damn. All her friends were going to go home and get laid. Macy was in for yet another long, lonely night if she didn't do something. Seth had already grown exasperated with his friends' exuberance and headed back to his car, but not before prying them apart long enough to make sure Candace was driving Macy home. Since Candace rarely drank more than a swallow or two, they'd dropped Macy's car off at her apartment and ridden together, but it touched her that he would look out for her. She took a deep, fortifying breath and followed him.

He glanced back at her as he popped open the driver's side door. Without hesitating, she walked up to him and put her arms around his neck. "Thank you."

"For what?" he asked, sounding genuinely puzzled. Seriously?

"For making *me* feel a whole lot better."

His mouth found her ear, sending a chill skittering down her spine when he flicked the lobe with his tongue. When he spoke, the warmth of his breath only intensified the sensation. "How 'bout I call you later tonight?"

Giddiness erupting inside her, she nodded into his shoulder, then stepped back and realized she was still wearing his hoodie. "Oh, here." As her hand came up to take it off, he caught it with his own.

"Looks better on you. Stay warm." So what if it had a big white skull with flaming eyes on the back and her fingers didn't reach the end of the sleeves? It smelled like him, and that was so good she might just sleep in the damn thing from now on. With one final dazzling grin, he dropped into the driver's seat. She'd begun to shuffle over to her friends when his voice called her back.

"Hey, Mace."

Desperately trying to hide her own smile, she glanced back.

"Happy Valentine's Day."

Damn.

Considering he was Ghost's best friend, Brian Ross sure was a sadistic bastard. He'd apparently been in on this ploy to throw Ghost and Macy together for a little Valentine's rendezvous, but he'd still agreed to let Ghost unknowingly give himself a galloping case of blue balls by letting him work the rest of the night.

Or maybe that had been his ploy all along, since Ghost sometimes got the impression Brian didn't really like Macy.

Yeah, he was a sneaky one.

Dermamania, Brian's business and Ghost's beloved place of work, had been trashed to hell and back in the midst of Brian and Candace's tumultuous genesis as a couple, and it had broken everyone's hearts. But at the moment, Ghost would have burned the place to the ground and roasted marshmallows over the open flames if it meant he could get out of there any sooner. It was no easy feat to sit on a stool and concentrate on precision when he had a raging hard-on that refused to subside because he couldn't get the memory of Macy's gorgeous tits out of his head or the sounds she made when she came. He was practically in pain.

Which was why, at nearly one a.m., when they generally tried to close, he wanted to cheerfully maim the trio that walked in the door and asked if they had time to get some needlework done.

NO, you assholes! I have a five-alarm situation here!

But all the other artists looked at him, deferring to him as usual in Brian's absence. That, at least, hadn't changed since he'd been gone. And they all knew Brian usually wasn't about turning away walk-ins if it was a small job and they were available. So Ghost wasn't about it, either—even if he had to grit his teeth as he told their clients, "Sure, no problem, come on in."

So the others wouldn't see the outright devastation on his face, he ambled over to his station to set up, trying to refrain from sighing heavily. Or throwing a cuss fit. He tapped out a quick text to Macy, letting her know he was held up. And then, because fate was a bitch, he got stuck with the client who was female and pretty and petite and must've worn the same damn perfume as Macy...or maybe her scent was just ingrained in his head forever. It wasn't that he deliberately tried to make comparisons, but Macy had lit a fire in his blood and it roared on unchecked. Right now he saw her everywhere he looked, and he would until he was inside her again.

Macy didn't text back. Which, in her condition, wasn't good.

His client perched on his table and looked up at him with

big blue eyes. She'd picked out two little cherries as the design she wanted, which he could bang out in ten minutes. Maybe fate was smiling upon him at last.

"Where do you want it?" he asked her and groaned inwardly as she whipped her shirt off to reveal a black bra that thankfully covered everything except her upper swells. But that was the spot she indicated with an almost seductive slide of her finger.

"Here, please."

This was just what he needed. He inhaled, trying to clear the fogs of lust from his brain, and concentrated on Winds of Plague blaring over the sound system. "Drop the Match," indeed. Macy had better not pass out before he could get to her; he had a lot of frustration to work out.

Five minutes into the design, Starla made the announcement they all dreaded to hear. "Oh, hell. Psycho ex incoming."

It was met with the usual panicked chorus of "*Whose?*" —they all had them, unfortunately—but Ghost had a familiar sinking feeling in his gut without even looking up. His own psycho ex was like a bloodhound. He'd been back in town for six hours, and she'd already sniffed him out. He knew it.

The door dinged as it opened. Starla cheerfully called out, "Hi, Raina!"

Damn, damn, triple damn. He still didn't look up, even as Raina struck up a brief conversation with Starla as if the two had ever liked each other. Starla, bless her, was trying to run interference for him, but she wasn't having any luck. Raina made a beeline for him.

"Hey, you. When did you get back?"

That throaty voice, purring into the mic at their gigs, purring into his ear, had once driven him wild. Now it was like nails down a chalkboard. Finally, he threw her a glance. Tiny, ferocious and—he couldn't deny it—completely fucking crazy from her multicolored dreads to her heavy black boots, she wasn't someone he'd wanted to welcome him home tonight. Shit. "Today."

"Brian said it was your grandma. How is she?"

Brian had even talked to her? Ghost channeled every bit of focus on the line he was drawing. His client was watching this exchange with amused interest. "Hanging in there."

"That's good. She's a sweet lady. Tell her I said hi."

She won't even remember who the fuck you are. She barely remembers who the fuck I am. "I'll be sure to do that."

"Do you have time to do something for me after you're finished?"

Seriously? "Something as in..."

"Well. I thought I might get you to cover this up." She let her coat slip off her shoulders and lifted the hem of her lacy black shirt, revealing her milky skin and turning so he could see the lock tattoo on her lower back. He'd given it to her. And the matching key was still in a similar area on his own back.

He couldn't resist a chuckle as he went back to drawing. Yeah. Completely fucking nuts. "Do you think that's good practice? Is there some reason why I have to be the one to do it?"

"Well, you did it in the first place."

"Yeah, so?"

"And I kind of want it gone."

"Then go have it lasered. If I cover it up, it's just going to be something else *I* did. Right?"

She scoffed and let her shirt fall, shrugging her coat back on. "Well, I'd just rather get it covered, and you're the best."

"Brian could do it if you come back another night."

"Brian hates me."

And I don't? Luckily, he refrained from saying it. There might have been a meltdown of nuclear proportions if he'd let it slip, and he tried to keep his drama out of here. Besides, he didn't hate the girl. He was too indifferent, really, to hate her. He just hated to see her.

"Raina, the fact remains that I'm busy at the moment, as you can see. And we're shutting down in a few. It's been a long day for me. If you want to come back some other time and talk about it, that would be awesome."

"Did you change your number? I've really wanted to talk to you. And since it was Valentine's, I was hoping—"

"I did change it. A while back."

"Avoiding me?"

He completely stopped what he was doing and turned on the stool to face her, pouring all the warning he could into his eyes and his tone. "Raina."

She huffed and gave an annoyed little toss of her head. "Fine. I'll leave. But we do need to talk. It's about the band. I asked Mark about coming out to Austin and singing with you guys again. He was all for it."

"Why? I thought you were done with that."

"I've just been feeling the itch, you know. Anyway. I just wanted to make sure you didn't have a problem with it."

"Are you fuckin'—" He broke off and sighed. "I'm not getting into it here, but I think that's a really, really bad idea, and you know it is too."

She sniffed and fell silent for a long, long time. Uncomfortably long. Finally, she said. "See ya," and flounced toward the door. He turned back to his client with an apology. God. It wasn't as if that was embarrassing as hell or anything. And two minutes after Raina left, he was getting outraged texts from Brian, whom Starla apparently had alerted in case there was trouble. Great. Interrupting the boss and his girlfriend on Valentine's night with this stupid bullshit. Now he'd have damage control there too.

And then there was Macy who, if she hadn't passed out yet, was waiting for him. Seeing Raina had been like dousing cold water on his hard-on.

Who the hell was he kidding? There was way too much piled on his plate, and with his nana finally going into the nursing home and the tension in the band due to his absence, the heap just kept getting higher. If he was honest with himself, he knew it wasn't the greatest idea to add Macy to the top of it. She didn't deserve to be yet another thing he'd cast aside or neglect altogether.

That didn't change the fact he couldn't wait to see her.

Chapter Five

Macy flopped away from the annoying sound blaring in her ear. She was about to contemplate unconsciousness again when her body suddenly acted on its own behalf before her brain could catch up. Her hand shot out for the iPhone—which her face had apparently been pressed against—and it took more than one attempt to slide the stupid freaking button all the way across to answer. The garbled word that came out of her mouth sounded something like, "Hulluh."

"You passed out, didn't you?" a deep voice accused teasingly. A voice she'd been hearing in all the torturous sex dreams she'd been having since, yes, passing out.

"No."

He laughed. Dark and rich, it made her rub her thighs together. She glanced at the clock and saw that it was almost two a.m. "Are you off?" she asked.

"Finally. I texted you earlier but I doubt you got it. How are you feeling?"

She did a quick assessment. Head throbbing, check. Stomach not quite right, check. Truthfully, she felt like crap. Somehow still horny crap, but crap all the same. And definitely not sexy crap that was anywhere near ready for a man to come over and make passionate love to her. "Um...I'm..."

"Yeah, I was afraid of that. I had kind of a bad night myself. It's okay."

"I'm sorry. I'm an idiot."

"There's always tomorrow. Or tonight, since it already is tomorrow."

"I wanted to see you," she confessed. "Where are you?"

"Driving home, now. But I want you to stay on the phone with me, okay?"

She rolled over on her back and got as comfortable as she could, smiling at nothing in particular. "Okay. What about your night? You said it was bad?"

"Torturous."

"Really? Why?"

"Just was."

"Tell me."

"Because I was so hard from what we did in the backseat that I couldn't even think about anything else. I'm hard right now, just hearing your voice, so sleepy and sweet."

The words shocked her eyes wide open, and all at once she was more awake than she'd ever been in her life. Would she ever get used to him? "Oh," she breathed.

His voice dropped even lower. "Where are you right now?"

"Lying on my couch."

"Hmm. I'd like for you to get up and go get on your bed. Will you do that for me?"

At the moment, she'd do anything for him. But she knew where this was going. Her heart began to thud double-time. "I've never done the whole phone-sex thing before." Nevertheless, she got up and shuffled toward her room, yelping as she sustained a bruised shin in the process.

"Well, good." Somehow that last word was full of wicked promise.

"I mean, I might not be very good at...talking. Like that."

"You don't have to say anything. I'll say it all. Believe me, right now just hearing you breathe will get me off. Leave your room dark."

Breathing she could handle; she was already doing way more of it than she needed for survival. Ignoring the lamps, she crawled onto her bed. He must've heard the covers rustle when she pulled them back.

"Take off the covers. I don't want there to be anything on the bed except you, right in the middle."

Heat flared through her. "Can I keep a pillow?"

"Just one."

The rational daytime Macy might've said this was a little

absurd. The still half-tipsy, aroused, middle-of-the-night Macy couldn't strip the bedding fast enough. "Are you home yet?" she asked him as she worked.

"Getting there."

She crawled back onto the mattress, now only with the fitted sheet and one pillow, and positioned herself directly in the middle. She put him on speakerphone as she settled. "I'm done," she said into the darkness.

"Are you still wearing the same thing I last saw you in?"

"Yes."

"Lose it."

The command in his voice shuddered through her. She wasn't used to taking commands; she was used to dishing them out. But there was something so thrilling, so forbidden about it that she couldn't resist. It was only the two of them here where the night would always keep their secrets, and it felt right.

He wasn't a guy for a slow, seductive reveal. She liked that. She usually wasn't much for foreplay, as a woman who got more from the action than the build-up. He'd always gotten lucky with her—or so she liked to tell herself—because he went in for the kill so fast.

"I'm pretty sure I lost my panties in your backseat," she told him.

"Oh, shit, seriously?"

Her shirt, skirt and bra landed in some unseen location across the room, and she lay back down. "Think you could find them and get them back for me? They're kind of a favorite pair."

"Hmm, maybe. What am I gonna get in return?"

She grinned. "My gratitude for giving back my rightful property?"

"I might want to keep them as a souvenir of the sexiest Valentine's night of my life. And they're so hot and red and lacy too. Were you *hoping* to show those off to someone tonight, babe?"

He was so bad. "Not necessarily. But I'm glad I did."

"Me too. Yeah. I can't even begin to tell you how glad I am."

"You do deserve something, though. I didn't get to return

the favor."

"You'll get your chance."

She mewled with frustration. He wasn't here to see her, and she wanted so badly to be naked for him like she'd never really been before due to the cramped confines of his backseat. She wanted to open her legs like a wanton and imagine him standing at the foot of her bed, his dark eyes drinking her in. She wanted that chance now and cursed herself again for her stupidity. "Okay," she whispered. "I'm undressed."

He groaned, as if just the thought of her naked was agony to his arousal. "You're so fucking hot, Macy. But you know, I wanted to imagine you lying there in nothing but those red panties. I was going to tell you to leave them on."

"I have others like them. Different colors, though."

"Which colors?"

"White. Black. Beige. And teal."

"Hmm. The black. Put them on for me."

"Are you serious?"

"Hell yes, I am. I need the mental image. Put them on."

"Twisted," she muttered as she climbed from the bed and was rewarded with his dastardly chuckle.

"You know it."

Once her task was completed, she settled back on the bed in her black panties. "Now what?"

"Now talk to me, I know you can do it. I'm there with you. What do you want me to do?"

Macy had begun to forget her headache, her questionable stomach and all the other afflictions she'd woken up with. "I wish you *were* here. If you want, you could still—"

"Shh. What do you want me to do?"

"Kiss me."

"Where?"

God, she was going to suck at this. But suddenly it didn't matter. "My mouth, at first."

"Just like I did in the car? Slow and teasing? Or rougher?"

She licked her lips just thinking about it. "Just like in the car. Slow and teasing to start off. Then rougher, like you can't get enough of how I taste."

"I couldn't. And I'm there with you now, and you're naked except for your panties, so you know I can't resist kissing your nipples. Run your fingers over them for me."

They were already torturously tight from his words, his voice. Now her fingertips drew them even tighter. Her head sank into her pillow as she arched into her own hands, taking the full, aroused heaviness of her breasts into her palms. She would offer them to him like this, cupping them underneath so he could kiss and lick his fill.

"You teased me in the car," she said softly. "You didn't put your mouth on my nipples. I wanted you to."

"I would do it now. I'd lick them and suck them until you couldn't take it anymore. I wouldn't take my mouth off them until you came, if you didn't want me to."

"I think I'd eventually have other uses for your mouth." This really wasn't that hard.

"Oh yeah? Tell me about them. I'm home, by the way. I'm getting into bed."

She smiled into the darkness, glad he'd made it safely given the content of their discussion. "What are *you* wearing?" she asked.

"What do you want me to wear?"

"My needs are simple. Get naked."

That evil-villain chuckle she was growing to love sounded in the darkness. She heard the tinkle of a belt buckle, the slide of denim being stripped off. "As you wish, my lady."

Oh *God*. This wasn't fair. She didn't know what he looked like naked. Before, she'd come back to earth to discover the indignity of having her shirt pushed up, bra cups pushed down, skirt bunched around her hips and panties dangling from her left ankle. He'd only had to zip up. No, not fair at all.

She could imagine, because he usually wore his shirts a little snug, that he had a fantastic body. And she'd held his cock in her hand, felt its thickness both with her fingers and in the devastating stretch of its intrusion into her body. The memory alone was enough to arch her body off the bed.

"Are you hard?" she asked, surprised at her husky tone.

"What the fuck do you think?"

She chuckled. "All the way?"

"Fully erect, baby. So hard it hurts."

"How big is it?"

"Uh, don't you know?"

"I'm talking precise measurements."

This laugh was less evil-villain and more jovial. "Why, Macy. A nice young lady like yourself, asking such a thing. I'm appalled."

"Oh, come on. Guys always know how big they are."

"Big enough that I should tie a bow around it and attach a little card that says 'To: Macy. You're welcome. Love, Seth.'"

She barked with laughter, amazed for a moment that they could go from red-hot murmurings to easy humor in a matter of seconds. "Keep this up and I'll text you a picture," he warned, further fueling her laughter.

"No freaking way!"

"Oh, but you want me over here busting out a ruler for your edification."

"*You* keep this up and I'm going to demand that you come over and show me in person."

"Feeling better now?"

"Mm-hmm." She writhed against her mattress restlessly. "Well...actually I think it's more that I just don't care how I feel."

"Ah. As much as I want that—and you have no idea—let's enjoy the ride until we get there. This will give us something to think about all day."

"As if we don't have enough?"

"Point taken."

Maybe he was a tease after all. Or he was worried she was still inebriated enough she didn't know what she was doing. "We got derailed," she said.

"You were about to tell me what else to do with my mouth."

She grinned as wickedly as he ever had. "But...it might be hard for you to do it. I'm wearing panties, remember."

His groan raised the hair at her nape. "You think I can't work around that? Slide your hand over the top of them. Tell me how they feel."

"Silky. Wet."

"I know your pussy is silkier and wetter than they are."

Her breath momentarily froze in her lungs, and she choked out his name. Her flash of chagrin only added to the aching heat under her gently rubbing fingers. "Do you want me to make sure?" she breathed in a gusty whisper.

"Slide your fingers in the side, not down the front. Don't touch your clit yet."

Exasperation shot through her. "*Please?*"

"No."

What the hell was she waiting on him for, anyway? He wasn't here watching her.

Except it was almost as if he were. Like if she touched herself without his permission, he would know.

"See, this is what I want to do to you. Leave those sexy little panties on; just pull them to the side while I go down on you. I might even leave them on while I fuck you."

She was pretty sure she was going to expire before any of this actually occurred. She whimpered as her fingers trailed through her wetness, careful not to brush the throbbing bud of her clit though it begged for attention. "What do you want me to do now?" she asked.

"Spread your legs wide. Rub your fingers through it. Get it wetter. God, I remember how you feel, how you smell. I can't wait to touch you again." His breathing had deepened, gone ragged, to match hers. She pictured him lying there, his hand wrapped around himself and stroking, as she pushed her fingers as deep inside her own molten heat as she could. Her hips arched up.

"I can't wait either," she whispered. "This is good, but it isn't enough."

"I know, baby. Tomorrow night. I'm going to take care of

you."

If she hadn't been such an idiot, it could've been tonight. Now. He would be sliding inside the slick, needy passage her own fingers couldn't adequately fill.

The mental image alone was enough to make her moan. "I need you here," she burst out. Quickly, she amended, "I need to come, Seth."

"You will. Tell me how it feels. Is it hot?"

"Hot. Burning up."

"Is it wet enough for me?"

"Oh yes."

"I want you so wet that I can slide in deep and fast and not hurt you."

Jesus. The only answer she could conjure up for him was an agonized sound halfway between a whimper and a sob. He'd done it like that before. He hadn't shown her any mercy. She hadn't wanted him to.

A strangled sound tore from his throat. "I'm close, baby. Are you?"

"If I touch my clit, I think I'll explode."

"Do it. And I need to hear you."

She pulled her fingers from her clenching depths and slid them over her swollen bud, biting down on her lip so hard she winced. Or maybe it was from the pleasure that zapped the last of her remaining senses. She didn't have to be embarrassed about letting him hear her cry out as she came—there was no other option. The release, so sweet, so needed despite everything that had already happened tonight, left her drained and panting in its aftermath. From his gasp and shuddering breath over the connection, she knew he'd gone with her.

She only wished he could have been here inside her, pressed against her, keeping her anchored to the earth.

Because she was floating somewhere around Jupiter. A whole other world sprawled wide before her, so far removed from her own.

She was looking forward to the visit. She just didn't know if she could live there.

Chapter Six

The morning dawned clear and beautiful...and planted a dagger between Macy's eyes. Despite the alcohol and the orgasms, she'd tossed and turned all night.

She couldn't even remember what she and Seth had talked about after the earth had moved; she only knew that the sleepy cadence of his voice was enormously sexy. Though she'd hardly been able to hold her eyes open by the time she hung up, she hadn't wanted to say good night to him.

There was no way she was going to make it in to work today, but she doubted any of the employees would miss her. She didn't amble into the kitchen for coffee until almost noon, and then she lounged in her pajamas—which she'd slipped into only upon waking almost completely naked this morning—until after two. Her phone was troublingly silent, but then if what he'd once told her was true, he slept late himself.

And she wanted to hear from him. Imagine that. Even in the back of her intoxicated mind last night, she'd taken some comfort in knowing she might wake up this morning having come to her senses. That her totally out-of-character behavior around him was simply the result of minor glitches in her normally mundane life. A person could take only so much monotony before they had to let off a little steam, right? Seth had been her pressure release. Unfortunately, the pressure had built back up overnight.

If he was still on board, she couldn't wait for tonight.

There was damage control to do in the meantime. By now, Candace would probably be at Brian's side at Dermamania, and Macy owed her an apology. Not just for the few tense minutes they'd spent discussing Candace's lifestyle choices last night, but for the past *year* they'd spent discussing them. Seth had been right with the whole live-and-let-live thing. As he'd said, if there was distance between Macy and her friends, it was because she'd put it there. The world wouldn't be crammed into her neat little unchanging box no matter how much she wanted it to be.

Candace's life was hers to live. God knows she'd fought hard enough to break free from people telling her what to do. Macy didn't need to be the one stark reminder of Candace's dark times before Brian had come along. The girl didn't deserve that, and Macy was going to start working on changing it. Today.

Still, walking into the tattoo parlor where her best friend spent most of her time away from home and class always gave Macy the shudders.

Dark sunglasses shielding her eyes, she drove to the parlor and deflated when she didn't recognize Seth's car in the parking lot. Not that he was the reason she needed to come here to do this, but seeing him would've been a perk.

Inside, the usual heavy metal was playing at thankfully tolerable levels and the banter was flying fast and furious. Candace was nowhere in sight.

"...all directly out of your friggin' minds," Brian was saying without looking up from the tattoo he was working on.

"Dude, that woman ranks off the *top* of the fuckability scale," the client under his needle said. Macy wasn't sure if arguing with your tattooist in the middle of the process was the smartest thing one could do.

"Agreed," one of the other artists—she thought they called him Tay—announced from across the room, where he was perched on a stool in front of the computer screen. "I'm staring at the evidence right now. I'd hit it like a big rig with no brakes."

"She's hot, okay, but she's got nothing on Maria Brink or Cristina Scabbia."

"Dude, you just have an Italian boner for Scabbia."

"Hey, fuck—" Brian took that moment to lift his head and address Tay, but his gaze landed right on Macy still standing near the door. "Oh, hey, Mace."

She grinned. "Would you be having this discussion in front of your girlfriend?"

One corner of his mouth tugged upward, and a dimple dug deep into his cheek. "She's privy to the never-ending hottest-chick-in-metal debate, don't worry. She knows she outshines them all."

"*Awww*," the guys said in unison, breaking into laughter. Tay muttered something that sounded awfully like "pussy whipped".

"Says the choad who has none," Brian fired back.

Macy pitched her voice higher to be heard over the bubbling testosterone. "Is she around?"

Brian nodded toward the back of the parlor. "She's in my office. Go on back."

"Thanks."

He watched as she skirted gingerly around the counter to the hallway. "And how was *your* night?"

If only he knew—and she hoped like hell he didn't. She realized she hadn't even thought to take her sunglasses off. Number-one hallmark of a hangover. Her grunted reply caused the guys to snicker.

She passed Starla, one of the two female artists, in the hall, and exchanged brief pleasantries. Then she peeked around Brian's office door to find Candace at the desk with her phone crammed between her ear and shoulder, typing furiously at the keyboard. With her hair pulled up in a stylishly sloppy bun, she looked a little tired, but her pretty face brightened when she noticed Macy, and she smiled and waved her inside. Good sign.

Macy pushed her glasses to the top of her head and shut the door before dropping into a chair across from the desk. Candace hung up her phone.

"She lives!" she said.

Macy rubbed her eyes, which were being assaulted by the too-bright bulbs overhead. "Well...sort of. I think."

Candace tucked a stray wisp of pink-and-blonde hair behind her ear. "So, spill. I've been waiting to hear this all day."

"Spill what?"

Her friend crossed her arms and sat back. "Oh, come on. Don't be like that. I'm not one to ask for details, because I know how you are. But I'm *dying* over here."

"Oh, it was nothing—"

"You did something. You were on his lap. Even if you only kissed him, it's still *something*. At last."

"Okay, so it was something. That's all I'm willing to divulge at the moment."

"You are nothing if not stubborn, woman."

"Listen, I'm not here to talk about him. I'm here because I need to talk to *you*."

"Do you want to go across the street to the coffee shop or—"

"No. Let me get this out." Sighing, Macy rubbed her temples. Why should it be so hard to say you're sorry to someone you knew as well as yourself? "I just...I owe you an apology. A really big one. And not just about how I acted like a complete bitch last night, although that's a big part of it."

Candace's eyebrows rose. She didn't comment.

"I'm sorry about the attitude I've had, how I try to talk you out of everything, and some of the things I've said about you and Brian being together. A million times, I'm sorry. You don't need to hear that crap. You're happy, and you deserve to be happy after everything you guys went through."

Relief washed over her friend's face, though somehow it made Macy feel worse rather than better. Candace must have been waiting a long time to hear her say this. "Thank you. That means a lot to me."

"You were always like a little sister to me, and I always felt like you sort of looked to me for guidance in a way, so seeing you stand on your own two feet and do your own thing was...well, it was awesome. But it was hard on me too. I thought I was going to lose you, and I'm still afraid you'll get fed up with me someday."

Tears welled in Candace's eyes. Macy tilted her head and studied her. She'd always been an emotional girl, but something about her wasn't quite right today. "I'm not going anywhere. I hate that you even think that."

58

"I know that, I was just being selfish and immature—" Before she could complete the thought, Candace bolted from her chair, and the two of them collided in a fierce hug at the corner of the desk. "I'll be better from now on," Macy promised.

"I love you just the way you are, Mace." Candace sniffled noisily into her ear. Macy pulled back from her and looked into troubled blue eyes, just now noticing the faint shadows underneath.

"Are you all right, though? Everything okay?"

Sighing, Candace stepped back and returned to her chair. Macy reclaimed her own, perching on the edge and hoping nothing was upset in her friend's world.

"Everything's okay, it's only that...well, Brian and I..." She glanced at the closed door and caught her bottom lip between her teeth.

"You aren't fighting, are you?" Macy whispered.

Candace shook her head. "No, not fighting," she whispered back. "I guess you could say engaging in a very serious, very intense ongoing discussion."

She had a feeling it had nothing to do with the hottest chick in metal. "What's up?"

"Well, I graduate in three months, you know. There's all these things I can do...and I had all these plans. But then I started helping him out here, and I love it. I want to be here, with him. And he feels like I'm throwing away years of hard work if I just hang my degree on the wall and keep working in his studio. I'm not throwing anything away as long as I'm doing what I love. I'm happy taking care of the business side of it so he can stay out front where he wants to be. I like knowing he's right down the hall." She sighed and pressed her fingers to her temples, bracing her elbows on the desk. "Am I completely psycho or something? Maybe he *wants* to get me out of here. Maybe I'm suffocating him."

"I saw you and Brian last night. He didn't look like a guy who was being suffocated, at least not in a way he doesn't enjoy."

"Yeah, I know that's not it. He's just thinking of what's best for me."

"I do see his point, and if you keep working here, your parents will all but *die*. He might be thinking about that too."

Candace waved her hand almost angrily. "They'll get over it. I'm not even worried about them."

"Yes you are. And he knows it. And he doesn't want them to hate him because he loves you, and he knows it's important to you that they don't."

She knew she'd struck a nerve when a fresh stream of tears trickled from Candace's eyes. Dammit, why wouldn't those people just leave them alone and let their only daughter be happy?

Macy sighed. "But there I go again, telling you what's what."

"No, you're fine. And I see his point too. But I'm also thinking of what's good for him, and he needs the help. Business is picking up, and he's got clients from all the surrounding areas coming in. He wants to open another studio. Why should he have to hire someone else when I can do it and I *want* to do it?"

"You'll get it worked out."

"I think he's smoking again."

"What?"

"He'd just quit smoking when we got together. Since all this has started and Ghost left and Connor moved away, I swear I smell cigarette smoke on him sometimes."

"Did you ask him?"

Candace nodded. "He said it must be from contact. I want to believe him, but I know how he is when he gets stressed out. It's not even that big a deal if he needs one every now and then—but he should trust me enough to not lie to me about it, right?"

"If that's really going on, then he's probably too embarrassed to admit he slipped up."

"I'm sure he is. I want him to know I won't judge him, but to tell him that, I'd be straight up accusing him of doing it and lying to me about it. So...damn, it sounds so petty, doesn't it?

We could have worse problems."

Macy shrugged. "That guy is crazy about you. Whatever is going on between you, you'll get through it."

Candace's eyes rounded. "Oh, I know that. There's no question. But seeing him upset, or even thinking he's upset, tears me up." She looked down and doodled absently on the desk pad. "When he hurts, I hurt."

The words seemed to lodge in Macy's head and reverberate. *When he hurts, I hurt.* What wouldn't she give to find a love like that? An image of Seth's troubled face as they talked about his grandmother last night floated through her mind. For the second day in a row, an unaccustomed sting pricked behind her eyes. She quickly shoved it back. "Brian's lucky to have you. You're both lucky to have each other. I think you guys need to take some time to sit down together, try to relax, and have a heart-to-heart. Get everything out there."

Candace smiled at her. "I need to talk him into a getaway for a couple days during spring break. I know he'll protest, but we're both here so much it's been a while since it felt like just the two of us."

"You definitely should. Get him to take you to his parents' condo in Destin."

"Ooh, I didn't think of that. That's a great idea."

"And let me borrow it this summer as thanks for making the suggestion."

Through her friend's laughter, Macy heard her cell phone chime with a new text message. A jolt of adrenaline shot through her, ratcheting up her heart rate and sending her stomach into a somersaulting free fall. Candace watched with a little too much interest as Macy clumsily drew her phone out of her purse. The display was still lit with the message.

Tonight?

A ridiculous-sounding giggle escaped her. Did he even have to ask?

Well...maybe he thought he did. She should have contacted him first—all along he'd been afraid her actions last night had been because she was drunk. Poor guy, she might've made him suffer needlessly.

Everything within her wanted to reply *When, where, what do I wear and what should I bring?* but that might have sounded desperately...desperate. Maybe she was, but she had to keep some shred of dignity, for God's sake.

So she sent back one word. *Absolutely.* He replied with a winky face and *Call u ltr.*

"Okay, what's up? Because you're grinning like a goon," Candace said. She tapped a pen impatiently on the desktop calendar. "Hot date? Please say yes."

"No comment."

Candace practically howled with frustration. But Macy was sure she put the mystery to rest when she swallowed all pride and asked, "So is he, uh, not working at all today?"

"Nope. Brian told him not to worry about coming in tonight since he was here so late last night—I could've killed Brian for actually letting him volunteer to work, by the way. But I heard Ghost say he was going to call the guys in his band and see if they could throw together an extra practice."

Interesting. She didn't know much about his band—just that he was the guitarist and they often played gigs in surrounding cities but didn't really have aspirations beyond that. He'd told her it was mostly a fun, blow-off-steam thing for him, and an outlet for any pent-up creativity he didn't manage to exorcise through his art alone. But he obviously loved it.

She'd never heard any of his music. She doubted she could give an objective opinion. Her main concern at the moment was what went on during these band meetings, practices or whatever. Hopefully no drunken debauchery that might delay him...or keep him from showing up altogether.

Great. Something else to obsess over.

Chapter Seven

"Nice of you to finally show up, G."

Ghost bit down on a retort that might not have been conducive to repairing some of the tension among the members of In the Slaughter. Then again, being confronted with assholic remarks from the much-maligned front man the second he walked in the door of Mark's home studio wasn't too conducive, either.

"Aw, I missed you too. All you worthless bastards."

The guys scattered about the room chuckled, looking glum. Ghost set his guitar case down and sighed when he glanced around and saw one of their five-piece was missing. He dropped into an empty seat and assumed the same sullen position as most of the others, arms crossed, mouth turned down.

Yeah, so even when he wasn't pulling a months'-long disappearing act, it was often hard for him to find time to devote to the band because of his work, and the guys gave him shit about it. But Brian needed him, and he didn't like letting Brian down. Gus, the other guitarist and his musical counterpart affectionately known as Little G to his Big G, often found it difficult to find time to devote to the band because he was off somewhere getting high.

"I guess no one's heard from him?"

No one had to ask who he meant. Heads shook in slow unison. "Couldn't even reach him," Randall said, rubbing his eyebrow ring the way he always did when he was worried. "I texted him earlier but didn't get a reply."

Ghost had received similar results. Mark bolted from his chair and paced a few steps away, a mass of nervous energy as he scrubbed his hands on his jeans. Onstage, that energy made the guy explode. Offstage, it sometimes made him hard to handle. "So fuckin' sick of this bullshit."

"What bullshit? So he wasn't sitting on top of his phone today. We did kind of put this together last minute, you know."

"Quit making excuses for him. It's always this way with him, and you know it."

"The guy's got a problem, Mark."

"That's not *my* problem, is it? But I'll tell you what is. The gig we have next month. The fact that one of our guitarists might be lying dead in a ditch for all we know, and the other has more important shit to do." His narrowed gaze landed directly on Ghost.

Aw, hell no. "Yeah, I did have more important shit to do. Way more important than you even know. But I can always go do more of it, if all I'm going to do is sit here and listen to you bitch."

"So that's how it is?"

"Yeah, that's how it is."

"We can't play without Gus, anyway," Eddie said, slowly twirling the drumsticks he held in both hands. "What's the point?"

"The point is we need to replace him." It was the statement from Mark they'd all known was coming for a long time. Grim looks exchanged among the others.

Sighing, Ghost pulled his cell phone from his pocket. He dialed Gus, not expecting much and not getting it, either. His voice mailbox was full. "While all of you sit around moaning about what's gonna happen to the band, has anyone thought about, you know, going to find him?"

"Why bother? Even if he's home, he's gonna be too messed up to play. He can't function when he's on that shit."

"Yeah, well, glass houses and all that," Ghost muttered. Mark sure wasn't in any position to throw stones. The only difference between Mark and Gus was that Mark *could* function when he was high.

He stood and shoved his phone back in his pocket. "Not that I wouldn't love to sit around and stare at y'all's ugly mugs all night, but I'd rather do something productive. I'll go find him."

"For *what*?" Mark raged.

"I'm going to tell him if he's not here and straight Saturday night, he's getting bounced."

"He's had way too many chances—"

"Agreed?" Ghost's voice overrode Mark's as he looked around at the other guys. "Last time I checked, this wasn't a dictatorship."

Randall and Eddie nodded, their gazes fixed warily on Mark. Mark huffed and turned his back for a second, then whirled back around. "You're wasting your time on him. I can have someone else here with one phone call."

Yeah, I bet you could. It was a commonly held belief that Mark would love to have his little brother positioned at the other end of the stage from Ghost and would jump at any chance to get him up there. The kid had talent, but Ghost had way more respect for one of the founding members of this group, even if the guy was having some issues.

"See you Saturday, then." Ghost slammed his way out the door and strode through the chilly twilight to his car. He'd just reached it when the door opened again and Mark called across the yard to him.

"Hey! Did Raina talk to you?"

"Briefly."

"What do you think?"

In reality, he couldn't give two flying fucks what Raina and Mark schemed up. He wouldn't let it affect him in any way whatsoever; he didn't want to give them the satisfaction. But the thought of them making plans around him made him seethe. "It's not cool with me, man."

"Aw, c'mon. We'll talk about it; it'll be fine. We're gonna fuck it up, dude!" Mark yelled, throwing the metal horns in the air and doing a wolf howl. Ghost dropped into the driver's seat and shut the door on his caterwauling.

Well, one thing was for damn sure. He couldn't wait to bury his troubles in Macy's sweet, warm body tonight. She'd made him the happiest damn guy on planet Earth earlier today when she let him know she was still with him on this thing. He definitely planned on showing her his gratitude. He didn't want to think about anything else.

Friggin' life and its interventions. He wished he could already be with her. It had been a draining day; he'd called his nana, and she'd basically called him by every name except his own. His sister had called him bitching about their brother, Scott, who was being his usual douche-bag self, having not seen Nana in months and apparently having no plans to. Because he just couldn't *face it*. Whatever. Couldn't be bothered to give a shit was more like it.

Some days he couldn't face it either. To see someone as strong and independent as she'd been...

He wouldn't think about it. That was what he'd come home for: to get a breather, to get time away, see his friends, do some work, play some music. Recharge his batteries, because he knew he'd have to go back soon. He didn't want to miss out on any good days she had left, but the good days were getting fewer and farther between. Days when Nana managed to maintain her mostly sunny disposition and didn't cut him any slack with her lightning-fast quips.

Macy was certainly helping matters. He hadn't talked to her on the phone yet today, so he didn't know how hungover she'd been or how mortified she was over what they'd done last night. And there was no question there would be some mortification; he knew her that well at least.

He would reassure her she'd gotten him through the day. If not for her soft, sleepy voice echoing seductively in his head, he might have broken something by now. Probably over Mark's head. Her whimpers and moans had haunted his restless dreams all night, and his one release hadn't been nearly enough—he'd had to take matters into his own hands again in the shower this morning to be able to walk normally.

He clung to her image like a kid with a security blanket, because who knew what sort of mess he would find at his friend's house. Hopefully not one that involved a morgue. Gus had been spiraling dangerously out of control for a while now, and things were already way past serious. All Mark and the other guys saw was the effect it had on the band. They seemed to have forgotten this was their *friend*. Their brother. And the yin to Ghost's yang, musically. He wasn't ready to give up on him yet. Or ever.

The simple frame house appeared dark from the street, the driveway empty of both Gus's truck and his girlfriend's Jeep. Ghost parked and killed the engine, then sat in indecision.

This most likely had been a wasted trip. He should just call Macy now, go be with her and forget about everyone else's fucking problems. He got out anyway and strode to the front door, pounding on it hard enough to wake the dead. And hopefully no one fitting that description was inside.

"Gus!"

The neighbors were probably going to come out shooting. He battered the door a few more times, rattling the three small squares of glass at his eye level. Peeking inside one of them revealed nothing but darkness in the living room. Impulsively, he gave the knob a twist, surprised when it gave and the door creaked open.

Well, this was probably wrong, but something told him to do it anyway. He hit the switch and flooded the room with sickly pale light, as all but one of the bulbs in the overhead ceiling-fan kit were burnt out. But that light was enough to disturb the snoring heap on the couch. Gus flopped over away from the disruption.

The breath left Ghost in a relieved rush. His friend was here. Not in jail, not lying in a ditch and, apparently, not dead. But the smell of alcohol was strong even from his position across the room. Hell, that was a good sign. Drunk he could deal with.

"Dude," he bellowed, striding across the room and yanking him over onto his back. "Wake your ass up."

Gus's eyes flew open, so bloodshot he could've had a double case of conjunctivitis. "Huh? The fuck you come from, man?"

"I've only tried to call you about a dozen times to explain.

And so have the guys, because we wanted to put together a jam session tonight."

Gus's bleary gaze tracked over to the clock on the bookshelf, taking a moment to focus on the time. "Shit."

"Shit is right. You're in a world of it if you don't pull it together. They're ready to toss you, kid."

Gus pressed the heels of his palms into both eyes. "I don't even care anymore."

"Don't say that. Where is your truck?"

"Wrecked it." He burst out laughing. It was a terrible, almost frightening sound, and it turned into a coughing fit. Ghost took a couple steps back in case he started spewing vomit. Once he subsided, he lay back and grimaced. "Wrapped it around a tree, totaled that fucker."

"When?"

"Two nights ago."

"Were you drunk?"

"Hell yes."

"What are you trying to do, man? Kill yourself? Or somebody else?"

"Naw. That bitch ain't worth that."

Ah. It all became staggeringly clear. "Great. When did she take off?"

"*Fuck* her."

"Okay. But will you look at yourself? It's no wonder she split. I want to leave you too, and I don't even have to live with you."

"So leave." Gus flicked a hand at him, turning his face toward the back of the couch again and throwing his arm over his head. "I don't give a shit."

This scene was so damn familiar, Ghost's hands began to shake. Except he had been the one in his friend's place. Brian had been the one trying to drag him kicking and screaming, fighting and cursing, back to the world of the living.

He had to turn away, fighting to fill his lungs with air. Old wounds he'd thought long since healed threatened to rip open and ooze again. Words he didn't want to remember ricocheted in his brain, replacing Macy's sweet sounds of pleasure that had been echoing there all day.

Brooke explaining to him over the phone why she'd left him. Her fucking weak-ass excuses. Each one of them an insult after the sheer magnitude of what she'd done to him.

It had been so long ago, it shouldn't have still been so close to the surface. But it was. It could be triggered by the simple sound of a particular voice...and not even hers. He hadn't spoken a single word to her in six years.

No other woman had ever fucked with his head like that. Not Raina. No one. No one ever would again. He'd all but sworn it in blood.

"You gotta get over this shit, man," he said, hearing the tremor in his own voice. Who was he to give that advice?

He was someone who knew how the guilt, the *I-should-haves* and the raw sense of betrayal could eat a guy alive, if he sat around and let it fester.

"I don't even know what she did," he went on, "and I don't care. Let it go."

"It's not even about—"

"Don't dick me around. I know exactly what it's about. You do this every time. I'm just amazed you're coherent."

"Give me time."

Oh god*damn.* Did he have to go and say that out loud? Ghost turned around and shoved his boot down hard on the couch cushion Gus was lying on. "Look, if I have to haul you back to my place and sit on you until you dry out, I will." *And you really have no idea how much I don't want to do that. I'm supposed to get spectacularly laid tonight.* He could already feel the anticipation draining away...until a miraculous flash of inspiration struck him. "Or better yet, I can dump you out at your dad's."

Gus's dad was a cop, and a big one at that. Hell, even Ghost was scared of him.

That got a reaction. "No friggin' way, man. You call my dad, and I'll kick your ass."

"*That's* funny. Look, if you really don't give a shit about life anymore, do what you gotta do. I know from experience nothing I say or do is going to change anything. But I'll tell you one thing—you skip out on practice Saturday, and you seal your fate with the guys. They're done. So am I. Think about that while you're prioritizing."

Gus was silent as Ghost stalked across the room. He switched off the light, bathing the room in the darkness Gus craved, before slamming the door behind him.

And breathed. That house had been...oppressive. Like the dark cloud hanging over his friend had begun to permeate his skin.

Fucking relationship drama. God, if there was one thing he didn't need. He'd had it in spades, and if Macy hadn't seemed like such a practical person with a decent head on her shoulders, he might have called off tonight no matter how his genitals might protest.

He pulled out his cell phone and, feeling like a tattletale, called Gus's parents to let them know they needed to check on him. His friend would want to kill him for it, but better that he was alive to do so.

And...well, that was all there was to do. Practice had been a bust. He'd been confronted with a pathetic ugliness he hadn't needed to see. But now he was done. Free at last. For a guy who wanted no strings with a girl, he was sure chomping at the bit to get to this one.

Chapter Eight

Macy's phone rang, and she leaped halfway across the living room to snatch it up. All night, she'd kept it within arm's reach, and of course he picked the one moment she put it down to call.

"I was starting to think you'd changed your mind," she said by way of greeting.

"Sorry about that. Had to handle some business with a friend."

"Everything okay?"

"Not really, but it will be as soon as I see you."

So he could talk sweet as well as sexy. She smiled and settled the phone between her ear and her shoulder. "I'm ready whenever you are."

"My place or yours?"

Considering she'd spent the evening cleaning like crazy? There was no way she was going to put all that effort to waste. Not that she was a slob, but she very rarely actually *dusted*. "Mine. Do you know where I live?"

"Are you kidding? I hide out underneath your bedroom window every night. I was really there last night, watching you."

She laughed. "Oh, really."

"No. What's your address?"

She gave him quick directions, and he said he knew the building.

No going back now, was there? Well, she supposed she *could*, but...who would want to?

"Are you dressed?" he asked.

"Hey now, we did all that last night. Let's just wait—"

"No, you goof. I meant are you decently attired such that

we might go into public without getting arrested."

Public? "Oh. Yeah, I'm dressed."

"Cool. I'll pick you up in twenty minutes." He hung up.

Okaaay. Nothing had been said about any public appearances. This wasn't a *date*. What on earth did he have in mind?

She was staring out her living room window exactly eighteen minutes later when his GTO purred its way into the parking space in front of her apartment. Purse already in hand, she bolted for the door, excitement churning through her belly.

Seth was already out of the car and striding around to the other side to open the door for her. She almost stopped in her tracks. He looked good enough to eat. And demand seconds. Tight black V-neck T-shirt, leather jacket and ratty jeans that broke over his boots just the right way. On his head was a black Fedora. He was definitely a guy who could pull off hats.

Dayum. Maybe she could take him somewhere after all.

"Wow," she said as she skirted around the door he held open. "You look great."

"Wow yourself," he said, his lopsided grin wreaking havoc with things down south.

Did they really have to go anywhere?

When the clean smell inside his car unleashed a torrent of flashbacks, she put the question to him as soon as he got in the driver's side. He planted his arm across the seatback and turned to look out the rear window as he backed out. The position gave her a great view of his neck. How she wanted to nibble that thick vein, lick it, feel his pulse throbbing inside.

"Well," he answered, "I hope you don't get mad, but Brian called a few minutes before I called you. There's a get-together at a friend's house, and he wanted me to go hang out with them. I shut him down, but when I was talking to you, I remembered everything you were saying last night, and...I thought this might be a good thing for you. If you don't want to go, say the word. We'll get sushi instead."

Ah, sushi, the one interest they did share. But she wasn't hungry. She shrugged. "I don't mind going. Candace will be around, right?"

His scoff had her lifting an eyebrow. "Have you ever seen those two in the last year when they're not attached at the hip?"

"Hmm. Do we have a certain measure of hostility about that?"

"I wouldn't say I have *hostility* about it." He straightened in his seat and zoomed out of her parking lot. "He's in a fool's paradise, and I hate it for him. That's all."

"Why do you say that? They seem pretty solid to me. She would never hurt him; that much I'd bet my life on."

"Every relationship I've ever seen is like a bubble ready to burst, and most of them do."

"Some of them don't."

"I guess I'm too cynical to think any of them around me are going to remain intact."

Insanely curious now, she glanced over at him, sizing up his body language as he manhandled the gearshift. If they hadn't passed through the yellowish wash of a street light, casting the tense lines of his face into stark relief, she might have thought these were simple observations of his.

"So who burned you?" she asked casually, smoothing her palms over her jeans.

He waved a dismissive hand. "An hour ago I was standing over the miserable, wasted heap of a good friend who would rather lose everything he's worked for than even make an effort to get over the woman who keeps walking out on him."

She didn't buy it, but if it was a conversation that was going to bring down the night, she didn't want to have it. "I'm sorry about that. But don't let it sour you. These things work out all the time, and sometimes they don't, but that's life." She shrugged and fell silent, staring out the window as the buildings gave way to skeletal trees missing their summer foliage. God, she hated winter.

The solid warmth of his fingers curled around her hand. She looked over to find Seth watching her in between glances at the road. "Didn't mean to get heavy on you, there."

"It's okay." At least she knew there wouldn't be any

weirdness on his end, if he had such a foul outlook on relationships. "Honestly...I wouldn't know about the drama, myself. The one serious relationship I had, it was just... nice. All the time. So any speculation on my part about these things is just me talking out of my ass."

He grinned and his thumb stroked over the back of her hand. "Well, in the interest of full disclosure, I've had more than my share...and I don't recommend it."

He had?

The two little words kept echoing in her head as their drive continued, as he parked among what must've been a dozen other cars at a house in the middle of nowhere, as they walked through the front door to a chorus of greetings from people who were strangers to her.

He'd had serious relationships? He'd been in love?

If ever a man existed that she would've pegged for never having succumbed to the lure of domesticity, it was Seth Warren. Wow. She couldn't even imagine the guy in a relationship that lasted more than one night. Or one night at a time, at least.

"Check him out, lookin' all *GQ* and shit." Some guy laughed, giving Seth's hat a thump.

Seth ducked the attempt. "Get off me, man. You wish you could make this look this good."

Candace slithered through the crowd and wrapped Macy in a hug almost before she realized it. "I'm so glad you're here," she said into her ear. Macy clung to her friend for dear life. *Save me.*

This was a get-together? It was an outright party, and it was definitely Seth's crowd. Ink and piercings everywhere. Heavy-metal riffs overlying obscenity-laced chatter. What the hell was she doing here? Whose freaking house was this?

Just relax. Go with the flow.

Candace appeared to recognize her distress. She disengaged herself and gently took Macy's upper arms, staring into her face. "You okay?"

Macy nodded.

"It's going to be all right. Do you need to drink?"

"Quite possibly."

"Let's get you fixed up."

She planned to nurse this one carefully, not wanting to end up like she had last night. No, she would go into this fully coherent...just with a tiny bit of the edge taken off. She was a nervous wreck.

But Seth didn't leave her side. They ended up in the spacious living room with about twelve others, Candace and Brian included. Sitting on the couch with him next to her, she slowly began to relax. It wasn't her crowd, and she was definitely the outsider here. No one was looking at her as if wondering what the hell she was doing there, though, and plenty of them had asked her name and what she did for a living and how she'd met Seth. Or Ghost. No one she'd ever met called him by his real name.

While other conversations went on all around them, she leaned closer to him. "How did you get your nickname?"

Everything about him seemed to freeze, and she swore a flush crept up his neck. "It's just a dumb name I got stuck with. No big deal."

"What was that?" Brian bellowed. He was sitting in a chair to their left with Candace perched on his lap, and apparently he'd overheard her question.

"Nothing," Seth snapped.

"No, no, not nothing. I heard. She wants to know about your name. Hey!" he shouted to the room in general. "Macy wants to know how Ghost got his name."

Laughter broke out. Macy lifted a brow at all of them.

Seth's eyes went round. "Oh, *hell* no, man."

Brian shrugged and grinned as he lifted his beer bottle to his mouth for a quick drink. "She'll probably find out sooner or later, right? Better to get it out of the way early. Well...let me rephrase that. If you don't tell her, I will."

"I still think you did it."

Brian clapped a hand over his heart. "That you would even think that of me wounds me."

"I'll wound you if I ever find out you did. I mean, you're the loud-mouthed bastard who told everyone we know about it."

"I'm totally lost right now," Macy admitted. But the exchange was fascinating.

"Don't be a pussy. Tell her," Brian said, nodding in Macy's direction.

Seth sighed, shaking his head and looking away. Debating, probably. What could be that bad? Macy looked to Candace for a clue, only to find her friend snickering into her boyfriend's neck. She must be privy to the big secret, then. Apparently everyone was.

"Many years ago," Seth began carefully. Those few words were all it took for the room to break up in riotous laughter. He waited patiently for it to settle before continuing. "I had this tattoo. And I don't exactly know how I got it."

"What? How can..."

"I got drunk at a party one night. I'm talking fuckin' hammered, falling-off-the-earth drunk. It was years ago, in Dallas, with some friends who live up there. Most of these assholes were there too, might I add...and I woke up the next morning only to discover a tattoo I don't remember getting."

"It's really not funny," Brian said, wiping his eyes with his thumb. "Except that it is."

"My ass, it's funny. It goes against every code of ethics we have."

"You want to talk about *ethics*? When there's a reason I don't let you give me ink?"

"So...what's the tattoo of?" Macy asked, setting off another round of hysterics. She saw quickly this was the really hard part. Seth wouldn't meet the gaze of anyone in the room. Several of the others began goading him to tell her. Once that went on for a while, he finally sighed and looked at her.

"Casper the Friendly Ghost."

Merriment ensued again. Macy couldn't resist the laughter. Finally, Seth cracked a smile himself, as if the humor of the situation wasn't entirely lost on him. "I mean, what the fuck? Casper? You're gonna let someone who's obviously inebriated get a tattoo of *Casper*?"

"I'm of the opinion it was a joke because they thought he looked like you. You'd just shaved your head for the first time. But that's not even as funny as where it is," Brian said.

Oh no. Macy dropped her face into her palm, having a pretty good idea where this was going.

"I can't even wait for him to tell this," Brian said. "Let's just say that for a while, from what I gather, any girl who went down on him found herself face-to-face with a cute little white ghost. It was *in the vicinity,* if you know what I mean."

The howls that followed were deafening. Macy simply moved her hand down to her mouth and watched how Seth was taking this. Remarkably well, she thought—although he was getting redder by the minute. Poor guy. That really was...bad.

"I got it covered up," he explained quickly. "But the damage was already done, and I made the mistake of telling someone I *thought* was my friend." He gave Brian a withering look. "Everyone was calling me Casper because of this son of a bitch. I somehow managed to divert it to 'Ghost'. I had to try to salvage some shred of coolness about this whole thing." He kicked Brian's leg. Brian yelped.

"Hey! You can't expect me to just sit on information like that. Deep down, I really was outraged on your behalf. Deep, *deep* down."

Seth swigged his beer. "Sure you were. Like I said. I wouldn't be surprised to find out you did it."

"Nope. I wouldn't voluntarily get that close to your junk, sorry. I left early and wasn't even there to defend your virtue. But if it's any consolation, if I ever found out one of my artists did something like that, his or her ass would get fired. Fast."

Seth grumbled a reply she couldn't make out.

"Maybe you shouldn't be so pissed," Brian said. "It could've been a hot girl who did it, and you might've had a good time."

"So what did you cover it up with?" Macy asked.

"Never again will I divulge the secrets of any intimate ink I have. Not to these guys, anyway." The look he gave her then sent a shiver down to her toes. It clearly indicated he wouldn't mind divulging those secrets to her.

As the jovial conversation went on, she thought Brian was probably wrong. There was nothing "friendly" looking about Seth, nothing that could be compared to a cute cartoon. He was the polar opposite.

Except she'd seen another side of him over the last couple of days, and she couldn't get it out of her mind. Before, there had only been the wisecracking tattoo artist and heavy-metal aficionado. The guy she could see hanging out with but never...*being* with at all. Now, he'd morphed into something else entirely—someone who did have cares and worries like everyone else, and who felt very deeply about them.

He was a loyal friend. He was devoted to his job. Even if they weren't exactly the friends or the job she would have chosen for the guy she was with, it counted for something.

She wasn't so dense that she didn't realize she was being sucked in by the magnetic lure of the bad boy, superficial though it might be. Okay, so maybe she had realized this attraction wasn't so crazy after all, and it could be good for the one thing she needed. But the coarse language and nonstop partying and loud music would wear on her nerves after a while—a short while.

She'd worry about all that later. Taking a pull on her beer, she watched him joke around with his friends. It was getting later, the music and chatter were grating, and she was ready to go home. With him.

And then everything *really* fell apart.

A girl walked in... Sashayed was more like it. Macy would've noticed her even if a nervous hush hadn't fallen over the entire room and Seth hadn't gone stiff next to her and uttered, "*Fuck.*" The girl's hair was predominantly blonde but shot through with pink, blue, red and purple and heavily dreaded. Her eyes were dark, and the smoky shadow surrounding them only accentuated their size in her pixie-like face. She was tiny and, beneath all the wildness of her appearance, breathtakingly beautiful.

At least, she was until her gaze fell on Seth and Macy

sitting side by side on the couch. Then she only looked scary.

Thankfully, a group of girls in the room bounded jubilantly toward her and the awkwardness dissipated somewhat as the crowd moved out of the room. Seth seemed to start breathing again beside her, at least. But she didn't miss the *oh, shit* glance he exchanged with Brian and Candace. Conversations began to pick up again around them all.

Seth leaned close to her ear. "I think that was our cue."

She drew her lips between her teeth for a moment, processing. She wasn't stupid. "I take it that was her."

"Her?"

"The one you didn't want to talk about on the ride over."

"I don't want to talk about her now, either, and I damn sure don't want to be in the same house with her."

"Look, it's up to you, but I don't see the big deal."

"I just don't want you to have to see what usually happens when she and I get within fifty feet of each other."

"Do you get into a brawl or something?"

He chuckled. "No, nothing like that. But it gets...ugly."

"That's fine. I'm ready to go anyway. Just let me find a bathroom first."

He gave her directions, not seeming too happy about it. She had to roll her eyes. Yes, she didn't go for the body-mod stuff—it freaked her out. But one thing she didn't shrink away from was confrontation. If that girl accosted her in some way, she might be surprised what she got in return.

As luck would have it, her path took her right in front of the bedroom where the group of girls had congregated. A sharp, "Hey!" halted her in her tracks, and she turned and leaned into the doorway.

"Yes?"

The Ex—whatever her name was—now had dark streams running from both eyes to her chin, making her look like The Crow. The three girls around her looked back at Macy uneasily, their hands resting lightly on The Ex's shoulders in case they had to suddenly restrain her.

"Who are you?" the girl demanded.

"Who are *you*?"

Inexplicably, that made The Ex laugh. "You'll find out."

"Then I guess you'll find out who I am too."

"Oh, it doesn't really matter. I know *what* you are." If the disdain in her eyes as she looked Macy up and down could have wounded, she would've dropped dead on the spot. "You're his fucking fantasy, see, and you're everything I hate, so that makes you nothing but his revenge fuck. And not just revenge on me but on some other rich bitch who put him through the ringer a long time ago. Once he throws you away, he'll be back where he knows he belongs."

"Jesus. Don't skip your next dose," Macy muttered, pushing away from the door to resume her hunt for the bathroom. She found the door closed with a strip of light glowing at the bottom. Great. Add to that a sudden burst of commotion and the sight of The Ex bearing down on her in the hallway despite her friends' restraining hands, and it was turning into a real shitty night.

This was what he was attracted to? Then what the hell was he doing with *her*?

It was all too ridiculous. She stood with her arms crossed and calmly watched the girl yell and sob while her friends tried to hustle her away, marveling there were people who still behaved that way over the age of twelve. Candace managed to sneak past the melee and came up to Macy's side, her eyes wide as saucers.

"Are you okay?"

Macy nodded toward the closed door. "Just waiting for the bathroom."

"Oh. Forget that. Here, I'll show you where there's another one. Get away from all this insanity."

Focusing on her breathing and taking one step at a time, she followed Candace's lead. Just because she didn't shrink from confrontation didn't necessarily mean she liked it. Especially when the other person looked ready to do physical damage to her. From behind her, she could hear Ghost join the fracas, telling the girl in a low, controlled tone to calm the fuck down. It apparently worked. She dissolved into sobs.

"What is that banshee's name?"

Candace led her into what looked like the master bedroom.

"Raina. I've only met her a couple of times myself. They broke up way before Brian and I got together. But she, ah, still has feelings for him, obviously."

"Obviously."

"She comes to the parlor sometimes. Brian has made her leave before. I even tried to talk to her and pretty much got the same reaction you did since I'm only a stupid rich bitch too, and Brian really doesn't give a shit about me and he's only going to dump my ass so why should she listen to me, and blah, blah, blah. Ghost has changed his cell phone number because of her. Apparently, when they broke up, she made threats about killing herself."

"Lovely. And you were knowingly plotting to put me in the middle of all this?"

"Just ignore it, Mace. Bad luck that she showed up here tonight. She doesn't come around that much. It's not a big deal."

Macy raised her eyebrows as a fresh wave of shrieking burst from the hall outside. Ignore *that*? She sighed. "He comes with quite the baggage, doesn't he?"

Chapter Nine

So, yeah, it was mostly his fault this had been delayed. But Ghost didn't think they were ever going to get back to Macy's apartment.

She'd made him proud tonight, though, and it had been worth it. "See? They're not so bad." He braked to turn in to her building's parking lot and chuckled. "At least, not all of them."

"No, not all of them." A little movement out of his peripheral vision caught his eye, and he glanced down to see she had twisted her purse strap practically into knots.

"Hey, I'm sorry about that. I really didn't think there'd be any danger of her being there tonight. I saw that a couple of her friends were there but ordinarily, that's not her crowd."

"Maybe her friends let her know you were there with someone."

"That's a possibility. You okay?"

"Yeah." Her voice was bright. Too bright.

"Are you sure?"

She nodded. "But I do want you to know that I left the whole fighting-over-a-guy thing back in middle school."

"Okay..."

"I don't know what the deal is with that girl, but I don't want any part of it."

"There's no *deal* with that girl."

"Well, just so we're clear. If that's some ongoing off-and-on thing—"

"*Hell* no. It's off. It's been off."

"—I don't need the drama."

"You think I do?" He pulled to a stop in the same space he'd taken earlier. "What, are you having second thoughts?"

"No, but frankly? I don't see how you can go from that to...me."

"Yeah, I'd love to get a look at whatever dude you hooked up with last too. See how we compare." He gave her arm a nudge and grinned when her jaw snapped closed, but he knew it wouldn't stay that way.

"But...well...it leads me to wonder if something she said might hold at least some merit."

"What did she say?"

"Basically that I was a rich-bitch revenge fuck for you."

He hoped she didn't notice—or that she couldn't see—the way those words made his jaw clench. *Damn you, Raina.* "Yeah, that sounds like something she would say. Don't worry about it."

"Well...am I? I just want to know what I'm getting myself into here. I don't like surprises."

He sat back and stared straight out the front of the windshield, sighing heavily. "Macy, I can tell you with absolute honesty that you are not a 'revenge fuck'. I don't screw people indiscriminately, so the very fact I'm here means I like you. Beyond that, I don't know what to tell you. Am I going to put a ring on your finger any time soon? Hell no. But you strike me as the type who wouldn't be looking for that from a guy like me, so it's all good, right?"

She only lowered her head, watching her fingers toy with the purse strap, and something surged in his chest.

"Macy? Is that cool?" As soon as the words left his mouth, he wondered if it was cool with *him.* A minute ago "no strings" would have been music to his ears. But in that split second when he'd asked and she'd faltered...a world of dreams had exploded in his head, an entire universe of *what if*s.

But whatever alternate universe had just infringed on their reality receded back into place, and she looked at him. "No strings, just fun?"

Now she made it sound so casual, too casual. There was nothing casual about the intensity of his want, his need, for her. Sitting in the dim light, she was stunning. Absolutely cover-girl gorgeous, and he knew in his heart this was another girl who could shred him all over again, really do a number on him. She could stamp her number right in the middle of his fucking forehead, and laugh about it.

Was he a fool of the biggest magnitude?

"Yeah."

"Cool," she said, sounding relieved. He was relieved by her relief. Whatever it took them to get out of his car and into her bed. Apparently his dick didn't care how big a fool he was.

"Sit tight." He felt her gaze on him as he jumped out and ran around to open her door, but hopefully she wasn't watching so closely that she could tell it almost pained him to walk. Excited was an understatement. He was threatening to bust the fly on his jeans. It was almost embarrassing.

After she got out of his car, she took his hand. Something about the simultaneous simplicity and enormity of her supple fingers curling around his fucked him all up inside, made something wild and protective ignite inside him.

Trust. She trusted him. Everything about him and his world was the opposite to her and hers, but she was willing to take this crazy gamble on him.

"What is it?" she whispered when he'd only stood there staring down at her like a dope for the last ten seconds.

He snapped out of it and shook his head. "Nothing."

"You can come in," she said, as if afraid he thought he wasn't welcome now or something. She dug in her purse with her other hand and came out with a jumble of keys. Together, they strolled toward her first-story apartment door.

For a second, he hoped things wouldn't get weird. Then he bitched himself out for acting like a little girl.

Of *course* things were about to get weird. He lived for weird.

But nothing prepared him for the "weird" that greeted him when Macy flipped on a lamp inside her place.

Okay, in all fairness, this was Texas and the country-and-western décor was, if not the norm, then pretty damn acceptable. But not among anyone he associated with. Everywhere he looked was leather and brown-and-white cowhide patterns. And the *trophies*. Jesus. She had a special lighted display case for them. He knew she rode horses a lot, but she must have been competing since she could walk to accumulate all of those.

Rows of them. Trophies. Medals. Framed pictures of her holding them as a snaggle-toothed little girl, then a gangly teenager, finally the gorgeous woman he knew. An older couple beaming with pride flanked her in most of them. Parents, probably. She bore a striking resemblance to the woman.

One picture in particular caught his eye. She was astride, turning a barrel in a cloud of dust. The photographer had caught the fierce, determined scowl on her face perfectly, and it didn't do any favors for his current erection.

"I had no idea I was in the presence of the Queen of the Rodeo."

"Obnoxious, isn't it?" she asked, wrinkling her pert nose and tossing her purse on the pale leather loveseat.

"Oh, sure. Totally obnoxious," he joked.

She laughed. "Well, I sort of...can't bring myself to get rid of them. For a long time after I quit competing, I packed them away. I didn't want to look at them, but in the end, I cracked. I guess it's my inborn competitive streak—I have to have the reminder that I accomplished something. Silly, right?" She actually seemed to be blushing.

It was insanely sexy.

"I get it," he said. "I feel the same way when I wake up and see the unconscious hookers and the tower of empty beer cans I built the night before. It's so hard to let go."

He struggled to keep the statement dead serious, and sure enough, he was gifted with an alarmed look from her wide hazel eyes.

Then, suddenly, she got it. Without him having to say a word or crack a smile, her body went off alert, and she laughed. "God, you're bad."

"So is there some reason why you quit racing?"

Her gaze flickered from the relics of her glory days to his face. There was a directness in that stare that threatened to undo him. "Candace never mentioned it to you?"

Racking his brain and coming up empty, he shook his head. "Nope."

"I was competing in Conroe when I was eighteen. I'd just made the last turn when—I don't know what happened. I don't even remember. But apparently, something spooked my horse, and I was thrown. Cracked a couple vertebrae among a dozen other things. I was black and blue all over. Ten weeks in a brace, plus surgery and physical therapy...it was...scary. My mare, Sugar, broke her leg and had to be put down." She nodded toward the picture he'd been contemplating earlier. "That's her there."

"Damn, girl."

Her lip quirked. "After I came out of all that, I just didn't have the fire for it like I used to. I still ride, still love it, but I'm way more cautious than before. In all things, I guess."

"I can see how that would happen. Do you still have problems?"

"Sometimes. But overall I've been really lucky. Very lucky. So I don't complain too much."

He opened his mouth to say he found it pretty incredible she would even want to look at a horse after something like that, but then being pulled from the mangled wreckage of his parents' car at six years old hadn't made him swear off vehicles. Just the opposite, really. He spent his spare time trying to fix them. The bigger the job, the more he liked it. But he'd never be able to mold that shredded mass of metal in his memory into anything resembling an automobile, even in his dreams.

She had caught him. "Were you about to say something?"

"Just that"—he struggled to contain the emotion threatening to crack his voice—"maybe we can compare scars."

There was little else he'd seen in his entire life more beautiful than Macy's smile. Maybe that was because, now that he thought about it, it was a fairly rare thing. "You'll show me yours if I show you mine?"

He winked at her. "That and other things."

The inquisitive way she was looking at him drove him nuts,

made him desperate to know what was going on behind those pretty eyes. One thing he knew for certain: there were depths in her he hadn't even begun to fathom. She intrigued him. Sorting her out would be no simpler than twisting that hunk of distorted metal back into mint shape.

"I'm going to get you used to me before it's over, you know," he said.

Her pink tongue swept across her top lip. Maybe her mouth was just dry, but he took it as an invitation. The tap dancing around each other was over. They were here. Alone. She was his and he was hers, if only for tonight.

"I'm getting a little used to you already," she said softly as he stepped closer.

"Just a little?"

She gave a slow nod, never taking her gaze from his. "Mm-hmm."

"It's a start."

Whisper-soft, he leaned down and brushed his lips across hers, savoring her intake of breath and the way it made her chest graze his. She was perfectly endowed. Way more than the handful most guys claimed was ideal—he'd always said *fuck that*; he liked the soft flesh to overflow his hands. He liked room to explore. Ample area to kiss and lick and suck. He didn't discriminate based on his preference, but he rejoiced when he found perfection. She was it.

A whimper escaped her throat when his tongue flickered against her lips, questing for entrance. She gave it, allowing her hands to creep up around his neck. Her flavor exploded on his tongue, sweet and sultry as a damn aphrodisiacal fruit. God. He hadn't counted on this gentleness. It was throwing him off, making him unbalanced. He groaned and sank his fingers into her silky hair, molding his palm to the back of her head. Reaching for the fire he knew was burning inside her, even if she was afraid to show it to him yet.

Breathless, she broke away, and the smolder in her eyes as she looked up at him nearly sucked the oxygen from him in turn. "My bedroom is...over there." She nodded to an open door across the room from them.

"Yeah? What awaits me in there? A genuine cow skull?"

She snickered. "Maybe. But most importantly, a really big bed."

"Mmm. In a hurry, are you?"

Judging from the glint in her eyes, the flush in her cheeks, she was. He'd never noticed before that she had freckles, just a light dusting under her eyes and across her nose. Her fingers stroked down his nape, sending gooseflesh down his back. "Don't you think we've waited long enough?"

"Good point." He stepped back slightly and swept his arm toward the door. "After you."

He'd been the last person she'd had sex with, and it had been the better part of a year. That was the longest she'd gone without having sex since she started having sex. Was that why she couldn't stop trembling? Should she say something before he got the wrong idea?

She'd never been this excited, this aroused. It couldn't all be *him*.

Taking the plunge, she tore her gaze from his and walked toward her room. She sensed him moving behind her, following closely. Between her legs, she was already slick and needy from his kiss, and if she didn't get out of this damn constrictive bra, she was going to scream. She needed his hands on her, soothing away the aches.

One lamp had been left on in her room for ambiance. Big ugly scar or not, she wasn't a lights-off kind of gal.

Some crazy compulsion made her turn around to close the door after he came in behind her—she didn't know why. It wasn't as if someone would be in the living room to overhear them. It just felt more...intimate. More—

The breath rushed out of her as his hard body pressed her roughly against the closed door. He swept her hair aside and fastened his hot mouth to the side of her neck, sucking hard. The outline of his cock branded her ass. Her heart rate soared out of control.

"Oh God," she gasped, grinding back against him. The movement gave him enough room to slide his hands under her sweater, up her quivering belly, and cup both of her breasts, kneading them with a gentleness that belied the hard-and-rough everywhere else. She only wished she were already naked for him. "Take it off," she pleaded.

His hands slid around to her back and deftly unfastened her bra. He lifted his mouth from her neck and sought her lips. She turned her head back and drank in his kiss like a starving woman as his fingers journeyed back around and played with her bare nipples beneath the loose bra cups. Dammit, she wanted the thing gone, but this was better than nothing.

It was all too much, and she couldn't get close enough. She couldn't see enough. He gave her space to shed her sweater and her bra; then he planted her right back in place, raining kisses over her shoulders and the back of her neck as his fingers worked the button on her jeans. She wriggled her hips as he stripped them down her legs. Thank God she hadn't worn boots or complicated shoes—she kicked off her flats and couldn't step out of the denim fast enough.

That left only her panties. Just as he'd promised on the phone last night.

Seth's breath gusted hot against her shoulder as his hand brushed the small of her back. Judging from the movements, he was unfastening his belt, wrenching at the button and—*oh God, yes*—yanking down his zipper.

"Let me see." She tried to turn, but he moved up so close behind her there was no way she could, not when every lean inch of his body pressed her against the door. And he was strong enough to stop any further efforts on her part. Not that she tried very hard.

"You're shaking," he murmured. He leaned into her, his nose nestling in her hair. She heard him inhale, felt his chest expand at her back.

There was no refuting his observation. No explaining it either. She shook as if it were twenty below in the room, but she was burning up.

His hands slid down her spine, fingertips grazing the thin seven-inch ridge of flesh nestled in the indentation. It had never had much sensation since it healed, but now...oh, it did. She felt his touch there more intensely than any other she'd ever known. Amazingly, she wasn't self-conscious about it, not with him. She opted out of bikinis these days, but Seth...in a way he carried his life story in his skin, right? He believed in that. He would merely see her scar as a little piece of hers.

His hands came to rest at the waist of her silk panties. Without conscious effort to move, she pushed back against his groin again, feeling the hard, smooth length of him press against the bare skin above her waistband. If she couldn't see him, dammit, she would feel him.

She gasped as the tip of his cock rubbed silkily across the flesh above her panties. The head was tipped with something cooler and even harder than his turgid flesh.

Her knees nearly gave. His piercing. She still didn't exactly know her feelings about it. But she did know it felt damn good.

He chuckled, a sound that made her think of a serial killer about to slip a garrote around her neck. "What's the matter?"

"Your...nothing."

"Hmm? My what?"

"Your piercing. It's...different for me."

"Different isn't always bad."

"No. It's just different."

"Okay."

"I mean, honestly I might run screaming if—"

"Macy?"

"What?"

He thrust his hardness between her legs so the bead rasped her clit. "Shut up."

His methods proved effective. She even spread her legs to give him better access, her forehead pressed against the door as she panted.

"Wait a second," he said. "Holy shit. What are you wearing?"

Until that moment, she'd almost forgotten. After his

turbocharged fantasies of leaving her panties on, she'd donned a pair of crotchless. "I thought you might appreciate it."

"Appreciate it? I think I'm in love."

It was said in jest, but an odd pang went through her.

"So wet for me," he murmured, keeping up the delectable movements that drew even more wetness from her core. One motion, one thrust from those powerful hips, and he could be inside her. So easy. She was almost mindless enough to beg him to do it. "Goddamn," he whispered as she undulated against his tip. "You're full of surprises, aren't you?"

"I'd rather be full of you."

He chuckled, and his teeth nipped her shoulder. She gasped. "Don't move," he said. "I mean it."

She'd never had a man take the upper hand the way he did. All of her lovers had been obsequious. Maybe that was what she'd always gravitated to, guys she could control. It wouldn't fly here. But she wanted to try, wanted to test him, to see just what he'd do if she disobeyed. Instead, she clung to the door and trembled as she felt him moving behind her.

There was the crinkle of a foil packet. The unmistakable sound of him unfurling latex down his cock with quick strokes. She moaned when his heat pressed against her again and two of his blunt fingertips zeroed in gently on the enflamed passage between her legs. She rose on her tiptoes when he pressed inside, testing, stretching. Her inner muscles had felt like liquid, but they gripped his intruding fingers with a strength that surprised her. His breath was ragged against her ear.

"Do you always get this wet?" he whispered.

She shook her head. It was the truth. If anything, there'd been times her *lack* of arousal with someone new distressed her. With him...it was the exact opposite. Her willingness, her need, her body's response to him, was a cause for major concern.

She didn't like the way he made her admit it to him. She didn't want to give him more power than he already had over her.

Suddenly, he removed his hand from between her legs and

reached down to catch her knee, lifting her leg and fitting himself between her thighs. Her muscles went rock hard in anticipation.

"Seth..." She tilted her hips back to meet his broad head, so ready for him to fill her. She'd take him all even if it hurt.

Could it be as good as it was before? It *couldn't*. Nothing could ever be that good again.

He rubbed the tip over her lips, down one side of the lace lining the slit in her panties, and up the other. She groaned and shifted, trying to capture him. There was no point in getting her any more wet; she was drenched. But he continued the elusive movements, teasing, making her beg. Making her open even wider in wantonness. Every time he passed it over her clit, his piercing wreaked havoc. Her body jerked, and she whimpered. He rubbed there, once, twice, harder...pressing...pushing up...

Desperate, nearly sobbing, she squirmed until he nestled into her entrance. Relief exploded through her, but then he didn't push right away. What the hell was he waiting for? "Seth!"

The low chuckle in her ear told her exactly what he'd been waiting for. Pressure built behind his thick head, slowly parting her. She tossed her head back against his shoulder and her fingernails dug into the wood of the door. Her breath seized. Her body locked. But he was relentless, taking her in one slow but persistent thrust she was powerless to stop even if she'd wanted to.

Oh yes. It was as good as before. Better.

"Holy fuck yes," he breathed against her neck. "Oh my God."

She choked out his name again. She felt...everything. Every nuance. The thick ridge of his corona. The bead underneath, now in perfect position to stimulate her G-spot. He was everywhere, all through her. Her body struggled to adjust, overwhelmed tissues quivering. She turned her head so he could kiss her with those gorgeous lips, and it was...

"Perfection," he murmured against her. "Have you thought about this as much as I have?"

As slowly as he'd entered, he began to withdraw. Sensitive flesh that had fought to accept him now fought to keep him in. Her only means of reply was a series of tiny whimpers.

"Have you?" he pressed, and she realized he wasn't going to give it back to her until she answered.

"Yes! Please..."

"Good. That's what I like." He filled her hard and fast, again and again, slamming her hips into the door. "You could've had me anytime you wanted, Macy."

If she made it through this alive...well, she wasn't sure what she'd do to atone for her survival but it would need to be something pretty momentous. Especially when his free hand squeezed between her body and the door and his fingers drew tantalizing circles around her clit.

When she grew so weak her legs wouldn't support her, he maneuvered them to her bed, laying her sideways across it. As hot as it had been having him behind her, she needed this. Face-to-face. His weight on her. So right.

She struggled to strip him of the shirt he was still wearing, but they didn't have time to bother with the jeans clinging to his hips. She'd have him naked before the night was over. He slid into her body again and she arched off the bed, wrapping her legs around his waist.

"Finally got you in bed," he murmured, capturing her trembling lips with his.

The kiss, deep, desperate, so heart-stoppingly *real*, ushered in her first orgasm without warning. He felt it, groaning into her mouth as she contracted around him. She loved how he stopped thrusting and grinded into her then, so in tune with her needs it was almost as if their minds melded as surely as their bodies.

Thoughts like that, she had to banish. But she couldn't, not when her brain was mush and her body quickly followed suit. Seth gentled his movements as she held on to him, letting her recover.

She knew from experience he wasn't anywhere near done. He was freaking Wonder Boy when it came to stamina. If by some miracle this became long-term, she was afraid there might be nights she just wouldn't have the energy to match him.

He grinned down at her. "That was sweet," he murmured, giving a twist to his hips that had her contemplating round two. "Took the edge off?"

"Mm-hmm."

He laced his fingers through hers and pinned her hands to the mattress, easing down to kiss and lick a path to her breasts. As he did, his cock slipped from her, and she gasped, her body clenching against the emptiness he left behind. Her nipples tightened in anticipation of his mouth. As he'd promised, he didn't tease her, this time taking one taut crest into his mouth and sucking deeply.

He released one of her hands, and a moment later, his finger slid into the lacy slit between her legs, and her thighs shuddered and closed against his sides. The sensations were just too acute, still sensitive from the ravages of her orgasm. "Mmm. Open up, babe."

She had to do it by increments, or she would fly into pieces. He waited patiently as she slowly let her knees drop apart.

His finger worked gently, maddeningly between her lips, swirling through her wetness but avoiding her clit altogether. All at once, she couldn't get enough of his touch. Her eyes flew wide as he slid down the length of her body, dropping kisses as he went down her tummy. His tongue flickered into her belly button, and then his lips teased the flesh at the border of her panties.

"These are so fucking sexy," he murmured. His lips skated over the lace that covered her mound. Her body clamped so hard on to his finger as he withdrew it that he cursed again. And squeezed in another.

By now his mouth was nuzzling her just above where his fingers disappeared into her body, and it was driving her wild. She throbbed, ached, writhed. His breath bathed her, each one a cooling burst just as searing as the heat. "Please," she whispered, not even knowing what she was asking for anymore. The slow thrust and drag of his fingers was only a miniscule reminder of what was to come.

"You want me?" he breathed. "You want my mouth on your pussy, sucking it until you scream, or my cock back inside it? Tell me how you need it, and I'll give it to you." His tongue darted once over her clit. She nearly had a seizure. Her hips wouldn't remain still, undulating against his plunging fingers in a perfectly sensuous and torturous rhythm.

As good as it was, it wouldn't compare to a blinding climax with him buried deep inside her, impossibly thick, impossibly hard. She *needed* it. "Your cock," she whispered.

"Hmm?"

Oh no, was he really going to make her do this?

"I want you inside me," she said. There could be no mistaking it that time. "*Now.*"

He didn't seem to mind the order. Quickly, he stripped his jeans the rest of the way off. At last. When he stretched out over her again, she cradled him between her legs and wrapped her arms around his naked flesh, her breathing harsh and irregular. Her trembling had never really subsided—now it doubled. His lips sought hers. She sighed as their tongues swirled around each other, tasting the faintest hint of herself on him. When he glided back into her body, the cry that wrenched from her throat must have sounded deceptively painful.

"Okay?"

"Don't stop."

That was the beauty of this, knowing he wouldn't, knowing he would take her there as many times as she needed to go. Confident now in her well-being, he unleashed his strength on her. She was more than ready for it, locking her ankles behind his back and hanging on for dear life, letting him exorcise all these months of accumulated frustration. She clung to him, taking it all and giving it back to him. Ecstasy had made her blind, but when he rolled them over so that she was on top, she vowed it wouldn't make her weak too.

A very fine sheen of sweat coated his chest, glistening in the lamplight. His body was nothing short of a work of art from his hard lines and planes to his ink; she'd only caught a glimpse of all of it but already knew she wanted desperately to run her tongue along those hip dips.

Later. The wicked glint in his eye was too enticing, and he felt too damn good inside her.

She squeezed her internal muscles and grinned at his reaction. His fingers bit into her thighs, and his chin tilted up. "*Fuck*, woman."

"Don't forget how much I like to ride."

He groaned in agony. "Crap. I'm dead."

She leaned down and grasped his chin, locking gazes with him. "I'll go easy on you."

His laugh sounded pained, and she couldn't help but enjoy the amazement in his expression. "Where the hell have you been all my life?"

She rolled her hips, and his voice became lost in a growl. His hands roamed up to cup her breasts, and she covered his fingers with her own, keeping up the pace and the angle that had him hitting all the right spots inside her. She'd wanted to deny there was something to be said for the piercing, but she'd have to be a fool—or a liar. When she leaned back just so...

Oh. My. God.

She gasped his name. Her rhythm became erratic, lost to passion. Pleasure, hot and molten, pooled low in her belly. Her first orgasm was usually her most intense, but he was going to shatter everything she thought she knew about herself and sex. One of his hands slid down so his thumb could circle her clit, and there was no fighting it. Her thighs locked down on his hips; her body clamped hard on him. The world exploded.

She collapsed over him as wave after wave swept through her, each contraction seeming to allow him deeper. So deep she didn't think she could take any more, but she did. He murmured insanely wicked things in her ear. And just as the maelstrom was ending for her, he was caught up in his own.

He flipped her underneath him as if she were nothing more than a rag doll, crushing her to the mattress. His sexy growl in her ear as he pushed deep and shuddered had her thinking enough naughty thoughts to keep them both occupied all night long. She stroked his back as he came, scoring him lightly with her fingernails. Judging by his shivers, he loved it.

"God, Macy," he groaned. Slowly, his hip movements subsided. She missed that rhythm immediately, didn't want it to end. So when he made a move to pull away, she locked her ankles around him and mewled.

His laugh sounded breathless. "It's okay. I'll just sleep here."

"Good."

"I'm not too heavy?"

She shook her head against his shoulder. Truthfully, she knew when she let him go...it was over. Reality would set in. She would have to look at him and know that he saw just how shaken she was. Who knew what naked post-coital vulnerability was showing on her face right now? She felt like crying. She couldn't speak.

He dotted kisses along her jawline, eventually finding her lips. She sighed as she opened to let him in, thinking it funny how a kiss had ignited her and now it was soothing her. Bringing her down. Calming her ragged breath, her racing heart.

They ended up lying on their sides, facing each other, legs a tangle she didn't even want to begin to figure out. She only wanted to enjoy the lazy, gentle brush of his fingers up and down her arm. Silence stretched out for a long time while she just looked at him.

"You must think I'm the biggest prude," she said after a while.

His dark brows dipped. "What in the hell makes you say that?"

"You having to shut me up."

"Naw. Prudish wouldn't be getting dirty in the backseat, having phone sex and...showing up tonight in crotchless panties. Damn, if I'd known you were wearing those all night..." His eyes closed as if savoring the mere thought of what he'd have done to her. "Let's just say we might've had to find a closet or something at my buddy's house."

She laughed. "I guess when you put it like that..."

"But, I can let you in on a secret. The little reservations and hang-ups you do have turn me on. Immensely."

"Really? Why?"

"It's a bigger challenge to get you to let go. And far more rewarding for me when you do."

So that was what all this was about. A challenge. Even that Raina girl had insinuated that. Oh well, how could she really be offended? At least he knew what he wanted, what he liked. At least he was honest. "I can see how it might be an ego stroke for you."

"That really has nothing to do with it. And don't get me wrong. I love a woman who loves sex and talking dirty." He reached up to rub his thumb across her bottom lip. Her eyes fell closed as his fingers trailed over her chin and down her throat. "But there's just something about hearing dirty talk coming from a nice, clean mouth. Any girl who says 'fuck' every other word can tell me to fuck her, and it's hot, but it doesn't mean as much as when you say it. If I can get *you* to tell me to fuck you, Macy, fuck you harder, fuck you faster...you'd better believe you're going to get it. You're going to get everything I've got, and then some."

How did he get her blood racing so fast so soon? Those very words he wanted to hear from her were crowding in her throat right now. She even pulled her bottom lip between her teeth to form the *f.* Just to test him. He seemed to be holding his breath, waiting. When she opened her eyes, she found his face so close their lips were almost touching.

"I do cuss, you know. I'm not Snow White here."

He exhaled in a frustrated rush, his warm breath tickling her mouth. "Dang and heck? You racy thing."

She lifted her chin, meeting his dark eyes head-on. "You've heard me cuss. And I have, believe it or not, been *fucked* before you came along."

Those eyes went even darker. "Oh, you've done it now."

Macy almost laughed as he rose over her, and his mouth descended on hers again, but two seconds later, all humor fled in the assault of blind lust that attacked her. He felt so good against her, strong and hard. She ran her palms over his smooth, marked skin, marveling at it.

She'd imagined him naked many times. But not knowing what lurked beneath his shirt, she'd neglected to fill in the tattoos in her fantasies. They covered both arms completely— that much she'd realized. Unlike Brian's vibrant riot of colors, Seth's tattoos were mostly black. The patterns swirled across his chest, a few tendrils meandering up his neck. Both his nipples bore silver hoops that glinted in the dim light.

"Why am I gonna get it? What have I done?" she asked innocently.

His reply was to don another condom and throw her knees over his shoulders. "You've been fucked before, huh?" he asked, angling her so that his piercing slid over her G-spot when he entered. "By the time I'm done, you'll have reassessed your definition."

She already had.

Hours later, he stirred beside her, and she reluctantly relinquished her legs' hold on his to let him get up. If she spent a little too much time admiring the view as he did so—*damn!*— well, who could blame her?

Tight butt. Firm thighs. The lingering ache between her thighs was testament that he knew how to use those muscles. The ink...well, she wasn't into it, but was it a deal breaker? Not in the least. She propped her head up on her hand and tried not to salivate as he moved toward the door.

"Got anything to drink?" he asked.

"All kinds of stuff. Help yourself to whatever you find."

"Want something?"

"Maybe I'll have a sip of whatever you're having."

She traced the ivy pattern on her sheets as she listened to him rummage around the kitchen. Searching through her cabinets, presumably for a glass, opening the fridge. It was strange having someone around. Strange, but nice. Even if he would be gone by tomorrow.

He walked back in a moment later with a glass of something—she couldn't see what. He handed it to her as he slid back under the covers, and she caught a glimpse of the glint of silver on his cock and the tattoo just above his pubic area, but she couldn't make out what it was.

The scent wafting from the glass she held reached her nostrils, and she took a sip, looking at him in surprise. "Apple juice?" she laughed.

"Yeah, so?"

"I just figured you'd go for something a little stronger."

"It was tempting. Actually, just so you know, I don't drink that much anymore. Every now and then I'll have a good time with friends, but not like I used to. Waking up in strange places with strange ink will do that to you."

"Good to know." She handed it back to him. He took a drink and set it on her nightstand, settling next to her again. "I didn't get to see. What did you cover up Casper with?" she asked. She tried to lift the covers, but it was too dark underneath.

"Ghostface."

She burst into laughter, and he followed suit. "From *Scream*? You did not."

"Naw, I didn't. It's still a ghost, but it's a scary-ass ghost."

"Oh, great. Now I have to come face-to-face with him whenever..."

"You'll learn to love him. It's a package deal. The monster in my pants and the monster lurking above."

"You have a lot of pride in your, erm, endowments, don't you?"

He cut her a sideways grin. "Am I hearing a complaint?"

"Nope, not from me."

"All right, then." She liked the way he looked at her, his gaze drinking her in from her eyes to her lips to the tumble of her hair down her arm. He reached out and touched a strand of it, curling it around his finger.

She didn't know if she should ask the questions burning in

her brain, but she wanted...no, she *needed*...to know more about who he was. He'd already shut her down once in the car. She glanced down and watched her fingertip trail around a curl of ink on his arm, taking the plunge. "How long were you together with Raina?"

"Three years."

Eyes widening, she lifted on her elbow and stared down at him. "Three *years*? How long ago did you break up?"

"About six months before you and I met."

Well over a year ago, then. That was somewhat of a relief, though she wondered why it had never come up before. "What happened?"

"You met her, didn't you?"

"But she didn't get that way overnight. You put up with it for that long, so there must have been something else. I'm sorry, I'm just insanely curious."

"It was cool to be that needed."

"Oh, come *on*."

"But I got over it."

"After three years."

"All right, you want the ugly truth? The girl was insane in the sack. She was insane in every other aspect too. She would go off on someone, or on me, in a heartbeat. It was fun. I got a kick out of wondering what the hell she would do next. We were like the death of every party, because we would get into a gigantic fight, and things would get destroyed...mostly by her as she threw them at me."

"So domestic violence is a turn-on for you."

He laughed. "Damn, when you put it like that, it sounds terrible. It wasn't *that* bad. She weighs all of ninety pounds. And it's mostly a front. She can cuss you six ways to Sunday, but if you say something that cuts her, she'll cry for hours."

"How did you meet?"

"Our lead singer introduced us. He knew her from Austin, where she used to live. She was in another band, but it was falling apart, and she did some guest vocals with us. When she and I hooked up, she moved here with me. She's hung around ever since."

"What happened? I mean, if it was all so much fun for you then—"

"She got pregnant."

Macy's heart skipped a beat as everything else froze. Not entirely certain how to proceed, she watched him closely and let him go on in his own time.

"The only other person on earth I've told this to is Brian, and I think even that was from shock. He was the one who was right there beside me when she called to tell me. Raina...she was excited. It scared the shit out of me. I mean, I might want to be a dad someday, but not any time soon, right? And I wouldn't wish her as a mother on anyone. Still, it was my responsibility too, so I wasn't going to run from it. But it made me realize how little I wanted to be with her. I mean, marry her? Or even deal with her for the next eighteen years while we raise a kid? That's what freaked me more than anything. Turns out it didn't matter. She had a miscarriage."

"Oh."

"Yeah. It was brutal. Sent her into a tailspin."

"What about you?"

"I guess I'd gotten used to the idea. It's a shock when suddenly everything you've been planning for and worrying about is gone just like that." He snapped his fingers. "I was pretty messed up too. But I knew by then I wanted out, right, but it only made her cling to me more, and I knew I couldn't leave her like that. I stuck it out with her a few months until I thought she was in a better place; then I had to bail. She had started talking about trying to get pregnant again, and I just couldn't deal with it."

Macy was silent while she digested what he'd just told her. Wow. She'd been expecting petty drama, not the life-altering circumstances that had led to their demise. And all at once she was ashamed of herself for making the crack to Raina about skipping her next dose. For all she knew, the girl was still dealing with the emotional fallout of losing her baby and the guy she loved in short order.

"I feel bad for her, and for a while I tried to be there for her if she needed me, but she would never take it for what it was. She wouldn't give it up. Then in typical Raina fashion, she started getting crazy on me *and* my friends, so...fuck her. It's done, I'm done. She's a big girl; she needs to deal with it."

"What about the other girl she mentioned?"

He'd been absently stroking her hair, but at her question, his hand froze. "Nothing to tell. I was a stupid kid. It wasn't what I thought it was." He scoffed and muttered, "Obviously," so low she could hardly hear it, shifting so that he lay on his back, staring straight up at the ceiling.

"Stupid kid or not, it sounds like it had a pretty serious effect on you."

"Listen to you, getting all deep." He grinned. He was a pretty good actor, she decided, but not that good. "Like I said, I was a dumbass. She was hot. I thought I was in love. I thought maybe she was too. She wasn't. End of story."

She sighed and laid her head on his shoulder. "What was her name?"

"Brooke."

She wanted to ask more, but the brusqueness of his reply clearly stated he considered the subject closed without even divulging the girl's last name.

"I was with my first boyfriend for a long time," she said instead. "We grew up together, so it wasn't really that I loved him in *that* way. He was just always there, you know?"

"Why are we tossing around the L-word so much?"

"Hey, you said it first."

"Then I'll be the first to shut it down."

"Fine by me." She searched her brain for another topic maybe he wouldn't shut down. Speaking of obvious love... "How long have you and Brian known each other?"

"Freshman year. I knew of him before, but we officially met in art class. He was like the big class star, at least in there. I got sick of it, so I went over to his table one day to tell him I thought his still lifes were okay but his perspective sucked. He said, 'Hey, fuck you.' After class, we beat the shit out of each other in the hallway and landed in detention together. Started talking about music. And a dysfunctional friendship was born. We still argue to this day over who won the fight. There's been more than one rematch."

She snickered. "Sounds like you two."

"We're a good team, though. Especially at work."

"How are you a team at a tattoo shop?"

"Well, see, he's stellar at portraits. When Brian draws someone's face, it looks more like them than *they* do. You've seen his work, right?"

"I saw the drawing he did of Candace. It's incredible."

"But he's not all that great at lettering. It's his dirty little secret, and I love to give him shit about it. I'm just the opposite. No way in hell I want to fuck up the face of someone's loved one on their body, you know? Shit makes me twitchy to even think about. So I draw up all his lettering, and he never throws any portraits my way. Give me a scorpion or a gecko or something any day, I'll bang it out in no time. But not Grandma Lucy."

Macy smiled at the way enthusiasm seeped into his voice whenever he talked about his and Brian's work. "That's really neat. I wish Candace and I had a story that exciting, but I can't even remember the first time we met. Our parents are friends. She was homeschooled, and I was pretty much the only person her mom would let her hang out with." She quieted for a moment, frowning, thinking. "Like with my first boyfriend, probably the only reason she puts up with me is that I've always been there."

"Oh, shut up. There you go again. Although I do hope for your sake that your parents aren't anything like hers. I don't know them, but I've heard Brian's horror stories."

"They're not. Just your typical nosy, meddling, occasionally embarrassing parents."

"Huh. I guess you're lucky to have parents around to be nosy and embarrassing. Mine didn't hang in there long enough."

She cringed inwardly. Another touchy subject. "I'm sorry."

He waved a hand. "It's all right. It was a long time ago. I'm not gonna go to pieces talking about it or anything."

"So your grandmother raised you after..."

"Yeah. She always said I was the only thing that pulled her through after the accident. My grandpa died when I was a baby, and my older brother was a dick from birth, so she was pretty much all alone except for me and my sister. Made me feel like there was a reason I walked away from the wreck with hardly a scratch, you know?"

"Of course there was a reason. Did you ever doubt it?"

"Through my teen-angst dumbassedness, I think I threw a few 'fuck the world, I wish I'd died instead of my folks' tantrums, but I got over that. Brian would always be there to kick my drunk ass if I needed it. Believe me, I fucking needed it."

"Sounds like he's been a really good friend to you."

He was silent for a moment. When he spoke, revulsion twisted his voice. "Brian is the brother I should've had. Instead of that sorry-ass motherfucker I got strapped with."

"What's the deal with your brother?" She racked her brain but couldn't recall him ever telling her why he hated the guy so much. He barely talked about him at all.

"He's an asshole. It needs no other explanation."

"There's got to be more to it than that. I'm pretty sure everyone has a relative they can say that about. But you...you take it to a whole new level."

"Yeah? Well, he takes being an asshole to a whole new level."

"It's just that I would think after the tragedy you guys went through, you would, I don't know, pull together."

"You'd think wrong." The chill coming off him was palpable. She lifted her head and frowned at him.

"What did he do to you?"

"Let's change the subject, all right? I don't want to fuck the night up now."

Stung, she settled her head back on his shoulder. "Okay."

He was right. She didn't want that either. She'd just gotten carried away putting together all his many scattered puzzle pieces. Something told her there wouldn't be a complete picture for a long, long time, if ever.

God, in the past few minutes they'd covered death, pregnancy and heartbreak—and his *brother* was the deal breaker? Weird. If she kept asking questions, he was probably going to get dressed and bolt.

She *definitely* didn't want that. Even more disturbing, she found herself wondering what it would be like to have this every night. The warm solidity of his shoulder under her cheek, his fingers lazily traveling up and down her arm.

It couldn't work. He'd made the terms clear in the car, and she'd agreed. Now that she'd let him in, she had to be on her guard. Lately she'd often thought he was different than he'd seemed when she first met him—the wisecracking, don't-give-a-damn-about-anyone-or-anything tattoo artist—but it was distinctly possible he wasn't. At least when it came to her.

How would she compare to the mystery girl who obviously splattered his heart all over hell, or even to the one he'd kept around because she was "insane" and exciting?

Macy had wanted to explore her wild side a bit with him...that's why she was here. She'd wanted to discover if she even *had* a wild side. She hadn't expected to feel duller than ever afterward.

Chapter Ten

The last thing he'd planned on was falling asleep with her snuggled at his side, her head on his shoulder like they were...a couple or something. One moment, they'd been lying in her bed in the peaceful semidarkness; the next, a swath of sunlight was hitting him right between the eyes.

Might as well make the most of it. He rolled over and groped for her warm body only to touch the coolness of empty sheets. Lifting his head and focusing, he not only saw visual evidence she was missing, but an aroma was drifting in from the kitchen that awakened parts of him that were famished for more than her body. He always woke up starving.

He wanted a shower, but first he tugged on his jeans and, leaving them unbuttoned, ambled out into her living room to investigate...bypassing a trophy saddle on the way.

Jesus, yes, the girl liked to ride. He could damn sure attest to that.

She was chopping vegetables at the counter in a silky pink robe thing that barely covered her ass. Moving quietly as he could on his bare feet, he sneaked up behind her and slid a finger under the hem.

Macy gasped and whirled, hazel eyes wide. "Dammit! Don't do that to a woman with a knife in her hand."

"You don't scare me," he murmured, leaning in to taste the sweetness of her neck. She smelled like warm, sugary vanilla. Tasted like it too. The scent had always barely teased him when he was around her, but now, this close, he could get drunk on it. Drunk on her.

Her knife clattered to the counter, and she sighed and wound her arms around his neck. The position raised the hem of her robe, and he took advantage, sliding his hands over the firm globes of her ass.

He loved how she was soft and strong at once, her muscles solid as any athlete's, the strength belied by the delicacy of her stature. Perfection, he thought yet again. He really wished he would stop it with that. Nobody was perfect.

She might damn well be as close as he'd ever get.

One quick tug and her robe fell open, baring those high, sweet, pink-tipped breasts. Something sizzled angrily on the stove, but it was nothing compared to the sizzle happening down south. He was as hard right now as he'd ever been last night, the sight of her luscious tits revving him until he was like a race car in the red.

"I'm going to burn the bacon," she murmured as his lips sought a nipple. For some reason, she made him think of cake frosting. A confection. Far too rich for his palate, but damn if he wasn't going to steal a bite if he could.

Thank God he'd put his pants back on. Thank God he'd put his wallet back in the pocket last night. Thank God there were more condoms in there. She was already shoving at his jeans, pushing them down his hips so that his erection sprang free. He pulled away from her and groaned as she encased him with her slim fingers. The first time she'd done that months ago, he could've blown in her gentle grip like a teenager. Just to be in her hands, *Macy's* hands, when he'd thought he never would be, had almost been too much for him.

"Hang on," she whispered and, stretching over to her left, turned off the knob on the stove and moved the pan to a cool eye.

He chuckled, but the sound abruptly died when she hit her knees in front of him. All the air pretty much waved bye-bye to his lungs. He shuffled backward until his ass met the edge of her kitchen island, and he braced his hands against it, trying to catch his breath. As she finally came face-to-face with the snarling, skeletal Grim-Reaper-ish ghost low on his abdomen, she paused long enough to glance up at him and smirk. Thank fuck, it didn't deter her. Her wet little tongue flickered over his tip and then circled it, and he let his head fall back with an agonized groan.

After three long, damp strokes up his dick, he was panting. Once he was glistening with moisture from her clever tongue, her hand curled around his base, her lips sucked in his crown. Slowly. Not even inch by inch but centimeter by centimeter. She worked him deep as his knees nearly gave out.

"Macy," he choked out, threading his fingers through silky hair still tousled from their wild escapades last night. He wanted to grab the back of her head and shove it, had to make a fist to keep from doing so. She whimpered as her hair pulled tight. "Sorry," he whispered, loosening. "I can't stand it."

She had yet to show him what he couldn't stand. Her tongue rolled around his shaft, teased at his piercing, and he growled. Her hand stroked him at his base. Her other hand came up to cup his balls. His entire friggin' life was focused between his legs in that moment.

But he didn't want to come down her throat. For that matter, he didn't want to come in a fucking rubber, either.

There were far worse decisions to have to make, he decided, than where and how to release inside Macy's willing body. But this kitchen island sure was an ideal height...

He was almost too far gone to stop her. Almost. Grasping her hands, he pulled them away as she glanced up at him questioningly. His cock fell from her mouth with a wet sound that almost made him change his mind. The memory of how soft, tight and perfect her pussy had felt wrapped around him was the only thing that gave him strength. He wanted to be there again, wanted to be there as often as she'd let him before she decided to move on.

Move on...maybe to some other undeserving asshole. The thought sent razor blades shredding through his chest.

He hauled her up to her feet and grabbed her around her slim waist, whirled and planted her on the island. She gave a soft laugh as a strand of dark hair fell over her eyes...stunningly beautiful, dreamy, come-fuck-me eyes. He insinuated himself between her thighs and reached for the back pocket of his drooping jeans. She glanced down at his dick. No drooping there. He was damn near pointing straight up.

Macy's pink tongue slid over her swollen top lip. He'd love to let it slide over him some more, but he was humming with too much adrenaline, too much pent-up energy. As much as he'd like her to suck him off, right now he needed to fuck. Hard. He needed her to never forget what he felt like inside her.

She reached for his cock while he tore the foil, one corner of that luscious mouth kicked up. "Magnum," she commented.

"You know it."

"Oh, yes, I do."

His task completed, he pulled her close, spreading her legs wide around his hips. "Seth," she breathed, the tiniest hint of urgency in her tone. "Go slow at first, okay? It...had been a while and..."

"It's okay," he whispered. He needed her, he needed her hard and fast, but one tiny hint of vulnerability from her and he also wanted to soothe her and protect her. And never, ever hurt her.

She took his gentle intrusion with her head back, her nails digging in his shoulders, her graceful throat exposed so he could watch the pulse flutter at the side of her neck. He could feel that same pulse in the clinging depths of her pussy. Her brow furrowed, but whether it was pleasure or pain or a comingling of the two, he couldn't tell. He held still while she shifted to angle her hips better for him. When she found it, he knew. Her expression smoothed over.

"Oh yes," he murmured, nuzzling the side of her neck. He moved one hand from her thigh to draw teasing circles around her areola with his thumb as he withdrew from her almost all the way. Only the very tip of him claimed the last inch of her. He slid back in, easier this time. She was so swollen, so tight. So perfect, contoured in just a way that stroked all his hot spots. Like she'd been made for him.

Every ounce of restraint he possessed was engaged right now, straining against the need roaring through his veins, holding it at bay. He wouldn't let go until he knew she was with him.

Her internal muscles squeezed him and he growled. God*damn*, he loved it when she did that. The girl had muscles in places that—

She did it again, and all thought shut down.

"Macy..." It was a plea. It was a prayer. If she needed it, he'd turn it into a fucking chant. He just wanted her, wanted to plunge into her over and over, needed to make her his.

"Yes, Seth, *yes.*"

She'd scarcely gotten his name out when he let go. Just like last night, her strong gripping heat brought out the beast in him, and he was hungry for her. Maybe someday he could imagine actually making love to this woman, but now wasn't that time. Her cries were music in his ears and when he looked down to watch himself disappear over and over inside her pink folds, so wet and pretty, the sight was almost his undoing. How many damn times *would* she undo him?

When she came, he felt it. Never in a million years would she ever be able to fake him out—she gripped him so hard and drew him so deep when she climaxed he couldn't breathe. Her thigh muscles went rock hard around his hips. Her nipples pulled tight. Color roared high in her cheeks. Right in front of him, she blossomed all over, and it was a thing of fucking beauty.

He followed her lead. How could he not? His chest constricted as his release shot through. For one moment, their gazes locked, and then their mouths melded furiously as he pumped his seed into the barrier between them. She drank in his moans and muffled curses and stroked his back as she squeezed the last drop from him with her own aftershocks.

"Oh my God," she sighed, that soft coming-down sigh he already recognized and loved. She drew his head down to rest on her shoulder as he struggled to catch his breath. Wrapped in her heat, in her arms, in her legs... *Christ.*

It had never been this way before. And that was why he needed to get the fuck out of here.

Needed to, but wouldn't. Because when it came to girls like Macy—like Brooke—he was a hopeless frigging sap.

He damn sure wished that name would quit crossing his thoughts. Whatever emotions Macy was pulling out of him, he wanted to push, shove and kick them back where they belonged. Her questions last night hadn't helped.

Macy was nothing like Brooke. They might've come from similar, wealthy backgrounds, but Brooke had been high maintenance to boot. He wouldn't have been able to afford that girl, something he realized now but as a kid with stars in his fuckin' eyes, he'd thought the world was his oyster. With her at his side, he could do *anything*. When she'd left, she'd given him a sharp slap of reality.

He lifted his head before he could fall asleep on his feet cradled in Macy's embrace. The glazed hazel eyes staring at him now didn't contain one ounce of the disdain he'd seen in the expression of the first and only woman he'd loved that day years ago. All he saw now were the ravages of very recent pleasure. Macy leaned forward and kissed him sweetly, stroking his tongue with hers, and the dark spot on his thoughts was washed away.

She eased back and stroked his eyebrow with her thumb. "You looked far away," she murmured.

"I'm back now."

"Where'd you go?"

He shook his head. "Nowhere you need to worry about." Only then did he step away from her, allowing himself to slip free of her body. She gasped softly and snapped closed her legs, pulling her robe over her flushed breasts.

There was something so sexy about a well-fucked woman. Especially when she came back to herself after an amazing orgasm and realized she was still sprawled wantonly on a piece of furniture in a moderately inappropriate place. Or a backseat. Macy had that look now, the slightly embarrassed *I can't believe I just let him take me here* look.

She cleared her throat and hopped down, her dark hair shielding her face. He grinned to himself and headed to her bathroom to take care of the condom. When he returned, she was back in her original position when he'd first entered the kitchen, whipping up pancakes.

"Hungry?" she asked.

Now that his sexual appetite was out of the way—well, for the most part—hell yeah, he could focus on less important parts of his anatomy, like his stomach. "And she cooks too," he said, pinching her on the bottom. She laughed.

"Well, a little. Don't get too excited."

She had him excited all right. It had little to do with her abilities in the kitchen. Of the culinary variety.

"We didn't burn the bacon after all," he observed, picking a piece and biting into it. It was good and crispy, just the way he liked it.

She laughed softly and he paused to watch her profile. As she tucked a strand of hair behind her ear, her hand visibly shook.

"You okay?" he asked, smoothing his hand up her back and massaging her shoulder.

She nodded almost before he could get the words out. She wouldn't look at him. "Mm-hmm. Great."

What the hell had happened here? He'd kind of sneaked up and laid siege to her, but she'd seemed to be into it. Maybe last night was supposed to have been *last night*, and this morning, she wanted him the hell out of her house.

No strings, right.

Okay, he could do that. It's what he'd promised her last night. But he found again that he didn't like it. A thousand and one things he could do to her pliant body zoomed through his mind. He wanted all day with her to knock some of them out.

"Coffee?" she asked, pulling mugs down from a cabinet.

Obviously she hadn't planned to kick him out right away. He was being a dumbass. "That'd be awesome. Black."

They sat down to eat at her bistro table in her sunny little nook, but the pleasure of the food was eclipsed by that of watching her hair sparkle in the sun. It was brown and silky, though the morning light cast a reddish halo around it. Several times, he glanced over his coffee mug to catch her staring at him. She would always drop her gaze to her plate or avert it out the window. She barely touched her own food.

"You're not eating much," he said.

"I'm actually not that hungry. I thought I was...but I guess I'm not."

"Feel okay?"

Her brows dipped briefly. "Oh, sure."

"Macy." Ghost reached across the table, sliding his hand over hers. Immediately, she turned hers over and grasped it. Might as well get it out there. "If you're feeling weird about all this, you don't have to worry. Don't think anything is different from what we talked about last night."

It really hurt to say. And maybe he was insane, but he thought the expression that crossed her face as she stared down at their joined hands was hurt too.

"I know that." Her voice sounded thick, as if her throat was closing in. "I had a really good time, though."

"Me too."

Her soulful gaze flickered up to his and back down. Dammit, they hadn't even scratched the surface. Why did her words have echoes of good-bye in them? Why the hell did sex always complicate things? It was just one body part going into another. Why couldn't it just be about the physical act, *please and thank you, catch ya later*?

But that was exactly what she was doing, wasn't it. *Again*. He should have friggin' known better than to go here with her. She'd already pulled this hot-and-cold shit on him once months ago. His running to another state hadn't cleared his memory of how pissed off he'd been. He'd thought surely she wouldn't run the same game on him now, but it looked as if she was ready to make him into a fool for the second time.

Damn if he was going to hang around and let her. Abruptly, he released her hand and shot out of his chair. Surprise flared across her face.

"Thanks for breakfast, but I'd better get dressed and jet," he said, jerking his thumb over his shoulder in the general direction of the door. "Gotta be at work in a couple hours, and I want to call Nana first."

"Oh...okay." Putting her palms flat on the table, she rose also, her movements slow and a little timid.

Curse the morning-after good-bye. It seemed ten times as awkward when all he really wanted was to drag her back into her bedroom and have his way with her for the rest of the day.

She dropped her gaze and busied herself clearing dishes. He lingered for a moment to help her, then headed to her bedroom to throw on his shirt and boots. When he finished and turned toward her bedroom door, she was standing there, having silently appeared behind him at some point.

"I meant what I said," she told him. "I had a really great time—I mean, that's an understatement."

Fuck, she was beautiful, and he wanted her. He wanted her right now. Wanted to tackle her into her unkempt sheets and make her cry out his name again.

So he did. Be damned if he would be making any walk of shame today.

Her startled gasp against his lips only fueled him as he crushed her to him and toppled them both back onto the mattress. She might as well give up on wearing her little robe around him; he yanked the sash and spread it open, palming her breast while she shook and writhed under him. Her thighs gripped his jean-clad hips and she rubbed her pussy against the hard shaft of the erection he'd never really lost from spending himself inside her.

He needed to finish what he'd started last night. He'd given her the option, and she'd chosen for him to fuck her, but right now he was craving another taste of the sweetness between her legs.

He kissed her with slow, deliberate sweeps of his tongue. He wanted her dying for him to do the same thing to her clit. Judging from her gyrations, her whimpers, she wanted just that. Pinning her wrists to the bed, he kissed a path from her lips to her left nipple, budded so tight. He licked it, sucked it, gave it the lightest pinch of his teeth.

Her head tossed. She was strong; sometimes her arms would jerk, and he'd nearly lose his grip on her. But he held her

115

fast. Her thighs rubbed up and down his hips, the heels of her feet pressed into his ass. She moved under him as if he were inside her, a slow, sensuous rhythm. If that was the way she liked it, he'd make note of it and use it on her later.

If there was one.

He slapped the thought aside. He'd make her come so hard there would be no question about *later*. She'd be the one coming back for more.

When both her nipples were wet and distended from his attentions, her milky skin splotchy with pink heat, he slid his open mouth down her belly. Lower, lower, flickering his tongue against her flesh. The farther down he went, the harder it became for her to move, until she was merely squirming as he pinned her legs down under his arms. As he nuzzled against her closely trimmed pubic hair, the scent of her arousal short-circuited his brain.

"Oh God, please..." she cried, the first words that had burst forth from her yet. Her wrists again threatened to break his grip.

"If I let your hands go, will you be a good girl and not touch me?"

"Why not?" she gasped, tilting her hips up toward him.

He evaded her. "All I want you to feel of me is my mouth and my fingers."

"Yes!"

"Even when you come, don't touch me."

The sounds tearing from Macy's throat were lost between whimpers and sobs. She managed to nod her head.

"Now, ask me nicely."

"What?"

"Ask me for what you want, Macy."

"P-please...lick me."

"Oh, okay." He licked the smooth inner side of her thigh.

"Shit. Not *there*."

He damn near burst out laughing. "My bad. Where? I can't read your mind, woman."

"Lick my *pussy*, Seth." He could swear her face went two

shades darker red.

"Thank you. I believe I will."

Christ, she was wet. And swollen. And sweet as the strawberries she'd put out on the table this morning. He kissed her tenderly, sweeping his tongue through her folds and collecting the taste of her juices. Her staccato sobs of moments ago turned into long, drawn-out sighs of pleasure.

His fingers loosened on her wrists, then released. Her arms remained obediently on the bed. He grazed his fingertips against her belly as he lowered first one hand and then the other, feeling her stomach muscles pull tighter under his touch. So sensitive. He tucked one arm under him for support and left one hand free to touch her. When she was ready.

"Feel good, baby?" he murmured against her.

"Sooo good."

He explored lower, letting his tongue slip over her entrance where her flavor was even sharper, tangier. Her thighs stiffened, and he remembered what she'd said earlier about being sore. She needed this right now. He moved his tongue in slow, soothing strokes around her tiny opening. The need to slide up and plunge his cock into it was there—it never left—but he ignored it. This was all about her.

"So sweet," he whispered. "I could do this all day."

"I could let you all day."

He moved his mouth up to suck her clit. As he drew on her with her moans echoing in his ears, he fluttered his tongue over it, sending her cries even higher. Her thighs opened wider. When he glanced up the length of her body, her hands were on her breasts. Hot as hell.

When her first orgasm swept her away, he slid a finger deep so he could feel her contractions. Incredible. He could swear her taste and scent sweetened and when he drew his finger out, it was coated in her honey. He slid it into his mouth for a taste, then back into her with another, hooking them upward to tease her upper wall.

She'd somehow not touched him through her climax. Now she seemed to realize she couldn't get him to stop without disobeying that order.

"Seth— I can't take it," she said, trying to squirm away.

"You can," he assured her. "You don't have a choice."

"Oh my God…"

He drew out his fingers, nice and wet from her arousal, and gently lowered them to tease the pucker of flesh below her pussy. Just like that, her breath caught in her lungs and, without even touching them, he sensed her thigh muscles go rock hard again. But she didn't push away; she didn't disobey and push *him* away.

"Have you ever been fucked in the ass, sweet Macy?"

He carefully watched her reaction. She pulled her lips between her teeth and shook her head, her forehead creased.

"But you'll let me, won't you," he cajoled as he exerted the slightest pressure with his finger. She was impossibly tight. Her chest suddenly heaved as if she'd just remembered to breathe.

"I… You'll hurt me."

"Afraid of a little pain, cowgirl?"

Her mouth quirked at that. "No. But I tend to avoid it if I have the choice."

"Well, you do, you know." A little more, and a little more, he pushed until the tip of his finger softened her tight ring enough to gain entrance. Millimeters. A centimeter. An inch. Macy's hands were gripping the bedspread, tugging it almost to her face. Her breath sobbed out. She didn't speak. Didn't stop him.

"How do you feel?" he whispered.

Her lips parted, her eyes opened, turmoil and agony writhing for dominance on her face. "*Dirty*," she bit out.

"That's what you wanted me for," he all but growled. His dick was going to cuss him for a bastard if he didn't get inside her. But he'd just have to take it. This was about leaving her wanting more. "Wasn't it? To get you dirty. That's why you know you're going to let me do it. After I leave and you cool down, you'll tell yourself you won't. But one day, you'll beg me for it, because you know there's more, and you know I can give it to you."

He could swear the word that left her lips was "*fuck*," and he couldn't resist a grin. Already loosening her tongue. He was knuckle-deep in her sweet heat, and sweat beaded on her brow. He eased his mouth back down to her clit and teased it with languid sweeps of his tongue, groaning at the sharp spice of her need. Oh yeah, she wanted it all right. She was practically dripping. While he distracted her with slow swirls of his tongue, he inched his finger deeper until she'd accepted all he could give her.

When she came, muscles clamping desperately on him, he slowly pulled it out. The keening moan that tore from her throat was a sound he'd hear in his dreams from now on.

It seemed forever before she settled. Her eyes were wet, her nipples beaded, her skin rosy. He couldn't take his eyes off her. She lay limp, panting, a thin sheen of sweat glistening on her skin in the light from her windows.

"I really can't take any more," she said weakly.

"That was hardly all day," he complained, lifting on his elbows, his knees and then climbing off the bed to his feet. If he stood and stared down at her for a moment admiring his handiwork, well, he figured there wasn't a dude on earth who'd blame him or who wouldn't do the same. Most of them would probably try to sneak a picture on their cell phones.

She drew her knees together, hiding her flushed slice of heaven from his view. Damn. He imagined the pout on his face as she did so was akin to a kid learning there was no Santa Claus.

Once she'd caught her breath, Macy giggled, lifting a hand to cover her face.

Well, that was a guaranteed way to dispense with any awkwardness with her. And he didn't want to find himself in that situation again. He trotted into her bathroom to wash his hands. Then, bracing on the bed with his hands, he leaned over and brushed his lips across her cheek. She turned her mouth to his. Knowing she tasted both of them as she kissed him offered no relief to his raging hard-on.

He pulled back. She whimpered, curling her fingers around the back of his neck, attempting to hold him to her.

"I have to go, lovely."

"But..." Her gaze drifted down to his fly, where he strained against his zipper. He smiled and traced her delicate jawline with his thumb.

"I'll catch you later."

Before she could reply, he was gone.

Chapter Eleven

"I'm ready to come clean."

Candace looked up from her steaming mug, one taupe eyebrow arched as she studied Macy from across the booth. "Is this about what I think it's about?"

Macy glanced around the coffee shop across the street from Dermamania. The girls had ducked in just before closing time to assuage a sudden craving for hot chocolate. "I'm pretty sure."

Candace grinned from ear to ear. "Not that I didn't know something was going on, but I'm glad you're finally filling me in. Spill."

Macy shrugged, feeling so out of her element. It wasn't that she didn't trust her friends or didn't like confiding in them about some things. She'd always prided herself on being the type who didn't spread her drama around for everyone's amusement, and swallowing that pride felt like choking down a bowling ball. Her face flamed, and she fanned herself. Candace broke into laughter.

"Damn, it must've been good."

"Oh, it was good."

Candace reached over and placed her hand over Macy's— she was wearing black-and-pink-striped fingerless gloves—and squeezed. "I am so happy for you. I've noticed a glow about you the past couple of days."

"Don't go picking out shower gifts or anything."

"Well, I know, but...you needed a pick-me-up. I take it he sufficed."

"More than. I just...I don't know. He's great."

"I feel a 'but' coming on."

"A big one."

"Macy, if you like him, go for it. Don't worry about anything else. When Brian and I were getting together, I wasted so much time worrying and—no offense—listening to *you* and everyone else tell me to forget it, that it would never work. I hurt him, I tortured myself...and for what? It didn't have to be that way. I should've trusted what I was feeling."

"You and Brian already had a lot in common, though. It's like he brought out the 'you' that was already there. You guys make a lot more sense than me and Ghost. All we have going for us"—she glanced around, leaned across the table and hissed—"is great sex."

"Hey, that's more than some people have." Candace winked.

"I'm afraid that's all it'll ever be. He's got a lot going on right now, you know? It's really bad timing. Not to mention the psycho ex."

Candace scoffed. "Don't worry about her. Everyone cringes when she comes around, and she likes to run her mouth, but I think she's pretty harmless."

"What's with this other girl who apparently broke his heart a long time ago?"

"Oh God. Brian told me a little about that—I don't think I got the whole story. Apparently this girl totally wrecked him, and he still gets bitter over it sometimes. That's all I know."

"Fantastic. That's exactly what I need—a man who's hung up on someone else." And it was essentially what Raina had been hinting at. "That whole baggage thing I was talking about. I could really do without that."

"I don't think it's so much that he's hung up on her. I think it's that he was fucked over, and it still pisses him off. Bruised that fragile male ego and all."

Macy thought about how he'd shut down at the mention of that girl. Oh, it had done more than bruise his ego. It had beaten it to a bloody pulp.

Candace twirled her mug slowly in her hands. "Brian is really loyal to him. They might talk a lot of crap to each other, but one of them couldn't jump off a bridge without the other close behind him."

"I gathered. And that's another problem."

"What?"

"Honestly? I get the feeling Brian doesn't like me. And I definitely wouldn't want to cause any problems between you and him or put you guys in a position to take sides if Ghost and I didn't work out."

As expected, Candace was already shaking her head. "Brian likes you—"

"Like he would tell you if he didn't."

"Knowing him? He would. But he's never said anything to me to indicate he doesn't, I promise."

"Okay."

"You have that line between your eyebrows. Stop."

Macy chuckled and drained her own mug, licking the last of the chocolate from her lips. "This could just as easily go nowhere, and I'll have stressed over nothing."

"Take it slow; give it a chance. Keep an open mind."

"I really don't think that's the kind of advice I need at this point. I'm beyond it. I...I can't quit thinking about him, Candace. It's driving me nuts. I'm trying so hard to be casual about it because..." She shook her head. "It just seems so impossible right now."

"Believe me, it's not impossible. If it worked for us, it can work for you."

"Does he strike you as the type who's looking for anything long-term? As much as I try to pretend I'm not, I am. I'd love it, you know? If the right guy came along, I'd be so ready to get married and have kids. I put out the vibe to him that I'm not into all that." When she really listened to herself, she let her head drop into her hands with a groan. "Do you hear what I'm admitting to? I basically lied to get laid."

"I don't know if you realize this or not, Macy, but you can be pretty standoffish. If that's the vibe you're putting out, he's probably doing the same thing. It's simple self-preservation."

"I'm not *that* bad." Macy lifted her head and searched Candace's face. "Am I?"

"I'm not one to give an objective opinion. I've known you my

123

whole life, I'm used to you."

"Great. In other words, 'You're a raging bitch only a best friend could love'. I had no idea I had so little self-awareness."

"Get over it. I'd have to say you're more a snob than a raging bitch. Oh, and maybe a control freak though you're better about that now than you used to be. But I love you anyway. So could he."

The words stung, the ring of truth biting deep. The Candace of old would never have said anything like that to her. Macy laughed to keep from crying. "It's only that I don't see what's so wrong about being set in my ways and wanting what I want, and liking what I like. And of course, *not* liking some things."

"The bottom line is you have to accept him the way he is and not try to change him. If you're not willing to do that, Mace, it really is going to be impossible. Give it up now, because I can tell you with absolute certainty, he won't go for it. I mean, he's a guy who'll tell you to fuck off and die if you try that on him."

"I know. I wouldn't do that. He is who he is. Just as long as he remembers that I am who I am too." Macy sighed, staring out the window at the neon sign of the tattoo parlor across the street. A light drizzle of rain beaded on the glass and slicked the street outside, but even so, she could see that Seth was over there. She could just make him out through the windows, and sure enough, his car was now parked at the side of the building. When had that happened, and how had she missed it? "Hey, I thought you said he wasn't working tonight."

Candace glanced over. "Huh. He's not. He must be hanging out. Looks like Kelsey and Evan are there too. When did the party start?"

Macy chewed on her thumbnail. He hadn't spoken to her since leaving her apartment. It had been days. She hadn't tried to contact him, either. Was it some kind of game, or did he really not care to talk to her? Whenever she tried to apply motives to him, though, she had to take a look at her own.

Yeah. She would *love* to talk to him. She just wasn't about to be the first one to pick up the phone and give him the satisfaction of knowing she needed him, of giving any truth to his final arrogant words before he'd left her lying lifeless on her bed wondering what the hell had just happened. For nearly an hour after he walked out, she'd stared at the ceiling in a daze. When she'd finally dragged herself up, aftershocks racking her every time she moved, she noticed he'd grabbed the hoodie he'd loaned her off her dresser and taken it with him.

It had only been there a little more than a day and she missed it. Missed picking it up and inhaling his scent.

Dammit, someone had to break the cycle. It might as well be her.

She looked across the table at her best friend. "Let's go."

It had been three days, and he hadn't heard a word out of her. Ghost might as well face it; she was a girl who stuck to her guns. He admired that. He mostly stuck to his too, except when it came to her, the gun he stuck to was perpetually cocked and ready to fire.

One excellent thing about his Saturday night was that Gus actually dragged in to practice, cohesively, no less, and they'd just about blown the roof off the house. They'd even started a bunch of new material. Seemed both the axmen had a lot of aggression to work out, and the rest of the guys had stepped up and added their respective flavors too. Even Mark had been happy. Neighbors had complained. It was an incredible feeling, what he lived for. By the time he left, he was still juiced up.

With nowhere to go and nothing to do. So he swung by Dermamania, thinking what a loser he must be to go to his workplace to hang out on his night off.

Nah. It just meant he had an awesome job.

"You know, if you're so fuckin' bored, I've got plenty you can do," Brian said as Ghost made his entrance.

"Ooh. I'm sure you do, loverboy."

"Jesus. I guess I left myself wide open for—shit, that's no good either."

Laughter erupted from artists and clients alike. "You know

I can't go a single night without you, Bri-baby. Is Candace not here? You and I can slip in your office and—"

"Please!" Starla cried. "Spare us."

"You know you love it, my little voyeur." Starla grinned as if to say there was no use denying it. Ghost hoisted himself up on the counter at his station. "What's going on tonight, kids?"

Brian shook his head. "Nothing here. Work, home, sleep."

"Come on, man. It's Saturday night."

"Says the guy who hasn't been *here* all day."

"Old ass."

He laughed at that. "I'm no older than you are, dude."

"He's just domesticated now," Starla said.

"Poor strapped bastard. Where is the domesticator, anyway?"

"Across the street at the coffee shop." Brian glanced up at him. "With Macy."

Shit. The pause had been so unnecessary, as were the little grins that passed among the others. Ghost could only hope he kept his expression bland and uninterested.

"Oh yeah? And here I was hoping you were gonna tell me they were in your office in the sixty-nine." Good. That sounded like something he would say.

"You wish." Brian's eye was caught by something outside the front windows. "Hell. It's my brother."

Ghost followed his gaze out to see Evan Ross and his wife Kelsey striding quickly through the light rain. Brian waited until Evan had pulled open the door before cupping a hand to his mouth and shouting toward the back, "Hey! Hide all the crack!"

Ghost laughed while he considered bolting. He didn't have one reason to be concerned that a state prosecutor was walking into his place of business, but Evan had a way of making them all feel like they had something to hide. Even when he was in jeans instead of a suit, the dude wore authority. He couldn't help it.

They laughed good-naturedly at Brian's joke, Kelsey walking over to give her brother-in-law a hug. Evan glanced around the shop with his all-too-assessing gaze, nodding at Ghost when he caught his eye. Always good to have friends in high places. Even if you never actually cared to see those friends.

"To what do I owe the dubious honor?" Brian asked, hopping up to sit on the counter as Evan turned back to him.

"Kelsey wants to get my name tattooed on her ass," he said, earning himself a smack on the arm and his wife's laughter.

And he could be pretty laid back too.

"Can't a guy visit his kid brother?" Evan asked once she'd subsided.

"Not if he insists on calling him kid brother."

"You should realize by now he only does it to annoy you," Kelsey said. "Where's Candace?"

"Off somewhere smoking up. Or mainlining. Or she might be getting coffee across the street. Where's Alex?"

"At Mom's," Evan said. "We're having the rare date night...though they might get more plentiful the closer we get to moving. She's trying to soak up all the baby-time she can."

"And so you come by to...get your name tatted on Kelsey's ass? *Ev* on one cheek and *an* on the other, right?"

Kelsey was turning redder than her cherry-red sweater, covering her mouth in her laughter. Evan shook his head. "You are all kinds of wrong."

"Hey," Starla piped up, "I just had an idea. You should name your next baby boy Kevin. It would be like a combination of both your names."

Brian's upper lip curled. "That's *lame*. God, you're lame, Star."

"We actually thought of that before we settled on Alex," Kelsey said, putting her hands on her hips in mock offense.

"That's because you're both sappy dorks."

"Ha. You talk smack, but we've all learned how sappy you can be too. It's only a matter of time before you have Candace's name on *your* ass," Evan said.

"Can I say for the record that I always throw out very strong hints to my clients that they should *not* tattoo a significant other's name onto their bodies? It's their skin; they can do what they want. But I don't care how long they've been together or how solid it looks. It never fails they'll be back here a few weeks later, sobbing to me that they want it covered up. Sometimes I swear you need to be a licensed counselor to go into this business."

"Aw, come on, Bri," Kelsey said. "You wouldn't get a tattoo of Candace's name? Even a little one? I know you would."

He grinned. "Oh, I've already got it, but it's somewhere you can't see."

"Too much information, Brian," Evan said as the room erupted in sounds of disgust.

Brian put a hand over his chest. "On my heart."

This time the gagging sounds were even louder.

"That is the sweetest thing I've ever heard!" Kelsey cried over it all.

"Are you slackin' off or what, dude?" Brian asked Evan. "Here I am, having to give your wife her romantic thrills and all."

"Don't let him snow you," Evan said, drawing Kelsey close to his side. But even he had a grin on his face.

"I always knew Brian was a closet romantic," she said. "I called it a long time ago, didn't I? It just took the right woman to bring him out."

Evan dropped a kiss on the tip of her nose, smiling down into her eyes. "Isn't that all it ever takes?"

"All right, get a room. And no more talk of me being romantic in here." Brian plucked at the front of his T-shirt. "I have an image to uphold."

Ghost had sat watching the rampant mushiness in speechless dismay. Macy's words in the car the other night came back to haunt him, when she'd said that sometimes things work out. He wished he could believe that for himself. Looking at the two relationships represented here, Brian's and Evan's, he could almost have hope. Of course, both of them were still in their infancy stages in the grand scheme of things. But he was beginning to realize he would be more surprised if

Brian and Candace *didn't* work out than if they did. In all the years he'd known him, Ghost had never seen his friend this way. And if Evan and Kelsey ever busted up...well, it would shake up the entire town.

He'd never felt deserving of it himself. He considered himself a confident-enough guy, but what in the ever-loving fuck could possibly be so appealing about him that another person would want to spend the rest of her life with him? He didn't get it. Like Gus, he was fucked up, only in different ways. And look what Gus's girl kept putting him through.

Candace and Macy took that moment to sweep in the front door, both laughing about something, but Macy's vibrant smile faltered a bit when she saw him. Not in disappointment, though. Her eyes brightened. He didn't know why or how, but he got the impression her heart had leaped into her throat. His had. Or maybe he was just fucking delusional where she was concerned. Nonetheless, he returned what smile she managed for him.

Kelsey and Candace rushed into a hug, both trilling with delight at seeing each other. Macy greeted Kelsey and Evan warmly, but Ghost didn't miss her gaze sliding over to him every few seconds. Because he couldn't stop looking at her.

Her cheeks, all flushed with the bite of cold. He remembered them flushed from arousal. Her bright hazel eyes— maybe he'd put the light there; it hadn't been there the first night he'd seen her before their interlude in his car.

She was one of those girls who remarkably had a different hairstyle every time he saw her. Sometimes curly, sometimes long and sleek, sometimes in a variety of stylishly sloppy updos. Tonight it was simple—one dark sweep tucked behind both ears under her off-white knit cap. Her ears were slightly pink too, and what he wouldn't give to take her home and warm her up...

Goddamn, she was out of his league.

"He was talking so sweet about you just now," Kelsey said as Candace moved to Brian's side and handed him the cup she'd brought in from across the street.

"Was he? He can be pretty sweet when he wants to be."

Brian sipped his coffee and hugged his girlfriend to his side. "I might keep her around for a while. As long as she acts right and doesn't give me too much lip. She's all right to look at, you know."

Candace smacked him on the chest. "So nice to know I'm wanted."

"Weren't you thinking of getting your master's and going for the LPC, Candace?" Evan asked. "There you go, Brian. You said you needed a counselor in the parlor. You'd have one."

The others laughed, but all at once, the atmosphere seemed to shift. Candace became very interested in the remaining contents of her drink, and Brian dropped his arm from her shoulders and promptly rubbed the back of his neck. Ghost cocked an eyebrow. Brian had hinted at a little bit of stress regarding Candace's future career goals, but he got the feeling now that Evan had just inadvertently dropped a major shit bomb right between them.

"I'm exploring options," she said carefully and looked up at Brian. He smiled at her, and the weirdness seemed to evaporate somewhat.

Ghost made a mental note to take Brian out for some one-on-one time.

As the lovey banter was resuscitated, he kept trying to figure out how in the hell he could get Macy off to the side without becoming a part of it all. His chance came when Brian decided he wanted to show everyone what he was working on. For all her hang-ups about ink and piercings, Macy loved to look at the artwork, so she followed the group. Ghost fell into step right on her heels. She was wearing some of those jeans with bling on the ass. As if he needed more reason to look *there.*

The sight had so captivated him that he almost missed it when Candace poked him in the arm as they all filed into the back room where they drew up designs. "I didn't know you were coming in tonight."

Macy glanced at him, smiled and ducked her head.

"Just hanging out," he said. "Thought I'd ruin Brian's night."

But flippancy was futile. He swallowed around the tightness in his throat as Macy moved beside him and her familiar scent filled his nostrils. Christ, she smelled so good. He wanted to pin her against the wall right here, breathe his fill.

The others engaged in chatter around him, giving Brian their compliments and opinions on this and that, but Ghost was concentrating too hard on not tenting the front of his pants to care much about what was being said.

"Have you changed your mind yet?" he asked Macy, damn near desperate to have that hazel gaze on him again.

Her delicate eyebrows dipped low as she looked at him. "About?"

"Miss 'I'll Never Get a Tattoo'."

"Oh." She laughed. "No, nothing will ever change my mind. Not that these aren't beautiful." She pointed to an elaborate floral design. "Especially that one."

"That's one of mine."

"Really?"

"He does have rare moments when he doesn't suck," Brian said.

"Shut up before I rip the metal out of your face."

"How rude!" Candace cried. Ghost didn't miss the little glance she exchanged with Macy. "Come on, guys, let's go back up front. Bri, I need you for a second." She tugged Brian's arm as she moved toward the door.

"Only for a second?" he asked, grinning as he followed with Evan and Kelsey.

"Well, when that's all you're capable of..." Ghost said, earning himself a middle-finger salute as Brian went out. Macy laughed, but it sounded strained, and she looked after the four of them as if she wanted to bolt out the door with them.

But she didn't.

Bless all their scheming little black hearts. As soon as the others were gone, Ghost stepped over and shut the door. Macy's eyebrows were practically in her hairline when he turned back to her.

"Hi," she said simply.

131

He could only stare at her for a moment, then blew out a breath and shook his head. "Damn, girl."

"What?"

"What, she asks."

"Well...*what?* I mean really. I don't know what to say, I don't know... I don't know what the hell I'm doing." She blew out a breath, her gaze on the floor in the vicinity of his boots. She pulled that luscious bottom lip between her little white teeth. Jesus help him, he wanted to do the same thing with it.

He waited until her eyes flickered back up to him. "You seemed to know what the hell you were doing the other night. And I liked that."

"That part's easy. It's this part I don't like. You know we're going to have to be around each other sometimes—our best friends live together. I don't want it to be awkward for everyone. Including us."

"Okay, so let's deal with it. Here and now. Do you want to keep seeing me? Don't worry about hurting my feelings or any shit like that. I'm a big boy; I can take it. But I'm not down for games at all. I let you have a few days' cooling off time, and I've been thinking too."

"Oh? What are you thinking?"

"Come on, Mace. You're beautiful, and you're accomplished, and any time a girl like you wants to hang out with a guy like me, you'd better believe I realize what a fucking idiot I'd be to pass that up."

"Maybe I don't want you to want me just because I'm...those things."

"All right, I didn't word that so well." He was opening his mouth to go on, but she held up a hand.

"Listen, Seth...I think we've done this all backwards."

"Backwards?"

She crossed her arms, her gaze startlingly direct under her cap. "Backwards for me. Typically, I get to know a guy before I land in the sack with him. That didn't happen here. In the beginning, that was okay. I didn't count on wanting anything more with you. I thought it would just be fun, like we said."

"So you're saying...you *do* want more?"

"All I'm saying at this moment is that I don't really know you...but I would like to."

Hell, if she got to know him, really know him, she might run screaming. This was a good thing, though. She hadn't run yet. He thought about all the nights he could spend slowly exploring her beautiful body without rushing to memorize it all before she booted his ass out of her bed and her life. All the hours he could spend inhaling the vanilla sweetness of her skin, her hair. Oh yeah, he wanted to get to know her better.

"Maybe we should cool off?" she asked.

All his sensuous fantasies ground to a halt. Cool off? That did not compute. "What?"

Macy cleared her throat, for the first time glancing away and absently studying the drawings on the board. "You could, I don't know, ask me on a date? A regular date?"

Do things the way she was used to having them done. Give her her comfort zone. He could handle that. But not without a little teasing. She might as well know that about him right away, if she didn't already. "Fine. I didn't want to have sex with you again anyway."

God, he loved her smile. Even more when it was accompanied by her laugh. She graced him with both at that moment. "Gee, thank you. I feel much better about this whole thing."

"You? I'm the one who was just informed about the whole cooling-off thing."

"It's not that I don't want to sleep with you again. Honestly? I want to drag you home right now. It's all I've thought about. But..." She sighed and shook her head. "I *have* thought about it, and I don't want to get caught up in something like that. It's not for me. I don't want a revolving-door relationship. I don't need someone blowing in and out of my life. Either you're going to be around or you're not. There's no in-between with me. If you can't deal with that..."

He stepped forward and took her hands in his. Warm and supple. But strong. Just like her. "Where should our first date be?"

She blinked up at him. In the bright overhead lights, her freckles were more prominent. And her lips too, pink and glistening with the gloss she wore. He wanted to taste it, touch her face, hell, plant her back against the wall right here, but he held off. Yeah, maybe his self-imposed restriction on getting involved had just been blown to hell and gone, but he didn't care. Not when she looked at him like that. What could it hurt to see where things went?

"In case you haven't realized," she said with a wink, "I really am an old-fashioned girl. You can decide."

"All right, but I think I should give you fair warning." He leaned down and put his forehead to hers, their noses nestling next to each other as she tilted her head up to meet him. "I'll give you all the dates you want. But that cooling-off thing? I can't promise you that."

The door closed on the last client of the night, and Starla rushed over to lock it. Ghost turned off the Lamb of God video blaring on the flat screens and glanced over as Brian emerged yawning from the back, truck keys in his hand. "I'm out," he said. "See y'all tomorrow." He turned to go back toward the rear exit.

"Bri. Hit the gym with me, dude."

He halted in his tracks. "You can't be serious."

"Come on. You need it."

"Not at midnight." Brian slapped a cap on his head with one hand and twirled his keys around his finger with the other. Candace had taken off, since she had an exam in the morning and the constant activity in the parlor wasn't conducive to studying. "I'm hitting the sack."

"Are you twenty-nine or sixty-nine?"

The devilish dimples appeared. "Twenty-nine with a sixty-nine waiting at home." The others whooped and laughed.

"Lucky fuck. I'm definitely hiding in your bushes tonight. Hey, but see, you can come with me and get all pumped up for her. She'll work it off for you."

"You're insane."

"What did we join the all-hours fucking gym for? Because we work crazy hours. Stop being a pussy, and let's go."

And so they found themselves on the way to the gym after Brian grumbled an explanation to Candace over the phone.

"Is it like having a probation officer or what?" he asked after Brian tossed his phone on the seat beside him.

"Huh? No. Not at all."

"So tell me where you see this thing going."

"What?"

"Don't play ignorant. It's been almost a year for you two, and she seems like a permanent fixture at the parlor."

Brian shot him a glance. "Have you got a problem with that?"

"Would it matter if I did?"

"As far as us being together? No. As far as her being a permanent fixture at the parlor, I value your input."

"Really."

"This ain't a dictatorship, man. I never intended it to be."

"So if I said the word, she'd be gone?"

"I wouldn't go so far as *gone*." Brian reached over to turn down Soulfly's "Prophecy". Then he sighed. "Look, I just don't want her identity all tangled up with mine. I don't want that for *her*. I keep telling her she should, you know, explore other options. She's a big help, but what the hell has she worked so hard for? I was too much of a fuck-up to go to college. But she did it, and she did it magna cum laude. I'm so damn proud of her and I don't want to hold her back."

Ghost grabbed Brian's half-a-foot-thick CD case and began idly flipping through it. "So that's what it was about. When Evan said what he did about her being an on-site counselor."

"Yeah, I know he was joking but there's...been some tension."

"You're being an insecure little bitch. You're still thinking you're not good enough for her."

"Hey, fuck you."

"That's all it is, dude. What you're saying is your life—*our* life, really, since I do what you do—isn't good enough for her." *Or someone like Macy.* "Admit it."

"That's not it. I barely keep her parents off my ass as it is. They're just now getting to where they'll look me in the eye. I wouldn't give a shit, but it matters to her, I don't care what she says."

"Then maybe you not caring what she says is the problem."

Brian drew a long breath in through his nose. Blew it out. Ah. He'd hit a nerve. "Her fuckin' mother, man. After Candace and I got together, Sylvia pulled me aside and was all 'Just promise me, Brian, that you'll see to it she finishes school'." He shook his finger in the air, taking on a high-pitched, scolding tone. "'And don't make me a grandmother yet!' Like I'm hell-bent on making her drop out and knocking her up. Shit. I need a cigarette."

"Still? It's been months."

"It really hasn't."

"Damn. You fell off the wagon."

"Just a couple times."

"Well, I'm back now, and I'm telling you straight. Cut it. The fuck. Out."

"I know. The gym was probably a really good idea tonight."

"I'm tuned in to you, dude. But despite how perfect you and I seem together, I could never be with anyone who has no Acid Bath in his collection." He closed the CD case and put it aside. "All joking aside. You gonna marry her? This is the one out of seven billion?"

"It is. And I am. I've got to. It's like...sometimes..."

"Speak."

"Sometimes I think I'm not going to make it another day without getting a ring on that girl's finger and changing her fucking last name from theirs to mine. I'm going to spend the rest of my life with her, and I want it to start *yesterday*."

"Then do it already. I knew something was eating you up. You're like a friggin' caged beast—it's all over you, and you're smoking again, for fuck's sake."

"I already sent her running once. It's not right for her yet. It has to be right."

"Yeah, but you're solid now. Look, stop stressing out. Candace is cool with me. She's a big help and I can't see her stirring up any drama. The girls like her. If she wants to hang around us that much then God bless her. And please, go ahead and ask her to marry you before your head explodes."

Just a few nights ago, he'd been singing the complete opposite tune to Macy. What sunshine and rainbows had she injected into him since then?

"All she's thinking about right now is getting through graduation. I don't want to sabotage her with my alpha bullshit."

"I do have one beef with her. She spooked all your groupies. I kinda do miss them." Brian laughed as he turned into the gym's parking lot. Ghost grinned to himself. That was more like it. He sounded like his old self. Brian was a volcano sometimes; he had to blow his top to someone before he could settle back down. "And I'd love to stand up for you, but don't expect to get me in no tux. Unless I can rip off the sleeves, add some chains or something."

"Don't worry about that. I think elopement would be our only option. Between my family and hers, can you imagine the circus any wedding of ours would be? My mom's ready to put a hit out on Candace's mom as it is."

"No way, man. This wedding *has* to happen if only to see your moms scrap with each other. I'd pay good money for that. Hell, I'd wear a tux for that."

"Any more problems out of Raina?"

Well, there was a good-mood killer. Raina had texted him five times today. He'd bet money that Mark, that son of a bitch, had given her his number. Why those two didn't just fuck each other and forget about him, he didn't know.

She'd wanted him to know how immature he was being for resisting her return to the band. How it must mean there were still feelings he wouldn't admit to. Ha.

"Aside from driving me nuts? No."

"You don't think she's going to scare Macy away?"

Ghost scoffed. "Macy would wrestle that girl down, tie her in a half hitch and throw her hands in the air. Raina's all talk."

Brian killed the engine. "I'm thinking you might be right, if what Candace says is true. The exterior is deceptive."

"Right? I think that could be said for us all, though. What do you think about her? Honestly."

"That she's kind of stuck up on her own pedestal. I probably need to get to know her better, though."

"Yeah. Coax her down, and she's cool."

They grabbed their bags, exited the truck and headed toward the building. From what he could see through the glass wall, looked like they would have it mostly to themselves, which was a good thing. A few people were walking on treadmills or working the ellipticals.

"What's going on with her?" Brian swiped his card key and pulled open the door. "You put me under the gun; now it's your turn."

Damn. He couldn't help the Cheshire cat grin that spread across his face when he thought about seeing her again. Touching her, tasting her. She was the last damn thing he needed right now. There was all the crap over Raina, the band, his nana. But she was the only thing he had to look forward to. The only thing that made him think he would get through it all okay.

That was...scary.

"I'm just gonna let the chips fall where they may, brother."

Chapter Twelve

Macy's parents' ranch lay on the outskirts of town, nestled away from the rest of the world within a solid barrier of pine trees. She maneuvered the winding tree-lined driveway in her Acadia with Jason Aldean serenading her from the stereo, shaking off the stresses of the workday. There had been many.

Ever since getting her business degree, she'd managed her parents' local outdoor-sports store while they mostly enjoyed retirement. It was a good gig; she couldn't complain. But there was a certain employee who was getting a *lot* of complaints lately, and she wouldn't abide that. It wasn't her favorite thing to fire someone, but it looked like it was coming to that. She'd need to talk to her dad about it.

But this had always been her oasis, the place where she could leave everything behind. She looked forward to the days when she gave Jared's six-year-old daughters, Ashley and Mia, their riding lessons. They were eager students, which made them a pleasure to work with. The girls reminded her a lot of herself at a similar age, fascinated with the beautiful equine majesty, determined to harness all that power any way she could. That fascination had fueled her for years, and she wanted to pass on what was left of it to anyone willing to accept it.

She turned a corner, and the unfamiliar sight of Jared's massive, gleaming red Chevrolet dually pickup came into view, parked near the arena. Macy frowned. Usually his mother brought the girls for their lessons, which was fine with her. It dispensed with any awkwardness, and Mrs. Stanton would stay around and chat with Macy's mom until they were done. Their frequent visits with each other had been how Macy ended up roped into this deal in the first place, but she didn't mind that.

What she did mind was unexpected encounters with her first lover, and memories of her most serious, longest-enduring relationship, when she had a date with Seth tonight.

"Great," she muttered, pulling around to the old-fashioned red barn and parking beside the truck. Ashley and Mia had taken up residence on a bench by the duck pond, their favorite spot aside from the arena. They hadn't even noticed Macy drive up. Their dad stood with one boot hooked in the fence, talking on his cell phone. He turned and waved when he saw her.

This so wasn't what she needed. Jared Stanton was as single as they came now, and she remembered how he'd told her he wanted to dance with her at the bar the other night. It didn't seem like a coincidence that he'd shown up this evening.

He'd always been just the sort of man she could really see herself settling down with. Stable, dependable, devoted to his kids. Someone with all her interests...heck, if she sat down and drafted a compatibility checklist, she could check off every box. On paper, he was perfection. And hot to boot.

They'd broken up not long after Macy had her accident. He'd wanted to be by her side but she'd chased him away in her anger and bitterness. He embodied too many memories of a life she'd turned away from. Shortly afterward, he married another girl in a rush. Macy had cried for days. When his twins were born only five months later, it all came a little clearer. He'd been trying to do the right thing, but in the end it was a dismal failure. His divorce had only recently been finalized.

"Hey," he said as she got out of her car, and quickly ended his call. Thanks to the very erratic Texas winter, it was considerably warmer today; she barely needed her light jacket, and he was wearing a blue flannel shirt that brought out his incredible eyes. "About time you showed up." A maddening dimple dug into his cheek. No way she couldn't return that grin.

"What? I am so not late. You, however, are half an hour early."

"Miss Macy!" the girls shouted in unison. Their ponytails, one brown, one blonde, flew behind them as they scurried over from the pond. They crashed into her, knocking her back a few steps as they threw their arms around her waist.

"Whoa there!" she laughed, hugging them back. "Glad to see someone appreciates me." She cast an exaggerated glare at Jared over the tops of their heads.

"You're appreciated, all right. Always have been."

Macy let his flirting go right over her head. "What brings you out?"

"Thought I'd see how you're doing, catch up...take you out to dinner with us, if you're interested."

"Oh...that's really sweet of you, Jared, but I have plans after we're done here."

The grin turned a little sad, but he comically slapped a hand across his chest and took a step back. "Still shooting me down after all these years."

"Stop that, now. Maybe I'll take a rain check, okay?"

He nodded without further comment and set out to help her saddle up Rose and Trinity for the girls. The familiar rituals were so much like old times, it unnerved her. If things had been different, and she hadn't been such a bitter über-bitch, maybe they'd be doing this for their own kids by now.

She slapped that thought aside before it could drag her down. She'd made her choices. Maybe they hadn't necessarily been good ones, but she would own them now. Too much had changed to go back.

"You look incredible," he said later, after they'd finished up and the girls scampered off for the duck pond again. It always took forever to wrangle those two up. The sun was just dropping behind the distant pines, and a chill breeze nipped Macy's cheeks before they warmed with his compliment.

"Thanks. You look pretty great too."

He propped the heel of his boot on the bottom rung of the fence and leaned his elbows back on the top. "You never did dance with me the other night."

She laughed, certain her blush deepened as she thought about what she'd been doing that prohibited any further contact with him. "You actually remember? You were three sheets to the wind."

"Naw! I had it handled."

"Suuure you did." *Just like I did.*

"I guess it's my fault. I should've grabbed you up right then."

She had absolutely no idea what to say to that. "I was...um, blocked in."

"Yeah, if that guy beside you could've killed me with looks alone, I might not be standing here right now. Is he...surely you're not *with* him, are you?"

"He's...ah...he's a friend. Of a friend. Friend of a friend's boyfriend, actually." *Who I happen to be sleeping with.* "We hang out."

"Is that who you're seeing tonight?"

"Yes."

"Macy. Seriously?"

He was starting to piss her off. "What, Jared?"

"He's just...not someone I'd imagine you would deal with very well."

"I think I know who I can deal with and who I can't."

"I know Candace is dating Brian Ross." He scoffed. "There's an apple that fell *way* far from the tree...and then got punted across the yard. I never thought you would get mixed up with any friends of his, though."

"I can't believe you're being so freaking..."

Judgmental. The same damn thing she'd been all this time. Not so long ago, she'd have agreed with him. She'd have chimed right in. *Brian's a thug. Look what he's doing to my best friend, filling her full of ink and turning her into a pin cushion. He's not good enough for her. He's going to hurt her.*

All thoughts she'd entertained, washed away with one simple statement from Seth the other night.

Brian is the brother I should've had.

And Candace loved Brian more than life. Candace wouldn't love someone who wasn't good enough for her.

"Look, Brian is great. I might not have realized it at first, but you know what? I couldn't have picked a better guy for her if she'd asked me to."

He held up both hands as if to fend her off, and she realized she was getting in his face. "I don't mean to piss you off. I just..." He straightened and took her shoulders gently in both hands. Always such a gentle touch, sometimes frustratingly so. She hadn't felt it in years. The sudden stark reminder made heat gather behind her eyes. "Macy, I always regret I didn't fight harder for you. I regret that I left when you told me to leave. I always hoped you didn't really mean it, or at least that you would someday realize you didn't mean it. But then I messed it up. Everything happened with Shelly, and..." He stared off at some point over her head, and she knew he must be watching his daughters play. "I don't regret that either, because it gave me Mia and Ash. But I saw you the other night at the bar with...that guy, and you looked more beautiful than I'd ever seen you, and if I could make everything right—"

Dismayed, she lifted her hand and covered his mouth with her fingers. "Jared? Stop. Okay? Don't."

"You wouldn't even think about it? Whatever you've got going with him is that important to you?"

"It's not even that, really. It's..."

What? What was it? If this offer had come a year ago, hell, two weeks ago before Seth came back, how would she have reacted? If she wanted to settle down and have a family, the perfect specimen was right in front of her. He came with a family already built in. She loved Mia and Ashley, and they loved her.

She and Jared had history. She knew his quirks, what would make him laugh, what would piss him off. That he loved everything she loved and disliked everything she disliked. That the back of his neck was an erogenous zone.

Comfort. Safety.

Seth...she didn't really know a damn thing about him except that he was loyal to his friends and family, she'd never seen a picture of him where he wasn't flipping off the camera or sticking his tongue through the V of his fingers and he had an ex so in love with him the girl had damn near lost her mind. That he really had never given Macy anything other than a string of violent orgasms and a "catch ya later". He made her feel the absolute opposite of Jared. Instability. Danger. Given the text he'd sent her earlier—*Wear a skirt 2night*—he only promised more of each.

God help her, she liked it. She couldn't imagine turning away now. It was unthinkable.

"Jared...ever since I got hurt, I've followed my head. I've been cautious to the point of almost losing my friends. I can't do it anymore. I've got to follow my heart this one time. My heart's telling me I need to go my own way, throw caution to the wind. Maybe it'll blow right back in my face, I don't know." She dropped her gaze and shook her head. "I don't know."

Jared sighed. His hands slid around her back and he pulled her into his arms, resting his chin on top of her head. She practically collapsed into him. He smelled wonderful, the clean, crisp scent of the outdoors—his favorite place to be.

Admitting all of that—to him of all people—had taken a lot out of her. Was she insane? Was she really following her heart, or just her freaking vagina?

"If you ever change your mind," he murmured, leaning his cheek into her hair, "you know where I'll be."

It was like déjà vu. Only the restaurant was dim and quieter than the bar. When Seth slid into the booth next to Macy, she shivered as his jeaned thigh brushed her bare one.

She'd acquiesced and worn a tight-fitting black skirt with knee-high boots and a green sweater, and there was no doubt in her mind why he'd made the request. Every time she remembered the other night in the bar, her heart did a swan dive to the pit of her stomach.

He looked...dangerous tonight. All in black, which wasn't unusual. It wasn't even really that he hadn't shaved in a couple days, and a shadow framed the darker brown of his goatee. It was his demeanor. She didn't know if he'd ever exuded raw sex like he did tonight. Like he'd thought about it all day and was to a breaking point in which he'd just as well put her on the table, spread her legs and make her his appetizer right here in the restaurant. The tension around his mouth, the look in his eyes, said it all.

"Never took you for a same-side sitter," she said, sipping the water the waitress had just sat in front of her.

"Ordinarily I'm not," he said after she was gone. "But how else am I going to get you off, if the mood strikes?"

Macy worked on swallowing that drink and placed her glass back down, struggling to maintain her composure. He leaned his shoulder into her, letting the tip of his nose trace the outer curve of her ear. "Ever since Valentine's, I can't get it out of my head. How much I wanted to make you come right there in front of everyone, wondering if you could hide it when you did."

"What if I couldn't? How embarrassing."

"Mmm. Maybe the stealth orgasm is something we'll work on. I picked a good place to start, right?"

He had. The backs of the booths here were higher than their heads. They were completely hidden from the people behind them. He'd specifically requested the corner. If the table off to their right remained empty, they would be all but isolated from everyone except the waitstaff.

Macy gulped more water, trying to dampen her dry throat. Already, her sex ached and pulsed for his touch, dampening her panties, and she couldn't look away from his hand as it rested on the table. Big, perfect, with long fingers just callused enough to make her skin sing with pleasure.

Oh Lord, please help me survive.

She had a feeling praying about whatever Seth Warren had in mind tonight would be sacrilegious.

As time passed and she kept wondering when he was going to get on with it already, she also noticed he could be a real charmer when he wanted to be. Their waitress already seemed to be in love. They might have a hard time getting rid of her long enough to...

That was probably just the way he wanted it. Upped the danger factor, didn't it?

Her fettuccine Alfredo came, and she attacked it. She'd

assuage the lust thumping through her veins with food. He laughed at her, commenting how he loved a woman who could eat. She fed him some from her fork, and he fed her a shrimp from his fingers, letting the tips linger on her lips until she flickered her tongue against them. His eyes closed.

"Damn, woman," he breathed.

"I want you." His eyes opened again at her declaration. His hand dropped beneath the fall of the tablecloth, and his fingers slid deftly under her skirt, bunching it up her thigh. In no time, he was tracing the edge of her panties.

"Here? Is this where you want me?" His fingertip just flickered over her clit, barred by the thin cotton panel.

She nodded and fused her mouth hotly to his. The little waitress was probably going to reappear any minute. Macy didn't much give a damn.

"Oh, hey," he said suddenly, breaking away from her mouth. "I almost forgot." She nearly screamed when he withdrew his hand from between her legs, but her aggravation turned into confusion as he reached into the pocket of his black leather jacket. Whatever he brought out was hidden in his balled-up fist. "Hold out your hand."

"What are you doing?"

"Just do it."

"Oh my God, Seth, if you're going to put something totally embarrassing in my hand—"

"Shh. Do it."

"But you—"

"Macy. Shut up. Do it."

She rolled her eyes and tried to glare at him, though she doubted it looked very convincing since she couldn't even begin to force her lips into a frown. "I didn't exactly mean I wanted to give away my autonomy when I told you—"

He leaned closer, so she could feel his warm breath across her lips, smell the wine on his breath. "Do you want me to touch you again? Do it."

Panting gently, trembling violently, she lifted her hand palm up with all the eagerness of someone about to receive a hand grenade. He kissed her, just a light brushing of his lips back and forth across hers, as he slid his fist across her palm, opened it and left behind the mystery item. The scratch of lace told her exactly what it was. She broke away and snatched her hand under the table with a gasp.

"Seth!"

"You asked for them back."

"Not in the middle of a freaking restaurant." Glancing down and seeing the flash of red between her fingers confirmed it: he'd given her back her Valentine's Day panties.

"We're not in the middle. Here's as good as anywhere."

"Really." She reached for her purse to put them away, but he caught her hand and shook his head.

"I want you to change into them."

"You're out of your mind."

"What?" He chuckled. "Don't worry, I washed them."

"But..."

"Come on, killjoy." He cast a glance back over his shoulder and then slid her hair back from her neck, leaning in to whisper in her ear. "I want to think about them covering that sweet, wet, hot, fucking *amazing* pussy of yours. When I strip you later, those are what I want to see."

She shivered despite herself. "You're so obsessed with my underwear, are you sure *you* don't want to wear them?"

He stilled and silence hung for a moment. For one terrible instant, she thought she'd made him angry. No chance. "Who's to say I didn't?"

She couldn't help it; she burst out laughing. "You are awful."

"And you like it. Admit it."

"And you're pushy. And presumptuous."

"No. I've just got your number, babe."

"*Really.*"

"I saw you, you know, that very first day you came into the parlor with Candace. All prim and proper, looking like your outfit cost more than my entire wardrobe. Also looking like you were ready to bolt for the door any minute. But you didn't, and

147

we were being offensive as all hell, and I saw you trying not to crack a smile. Mostly failing at it."

She remembered too. She remembered watching him when he wasn't watching her. He'd asked her if she needed anything, a drink or whatever, and she'd jolted like being hit with a live wire, quickly shaking her head and going back to her ebook while she waited for Candace to finish getting her first tattoo from Brian. Everyone had probably thought she was the biggest stuck-up bitch to ever walk in the place.

"I just... I was worried about her."

"Yeah? And yourself? Did you think one of us was going to tackle you and tattoo you against your will?"

"Of course not."

"Are you mother hen to everyone, or just Candace?"

It was too truthful an observation for her to take any offense. "I guess I can be that way with everyone, but Candace was really sheltered. I mean really. I thought she was making a huge mistake, and it was probably the first time she refused to listen to me."

"If she was so sheltered, I can't really get why you would try to perpetuate that."

"It just freaked me out a little."

"Did I freak you out a little?"

She looked him in the eye. "Yes."

"Do I still?"

"Yes."

"Good. Let me know if I ever stop; I'll have to think up something new." Just as he was leaning in to kiss her again, the waitress showed up, and he backed off, facing forward as Macy tried to catch her breath. His nearness had a way of stealing it from her.

The waitress collected their empty glasses and smirked a little as she began to turn away. "Sorry. Carry on."

Heat rose in Macy's cheeks. He glanced sideways and winked at her. Clearing her throat, she dared raise her hand above the table, the one still holding her panties in a naughty little pile of silk and lace. "So what about these?"

His dark gaze followed hers down to them. "Go to the ladies' room and put them on." The corner of his mouth kicked up. "Though I have no objection to you putting them on here."

"I don't think I'm that brazen yet."

"We'll have to work on that too, won't we?"

Chapter Thirteen

If someone had told her at any point before tonight that she would change her panties in a restaurant bathroom just to please a man, she'd have laughed herself stupid. Granted, she didn't get through the process without a little grin she couldn't quite wipe off her face. As she slid them up over her thighs and into place, visions of him sliding them off in the cramped confines of his backseat flashed through her mind, heating her flesh down there almost as if it were his fingers touching her. She had to lean against the door of the stall and try to calm her ragged pulse.

After all this fuss over them, if he ended up breaking her heart, she'd have to burn the damn things.

No thoughts of that now, though. They were still just having a good time, right? No hearts had been exchanged, and it would be a long, long time before they would be, if ever.

When she returned to their table and he slid out of the booth to let her in, she noticed with a pang of disappointment that the table across from them was now occupied by a couple with two little girls. That pang bit deeper when Seth took the seat across from her this time. She missed the feel of him at her side.

"I guess the mood passed," she remarked with a wry smile, picking a strawberry off the cheesecake that had arrived while she was away. He watched in rapt attention as she slowly bit into it.

"Oh, I wouldn't say that."

"Hmm, maybe if someone weren't all talk..."

The sound he made in his throat was almost a growl. "I'm gonna show you talk when we get back to my place."

Macy finished off her strawberry while her mind turned

that over. His place? Interesting. They hadn't made concrete plans beyond the restaurant; she'd just assumed they'd go back to her apartment again. She was going to get to see where he lived. Given his various interests, it was rather frightening.

"You're giving me ideas, you know," he said, picking up his fork and digging into his own dessert.

"Ideas?"

"I could name a few things I'd like to do with you and strawberries. And whipped cream."

She fidgeted, tempted to tell him to hurry this along already. Something about slipping into the red panties she knew he found so sexy had lit fires down below. He'd known what he was doing making her put them on. And now he was making her wait.

Freaking tease.

The waitress, on her way to the family at the other table, dropped off the leather folder with their check. As he reached for it, she put her hand over his. "Let me."

"No way. I got this."

"Let me pay my share at least. I *asked* you to take me on a date, after all."

"And I did, right? Because I wanted to, not because you asked me to." He winked and slid the folder from under her hand. "I'm an old-fashioned guy myself in many ways, you know."

She wasn't placated in the least. She hadn't asked him to bring her to one of the most expensive places in town, hadn't even imagined he would dream of doing so. It had been a pleasant surprise, because it was her favorite. But not something she *needed* or expected. Hopefully, he didn't have that impression of her, when she'd have been perfectly happy catching a movie or going to the sushi place they both loved.

And hopefully...well, she felt wretched for even thinking it. She had no idea about his financial situation, really, and no business speculating. But she hated the idea that he might think he needed to overextend himself just to make her happy.

Not to mention it brought back Raina's hateful words from

the other night, try as she might to keep them from echoing in her head.

After he'd taken care of the check, he helped her into her coat. He held the restaurant door open for her. He opened the car door for her. She didn't think more than a few seconds had gone by on the journey without his hand on her somewhere...whether it was resting lightly on her back or low on her hip or even at her nape, raising the fine hairs there. Even they craved his touch, it seemed. When he settled in the driver's seat, she cursed the console and gearshift between them. She wanted to scoot over until she could feel him all along her side, like she had in the restaurant.

Despite her aggravation with its obstacles, she adored his car. That he'd so lovingly restored it to mint shape gave her a little tickle in her belly. It made her think of everything else that could flourish in his careful hands.

"Your place, huh?" she asked once he steered out onto the street.

"Was there somewhere else you wanted to go?"

"Oh no. I just..." She broke off and laughed. "I am *extremely* curious to see where you live, I admit."

"Yeah? I hope you won't be disappointed with how normal it is, then. It's the house I grew up in. I try not to deface it too much."

"Ah. Family home."

"When my parents died, Nana moved down from Oklahoma to take care of us so we wouldn't be uprooted after what happened. After we all grew up, my brother was the first to take off, so that left me and my older sister. Nana moved back to Oklahoma after she saw Steph and I weren't going to starve or wander aimlessly into the street. Not every day, anyway." He threw her a grin. "Steph's a mother-hen type too."

She chuckled at his light-heartedness, but it sounded...lonely. Of course, she'd been surrounded by family all her life. Family and more friends than she knew what to do with. And the rodeo, though, all that had changed...

"But doesn't your sister live in Oklahoma now?"

"She was visiting Nana a few years back, and she met a guy. Moved up there, got married. Has two boys."

"Aw, Uncle Ghost." She gave him a playful pinch on the arm.

"I miss those guys, too. I really got to know them while I was staying there. I need to get back up there soon."

"Did you ever think of moving there yourself?"

"Not really. The whole time I was there, I couldn't wait to get back."

She didn't have to know him well at all to see the sadness that came over him when he mentioned his nana. He tried to hide it. He did it well. But even if it was only a split-second faltering in his expression or the briefest flicker of grief in his eyes, she caught it. She honestly didn't know how he was putting up such an amazing front. Laughing with her, flirting and talking dirty... Was he only trying to forget what was going on one state to the north?

His right hand was resting on the gearshift. Macy reached over and placed hers on top of it. "It's really bad, isn't it?"

He was a long time answering. She watched his throat muscles constrict as he swallowed. "It's bad."

"I'm so sorry. We don't even—"

"No, stop right there. The thing about Nana is she's more full of life than anyone I've ever known. And so genuinely *good*. To leave the life she'd made, and move down here to take care of us when she was grieving too... I don't know that *I* could do it, you know? I can just hear her in my head telling me not to worry about her, to go on living. It isn't that I don't worry about her, but... Oh, shit." He rubbed his eyes hard with his thumb and forefinger.

"What? Please tell me."

His discomfort was palpable. He rubbed the back of his neck, checked the mirrors unnecessarily. She began to think he wasn't going to answer, and she would have to accept that. But then he surprised her. "A few months back, she was having a good day, and I told her all about you. I have a picture on my phone I took of me and you when we were goofing around back when we first started hanging out, remember? The one where we're making stupid faces. She looked at it, and then looked at me and asked me what in the hell I was doing there talking to her when I should be here chasing after you. That's the kind of person she is. She really means it." He hit the blinker and sighed. "That's one of the last lucid conversations we had. All about you."

Macy gazed at his profile in such silent amazement, she hardly noticed when he pulled into a driveway and braked to a halt. Once he'd shifted into park, he reclaimed her hand and laced his fingers through hers. "I can't say that's what I came back for, though. My sister encouraged me to go home for a while, and I felt like I needed to check on things around the house, see my friends, get back to my music, just *be*. But I've thought it's pretty damn funny the way things work out. If you knew Nana, you'd know she almost always gets her way." He brought her hand up, brushing her knuckles with his lips. "Here I am, chasing after you."

She opened her mouth, but the words weren't there. Whether it was terror or elation that held them captive, she didn't know.

This wasn't supposed to happen. Oh God. Warmth pricked the back of her eyes, and she wanted to run. Wanted to stay. Because his lips were warm and full and wonderful, and she wanted them all over her body. Right now.

She lunged for him, and the voluptuousness of his mouth on hers sent her stomach into a free fall. It wasn't unlike the dizzying high of riding full gallop, and she hadn't allowed herself to do that in so very long...

Gasping for air, she pulled back, her heart slamming in her chest.

"What's the matter?" he breathed, leaning in and trying to recapture her. She let him, unable to resist. Just like the first night, just like every night they'd been together since. Unable to resist. Knowing she should. Helpless whimpers escaped her throat. His tongue slipped into her mouth. He let go of her hand, and she wrapped her arms around his neck while he smoothed his hand up her ribs and found her breast, squeezing gently through her layers of clothing.

Why did her body have to respond like this to him? Why couldn't it have craved Jared's touch this much? She never would have left if it had. Under Seth's hands, she came alive. She unfurled, smoothed out, blossomed. He felt so right, even when everything else was so wrong.

"Let's go inside," he murmured against her lips. Macy couldn't imagine letting him go, but she figured if she didn't, they would only have another bout of vehicular sex. Nodding, she leaned back when he released her. "Sit tight."

As he made the quick journey around to open her door, she gazed up at the house in front of her. Very pretty, traditional beige brick with gables. She slid from her seat after he popped open the door, taking a glance around. Nice enough neighborhood with similar houses cramped together along both sides of the street. Quiet. Most of the lights were already out; she had the feeling they'd been out for hours.

"I take it you can't play your music very loud here."

He closed the door, grinned and tugged her toward the front porch. "Might explain why I don't hang out here that often."

There was a chill in the air tonight, exacerbated by the heat she'd just felt in his car, in his arms. She shivered impatiently in her coat while he unlocked the front door, and then he was pulling her inside and pushing her against the wall, and there was nothing but *him*, his kiss, the strength of his body overpowering hers. She grabbed his collar and matched his ferocity with her own. When his lips left hers to kiss a hot path to her neck, she turned her head and noticed the still-open door.

"Seth...the door..."

"It's dark."

"You can't—"

"Shut up, Macy."

Damn herself for ever telling him she needed someone to shut her up. Then again, she thought as he pushed her skirt up her hips, it might have been one of the most beneficial requests she'd ever made. His fingers, still cool from the outside chill, seared the burning flesh between her legs, and her knees buckled. She grabbed on to his shoulders to hold herself up.

"So hot," he said, brushing his mouth back and forth across hers in that devastatingly erotic way he had. "So fucking hot, Macy..." Big hands slid under her ass and lifted, planting her back hard against the wall. She wrapped her legs around his hips, arched into him and practically purred. He had to let go of her to unzip his pants, and she clung on haphazardly, praying he would hurry.

Five feet to their left, the front door still stood wide open, and a chilly breeze brushed her left thigh. Out on the street, a car cruised slowly by, and she gasped, though being seen wasn't even a remote possibility.

Who was she kidding? At the moment, she might not care if someone walked up to the door and watched. His cock, in all its fully erect glory, slid along her damp panties, abrading her clit through the lace. Her grip on him tightened in desperation. One tiny shift in position and he'd be able to...

"Condom," she gasped. Holy crap, they couldn't forget. He'd already impregnated one girl, for God's sake.

"Fuck." Whirling her around, he deposited her on a nearby couch while she tried to get her bearings in the pitch-black room. He was nothing but his darker shadow looming over her, but she could see him swiftly pluck his wallet and pull the little packet out. As soon as he had it over the tip, she reached up with both hands and unrolled it down his swollen length. He released a shuddering breath, barely seeming to hold himself in check long enough for her to accomplish the task. She expected him to fall on her when she finished, but he hauled her up by her wrists and put her back in her former position, against the wall.

She laughed, and he chuckled against her throat. "I *really* wanted to do it like this," he said.

"I really wanted you to."

"Naughty girl." His fingers, gripping her cheeks, crept

inward to pull her panties aside. She groaned and panted as he tested her wetness and then positioned himself with a growl that sounded more animal than human. Without wearing a stitch less clothing than she'd had on two minutes ago, she was about to have sex against a wall. In front of an open door. That was a first.

"Oh!" The blunt intrusion whipped all thought out of her head, had her climbing him in an initial effort to escape the burning stretch as their breath mingled. His grip on her tightened, not letting her get away. She whimpered as he went deeper than her overly greedy body was ready for.

"Jesus," he muttered and kissed her, slow and melting. All at once, her muscles seemed to respond in kind, relaxing around him, going liquid. He slid inside until she was held tight to his groin. An exhale of relief escaped her. When he began to move, it wasn't with the urgency she expected given their rushed beginnings. It was with a slow deliberation that would destroy her.

"Seth, oh God..."

It was a good thing he was strong enough to hold her; she had no strength. She constricted around him, tighter and tighter, and she knew he felt it from the sounds he made. Sharp pleasure sparked in the front of her belly and glowed outward until nothing existed but the feel of him inside of her and the taste of him in her mouth. Heat. She turned her head toward the breeze coming in from the open door, hoping to find some relief for her flaming cheeks. Another car eased by out on the street. Seth sucked on the side of her neck, and she smiled at nothing in particular.

The fear, the need to run that had gripped her out in the car...it was still there, somewhat. And it was too late. If she'd wanted to flee from Seth Warren and everything he made her feel, she should have done it from the first moment she'd met him. She shouldn't have let him anywhere near her. Every time they were together, he chipped away at her resolve. That very first night last year, she hadn't been able to *not* run away from it afterward. Now, she didn't think she could do it if she tried.

He shifted his hold on her then, hoisting her up, moving first one arm and then the other until he was holding her with his forearms under her thighs...and something happened. Was it his piercing? Or his adjusted angle... Her breath caught, mouth falling open as her head fell back. That spark of pleasure, he was stoking it into a full roaring inferno, higher and higher with every thrust. A cry wrenched from her throat, and she prayed the neighbors couldn't hear, though a second later, she was beyond caring.

"Oh, baby, if you get any tighter on me I'm going to fucking die," he said.

"Seth, you're... What is... God!" Pure molten ecstasy radiated from her sex; the back of her head met the wall with a thud as he pushed deeper into it. Her muscles began to jerk. Her nails dug hard into the leather of his jacket. She had no control now; it was all his, and he liked it that way, didn't he? She couldn't resist trying to squirm away from the intensity even as she strained toward it.

"Where you trying to go, huh? Come on me, Macy. Come on me, or I'll take you outside and make you scream right there on the front lawn for the whole fuckin' neighborhood to hear."

The surge of panic and excitement at his words flung her over, even as she knew if every orgasm before had been mind-blowing, this one would surely seal her fate. There was no help for it. She wrapped him in a death grip, biting the leather on his shoulder to keep from shrieking as pleasure ripped so hard down her middle it was almost painful.

He rasped something her pleasure-saturated brain couldn't decipher, churning harder against her. His new exuberance brushed her clit, catching her at the peak and flinging her higher. She cried out and sobbed and scratched at him, might have even slapped at him, before exhaustion pulled her under and she went boneless between him and the wall.

Slipping free and then scooping her up in his arms, he kicked the door closed and managed to hit a nearby light switch. She only knew because the blackness behind her closed eyelids was suddenly...less black. Her mind hadn't rebooted yet.

By the time she finally managed to pry her eyes open, she was lying on a bed in a dimly lit room.

"Still with me?" he asked, smoothing the hair back from her forehead.

"What the hell was that?"

He laughed, propping his head up on his elbow. "The hottest fuck I think I've ever had."

Macy's brows drew together. Would he ever think of what they did as more than that? Was she insane that she wanted him to?

"What's the matter?"

"Am I...wet?" Something was definitely going on; her thighs were damp. Oh, God, the condom hadn't broken, had it?

"Is that the first time that's ever happened to you?"

"What?"

"Baby, that's all you." He trailed one fingertip up her leg. "The G-spot is a thing of wonder."

Seriously? She'd never believed in all that female ejaculation stuff. Candace and Sam had debated it once, she thought, but she'd tuned them out...like much of what Candace had said about sex with genital piercings involved. She still felt wretched about the way she'd treated her friend despite all her apologies. "Are you sure?"

He gave a wry laugh. "Oh yeah. You can bet I'm fucking sure when I make a woman do that." In one fluid motion, he stood from the bed. "Let me get you a towel."

Embarrassment roared high in her face, and when she covered her face with her hands, she realized her legs weren't the only things wet. Tears covered her cheeks. She sat up, staring at her damp palms in dismay. What the hell did he think of her now? That she was a broken, emotional, sexually repressed nightmare? Cruelly enough, the thought only made more tears drip from her eyes faster than she could frantically wipe them with the sleeves of her sweater.

"Macy, baby, what's wrong?"

At the sound of his voice, she leaped up, panicked, thanking all that was holy her legs were able to hold her. She couldn't suffer another indignity tonight. "Nothing. Can...can you take me home?"

"Wait, no. *Shit*, did I do something?"

This wasn't how things were supposed to go, not at all. This was supposed to be fun. Where was the fun? Where was all this emotional crap coming from?

"Talk to me, dammit. I can't fix it if you don't talk to me."

"I don't need you to fix me," she snapped and immediately wished she could've caught those words before they escaped. He froze midstep, a furrow appearing between his brows.

"I didn't say I was fucking going to fix *you*. You're not broken. But something's got you all fucked up, and maybe I can fix *that*. There's a difference."

"Is there? I just..." She exhaled deeply, then took slow, measured breaths, struggling to send the tears back where they belonged even as she scrubbed at them. "I'm sorry. Typically, I'm not a crier."

He raised a skeptical eyebrow. "Okay."

Great. He'd already suffered one psycho ex. She hoped he didn't think he was standing in front of the next one. She chuckled without humor, giving up her battle with her own emotions and looking down to toy with her fingers. "It's not your fault. It's not anything you did."

"I think I'd rather hear that it is. At least then I might be able to do something." He came closer and handed her the towel he'd brought. Thankfully, he didn't watch as she swiped at the remnants of her earlier pleasure and the emotional pain that chased it. He ambled away, shoving his hands in his pockets and sightlessly staring at some pictures on the dresser. She had to strip off her panties—she'd have to get the other ones out of her purse.

"Don't you think it's pretty obvious how this will end?" she blurted.

He looked at her then. The bitterness in his reply wrenched something inside her. As if the words dredged up old hurts she couldn't possibly imagine. "Yeah. I guess I do."

"Then why am I here?"

"I don't know, Macy. Why are you? I don't feel like *I* have to explain what you're doing here, after what I said to you in the car."

"You don't believe these things ever work out. I'm surprised you would even want to try."

"Maybe at last I see something worth the risk."

She didn't want to resist the smile teasing at her lips, but she couldn't trust it yet. "Really?"

"Well, not so much when you're a sobbing mess or a mopey drunk, but—" He ducked to avoid the pillow she snatched up and tossed at him. "Just kidding. I even like you then."

"I can't imagine why."

"Jesus. I don't know how someone as beautiful and accomplished and awesome as you ever took such a hit to your self-esteem. Can you explain that, please?"

"My accident—"

"That's all it was. An accident. It could've happened to anyone. It happened to me, every little kid's nightmare. It's hard; I know it is. But you don't let it defeat you."

She nodded, still sniffling. "I did let it. It...I feel like it took away my identity. It made me afraid. I even became afraid of my friends when they started changing around me. I felt like my world was snatched from under me once, and I got it back, but...what if I'm not so lucky next time?"

He crossed to her, tipping her chin up so she was forced to look at him...not that she thought she wanted to look anywhere else at that moment, or ever. Some unnamable emotion shuddered through her chest as his warm, gentle hands cupped both her cheeks. "Stop. Being. Afraid."

Was she so afraid because she'd found the one person with the tools to put her back together again? He'd suffered a loss so profound she felt like an idiot little child complaining about the boo-boo she got when she fell off her horse.

Those eyes. She often thought they could swallow her up. Now she was sure of it. His thumbs gently smoothed the last of her tear tracks away. "And don't be embarrassed with me."

She bit her lip, watching him watch her, wondering what

he was looking for in her eyes. He should know if she had the answers to all the many mysteries of her soul, she would have damn sure given them to him for present and future reference.

"When we're together, I *want* to take you places you've never been before," he said. "That's what I signed on for, remember? Don't freak out on me when I do it, unless you're ready to walk away from this whole thing."

"I'm not walking away," she whispered. He lowered his face to hers, and she leaned up to kiss him before he could make it. Echoes of pleasure rippled through her belly at the touch of his lips. He pulled her closer, and she realized how brutally hard he was against her. That couldn't have happened in the past few minutes. "Wait, Seth...you didn't?"

He shook his head, brushing noses with her. "No. You kind of collapsed on me. Thought I'd get you in bed and recovered first. Don't worry about it."

She grinned, reaching up to stroke his dark eyebrow. "You know, I do think I'm all recovered now."

"Oh yeah? Well, then, in that case..." She squealed happily as he toppled her back on the bed.

Chapter Fourteen

It was three a.m. He was so exhausted he could barely move his arm, but the utterly relaxed and tranquil woman beside him made all the effort worth it. It would've been worth it regardless, but...damn.

She lay on her stomach with her arms tucked under her and a peaceful little smile on her face, her nude body long, lean and shimmering in the dim glow of the lamp. He traced light trails across her back with his fingertips.

Who the fuck was smiling down on him for this to have happened?

"Mmm," she said, the first utterance either of them had managed since collapsing in a heap of tangled limbs, sweat and euphoria twenty minutes ago.

He echoed the sound, leaning over to kiss her shoulder and smell the dark, vanilla-scented hair spilling over it. No matter how tired he was, he couldn't stop touching her.

He was so screwed. In the very best way.

"Are you thirsty?" he asked.

"Mm-hmm. But don't get up yet. This feels good." She sounded so drowsy and so fuckin' cute. Her skin was a delight, smooth and soft and, except for the scar up her spine, otherwise unblemished. He moved until his head lay on her upper back so he could watch his fingers trace the line. A little tension crept into her muscles but flowed easily out as he kept caressing her.

Its presence obviously bothered her. And it wasn't a keloid, which he was never inclined to fuck around with. If only she weren't so damn anti-ink, he could create a masterpiece for her. Before he realized it, he was tracing outward from it, a design unfurling in his head that encompassed the straight line and extended outward into meandering patterns. Maybe something with vibrant green ivy, or...

"What are you doing?" she murmured.

He kept right on drawing. Damn, it would be gorgeous on her. "Designing the tattoo you would never let me give you."

To his surprise, he wasn't met with sudden, harsh rejection. She shifted under him, and he slid his head back to the pillow to look into her face. "Over my scar?"

"Check it." He pulled his left arm up for her to see, pointing at one thick black swath of ink in his design. "Right here. Feel? That's where a bone was sticking through my skin after the wreck. The scar is ugly as hell."

She drew her fingers lightly across it. "Wow. I'd never thought of that before. Covering a scar with a tattoo, I mean."

"It's not for everyone. Some might take several sessions. Some might hurt worse, if that's a factor. I think you'd be a good candidate, though. It's thin, and even if I didn't cover it, I could make it less noticeable. I mean," he smirked, "people would only be looking at how awesome your ink is."

She lay quietly for several seconds. "Something to think about, I guess. I don't know if I could ever do it, though."

"Well, you know," he said, turning onto his back and tucking an arm behind his head. "Do it for the right reasons, or don't do it."

"It's not about vanity, really. It's the reminder. I don't know if changing it or covering it would help."

"It would at least be a reminder of something else. Turn it into something beautiful."

Macy's hand slid over his chest, and she rose over him, her breasts and her long hair brushing him as she leaned down to give him a kiss. "Thank you."

At that moment, the way her hazel eyes drank him in, he didn't want to change one damn thing about her. "I think you're beautiful the way you are. I just want you to feel better."

Her lips curled upward. "It's all a front, isn't it?"

"What's that?"

"You are nothing like the image you project."

"So I'm a fake now?"

"No, not a *fake*. Jeez."

He laughed, and she leaned down and bit him. "Naw, I get you. There is some show, I can't lie. But it's still who I am. It's an outlet. My music and my job, it's how I get out all the crazy shit that goes on in my head. Stuff I can't let out in *polite society*, ya know. Only...I'm so rarely in polite society, I don't know how to behave in it anyway, so there."

Macy's half-smile began to tremble, and then she broke into a full-fledged fit of laughter. It was infectious, and he couldn't help but join in as he sat up to face her. "What's so funny there, killjoy?"

"I'm just... I don't know if I should even say this. Might freak you out or make you mad or something."

"If it doesn't involve you putting your clothes on right now, it won't."

She trailed her finger along one of his tats, not looking him in the eye. "I'm thinking of what it would be like to take you home to meet my parents."

Mad, hell. He experienced a joy eruption that the thought had even crossed her mind. "Oh yeah? What would they think?"

"They're good people, you understand, but you aren't exactly what they would expect. They're very outdoorsy, very down-to-earth. My dad can be really loud and funny, though, and he doesn't care about pissing people off. I think it'd be hilarious to see you two go head-to-head, that's all."

"Your dad sounds like my kinda guy."

"Then maybe we'll get to see how that goes," she said shyly. "I have to warn you, he'll probably have you camping and fishing and hunting with him before you know it."

He'd never had his own dad around to do that kind of stuff with. At least not that he could remember. "I'd be down for that. As long as I ain't gotta get on no fuckin' horse."

The hand drawing tantalizing lines along his skin suddenly shoved at him. "Oh no! Tell me you don't hate horses."

He caught her wrist and shoved her down on the bed, rising over her. "No, no hate. I simply don't feel the need to get

165

on top of one. You, on the other hand..." God, would he ever inhale enough of her scent? She sighed as he trailed his lips down her neck.

"Fair enough. You might discover, though...oooh..." He kept moving down, licking a path around her pert little nipple. "...might discover a love of riding that will stay with you for the rest of your life."

He might discover a love for her that would stay with him for the rest of his life, if he kept this shit up. Beautiful, soft, sensitive Macy...a tough little nut to crack, but so warm and sweet once he did.

"You can't possibly be ready to go again," she said. At that, he rose up on his knees and guided her hand to his erection.

"Does this look not ready to you?"

"My God. You're supernatural."

"Or you are. It's all you, baby."

She sat up, stroking him lightly in her hand as she gave him a coy glance from under a swath of dark hair. That look right there, it would be the death of him. Especially with her mouth hovering so close to his dick, when all he wanted was to plunder between those pink lips. "Oh, please. I'm supposed to believe that?"

He gave an exaggerated glance around the room, left, right and back down to her. "You're the only one here. Unless I have a leftover girl stashed under the bed. I don't think I do. I could check."

"That's okay, thanks."

"No other girls? Come on, Macy. If you want to be with a guy like me, you have to be understanding of my needs."

There it was. The look of utter *is he kidding or not?* confusion in her hazel eyes. Cracked nut or not, he'd known her skittishness was still in there somewhere.

"You said it yourself, babe. I'm supernatural. You're a great lay, but surely you don't think one woman could ever keep all this man satisfied."

"I would advise you not to say things like that to a woman who has your most precious *manly* asset in her hands."

Grinning, he cupped her face and tilted her up for a kiss. "You know I'm full of shit, right?"

"Sometimes it's hard to tell." Macy was actually pouting. Damn, she was hot.

"Yeah, well don't worry. Women are crazy. One at a time is all I'm willing to take on." She gave his thigh a wicked pinch, and he yelped.

"Hey! Watch it with your fuckin' Hulk hands."

"I don't have Hulk hands."

"They may look small and dainty, but you could break boulders with those suckers."

"I can do this with them too." She ringed his cock with both, slowly and gently drawing them toward the tip and down to the base. All the breath rushed from his lungs. He plunged his fingers into her hair, resisting the urge to push her mouth toward him.

"That's good," he rasped. "I like that much better."

Macy shifted closer, one leg on each side of his knees. Oh, fuck, yes. Her eyes flickered up to his, pure evil in their depths. She licked her lips. "Do you want me to suck it?"

It was like asking if he wanted to take his next breath. He throbbed between her hands, and that distance between her lips and the head of his cock? It needed to diminish very, very soon. "Suck it, Macy."

"I'm not taking orders right now. If you want it, you have to ask me nicely."

"Goddammit! *Please* suck it."

"That wasn't nice. You can't cuss, and let's make it interesting. You can't say 'suck'."

"Hey now. You did."

Her lips curled up. "My mouth. My rules."

She was so going to get it later. "Macy, queen of my universe, I beseechingly request you place your sweetest of lips upon my manhood and make it your lollipop."

"Oh my God. That was kind of awesome." Grinning fiendishly now, she watched the maddening motions of her hands for a long time—now stroking one, then the other over him—and he thought he was going to scream. "Hmm. I acquiesce."

The unadulterated pleasure of her tongue slicking up the underside of his dick was more than he could take. She left no part of his length unexplored by those wet, delectable swirls, even toying with his piercing, giving it little flicks he felt all the way up his spine. When she finally enveloped him in the bliss of her mouth, sucking her way little by little toward the base, he was panting.

He gathered her unruly hair into a ponytail and held it in his fist, needing some measure of control over her devastating assault on his senses. Whoever the guy was who taught her to suck cock, he wanted to buy him a beer and punch his fucking lights out.

Her desperate little whimpers around him made his nerve endings sing. Her hand squeezed tight around him, only prolonging the agony, but he wasn't complaining. He would, however, totally return the favor later, and he wouldn't rest until he completely robbed her of her powers of speech.

If he couldn't tell this girl how amazing and beautiful and breathtaking she was, he would show her, and then leave her no way to argue with him.

When he came, he meant to push her back. He really did. But the moment his hands tensed in her hair and his cock jerked in her mouth, she sucked him to the back of her throat and grabbed his ass with both hands. He was lost. It was all he could do not to tumble over her, and he ground out words he wouldn't remember later but would have surely damned him after her earlier no-cussing request. She didn't let him go until she'd wrung every blessed drop from him, and then he fell to his side, panting.

"Damn, girl."

Macy slid alongside him, fitting as if she'd been made to go there. He wrapped her in his arms and struggled to catch his breath and fight off thoughts like *that* one. With the warmth of her silken skin seeping into his, though, it was a losing battle.

"What?" she asked innocently.

"*You're* supernatural."

For a second, her little teeth sank into his shoulder, making chills skitter across his chest. "It's all you," she said sweetly and kissed away the sting she'd left.

He couldn't wait one more minute to feel those swollen lips on his. Tilting her face up, he captured her mouth and rolled her on her back, intent on kissing her for the rest of the night if he could. She trembled and cradled him against the curves and slopes of her body, running the sole of her foot up his leg, stroking his back and scoring it lightly with her nails. Fuck, she was exquisite. Her little whimpers resounded in his head. Another couple of minutes, and he'd be ready for yet another round of her. Who was he kidding about fighting his feelings? He wanted her every fucking way he could have her.

By half past four, Macy was beginning to think he'd never let her sleep again. And that was fine with her. But since they'd kicked up a good appetite with the workout they'd given each other, she was almost glad when he dragged her near-lifeless body from the bed to scrounge up something to eat. It was a chance to look around his house too.

Wearing the shirt he'd worn to dinner, which reached well past mid-thigh on her, she roamed around his living room while he rifled through the cabinets in the kitchen. On the mantel were several framed family photos, and she had to grin when she saw one of Seth in his younger days. Finally, a picture where he wasn't flipping off the camera. He was dressed as if on a beach vacation, with his arm around a petite blonde with his same smile and dark eyes. His sister, maybe? Stephanie? She was cute. And Seth...he looked a hundred percent different with hair. She'd been right in her assessment: it was dark brown, thick and even sported a bit of curl. A couple tattoos peeked from under his T-shirt sleeves, but nothing like what he had now.

No doubt about it, he'd been a doll then and he still was now, just...a little scarier-looking doll.

The next photo to the right was obviously his parents. He looked like them both, and their big happy smiles almost brought tears to her eyes. *Every little kid's nightmare.* She had the sudden urge to call her parents right then...though of course they would ask what she was smoking to call them at nearly five in the morning if she wasn't dying.

Sweeping her gaze across some of the other pictures—more of him, his sister's family and an older woman who could only have been his nana—she realized his brother must be absent from them all. No guy resembling him or near his age was to be seen anywhere.

"What are you up to in there?" he called from the kitchen.

"Just looking at your pictures."

"Ugh. Don't get too acquainted with that guy."

"Who, you? I *like* that guy. Then and now."

He chuckled and came into the living room bearing chips and a couple sandwiches on a plate. "I eat out a lot," he told her apologetically. "It's just me, so..."

"This is fine. Thanks."

He put the stuff on the coffee table. "I forgot drinks. Hang on."

She continued her perusal as he trotted back to the kitchen, moving to his massive CD collection. It took up an entire bookshelf. He'd even begun stacking rows on top of rows. Some of the band names...they made her cringe. "Oh my God."

"What?" he asked, coming back in behind her.

"This stuff..." She started laughing. "You have it alphabetized."

"Yeah, so?"

"I don't know, I just find something funny about having your death metal in alphabetical order. Bringing order to chaos, I guess? I mean, God forbid you get Cannibal Corpse and...*Cattle Decapitation* out of order or something." She turned to him, her eyes wide. "Cattle Decapitation? Seriously?"

"Don't hate. There's a lot I could say about that twangy yee-haw shit you listen to."

"Yeah, but—"

"Yeah but nothing."

"Fine."

"If it makes you feel any better, that's just stuff I've accumulated over the years. I don't necessarily listen to it all the time...or even like all of it."

"Oh. Good."

"But Corpse is fucking awesome."

"Great. So how do you 'accumulate' this many CDs?"

"By finding them littered around someone's house after a night of drunken carousing."

Since she was slowly but surely learning to take everything he said with a grain of salt, she shrugged that one off. "Who's your favorite band? Not that I'll have heard of them or anything."

"In Flames."

"Hmm."

"And it's not chaos."

She moved to sit by him on the couch and popped the top on her drink. "It sounds like it to me. I just don't see the appeal. It gives me a headache."

"It's raw power. It's brokenhearted and pissed off about it. The music itself brings order to chaos. Listening to it, playing it, for me helps me work out all the ugliness. It lets me vent. It helps me control my emotions—I can step back and view them from a distance, look at them and explore them without doing something I'll regret. It's like...a controlled burn."

He spoke so passionately, so earnestly about it, she couldn't help but be transfixed. "That's...interesting, I guess. It's therapeutic for you."

"Exactly. But not just that. I enjoy the hell out of it. I'm sure I would no matter what hand I'd been dealt." He bit into his sandwich, and she stared across at his collection, a little jealous that he'd found an outlet. She had none. Her emotions had been bottled up for so long she didn't know what would happen if she pulled the cork. But given her unbidden tears and her lashing out at him earlier tonight, she had an idea now.

"I would listen to some of it."

"You don't have to. I was just explaining my reasons, not trying to push them off on you."

"But if it means so much to you, if it's such a big part of you..." *It would help me know you.* "You could play me your favorite song; how about that?"

"I could never pick only one."

"A few, then. And tell me about your band. Do I dare ask the name?"

"In the Slaughter."

"Cheerful. But not so bad, considering."

He laughed. "Well, the guys rejected my proposal of Misanthropic Motherfuckers. I can't imagine why."

"Me either."

He jumped up. "Let me get my laptop, and I'll play you some Flames. There's this one song of theirs we cover a lot. It's called 'The Jester Race'. You'll get an idea of what you'd hear if you ever came to a show." He reached down and flicked her nose. "Which you should do. We're playing next month in Austin."

"Oh, ah...I don't think I could do that."

"Why not? Brian and Candace come out and see us when they can. Maybe they could come too. You wouldn't be on your own."

"It's not my thing. Really. It is *so* not my thing. I'd listen to it but having it live in my face is another matter."

He scoffed. "Yeah, but...it's a little different. I'm asking you to watch me perform. You'd probably never get me on a horse, but I'd still watch you race."

"You don't have to worry about that, do you?"

She dropped her gaze when his face darkened, staring down at her hands while her fingers fidgeted anxiously with one another.

"I wish to fuck I did," he said with such sharpness it snapped her head back up. "I wish I'd known you back then, Macy, because you wouldn't have given up *shit.* The doctors cleared you to ride, didn't they?"

"You don't know—"

"I'm asking. They cleared you to ride, didn't they?"

She glared at him, her pulse pounding in her temples. "Yes."

"You said yourself it was your identity; it's who you are. Who let you throw in the fucking towel on yourself?"

"No one! It was my decision, and everyone around me respected it." Everyone she'd let stay around her, that was.

"And you made that decision out of fear, didn't you?"

"There's nothing wrong with being afraid. Are you going to tell me there's *nothing* you're afraid of?"

"There's plenty I'm afraid of. But there's nothing that would stop me from doing what I love to do. Nothing."

"Then I guess that's where we're different," she said. "I don't even know why this is an issue. It was years ago. It's done. I still ride, it's not like I'm phobic. But no one's going to make me do what I don't want to do."

"Only, you want to do it. You *have* to want to do it."

"If I wanted it that bad, I'd do it!" But the betraying tears were filling her eyes. Shit! She didn't want to call his attention to them by scrubbing them away, but neither did she want to let them spill. She dropped her chin to her chest, squeezing her eyes shut. *Go back, go back...*

"How different are you from the way you were before your accident?"

"Ask Candace," she snapped. "She can tell you."

"I'm asking you. Because the girl I saw in those pictures at your place...she looked fearless. And proud."

"That girl still wouldn't have gone to a death metal concert."

"That may be, but she never thought she'd be running from herself either, did she?"

She gave a humorless laugh and shook her head. "I don't know why you're doing this. What the hell are you trying to prove?"

Sighing, he dropped down beside her. The warm comfort of his hand stroked up her back, under her hair, and his fingers kneaded her gently. "I didn't mean to blow up at you. It's just something that's been on my mind, and the opportunity came up to get it out there."

"*What* exactly has been on your mind? Clue me in a little."

"Nothing about you was adding up. I don't have to ask Candace how awesome you were at your rodeo-queen stuff. I could see it. But what I saw there that night at your place, in those pictures, it wasn't what I was seeing in *you*. This shouldn't be a woman who needed anyone to 'shut her up' because she's so cautious. This should be a woman who kicked ass and took names. Who tells other people when to shut up." He gently brushed the hair back from her ear. "I still see her, you know. I think you should let her out to play more often."

Macy sniffled, suddenly unafraid to let him see that tears were dripping one by one from her eyes, splattering onto his shirt she wore. "I can tell you the precise moment when I locked her up," she said softly, voice quavering as much as her hands.

"Tell me."

"When I woke up in that hospital bed, and...I couldn't move." He pulled her closer, putting his lips to the side of her forehead. She sucked in a strangled breath and faced the darkness of that moment for the first time since she'd shoved it into the furthest recesses of her mind. "I didn't understand at first; I thought I was paralyzed. But I should've known I wasn't, because, oh my God, the pain. I hurt all over. I broke bones other than my back, mainly ribs, because my horse fell over me. My entire body looked like it was in a cast. I had a concussion, and my head was wrapped up. I freaked out. My mom burst into tears. It was relief on her part, because I was awake and coherent, but it scared me even more, because I just knew she was crying because I'd never walk again."

He was silent, just holding her, letting her go on in her own time. "You mount up knowing all the risks," she said after a few moments. "I always knew them. I had friends who got hurt, and I'd even been thrown plenty of times myself. When you think you're invincible, though, like I did, it's easy to believe it's all worth the risk. I only found out that it wasn't. Not to me."

She thought about Jared and how she'd told him to get away from her until he listened. She'd done the same thing to a lot of her friends. Hell, if her parents hadn't been stuck with her, she'd have sent them packing too. They were all stark, painful reminders of what she could no longer have, what she could no longer do. Rather, what she wouldn't let herself do.

Candace and Sam, they hadn't left her. But they hadn't been part of her rodeo life, and she'd clung to them, perhaps more than anyone else. It was no wonder any rift in those relationships threw her into a tizzy. Those two had been her lifeline. Still were in ways.

"I can understand," Seth said after a long silence. "I don't like it for you. I want to see you doing what you love. You deserve that. But I definitely understand."

"Everyone deserves that, don't they? But it doesn't mean they get what they want. Thank you, though."

"I stand by what I said. I wish I'd known you back then. I wish I'd...been there for you."

She scoffed. "I'd have chased you away."

"Baby, a little something about me you might not know yet...I don't run that easily. And you don't scare me."

Chapter Fifteen

The sun hadn't peeked over the trees yet, but it had to be getting close. Seth had done more than get his laptop to play her some music. He'd brought out his guitar and amp. She now knew he played *melodic* death metal, and she'd been introduced to an overview of In Flames' discography and evolution. Despite her reservations, and the fact that a deeper understanding of the music didn't dispense with the slight headache it gave her, watching him play thrilled her. To see the muscles flex in his arms and chest, to witness the passion and power he put into every note. What was once an adamant *no* about going to one of his shows turned into a *well, maybe, someday*. With a lot of Advil on hand.

She wouldn't tell him that yet, though. Make him suffer. He didn't seem to mind doing the same to her.

"Here, I think you'll like this," he said, sitting on the ottoman opposite her with his guitar in his lap. "Probably more your speed."

She perked up. "Really? I can't wait to see what you consider my speed."

Seth chuckled and cleared his throat. He let the suspense build for a minute, then the unmistakable opening strains of "Sweet Home Alabama" filled the air.

Macy laughed in delight, clapping her hands. But that wasn't the only surprise he had for her; her jaw fell open as he began to sing the lyrics in a clear, flawless voice. Was there anything this guy couldn't do well? She didn't know what to focus on. The mesmerizing movements of his long, graceful fingers on the fret, or his delectable mouth forming the words she'd known by heart ever since she was a little girl. Hell. It didn't matter where she looked. His bare, inked chest, his tattered jeans or his skillful hands. He was the whole package.

"Awesome," she breathed as he finished with a flourish.

Grinning sheepishly, he picked out a few more chords. "Thanks."

"What on earth possessed you to learn to play that?"

"Hey, I have respect for the classics." His gaze went to a point over her left shoulder, toward the area where the family pictures were gathered. All at once, his eyes unfocused, and his jaw tightened almost imperceptibly. "One of the few memories I have of my dad was of him playing that song."

"Well, I think he'd be very proud."

She wanted to kiss the little smile that teased his lips then. "That's kinda the thing. I probably haven't done much else he'd be proud of, so I decided to strive to perfect that one thing."

"I doubt that." Stifling a yawn with her hand, she checked her watch. "Wow. I don't think I've stayed up all night since... Hmm. I don't know if I've ever stayed up all night."

Seth pulled his guitar strap over his head and set the instrument aside, and she couldn't help but think he was grateful for the change of topic. "It's been a while since I have. You're a bad influence."

"I should get home, let you sleep. Are you working tonight?"

"Shit. Yeah. I am."

"Oh no. You'll be a zombie."

"I'll be all right." He moved to sit next to her on the couch. Without even thinking, she snuggled up to his warm, bare chest. It seemed equally natural when his arm settled around her shoulders, hugging her close. "You don't have to go anywhere, you know. Unless you want to."

Peacefulness suffused her. That scent, his scent, the one she could never quite get out of her head when she wasn't with him, enveloped her. "Mmm. I'm glad you said that. I could sleep right here."

"Whatever you want," he murmured, his lips brushing her forehead.

She was just beginning to doze when his cell phone came alive in the dead silence, the frantic riffs of his ringtone nearly making her jump out of her skin.

"The fuck," he grumbled, and she shifted to let him get up. "Everyone oughta know better than to call me at six in the goddamn morning."

Grinning drowsily at the sight of his denim-clad ass as he walked across the room to retrieve his phone, she snuggled into the corner of the couch and laid her head on the arm. Without him under her, it was a little chilly. Damn, he had a nice back. Nice shoulders. Nice everything. The ink only accentuated the lines and contours. She wanted to lick every—

Macy didn't know what alerted her to the change in atmosphere, but she sat up almost without conscious thought. Maybe it was his demeanor as he checked the phone display, maybe there was a barely perceptible stiffening of his muscles she sensed even from across the room. Maybe it had simply taken some time for it to sink in that a call at an ungodly hour when everyone should "know better" was never a good thing.

Whatever it was, she knew before he lifted the phone to his ear that it was bad, and the urgency in his voice when he answered confirmed it.

"Steph? What's wrong?"

His nana. He listened for a moment before darting toward his room. Macy leaped to her feet and followed, heart racing. "Fuck. *Fuck.* Is she...? I'm coming. Just...no! I've got to be there. I'll be all right... Yeah, well, dammit, I shouldn't have let you talk me into coming home in the first place. I'm on my way, all right? Keep me updated."

He was already snatching clothes out of his closet and tossing them on the bed when he threw the phone down on the mattress. It bounced and hit the floor; Macy stooped to pick it up. What the hell should she say? What should she even ask? He had all but forgotten her presence, though she understood that completely.

Finally she blurted the only thing that really mattered to her at that moment. "Are you okay?"

He paused long enough to rub his eyes hard with his thumb and index finger. He didn't answer. From several feet away, she could see the trembling of his hands.

"What do you need me to do? Let me help," she tried again, hoping to get some constructive response that way.

"There's nothing you need to do. I'll drive you home and head out."

"Seth, listen to me. I know you're upset, and I know all you're thinking about is getting to her, but you've been awake all night, and you do *not* need to be on the road right now."

He grabbed a duffel bag from the closet and carelessly shoved a handful of T-shirts into it. "I'm fine."

"You're not fine. You could—"

"Baby, I've got enough raw adrenaline pumping through me right now to never need to sleep again. I got this, okay?"

"At least let me call Brian. Maybe he can go with you or something."

"Hell no, I'm not gonna bother him with this."

"You know he'd want to help."

"I know. Which is exactly why I'm not calling him."

"Then let me go with you. Or even get you a plane ticket. *Anything.* Please."

"You driving wouldn't be any better than me. And I appreciate the offer, but you know I'll have been able to drive to Oklahoma in the time it would take me to get through all that bullshit at the airport."

Dammit, she wasn't making a single dent. He didn't even look at her, just spouted his retorts as he continued his frantic packing. "Seth, can you honestly tell me your nana would want you to put yourself in danger?"

His shoulders slumped. Then he dropped the shirt and bent over the bed, holding himself up with his fists, breathing deeply. She stepped forward and smoothed her fingers over his shuddering back. "Just a few hours' sleep and I bet you'll be good as new."

"There's no fucking way I could sleep right now."

Any little thing could set him off again. She knew that, but she had to ask. Swallowing her anxiety, she said, "What happened to her?"

"A stroke, they think." Standing straight, he picked up the shirt and whipped it down into the bag with a violence that made her step back. "Son of a *mother*fucker."

"Don't blame yourself for not being there. You said yourself she wanted you here."

"I know that."

"So let's think about this and—"

He surged into action again. "No, fuck it. I'm going."

"Then I *am* going with you."

"Yeah, right."

The way he brushed her words off as if she didn't mean them stung her. "We can take shifts and keep each other awake. I know I'll be in the way once we get there, but we'll figure something out. I only want you to be safe. Hey." Catching his arm, she made him look at her. The raw pain in his eyes stole her breath for a second. "I'm serious."

"Macy..."

"You wanted to be there for me back then. I want to be here for you now."

Suddenly, he wouldn't meet her gaze, and a black pit opened and yawned wide in the bottom of her stomach. She might be overstepping the boundaries of this relationship...whatever this relationship was. He might very well not want her intrusion into a private family matter. And while she could understand completely, the pain that ripped through her at the thought was so sharp and *real* that, for the second time in less than a minute, she could hardly breathe through it.

He couldn't do this. Not now.

"Macy, this is..."

"Whatever else this is, you're my friend. I would do this for any of my friends." It was the truth, even if she was minimizing for her own sense of self-preservation.

"I was only about to say this is *crazy*. You have stuff going on, you have a job—"

"And I work for my parents, who are extremely understanding and capable people. I can find a way back somehow. Candace and Sam can come get me; they'll love a road trip, and we need girl time. I won't be in your way."

When he reached up and stroked her cheek, a little of that emptiness closed up. He wanted her. Even if she couldn't stay with him, it was all she needed to know...that he wished she could. "You wouldn't be in my way. I'd keep you with me if you could stay. I'm sure I won't be back this time until...it's over."

"I know. I'm sorry you're going through this."

"You're incredible, you know that? I wish she could have met you."

Macy reached up and took his hand from her cheek to hold it against her chest. With her other, she stroked the back of his neck, feeling the tension straining his muscles. "Hey. She still might. Don't think like that."

"It sounds...pretty grim."

"Then let's get you to her. Okay?"

He enveloped her in his arms, squeezing the air from her lungs and holding so tight she almost couldn't fill them again. She returned the embrace just as fiercely.

When he hurts, I hurt.

The tears that welled up then, they weren't such a bad thing, and she let them flow. They weren't for herself. They were all for him.

"You're in love with him, aren't you?" Candace asked.

Macy glanced out the window of the convenience store and balanced the cell phone precariously between her ear and shoulder as she grabbed drinks out of the cooler. Outside, Seth was filling up his car with gas. The sight of him in his hoodie and ratty jeans with the early morning sunlight glinting off his aviator sunglasses made her heart flip over. A brunette walking by him in sprayed-on, low-slung jeans and a teeny T-shirt nearly tripped over her own feet checking him out. He tipped his chin up at her. Macy rolled her eyes.

"I don't really—"

"Ma-*cy*."

"I might be...a little bit in love with him?"

That made her friend laugh. "A little bit? That's like being a little bit pregnant or something. It doesn't happen."

"I have a serious question to ask you."

"Okay?"

"What do you honestly think the future holds for either of us? You or me. I mean, thirty years from now, are we still really going to be with these guys, coming home old and gray from the tattoo parlor? Listening to heavy metal all the time while we try to keep them from cussing around the grandkids?"

"I'll be with mine, whatever he's doing. Without a doubt."

"I just feel like their very profession allows them to revel in their Peter Pan syndrome or something."

"Brian is serious-minded, though. He's thinking ahead. He knows he won't do this forever, most likely, and he's looking at opening a few more parlors around the area. Plus, let's face it...he'll inherit someday, and so will I. So will you." She laughed. "Well, I'll inherit unless my parents finally disown me."

"Oh, that'll never happen."

"I've decided you must be right. They would've done it already. And hey, it's not like Ghost is a slacker. He's not going to spend all his time laid up on your couch."

"I know."

"So stop worrying so much. God. It's so funny. Here I tell you *not* to worry, and your advice to me was always to worry my ass off."

"All right, already." Macy put their snacks on the front counter and dug her wallet out of her purse. "You'll have many hours to put me under fire on the drive back. We're all set for you guys coming to get me, right?"

"Yep. Just text the address when you get it, and we'll be on our way. Tell Ghost that Brian will call him in a few minutes when he gets out of the shower. We're sending good thoughts for his grandmother."

"I'm sure he'll appreciate that. You guys are the best."

"Thanks so much for going with him. Brian was so relieved to hear he wasn't driving up there upset and alone. He really needs you right now."

She opened her mouth to contradict that, certain that despite all her protesting to the contrary, he'd have been fine whether she was with him or not. But she let those words die in her throat, saying her good-byes to Candace and thanking the cashier instead.

Before they'd left his house earlier, he'd certainly held her like he needed her. She couldn't think of that moment without her stomach clenching in equal parts fear and jubilation. If the last twelve hours with him had been such sexual and emotional insanity, what would life with him be like?

He breezed in the door just as she turned toward it. With his sunglasses pushed to the top of his head now, she could see the weariness setting in. The shadows under his eyes, the downturn of his mouth. She was ready to fall flat on her face too. But she injected as much brightness into her voice as she could. "I talked to Candace. She and Sam are coming. She said Brian will call you in a few minutes."

"Cool."

"I got us the biggest coffee they offer. Let me drive now, okay?"

He handed her the keys without comment and moved on to the restrooms in the back. Not even a protest. Yeah, he was exhausted.

Five minutes later, they were on the road again. She'd learned how to drive on a stick shift—her dad had insisted—but it took some time for her to re-acclimate. He was a good sport and laughed when she almost rolled back on a hill and then lurched forward.

"Hey, you're here for my safety, remember."

"I've got this! It's just been a few years." *Like, almost ten.* But he didn't need to know that. "I'll try not to stall your baby."

He patted the dashboard. "It would take a lot to stall my Goat." She glanced over as he leaned his head back and yawned, wishing he would try to grab a couple hours' sleep at least. He probably wanted to make sure she wasn't going to leave his transmission lying on the road first.

Another mile or so later, she became intensely aware of the

weight of his stare on her. His eyes were completely hidden behind his shades now; for all she knew, with the way his head was leaned back, they could've been closed. They weren't. She could feel it. "What?" she asked, fidgeting in her seat.

"I think you're the first person I've ever let drive this car besides me. And you look incredibly sexy doing it."

"Pfft. I'm a mess." He'd dropped her by her apartment long enough for her to change, scrub her face clean, brush her teeth and slick her hair back in a ponytail. She needed a good night's sleep herself, but mostly she needed a shower. And to think she might actually meet his sister in this condition.

"You're gorgeous."

So was he. If it had never jumped out and violently beaten her over the head before, it did then. The dark shadow on his jaw was intensified this morning. Despite their circumstances, she longed to feel it rasp against her skin again. He had the best damn mouth she had ever seen in her life, and he knew how to use it.

"Now I know you're sleep deprived," she said, heat tingling up her cheeks, which were remembering all too well what that scruff had felt like as his body moved against hers. Into hers. She had to resist the urge to put a hand to her face. Her pulse grew ragged. "You're hallucinating."

"No. I'm seeing more clearly than ever, I think." As he reached over and brushed a stray tendril behind her ear, she shivered at the touch of his fingers there.

What did he mean? She tried to swallow the lump gathering in her throat, but it only remained there, choking her. Something was growing between them. Something big. She felt powerless against it, and God knew she didn't like powerless.

You don't like it, but you've sure let it own you for the past several years, haven't you? Not as tough as you thought you were.

She sipped her coffee, hoping he didn't notice how her hand shook.

"I know this whole thing, it's been a lot to dump on you when we're...friends. Fairly new friends, at that. I've never had a chance to do anything like this for you. But I want you to know, Macy, no matter what happens, I'll never forget this. I've got your back for anything you ever need me for. *Ever.* No questions asked."

Friends. That word hadn't tasted very good in his mouth, she could tell. She wasn't comfortable with it either, even if she was the one who'd thrown it at him earlier. To hell with self-preservation. Her regret at that moment was so immense, it eclipsed everything else but the need to tell him the truth: she wanted so much more than to be his *friend.*

"Seth, I didn't mean—"

His cell phone took that moment to come to life, blaring what even she knew was AC/DC's "Big Balls". Why he'd chosen that as Brian's ringtone, she didn't know and didn't dare ask.

The mood shattered as Seth answered the call. Macy inwardly cursed Brian's timing and refocused on the long road ahead, tightening her grip on the steering wheel, heart thudding dully. Despite her exhaustion, suddenly she'd never felt more awake.

She needed to get a grip, so maybe Brian's timing wasn't so bad after all. Seth was in the middle of a family crisis. Now wasn't the time to add her conflicted emotions to his turmoil, no matter how they begged for her to express them. She would be there to comfort him until her friends came, and then she would leave and let him deal with his grief. When he came back, maybe they could pick up where they left off.

Her body still tingled with aftereffects of last night's sex marathon, and being in this car, with its *backseat*, was no help. At all. No wonder she was frazzled. She'd probably never be able to ride in this vehicle without thinking of that first encounter many months ago.

The very fact she'd met up with him that night was telling— the first crack in her cautious outer shell. She still didn't know what had come over her, but when she ran into him at the sushi bar and he asked if she wanted to hang out later, her "yes" had been immediate.

Loneliness? Boredom? Maybe both, maybe a lot more.

Candace had just begun messing around with Brian, Sam had Michael, and Macy had...no one.

Nothing had happened, at least not that night. They'd only talked. She hadn't lied to her friend when Candace grilled her about it a few days later, but she'd tried damn hard to hide the disappointment she'd felt—disappointment she tried to talk herself out of. As bad an idea as the whole thing was, she hadn't been able to help herself. Surely this edgy, razor-witted, dangerous-looking guy had more in mind for her than *hanging out*.

As it turned out, it hadn't taken long for him to show her.

She glanced over at him now, found that he'd finally settled down after hanging up with Brian and appeared to be dozing with his hood drawn over his head. Good. She let the memories of their second meet-up engulf her.

The way he hadn't kissed her mouth. She'd gone in for the move first—imagine *that*—and he'd grasped her chin and grazed the side of her neck with his lips...oh, those lips...before scoring lightly with his teeth. She would never, could never forget that. It had been so disconcerting and wildly erotic for him to deny her the taste of him when she was starving for it. He'd had her without another modicum of effort.

After that one intensely vivid moment, the rest was a blur of pleasure. Of desire trumping dignity. Probably good that she couldn't recall the exact things he'd gotten her to say or the positions he'd had her in so he could get to her in the cramped confines. The degree of difficulty had only made it that much hotter.

He gave her the best sex of her life. But that wasn't something they could build a *relationship* on. It should be a perk, not the foundation.

Things like this, though. Being there for each other through crises. Caring. She had no doubt she could call him for anything and he'd be there, even before today. That's what it was all about, right? And they had that going for them too.

She didn't want to end up like Raina. That thought terrified her more than anything. He could be making the girl sound worse than she was, but Macy had witnessed the crazy firsthand, and she seemed *ruined* over him. When he was done giving Macy all the addictive sex she could handle, would he then cut her loose too? Would he stick by her if they faced something major and life-changing?

"Having her back" for a favor every now and then was a damn sight different than having it forever.

She wanted forever with someone. She was ready for forever. *Please, God, don't let me be wasting my time.*

Chapter Sixteen

"Oh, what the *fuck.*"

Seth's voice yanked Macy from a fitful sleep...if what she was doing could be called that. She never could get comfortable or relaxed enough in a car to fully achieve it. Whatever the case, he startled her so that she was upright and wide awake almost before the final *k* left his lips.

By all appearances, it was early afternoon, and he was nudging the GTO to the curb on a quiet-looking street lined with quiet-looking houses. They had made it to his sister's, presumably. And he wasn't happy.

"What's wrong?"

"That." He pointed through the windshield at the shiny black Tahoe with Texas plates parked in front of them. "*That* is my sorry motherfucker of a brother."

"Oh. You didn't think he'd come?"

"Why the hell would he? He hasn't done shit so far; why start now?"

"Well..." At a loss and a grave disadvantage, Macy fumbled for something encouraging to say and gave up. Nothing her sleepy brain could conjure would magically undo what appeared to be years of animosity. "I'm sorry."

"I can't believe Steph didn't give me the heads-up he was here."

"Maybe she didn't think you'd come if she did."

"I wouldn't have. I'd have at least gone straight to the hospital like I wanted to in the first place. If she's got some kind of family reunion kiss-and-make-up shit in mind, she can hang it up."

Here was an angle she could take, maybe. "You're her brothers. She needs you both. Whatever's in the past, put it aside for her and your grandmother. You all need each other now."

"I need that asshole like I need—"

"Yes, everyone knows that. Listen to what I said, please? Am I not right?"

He hadn't killed the engine yet. He could still dart away and avoid this altogether...for now, at least. He'd have to face it sooner or later. She could see the calculations going on behind his eyes. And the pain. Maybe leaving right now would be for the best. She didn't like it, but the last thing she wanted to get caught up in was drama in an unfamiliar family. Sam and Candace were only a couple hours behind them, maybe three. If Seth's driving away right now would keep the peace until her friends could get here and rescue her, hell, she should be all for it.

"Whatever you want to do," she told him quietly.

He deflated. His brief nap had invigorated him enough that he'd seemed okay when they swapped driving duties at the state line, but now she watched the lingering exhaustion take hold of him, absolutely sapping what remaining energy he had left. Reaching up, he turned the key off. Everything about the motion seemed like a slow defeat.

What could be as bad as *that*? What was waiting for him in there?

"Maybe you should clue me in a little?"

"Macy, I honestly don't have the strength right now. You'll find out soon enough."

Adequately mystified, she turned her attention to the pretty white frame house beyond the small but meticulously landscaped yard to their right. As she watched, a blonde woman stepped out onto the porch with a toddler on her hip, waved and descended the steps. The same woman from the pictures at his house.

Seth popped open his door, and Macy followed suit, getting out and trailing him up the walkway. She stood without speaking while he and his sister embraced as best they could around his nephew—who was adorable—and then stepped forward into Seth's reach when he turned back and held his arm out toward her.

"Macy, sister. Sister, Macy."

"Stephanie," the other woman supplied. To Macy's surprise, she rushed forward and pulled her into a one-armed hug too. "Thank you so much for coming with him."

"It was no problem, really. I'm sorry about your nana." Despite the somberness of the exchange, she had to chuckle as the little boy on Steph's hip grabbed her hair in a death grip, and Steph joined in her laughter as she worked to extricate her.

"I never have that problem," Seth deadpanned as Macy came free. He rubbed the shadow on his shaved head in demonstration.

"Well, if that's what I have to do to stop having that problem, I'll pass." Steph took her little boy's hand and waved it at Macy. "This is Matthew, and yes, he loves long hair. And dangly earrings. Come on in, you guys. You look exhausted."

"Hold up. You could've warned me he was here, you know. I mean...*dammit*, Steph."

"Are you being serious? Don't you think it's time you got over it?"

"No, I fucking don't. That's not some shit you just get over."

"Jesus, Seth, you have a beautiful, obviously wonderful angel of a girl right here." Macy nearly jumped backward when Stephanie indicated her with a sweep of her free arm. What the hell did *she* have to do with anything? "So what does it even matter anymore?"

It all clicked into place. Oh, God. It was over a girl. Some other girl. Macy shifted uncomfortably, more convinced than ever this had been a very, no, *excruciatingly* bad idea.

"I don't give a fuck about the girl. What I give a f—" He seemed to catch himself when Steph smacked his arm and jerked her head toward his nephew. "What I care about is that I'm blood related to someone who'd even *do* that sh—stuff. You should take note, you know. If he'll screw me, he'll screw you."

Steph sighed with weary resignation. "I'm sure we won't have to deal with him for long. Once it's all over, he'll disappear again. Just play nice for now, please?"

"I guess she's here too?"

"She's here."

"If he starts up with me, I'm gone."

"Fine. Fair enough." His sister turned and went up the steps. Seth looked at Macy, who stared back with something akin to panic as the screen door banged shut.

"This is about some *girl?*" she hissed at him. "Thanks a lot for warning me."

"It's..." He shook his head and turned, clomping up the steps. Practically leaving her standing there. "It's just fucked up." As she considered bolting for his car and jacking it all the way back to Texas, he stopped and looked back at her. "I didn't expect all this, you know. If I had, you wouldn't be here. I'm sorry."

If he was trying to encourage her, he was failing miserably...but he wasn't trying, she decided as he pulled open the screen door and stared at her expectantly. He had closed down, turned off. She'd watched it happen in the car. It wasn't exhaustion—or it wasn't only exhaustion. It was emotional shutdown. The grimness she'd only seen flashes of since he'd come back had overtaken all remaining good humor in his features.

Whatever this was, he definitely wasn't over it by now. Where did that leave her?

Aching like hell, that was what. It hurt. Anger bubbled up, but as she'd told herself in the car, she had to get a grip. Now wasn't the time, and she'd be going home blessedly soon. Maybe she'd have a good long while to step back and mull it over while he stayed here. *Just a couple more hours. Hang in there.*

She brushed past Seth into the house as he held the door for her, almost afraid of what she would find. No one was in the living room, but voices drifted in from what must be the kitchen up ahead. She waited for Seth to come in and lead the way, wiping her damp palms on her jeans.

And stopped in her tracks.

A man had stepped into the doorway...and he could've been

Seth himself, only...well, with hair. Just as he'd looked in that picture at his house. Identical.

Freaking twins. God, there were *two* of him?

Only this guy was another animal entirely. His clothes were expensive. Not a rip or tear or even a worn spot in those starched jeans, and what skin she could see on his arms carried no trace of ink.

Wow. Just...fucking wow.

Seth greeted him, shook hands with him, but he did so coolly. Macy was waiting for her own introduction—his name was Scott, wasn't it?—when a very tall, very beautiful blonde came in behind Seth's brother and took her place beside him. She wore slim black pants and a flowing blue top that did nothing to hide the fact she was also very pregnant.

Macy felt Seth freeze up beside her. If that were even possible given the tension already coming off him in waves. Had he not known?

"Seth," the blonde said, "how have you been?"

"I've been great. I see you're...doing well."

She dropped a delicate hand—her left hand, big sparkling rock on her finger—to her swollen belly and laughed as Scott settled his arm around her shoulders. "I guess if you can call this 'well'."

"Yeah, you...look great."

"Doesn't she?" Scott asked. "Brooke's the hottest little mama around." He nuzzled her ear and she giggled.

Brooke. *Brooke?*

The Brooke?

Oh, hell no.

Forget Seth acting a fool; Macy herself was ready to launch at this guy's throat on his behalf. Fucked up, he'd said. Yeah, that was an understatement. This was *all kinds* of fucked up.

And now the twin-brother-hopping Brooke was pregnant, and apparently, Seth hadn't known.

Through the rushing in her ears, she was vaguely aware the conversation went stiltedly on. How humiliated must he be for Macy to see this? She wanted to get him out of here, because he was going through enough, and now he had to face this too. Everything she'd told him in the car was off the table. They definitely should not have come here.

But for God's sake, he could have told her. He could have trusted her that much. Though if the tables were reversed, could she have done the same?

"Aren't you going to introduce us to your girlfriend?" Scott was saying. Macy snapped out of her funk, realizing she'd let herself stand back ignored for too long. She was opening her mouth to reply when Seth opened his. Oh, did he ever open it.

"I don't know. Is it safe?"

Macy had the irrational thought that the elephant in the room had just surged forward and trumpeted and trampled everything in its path. The painful, forced formality towered into full-blown hostility as Scott glared at Seth with a look that could burn through steel and Brooke dropped her gaze to the floor. Stephanie entered the room cautiously at their backs, looking ready to throw herself between the four of them if need be.

Macy stuck her hand out practically in Scott's face. "Macy Rodgers. Very nice to meet you."

He blinked and looked at her, taking her hand briefly. "Scott Warren. You too."

She swung her hand to the blonde. "Brooke, was it?"

Looking relieved, she nodded and shook also, but Macy didn't miss the tremor in her hands. "Brooke Warren."

"So nice to meet you too. How far along are you?"

"Seven months."

"Wow." She gave Seth's arm a backhanded smack. "I hope I look that good when I'm seven months."

Brooke looked confused. "Oh, are you...?"

"God, no. Just, you know, someday." She linked her arm through Seth's and beamed up at him. A hint of a smile played around his lips as he stared back.

"O-of course," the other girl stammered.

"Listen, I'm about to fall down from exhaustion, let's go sit and—"

Stephanie, who had just begun to breathe again, jumped all over Macy's suggestion. "Yes! Let's all sit down for a few minutes. Seth, Macy, I have drinks and snacks out for you guys. You must be starving. You can freshen up, and we'll go see Nana."

"Any change?" Seth asked. "I'd rather not wait."

"I know, sweetie, but she's stable. Let's take care of you first." She bustled them into the kitchen like the mother hen Seth had said she was. Macy didn't miss the mouthed "thank you" she sent her way as they took places around the dining room table and a smorgasbord of chips and sandwiches and drinks.

It was still awkward, and that awful tightness continued to hang in the air, but the fear that violence might erupt at any moment slowly ebbed. The situation had been addressed. Scott seemed to know Seth hadn't forgotten and wasn't going to forgive. The two of them hardly looked at each other, spoke even less. Macy, Brooke and Stephanie carried what conversation there was.

Under the table, she sought out Seth's hand, held it tight. He didn't eat. His constant fidgeting and checking his watch plainly said he didn't want to be here, and Macy couldn't help thinking if she wasn't here, he would get in his car and go to the hospital, where he wanted to be. She was holding him up.

Leaning over, she put her mouth close to his ear. "Can I talk to you for a minute?"

He nodded and stood, pulling her with him, telling the others they'd be back. They walked out front to where his car was parked, Macy crossing her arms against the chill the weak late-February sun couldn't eliminate. A headache was blossoming at the back of her skull and she pulled out her ponytail holder. For a moment they were silent as cars passed on the street and a group of kids biked by them. She barely even knew where to begin.

"I'm sorry. If you want to go, let's go," she said at last. "Sam and Candace can pick me up at the hospital."

"It's all right. I friggin' hate hospitals, and I'm sure you do too, so no reason to subject you to that. Are you cold?" He made a move to unzip his hoodie, but she stopped him.

"I'm fine. And really, it's not a big deal. But Seth? I so wish you'd warned me what I was walking into."

The look on his face said she didn't need to tell him that. "Fucked up, right? You handled it like a champ, though. Thank you for that."

She gave him a little smile and flipped her hair back in an I-ain't-scared gesture. He chuckled. "So I guess you don't want to talk about it now, either," she said.

"Well, it's out there. You got any questions, shoot."

"I take it this girl... How did it go? Was there a competition for her between you and your brother, or what?"

"I guess there was, only I didn't know about it. She left me for him. It's been...Christ, almost seven years. They took the pussy way out, practically disappeared into the night together, and I hadn't laid eyes on either of them since. Until today. Had no idea she's pregnant."

"You loved her."

"Yeah."

"Do you still?"

She would have thought he'd expect that to be the next logical question to leave her lips, but he looked staggered by it. Her heart sank. Hostility between him and his brother she could understand. You just didn't do that to someone you cared about. If he wanted to carry the grudge around with him for the rest of his life, that was his business. Unhealthy, maybe, but his business.

How he felt about another woman while Macy was becoming increasingly more involved with him was her business.

"It's like I can't disentangle my feelings for her from my hatred for him. Does that make sense? I can't say that I love her, no. But I'm always gonna hate him. Every fucking day, I'm gonna hate him. When I think about him, I have to think about her, and I get pissed off all over again."

"Do you hate him *because* of her, or was that the nail in the coffin?"

"He was always an asshole. But then, so was I, so can't blame him there. I don't know. We never had much more than toleration between us, even before shit went way south."

"So...the tattoos, the music, the piercings...I mean, what are you trying to do, distance yourself as much from your twin as possible?"

"Jesus, Macy. I am who I am. Not to rebel, not to piss anyone off, and *damn* sure not for any fucking reason related to that douche bag in there."

"That wasn't... I shouldn't have said that. I'm sorry."

Now that the can of worms was open, though, he couldn't seem to put the lid on it again. "I guess my brother was an upgrade. Same package, bigger ambitions. And she was right, too, wasn't she? As it turns out. So...whatever."

"What are you *talking* about? As sure of yourself as you've always been, you can't possibly believe that."

"I know what I believe about myself." He gestured toward the house. "But I also know what they believe about me."

"Well, who cares about them, then?" One corner of her mouth tugged upward. "Fuck them."

It was worth it to see his eyebrows shoot up, to see a genuine grin brighten his face. All it had taken was an f-bomb from her. But his next words had her losing her own smile, and he wouldn't look at her as he said them, instead watching the toe of his boot dig into the ground. "You would wreck me, you know that?"

"What?"

"If you ever run some shit on me like she did. I've known it from the start. I guess I'm a glutton for punishment. I've crashed and burned too many times, but here I am, asking for more."

Her heart lurched. She stepped forward and grasped the zippered edges of his hoodie, making him look at her, waiting until she had his full attention again before she spoke. "Hey. I'm not her. I'm not anything like her. Don't project that onto me. It's not fair, and you know it. As soon as I put together what had happened, I was disgusted. If you think I'm that kind of person, that I would do something like that to you, then..."

Then what? If he was that wary and mistrustful...what future would they have?

His fingers were surprisingly warm as he reached up to take hers. "Now, I shouldn't have said *that*. Dammit. It just...brought a lot back. Seeing them. I'm sorry."

"Maybe this will give you a chance to work through some things."

"Right. Can I ask you something?"

"Sure."

"Where did you go after that night, that very first night we were together?"

Macy's breath caught as shame burned through her middle. His dark eyes searched her face.

"You quit talking to me," he went on. "More than that, you avoided the shit out of me. Do you remember what you said to me, after we were done? You told me not to tell anyone."

That's right, she had. It wasn't as bad as it sounded, though, he had to know that. She shook her head, but he continued. "What, I was good enough to bang a few orgasms out of you, but I wasn't good enough for your friends to have a clue?"

"That's not what I meant. I'm not one to talk about stuff like that, even with my best friends. Ask Candace and Sam when they get here, if you want. I didn't know if you were the type to run and brag to Brian you'd got it on with his girl's best friend. Yes, I was a little embarrassed and a little confused and wondering what the hell was up with myself. But my asking you not to tell anyone wasn't commentary on *you*. It was on me. I promise."

She hadn't meant to hurt him. She hadn't thought she *would* hurt him, or even that she could. Back then, especially, he'd seemed so...invincible. Impervious. Yeah, she'd really thought he might boast to his buddies that he'd managed to nail Candace's frigid best friend in his backseat, and she would die of mortification, and that would be that. But no. As far as she knew, he hadn't breathed a word of it, and he wouldn't have even if she hadn't asked it of him.

Reaching up, she captured his face between her hands. She could look at that face forever, she realized. So full of character, so beautiful. She'd laughed more with him in the past couple of weeks than she had in the entire year. And she had to leave him. The thought of not touching him, not hearing his laughter in her ear or seeing that devilish glint in his eyes for who knew how long, laid her heart wide open.

"I'm really going to miss you," she said, hating how banal it sounded. If those damn threatening tears began to win out, she was going to have to let them. They would speak more for her feelings than her voice ever could.

A little bit in love, my ass.

"Macy..." Her transition into his arms was seamless; she didn't know if she went into them or if he pulled her in first—it was simply a fluid, instinctive motion. As if they both knew she belonged there.

"I don't know what to say," he breathed into her hair, squeezing the air from her. "Fuck. Just wait for me."

That was all he needed to say.

"I will."

Chapter Seventeen

There were so many reasons he dreaded her leaving. For one, once she was gone it meant he would have to face what was waiting for him at the hospital, and he didn't know if he could take it. For another, he'd be left staring at the happy fucking baby-making couple without her comforting voice of reason at his ear or her calming presence by his side.

Last but most importantly...God, he hadn't realized just how much he was going to miss her until he watched her friend's car pull up front, and it hit him like a kick in the gut.

"There they are," she said quietly, standing from the porch swing where they'd been swaying mostly in silence for over an hour. Without her warmth curled almost protectively against his side, the cold seeped in, but she didn't let go of his hand as he stood and followed her down the steps. So there was that.

Candace bailed out of the passenger's seat and rushed forward, hugging him and saying how sorry she was for everything, how she and Brian were there if he needed anything done back home, but he heard it and watched it all through a fog. Brian had already told him that on the phone. Told him to take all the time he needed, and he would still have a job whenever he was ready for it.

Damn, he hated letting him down or leaving him in a bind.

He wanted to ask Macy to stay. At least for a day or two. The impossibility of it didn't make it any easier to resist. Her friends had already come all this way. She had a life, and he wasn't a permanent-enough presence in it yet for an interference of that magnitude. Besides, even if by some miracle she didn't shoot him down cold, it would only be that much worse when she finally did go back. He was getting way too ahead of himself, dumping all this on her. She'd end up running before they even had a fair shot. Hell, he was damn lucky she hadn't already.

"You are a saint," Candace was saying, hugging Macy now. That much he knew, and he hoped Macy did too. She was an angel on earth to go through the last twenty-four sleepless hours with him.

"I'm a sleepy saint," Macy said. Her eyelids drooped a little. He'd thought a couple of times she'd been dozing on the swing. Still, she was beautiful, her skin a little flushed from the chill, her hazel eyes no less clear for the apparent drowsiness.

"I bet. We'll leave you alone and you can sleep all the way home."

Samantha came around the front of her SUV. "I brought pillows and a blanket for you, even."

"Bless you." The two exchanged a quick hug and Macy asked if she could retrieve her purse from Ghost's car.

He got it for her, making sure his fingers brushed hers as he handed it over. Her gaze met his, held there and spoke volumes her friends couldn't hear. There were no words, anyway. Maybe that was part of his fucking problem; he never knew how to say the words to keep someone from leaving him. Macy was different from anyone he'd ever been with, though. She would understand.

Yeah. He'd thought that about Brooke once too, hadn't he? And she was pregnant with his brother's kid. In the beginning, he'd even thought it about Raina, who was so much like him on so many levels that surely there was no *way* they couldn't work out. Eventually, their explosiveness together had only resulted in their self-destruction.

Don't think about that shit, man.

There was way more pressing crap to worry about.

"I guess...we'd better get on the road," Macy said, shouldering the strap of her purse then stroking the back of his hand with her thumb.

"Yeah." He had to resist licking his lips with his need to kiss her.

"I'd feel bad not saying good-bye to everyone..."

"I'll tell Steph for you; she understands. As for the others, don't worry about it. Really."

"Okay."

"I wish you didn't have to go."

At his blurted words, her expression seemed to drain. Was that good or bad? He knew she couldn't stay; he wasn't that dense. All that mattered was that she would if she were able. When her eyes filled with tears, he decided it must be a good sign. Sam and Candace returned to the car, giving them their privacy.

"Everything is going to work out for the best," she told him, gently taking his shoulders in her hands. "You have to believe that."

"I know it will."

Standing on her toes, she pressed her lips to his, lingering until he was just getting ready to crush her in his arms, throw her over his shoulder and run away with her caveman style—and then she pulled back, stroked his cheek once and turned away. Taking her sugary vanilla scent and her quiet reassurance with her, leaving him to face some harsh, cold realities all on his own.

But that's the way it had always been. That's the way he'd preferred it. What was different now?

"I'll call you," he said lamely, just in case it wasn't obvious. He wouldn't last ten minutes without needing to hear her voice.

"You'd better."

He opened the back door for her, watched as she got in and buckled up. He told Samantha to drive safe. Macy's gaze met his as he shut the door; he didn't break the connection as the car pulled away, even as it drove down the street and he couldn't actually see her anymore.

Then they turned the corner, and she was gone.

He didn't go back in Stephanie's house. There wasn't anything for him in there right now. He'd be a comfort to his sister and her family once that bastard wasn't under her roof, but right now, there was little short of a fire that could make him share oxygen with Scott.

Bad enough they had to share DNA. And a face. Macy had asked if he was trying to be different from his brother, and he wasn't—they'd always been like night and day. They hadn't shared any of the same interests except in one huge, glaring example...it wasn't enough to have the same taste in women; no, they had to have the same woman.

Macy had said it all. Fuck him. And fuck Brooke too.

It was too beautiful a day for this much gloom. He made the drive to the hospital on autopilot, bracing himself the whole way. The depressing, all-too-familiar smells inside the building turned his stomach, but he steeled himself and trudged on, knowing that the atmosphere was going to get way more fucking familiar in the next few days, weeks...however long it would be.

God, how he wished things could go back to normal again. For himself, for his nana.

The information desk told him where to find her and soon he stood frozen in the door to her room, practically deaf and blind to the bustle of nurses and white-coats in the ICU. It was all he could do to breathe. She looked so frail, almost nonexistent beneath the blankets except for her cap of white hair and the little points where her feet rested under the blankets. What must've been a dozen tubes connected her to this machine and that.

He'd really fucked this up, thrown away his last chance to say good-bye to her, to tell her he loved her and have her hear him.

Dragging a chair to her bedside, he sat heavily and took her thin, tepid hand in his. Was it just yesterday he'd been so stoked to take Macy out on their first real date? It felt like ten years ago. His grandmother would've liked her. She also would've been able to tell him how to deal with Scott, or if nothing else, she would've yanked him in line and told him to quit wasting mental energy on something so worthless. It had broken her heart to see the two of them divided in such a way, but she'd known where to place the blame. Scott hadn't just hurt Seth, he'd hurt her, he'd hurt all of them. He'd run away like the fucking little weasel coward he was so he wouldn't have to hear crap from anyone about what a piece of shit he was being.

Hell, maybe Scott had the right idea. Do what you want to do, no matter who you hurt or how much, live your life the way you want and to hell with everyone else. They were all going to end up right where his grandmother was someday, right? Might as well make the most of it, and it seemed to be working out awfully well for that rat bastard. Financially well-off and a baby on the way with the woman who was supposed to be someone else's wife.

Every time he thought about the nights he and Brooke had lain together and talked about getting married, he wanted to tear walls down with his bare hands, wanted to jump out of his skin because it felt covered in slime from letting himself fall victim to a betrayal like that. It wasn't so much for what he'd lost—not anymore—but for the fool he'd been. Had she been fucking Scott even then? He didn't know and he never would. The only minor, infinitesimal satisfaction he had from that entire situation was that he knew he'd been Brooke's first. *Yeah, smoke on that, motherfucker.* Not that Scott probably even knew. When was the best time to tell your husband his identical twin brother had popped your cherry? Try never.

The machines beeped and pumped and did whatever they were doing to keep his grandmother alive. At that moment, he was barely hanging in there himself. His mind spun on his current drama to keep from dealing with the reality in front of him.

She was dying. And he couldn't fucking take it.

The images he'd been deliberately pushing back flashed their way through his turmoil then, and he shuddered, breathing hard through his nose to keep from losing it. Playing hide-and-seek behind the house, listening to the awesome bedtime stories she always told him to put his hyper ass to sleep, her holding him and rocking him and somehow managing to keep it together while he cried and wailed for his parents. She'd lost them too.

Maybe his mom and dad would know how to deal with everything too. But they weren't here either. They'd gone away, like most everyone else in his life. They weren't with him in spirit, they weren't comforting him, and anyone who said otherwise was full of shit. He was alone.

The emotions tore through and ripped him to pieces. He dropped his head to where his hand clutched his grandmother's and sobbed.

"I know we promised to let you sleep, but I have a question."

Macy turned from her blind perusal of the passing landscape and met Sam's gaze in the rearview mirror. "I probably won't be able to sleep until I'm in my bed, anyway. What?"

"We debated this all the way up here."

"Okay..."

"Is he pierced?"

"Sam!"

Her friends' mingled laughter was like a balm to her soul. What would she do without them? "I'm just joking," Sam said. "Sorry. It's just way too serious around here; I can't help it."

"I know you can't."

"You really are gonna keep it in the vault, aren't you?"

"Yep. And speaking of vaults, Candace... What has Brian told you about Brooke? Anything?"

"No, nothing really."

"Wow. Those guys have a blast-proof vault, then."

"Is he holding out on me? What is it?"

"If *Brian* hasn't told *you*, then I'm sure as hell not going to. I was just curious what you knew."

"Men and their vaults," Candace grumbled.

"Hey, we have a vault too," Sam said. "It's just that *usually*, it's in a centralized location and we all three have keys to it." She shot Macy a comical glare over her shoulder.

"Not this time. Sorry."

"Who's the Brooke chick, though? Clue me in at least a little. I know absolutely nothing."

"She's an ex."

"He still hung up on her?"

"There are some...lingering anger issues. That's all I'm going to say on the matter."

"Tear through 'em. She ain't got nothing on you, babe. Right?"

"At least you're not blood related to the most prominent ex," Candace put in. Macy smirked as she pulled her cell phone out of her purse. God, wasn't that the truth. Brian had dated Candace's favorite cousin before the two of them hooked up, and it was still a source of contention with Candace's suffocating family.

She sent a quick text to Seth. They'd been on the road for over an hour; surely by now he'd gotten to the hospital. A feeling that he wasn't okay churned in her gut, and that more than anything else was keeping her awake.

Of course he wasn't okay. She wouldn't be okay in his situation either, but she couldn't stand not being there. He was practically alone with his ex, a brother he hated and a sister who, while her intentions were good, was probably going to push the whole get-over-it thing until he snapped.

Hope you're okay, I promise not to stop thinking about you.

She chewed her bottom lip. Too much? Did he give a crap right now if she was thinking about him or not? The words seemed to stand ten feet high on her little display. Before she could talk herself out of it, she hit Send and threw her head back against the seat, rubbing her eyes hard with her thumb and forefinger.

"Okay, Mace?" Sam was watching her in the mirror again.

"I'm...not really, no."

"Please try to get some sleep," Candace said. "You'll feel better."

"Can you make sure Brian checks on him a lot? I mean, there's things he won't talk to me about yet, you know?"

"I won't have to make sure. He will. He'll probably be making a trip to see him, but he wasn't able to today."

Was there any reason she couldn't do the same thing? But no, she was being ridiculous. Acting like a lovesick teenager or something. Seth needed to handle his business without her hanging around. In the meantime...

Thanks to him, and last night—and this morning—there were a few things she needed to work on herself.

Her phone chimed with a return message. *Im ok. Thx. Cld rlly go 4 some sushi rt now tho. :)*

It wasn't exactly what she'd hoped to hear, but oh well. At least he earned points for the memory he conjured. She wrote back *Me too* and resolved to take her friends' advice to try to catch a few minutes' sleep.

Chapter Eighteen

The ringing of her phone tore her out of the deepest sleep she'd experienced in her entire life. Macy's head jerked up from the pillow.

She made a clumsy grab for the phone on her nightstand before reality had swept the cobwebs from her brain. It might be Seth; something bad might've happened—

The bold letters on her display told her it was only her mom.

She answered and flopped back onto her oh-so-comfy pillow.

"Where are you?" her mom asked before she could get her greeting out.

"I'm home. Asleep." *And that asleep part? I'd like to get there again.*

"Well, I figured. But you never called. And it's two in the afternoon already."

"Sorry to make you worry."

"Is everything all right?"

"Yes."

"Will you tell me now what's going on?"

Ugh. She'd rushed through her explanation yesterday morning when she'd called her mom because she hadn't wanted to tell her the situation and deal with her game of one hundred questions.

"Everything's fine. I told you I was helping a friend."

"You said you were helping a friend get to Oklahoma. It must be a friend I don't know, because Candace and Sam don't have family in Oklahoma."

"Don't you think I might have friends you don't know at

this point?"

"You're being evasive. I can only assume you have a man."

Oh, Jesus. "It's a...male friend, yes."

"I guess we shouldn't have invited Jared over for dinner tonight, then."

Macy shot bolt upright. "You did *what*?" She always had dinner with her parents on Sunday nights; what in the world possessed them to do this?

"He came here this morning, Macy, and he looked pitiful. He'd gone to your apartment looking for you yesterday, but of course you were gone all day. He said he was worried about you, but I told him what you were doing."

"And he said...?"

"Nothing. Just visited with us for a little while. As he was leaving, your dad told him to come back tonight, and the two of you could talk."

"Oh, *Mom*."

"Don't yell at me; yell at him. You know he was practically planning your wedding to Jared from the time you were twelve. He loves him, and so do I. We want to see you work things out. *Jared* seems to want to work things out."

"*I* don't want to work things out."

"Are you positive about that? You loved him so much. I know you did. And I saw you two outside Friday."

"Jared's on the rebound, Mom. His marriage just fell apart. It isn't love, it's...nostalgia. Or something."

"I don't believe that. I believe he never got over you."

Damn, what was it with the exes? Try to hook up with someone else, and they buzzed out of the woodwork like angry hornets. Macy had the irrationally hilarious thought that they should introduce Jared and Raina, but she bit her lip on that laughter.

"If he's going to be there, then I can't come."

"Don't do that. How rude. If nothing else, he was your best friend. He misses you."

She lay still in her bed and listened to her own heartbeat and the rain she'd just realized was spattering against her window. "Mom...what would you say if I told you I'm thinking of racing again? Not anything serious," she quickly amended. "Just...getting back into it a little. See where it goes."

"What would I say?" She could already hear the joy bubbling up in her mom's voice. "I'd say I think you definitely need to come to dinner tonight."

So she found herself walking past Jared's dually parked in her parents' driveway—he was early—and trudging up to the front door at seven o'clock. She felt like absolute crap, still out of whack. After all this, she probably wouldn't sleep a wink tonight. Seth had called her an hour ago; he'd sounded tired but okay. He hadn't talked long, and she hadn't bothered to tell him where she was going. There had been no change in his grandmother's condition, and the doctors weren't optimistic. He'd slept in as long as she had.

It had been so good to hear his voice. She'd heard it in her dreams all night, but they'd had nothing on the reality. Now she needed only to endure her parents' scheming and get back home. Reflect on the past two days and think. And remember.

Oh yes. Remember. Now that she was back, somewhat rested and not living on raw adrenaline, ten seconds couldn't go by without a flashback to Friday night. It shouldn't be that hard to hang on to those feelings and get through this.

She didn't bother ringing the bell. The scents of home were a comfort as she entered the rambling two-story ranch house; ordinarily, she really looked forward to seeing her parents each week. A little guilt lanced through her tonight, though. She hadn't exactly been forthcoming with them, so they probably had their hopes up for a reconciliation. And she doubted Seth would like it if he knew she was having dinner with her ex when he had nothing but hell with his own.

It was no big deal, though. If Jared started anything with her, she'd just shut him down again.

"Macy?" Her mom's voice drifted in from the dining room over the rumble of male laughter. "We're in here, hon."

She followed the sound, managing a smile for everyone as she entered. Her mom and dad came around to give her hugs, and Jared rose from his seat, his knock-you-down blue gaze lingering on her a little too intimately. Maybe seeing a little too much. Sam had always suggested guys could subconsciously smell sex on a woman, and it brought them sniffing. But it had been two days since Seth had spent the night with her. Surely the remnants of catastrophic pleasure were all gone by now.

She greeted him with a smile and quickly took her usual seat, which was thankfully *across* the table from him. Her mom had already set out the food, and she dished some up and ate without really seeing anything going on around her. Vaguely, she heard her dad ask Jared all the usual questions about his family, his parents, how work was going, his new John Deere, the remodeling he was doing to his house...etcetera, etcetera. She couldn't be bothered listening to the answers.

Her cell phone buzzed in her jeans pocket. Hiding her movements under the table lest her mom throw out her phone because she was fanatical about table manners—Lord, imagine Seth getting his hand up her skirt *here*—she fished it out and sneaked a glance.

Seth was usually a sparse texter, but he must want his message to get across loud and clear tonight. *Call me when you go to bed. Need to listen to you moan my name again.*

Heat crept up her face; she could practically feel herself turning red. It was as if he'd just said those words in her ear. Squirming in her chair against the ache building in her sex, she quickly lifted her gaze and focused on her still-full plate.

Jared was watching her. She felt the weight of it without looking, and when she dared a glance upward, her suspicions were confirmed. There was something vaguely hungry about the way he looked at her, and she wondered if the man across from her was anything like the boy she'd pushed away years ago.

But even that predatory look would never, not in a million years, incite such a riot of passion in her. Not like those words on her phone's display, which seemed to be burning a hole in her jeans right now.

"What's wrong with you?" her dad said. She heard it, processed it, but for a moment, didn't even consider that he was talking to her. "Hey! Daughter of mine."

She started in her chair. A quick glance around showed not only Jared's, but all eyes were on her. "What?"

"You're off in outer space."

"Just tired, Daddy."

He scoffed. "Aw, poor thing."

"Don't give me a hard time," she said, grinning and picking up her fork mostly for show.

Her mother frowned at her, not fooled for a second. "You have seemed preoccupied the past couple weeks. I noticed even when I talked to you Friday, you barely heard a word I said."

She'd talked to her mom Friday? "I don't know why. Everything's fine."

"Are things at the store okay? Everyone behaving?"

"Yeah, it's good."

"How are Candace and Samantha?"

"Everyone is great, Mom. Nothing is wrong."

"I talked to Candace's mother today. She said her and that Ross boy are still going strong. She never has much to say other than that, though."

That Ross boy. Poor Brian. It was like he didn't even have a first name. "Yep. Strong."

"I just hope she doesn't get pregnant," Macy's mom fretted.

Seriously? "Mo*ther.*"

"Well! It would kill Sylvia, you know it would."

"I'm sure they'll be fine. They're adults, you know."

"Is he going to marry her? Has she said anything?"

So Jennifer Rodgers could run to her BFF Sylvia Andrews and report back about the goings-on in Brian and Candace's life? "I don't know. She hasn't even graduated yet. Give them time before you start planning bridal and baby showers."

"I don't think Sylvia's too excited about planning anything where they're concerned."

Except maybe how to get Brian out of her daughter's life

without looking too guilty. "Well, she needs to get over it, and maybe you could try explaining that to her."

"She's doing much better about it now than she was when it first blew up. That much I can say."

"Blew up" was an understatement. It had been ugly. Candace's brother James had tried to destroy Brian and everything he'd worked for. Macy hated to think about it. She'd had to come forward with information that could've taken James down in return—and probably would've brought shame on the entire Andrews family. It had taken everything she had in her to do it.

But Brian hadn't been angry at her for her indecision about confessing what she knew. And it had all worked out in a truce, albeit a very tense one.

"This is all very interesting," Macy's dad said, "but what's this about you wanting to race again?" She didn't think she'd seen him grin that big since before she'd gotten hurt.

Jared had been cutting his steak. His hands froze. The hopefulness that bloomed on his face as he slowly raised his eyes to hers broke her heart. "Really?" he asked.

"I'm not so against the idea anymore."

"That's awesome. You should come out for the roping next weekend. I'll set up the barrels for you; you can make a few runs. Get some practice in. I know everyone would love to see you."

All her old friends? Half of them would probably throw rocks at her. And at Jared's house? No, thanks. "Oh no, that's... I'm not ready for all that yet."

"I'm inclined to not take no for an answer." Ugh, and there was the smile that had charmed her right out of her virginity at an age that would probably make her parents reassess their feelings and throw him out of the house if they knew.

"Well, you might just have to," she fired back, sounding more flirtatious than she'd intended. It was a little too much...Jared staring at her across the table like he wanted to eat her alive, and Seth texting her under the table about her moaning in his ear. And she still didn't think she'd come down from Friday night. She'd be riding that high for a long time yet.

Jared put a hand thoughtfully to his chin. "What kind of blackmail can I resort to? Your parents are sitting right here. Hmm..."

Yeah, you just go there, buddy. My dad has guns. Lots and lots of guns.

Her parents laughed at that, and he joined in, giving Macy a wink.

"Seriously, though. Saturday around noon. Come on out."

"You really should go," her mom said. "It would be good for you to get out."

"I do get out."

"Yes, but..." She trailed off, and Macy raised her eyebrows, her mind supplying the end to that thought. *...it would be good for you to get out with different people.*

Oh no. They weren't about to start *that* up, were they? She wondered just how much Jared had told them. Her parents had always been accepting people, but if Jared had made it sound like she was hanging out with a thug, that would change. She was her own person; she did what she wanted to do. But she was close with them, and their approval was important to her. It always had been, and for most of her life, it had always been fairly easy for her to attain.

Jared had better not tarnish their image of Seth before they even got a chance to meet him. Who was she kidding, though? He'd probably be fairly adept at tarnishing it all on his own once they did.

While she stewed over it, the others took a trip down memory lane over dessert, and before long her mother was pulling out old photos of her and Jared and their friends, and all that crap.

She smiled and chatted and reminisced with them, but underneath it all, she only wanted to bolt from the table. Why did she ever have to open her big, fat mouth?

"I hate to break up the party, but I'm still really tired," she announced, easing out of her chair.

"Oh, so soon?" Her mother looked crestfallen. "The coffee

should be ready in a minute."

"No, thanks. I lived on coffee yesterday. I'm coffee'd out."

"Will you please call me when you have time to talk?"

And when would that be? "All right, Mom."

Jared stood as she edged closer to the door. "Can I walk you out?"

Shit, she should have seen that coming. And it was like insta-happiness dawned across her parents' faces. Seething, she shrugged and hoped the fake smile she plastered on wouldn't give away her aggravation. "Suit yourself."

She kissed her parents good-bye as Jared went into the foyer, making sure he'd be able to help her into her coat and open the front door for her. She let him go through the motions without a fuss, thinking how none of it meant as much as when Seth had done similar things. Maybe because she hadn't expected it out of a guy like him. Or maybe because when Seth had done it, it hadn't reeked of desperation.

The thought made her sad all of a sudden. Jared hadn't done anything to deserve her annoyance, really, except still care about her at a very inopportune time.

"Please come by Saturday," he said as they strolled out into the chilly night. His warm fingers curled around hers. "The weather's supposed to be great."

She tugged her hand away and shoved it into her coat pocket. "Jared, I need you to stop this."

"What?"

"I explained to you Friday."

"I'm just trying to be your friend."

"Then I'm going to have to ask you to stop that too, if this is the way you go about it. Getting Mom and Dad involved was *not* the thing to do."

"I'm sorry about that." He leaned against the front fender of her Acadia, looking as if he was getting comfortable, and she sighed. "I got to thinking yesterday, and I sorta got beside myself, I guess. I wanted to talk to you some more. Then you didn't come home all day—"

"What did you do, camp out on the street?"

"No. I checked once in the morning and then tried again in the afternoon."

She narrowed her eyes. He'd gotten "beside herself" thinking she'd spent the night with Seth. "You don't have to worry about me. I'm a big girl. I can make my own decisions; I can take care of myself."

"Macy, you can do better than that guy."

Hell no. She lunged for her car door handle, elbowing him out of the way when he tried to intercept her. "I don't owe you any explanations."

He won, grabbing the handle before she could open it. "I'm sorry, okay? But listen to what I'm saying. You *know* it. In your heart, you know it. It's never going to work. You think *they'll* go for it?" He pointed toward her house. She stopped trying to pry his hand away and glared at him as her breath burned her lungs. "You think they'll welcome *that* in their house?"

"It's not up to them."

"Don't go like this. Please. Just think about coming over Saturday. I swear I won't get out of line. I have the girls this weekend. They would love to see you there. It would make their weekend, Macy, really."

Oh, that wasn't fair. "You've proven you won't back off when I tell you to, so no. I'm not putting myself in this situation again."

"What if I promise I'll be good?" He grinned at her.

"No."

"Just tell me what it's gonna hurt. You can see some old friends, laugh about old times, get a little piece of your old life back. I want to help you with that, if nothing else. You were awesome. If I can be a little part, a *tiny* part, of you getting back to that, then hell. I want in."

Jared wasn't supposed to be a part of her getting her old life back. She searched his face, looking for any signs of insincerity. Or veiled lechery. Nothing was there except his earnest, pleading blue eyes.

"Jared..."

"Come on. Just one day. If you don't have fun, I promise I

will never, ever bug you about hanging out with us again."

She crossed her arms, glared at him some more, chewed her bottom lip. Finally she released her breath in a huff, dropping the defensive stance and trying for her car door again. This time, he let her. "Fine! All right. I'll freaking come over." After opening the door, she put her finger in his face. "Listen to me. You try one thing, you *say* one thing that even remotely offends me or pisses me off, and I'm out of there. You got that? I'm serious, Jared."

He'd been grinning like the Cheshire cat, but he dropped all expression at her tirade. "I got it. I do. Yes, ma'am." He saluted her.

She rolled her eyes and escaped into the interior of her car, yanking her keys from her purse and jamming one in the ignition.

"Saturday. Noon," he said.

"I know."

"Good night, Macy." With a final grin that had a little too much triumph behind it for her liking, he shut her door.

Seth's sleepy voice as he answered his phone was the best damn thing she'd heard all day. Chuckling, she pulled her own covers up to her chin. "You were asleep."

"Yeah," he yawned.

"But you answered on, like, the first ring."

"Been waiting on you."

"Really?"

"You didn't answer my text earlier, though, so I didn't know if you'd call or not."

"Sorry. I was at my parents' having dinner." Her brow furrowed. Should she tell him her ex-boyfriend was there? Or that they were hanging out this weekend? Was he the type to get mad about something like that? If he was, it probably wouldn't be worth the drama. Wasn't like he had anything to worry about.

His laugh was slow and warm and...oh, what she wouldn't

give to hear it beside her instead of across a state line. She rubbed her thighs together restlessly.

"That's awesome," he said.

"Why?"

"Call me deranged, but if I'd known you were at your parents', I probably would've kept it up."

Thank God he hadn't known, then. She would've been glued to her phone all night, and her mom might have flipped out. "You must feel a little better."

"Well...I'm all right."

"Everything...the same?"

"Pretty much, yeah."

She wanted to ask how things were going with his brother, but that would probably be the last thing he wanted to talk about. "Where are you?"

"Stephanie's guest bedroom."

"Hmm. I guess you have to be quiet then."

"I've got no problem with that." His voice dropped to an intimate timbre that made chills run from the tips of her toes to the roots of her hair. "I already miss you, Macy."

She'd missed him before she'd gotten in Sam's car and rode away. Her hand, which had been resting on her belly, inched downward of its own volition. To think just a couple nights ago...

"Can I take your mind off things?" she asked softly.

"That would be fucking splendid."

"I was thinking about something earlier, just before I called you." Her heart rate accelerated. She hadn't exactly intended on letting him know just yet where her thoughts had been wandering, but if he wanted to occupy his mind with other things, she was certain she had the solution.

"Uh-oh."

"We're actually only *three* hours apart if we meet in the middle."

"Are you being serious?" All humor had left his voice.

She pulled her lip between her teeth and considered for a

moment. "If you're up to it, absolutely. Not like this minute, because I need more sleep, but I just want to see you. I want to be there for you when I can. If you need to get away and you can't come all the way home...I'll come to you, I'll come all the way if you need me to, but... say the word and I'm there."

"I'm... I don't know what to say, really."

In the darkness of her room, she cringed. "Too much? I'm sorry."

"No—"

"You're dealing with something I have no experience with and I don't know what to do to help. So tell me if I need to back off."

"You're helping me by talking to me. By being there. By doing every damn thing you're already doing." He was quiet for a minute. She was tempted to fill the silence herself, but she let him have it. "This is more bearable because of you."

Her heart warmed, and she wanted so much to feel his lips on hers she might have driven those six hours right then, sleep be damned. That she wanted to be his any and every way she possibly could, both physically and emotionally, was a revelation that knocked the breath from her.

Cautious Macy had fallen for the very kind of guy that should send her running for the hills.

That *had* once, but she had her bearings now. She had a little of her old self back. Tiny, but it was there, and it was all thanks to him. She owed him far more than he could ever owe her.

"Are you off Saturday?" he asked.

Saturday. She was supposed to go to Jared's Saturday. But if it came down to one or the other...there was no question.

"Yeah. I'm usually off on weekends."

"Hmm."

"What are you thinking?"

"I'm thinking by then I will damn sure need to get away for a few hours. I'm thinking overnight."

"Are you sure?"

"I'm not sure I *should*, but..." He gave a frustrated growl.

"Shit."

"Whatever you think," she said quickly. "I don't want to pull you away if you need to be there."

"I know that, baby. But I wouldn't be considering it if I didn't need to see you, too."

"You have to take care of you. I don't care if we just talk all night."

"Oh, I think we can find more to do than that."

Chapter Nineteen

It had been the longest week of his life. Whether it was the anticipation of seeing Macy or the absolute devastation of basically being on a death watch, he didn't know. The two factors simply amalgamated into one long, never-ending stretch of agony.

He felt better the instant he got away from the sterile hospital smells and on the road, putting miles between him and that damned place and eating up the ones that separated him from his girl. He ate them up a little too eagerly, resulting in a speeding ticket halfway to Fort Worth. It didn't even matter. Minutes after getting back on I-35, he was flying again.

She would probably get on his ass about that if she were here. He could almost hear her, and it seemed even her imagined nagging made him grin. He supposed he wouldn't do either one of them any good if he got himself killed, so he managed to ease off the accelerator a little. The closer he got, the calmer he got.

Macy had booked the hotel room and texted him the directions. She'd also said she would call him when she got there, so even though she'd left home earlier than he had, he figured as he pulled into the parking lot that he must have beaten her.

Well, given the fucking ticket tossed over in his passenger seat, it was no wonder. At least the cop had let him go without searching his damn car. His appearance didn't exactly present him as an upstanding citizen.

After parking and stretching his legs for a minute, he grabbed his cell and dialed her. It was a perfect day, the sky a flawless, early spring blue. He stared at the cars zooming past on the interstate while he waited to hear her voice again.

"Do *not* tell me you're already there," she answered.

"Yeah, I am. Where is your slow ass?"

"Hey, now. I'll show you *slow* in about...twenty minutes, according to my GPS."

Oh, hell yes. "A'ight, then. Just making sure I wasn't about to get stood up."

"Not in a million. See you soon."

"Be careful."

While he waited, he texted Steph, then called and shot the shit with Brian for a few minutes. The dude sounded frazzled but hid it fairly well. If Ghost hadn't known him for half his life, he might have missed the strain.

Did Brian think the same about him? Probably. Weren't they just a couple of miserable clods. But brighter days lay ahead. They had to. He could put a bug in Macy's ear that she needed to get her best friend to drag that guy away and fuck him senseless for a few days. He'd be a new man.

A burgundy Acadia caught his attention as it whipped into a parking space a few down from him, and he said his good-byes to his friend.

All through the week while he'd been away from Macy, he'd told himself she couldn't be as beautiful as he remembered, he couldn't feel for her this much this soon. He'd spent days having to look at Brooke, whose beauty was like a knife carving his heart out all over again. When Macy came around the back end of her SUV, her bright smile all for him, she was like a balm to his ragged senses. His breath fled him. He literally couldn't take in air for a moment; he damn sure couldn't speak.

She couldn't know she did this to him. Not ever. How could he give someone that kind of power over him, when every time he'd allowed it to happen before, everything had gone to shit?

Macy flew into his arms, and he held her with all the conviction and determination he had in that moment to keep her at a distance. To not get so crazy so fast. It wasn't smart, and he knew it; he just didn't think good sense would be enough to trump his need for her. He was so fucked, careening madly down the path to getting his heart splattered all over hell.

And grinning like a buffoon the entire time.

Her scent engulfed him. Warm vanilla, even sweeter than he remembered, tempting him to eat her alive. She made a little helpless sound in his ear, and he damn near lost control of himself.

"You okay?" he asked, wondering at her exuberance. They'd talked a lot in the past week, almost every night, but he realized they'd mostly talked about what was going on with him. What hurts and stresses had she come here to work out? He simply couldn't believe she was only here to see him, but he had all night to get to the bottom of it.

She nodded against his neck. "Mm-hmm. Long drive. Glad to be here, glad to see you." She gave him another squeeze, and he set her feet on the ground, only then realizing he'd lifted her.

"You look... You're stunning, Macy."

A blush rose in her cheeks, and he couldn't resist reaching up to caress them with his thumbs. Had no one other than him ever told her that before? It was most likely an idiotic assumption, but even so, it pissed him off. Any man she'd belonged to who neglected to praise her every damn day was a damn fool.

"Thanks. I feel kind of wilted after being in the car all this time."

"Wilted, my ass. You're in full bloom, baby." He ducked as she laughed and swatted at him. "Hey, are you hungry? The city is our playground. I know we can find good sushi around here."

"Mmm. Yes, I'm hungry," she said, running her finger underneath his chin and getting an instant reaction from down south. "But the food can wait awhile."

Damn straight it could. Somehow he made it through the next few minutes, waiting while she checked them in, unloading her bags for her, finding their room. It all passed in slow fucking motion. Lust had sucker-punched him. He hoped that woman knew what she'd signed on for, because he kept thinking he was going to go to hell for all the things he wanted to do to her.

"I can't help but feel naughty about doing this," she said as she fitted the key card into the slot. "It feels like some illicit affair, sneaking off from life, meeting up at a hotel..."

He grinned and hauled their overnight bags inside, dropping them by the door. "Then that's what it is."

"Secret lovers. That aren't exactly so secret anymore." She glanced around the room. It was nice, cool, dim from the closed curtains. Hell, he didn't give a fuck about the room. He only gave a fuck about the bed and the woman in the room.

"Oh yeah? Who knows you're here?" he asked.

"You know...no one, actually. I didn't even tell Candace or Sam where I was going."

"I hope there was no important reason for that, because Brian knows. So Candace probably does too."

Macy muttered something that sounded like, "That isn't necessarily true," as she leaned over and tested the softness of the bed, but he couldn't be bothered to ponder over it. All he could focus on was the way her blousy brown shirt cinched at her little waist and those fucking ass-bling jeans molded to her butt.

"Secret lovers, huh?" he said, moving toward her. She turned around and gave him a little smirk, taking a step back for every one he took forward. She wore her hair long and straight, and it spilled around her shoulders, inviting his fingers to sink into the heavy, lustrous silk of it. "That the way you want it?"

"No. I didn't mean that. Like I said, we aren't so secret now."

And she didn't mind. Jesus H. Could he love this girl the way she deserved? He could love her with everything he was, and still it wouldn't be enough. He would fuck up somehow, because that was what he did.

She'd stopped her teasing retreat from his advance and stood still now, big hazel eyes watching his approach until she was looking right up into his eyes. Unflinching. Open. Her breath came a little quickly; her pulse fluttered at the side of her neck.

Would he ever get used to this breathless, speechless,

fucking stupefaction she instigated when she was close to him? It all seemed so fragile... One wrong word, one wrong action from him and the whole thing would crack. He only knew how to really communicate with girls like Raina. Brash, in-your-face girls who knew why they were here: to fuck and fight and above all have a good time.

Not girls like Macy, who looked at him with expectations beyond what he could give them physically. Girls like that should know to go elsewhere to get those needs met. Brooke sure as hell had. She'd even known right where to go.

"Why'd you come here?" he asked, gently brushing back a lock of hair straying near her eye.

Confusion flitted across her delicate features. "What?"

"I'm sure it's not about walking on the wild side anymore—hell, we never even really got there, did we? I've been a sucky tour guide."

"Seth, you've said and done things to me no one else has. *I've* done things and thought things and said things I never thought I would. So, no, you haven't been a 'sucky tour guide'. You've been...perfect. For me, you've been perfect." She took his hand, the one that hadn't quite been able to stop touching her hair, and let her fingers slide through his. "I even talked to my parents and one of my old friends about racing again. Baby steps," she added quickly.

Pride practically exploded in his chest. "Babe, that's awesome."

"Well, thanks for confronting me about it."

"It's all you. All I did was give you one little nudge."

"Yeah, but...it was a nudge no one else would give me. And you did way more than that."

"Oh? Like what?"

"I know I can be sort of a closed book sometimes. You get me to open up. You aren't afraid to do that. It means a lot, that you would make the effort. At that moment, it was like you knew me and what I needed to hear better than anyone else ever has."

Again, she was able to put something out there that

strangled his heart in a chokehold and tied his friggin' tongue up in knots. So he did the only thing he knew to do—pulled her in his arms and put his mouth on hers. If he couldn't use it to speak to her right then, he could use it to make her feel good. To get closer to her.

A sigh escaped her, and he drank it up, drank her in, sliding his hands down to her ass to pull her tight against his aching cock. She whimpered against his lips, and her tongue slipped between his teeth, teasing and tempting his until he plundered her back. Her body trembled and heated against his, and when she pulled away to look up at him, her eyes were a little brighter, her lips a little fuller.

"Why didn't you kiss me the first night we were together?"

Seriously? "Couldn't give you everything up front."

Her fingers curled around the back of his neck, warm and tantalizing. She wet her lips, and the knowledge that she tasted him there made his hands clench on her. "You gave me everything later."

He leaned in, sliding his lips across hers. "Not everything." When she parted her lips to invite the invasion of his tongue once more, he eluded her, instead trailing his mouth down her jaw and her sweet-smelling neck.

"Tease," she chided, but he heard the tremor in the word. Chuckling, he reluctantly let go of her and stepped back, leaving her panting gently and staring at him in bewilderment.

"Undress for me," he told her.

"What about you?"

"In due time." He sat on the bed and leaned back against the headboard. "Do it."

Expression unreadable, she regarded him for a few seconds, and he wondered if she might refuse despite the fact he'd seen her naked often enough.

"You're feeling like a bad girl today, remember," he prompted her. "You've run away from life to meet up with your clandestine lover in a distant city, and no one knows where you are. You're his for the night. It scares you a little, doesn't it." Her quick intake of breath caused her breasts to swell briefly, beguilingly. He couldn't take his eyes off her, watching the effects of his words soften her body. "But it also gets you hot."

"Sometimes I think you know me a little too well." Even as she said it, her hands slipped under the bottom of her shirt. Agonizingly slowly, she peeled it upward and over her head until her hair came free of it with a soft swish and settled back around her creamy, naked shoulders. His mouth ran dry at the sight of her lacy red bra, cut so low if she but moved, he might catch the slightest glimpse of the upper edge of her areola.

Aw fuck.

"You're wearing the red panties, aren't you?"

Her head fell back, and she giggled in a way that made him think of a demonic seductress. She should have a red devil tail twitching around her feet. Then, giving him an impish glance any porn star could learn from, she popped the button on her jeans, lowered the zipper and slid them down over her hips with a slow wiggle. Kicking them free, she shook her hair back and looked at him, waiting for his next move.

He knew what he wanted that move to be. Pinning her sexy ass down on the bed and having it six ways to Sunday all night long. He wanted to tie her up, take away the control she so desperately needed in her life, make her give it all to him.

Instead, he said, "Come here."

She wet her lips and obeyed, hips swaying hypnotically. If he were a lesser man, the mere sight of her advancing on him would be enough to make him come all over himself.

He'd known from the first time he'd seen her—freaked out and practically cowering in the parlor—that underneath the demure exterior lurked a passionate, confident and devastatingly sexual woman. She'd never disappointed him.

"So if I'm yours for the night, what are you going to do to me?" she asked. He let his gaze roam her body. She was within reach now, standing at the side of the bed; he just didn't know what he wanted to reach for first.

"What do you want?" he whispered.

Never taking her eyes from his, she unhooked her bra and let it slide from her arms. He swallowed against the sudden dryness in his throat. Suddenly there was no question what he wanted to reach for first.

Sitting up and turning toward her, he grasped her hips and pulled her in between his legs. Her breath hitched and shuddered and her skin felt like warm satin underneath his palms as he pushed his hands up her belly to cup the firm weight of her breasts. "Fucking gorgeous," he murmured, leaning forward to catch first one nipple and then the other in his mouth. Her knees quaked where they were pressed between his thighs, and her hands grasped fistfuls of his shirt as she whimpered.

He loved the sound of that. He drew her deeper, sucked her harder, circling her hard little nipple with his tongue, all in an effort to send her moans to a crescendo. Her head fell back, a movement that only bowed her lithe body into him more. The scent of her arousal flared his nostrils, and if his erection had been threatening to bust his fly before, the situation was twice as dire now.

Hooking his wrist under her knee, he hauled her leg up until her bent knee rested on his thigh. She gasped and immediately rolled her hips toward him, wordlessly begging for him to touch. He didn't keep her waiting, slipping his fingers between her parted legs but making sure to stay on top of the damp fabric for now. He moved his attentions from one wet, beaded nipple to the other one he'd been mostly neglecting.

"Oh, Seth, please," she panted, angling her body so that his fingertips brushed her clit. A jolt went through her; her hands clenched him tighter. Any more and she was going to tear off his shirt. He didn't give a shit.

"You didn't answer my question," he said against her puckering flesh.

"Wha...?" The breath left her as he sucked again. He didn't let her have it back for at least another minute, teasing her nipple, strumming her clit.

"Why you came here. I asked, you never said."

"To see you." Her voice was lower, fuller, desire-drenched, and damn, he got off on it.

"To fuck me."

"Not just...no, I...oh, *God.*" His fingers had just bypassed the fabric barrier between them and her pussy. So wet, so soft. In one frenzied motion, she put all her weight on her knee and lifted her other leg until it rested on him too, opening herself more.

"No? So if I stop, then—"

"No, don't stop!"

He chuckled. She was lying to herself if she thought she didn't need this. Maybe he was lying to himself to think she needed anything *more* than this.

What if he loosened her up sexually only for the next fucking bastard who came into her life to reap all the benefits?

Oh, goddammit, no. He snatched his hand away, grabbed her by the hips and threw her on the bed sideways, rising up over her and damn near ripping his shirt off as she watched him with a kind of feral apprehension in her eyes. It didn't stop her from grabbing his jeans and working them until she held his cock in her hands. Fuck, he was hard, so hard it hurt, and sweet relief was only a few inches away. Between her legs or between her lips, he didn't much care, only knew he had to get in one place or the other, and he had to get there fast.

"Are you on the pill?" he rasped.

Her eyelashes flickered as she looked up at him. "No. Sorry."

And so his dreams of sinking uninhibited into her wet heat and not leaving until he came died a screaming death. It was all right. He just wished he'd had the foresight to get the condoms out and have them close at hand. By the time he returned to her with the little foil packet, he was no less ravenous for the pause. She wasn't either, apparently, because she grabbed it from him and had it opened and his dick sheathed in latex almost before he could blink.

"Panties off," he demanded, and she made even quicker work of stripping them. He shucked his jeans. Her hungry gaze roved over him, and she stretched her arms above her head, already knowing what he liked without him having to ask.

"I thought you liked them on," she said huskily.

"I don't want a fucking thing keeping me from touching every inch of you I can."

A sigh shuddered from her. Jesus Christ. Her long, naked body gleamed in the dim light. All his. Her gaze dropped to his cock, she licked her lips, and that was the last thing his dangerously thin control could take.

He hadn't slid his fingers inside her, hadn't stretched her, hadn't prepared her. He wanted the sweet shock of her impossible tightness, wanted her squeezing him until he couldn't breathe, wanted to see the answering sensations pass across her face.

He spread her knees wider. Let the head of his cock slip through her gathered moisture and thrust once, hard. Her fingers wrenched the bedspread above her head. Her lovely face pinched in agonized ecstasy. He made it only halfway before he couldn't take any more of the friction, drew back and thrust again to ease his entry.

A dozen curses must have fallen from his lips, but he was beyond knowing or caring what he said. Only when she'd taken him all did he stop for a moment, breathing harshly while her legs trembled around his hips. She shivered all over, in fact, even inside where he could feel every movement magnified a hundredfold around his too-engorged shaft.

Scared, hurt, tuned on...whatever she was right now, he was right there with her. It was all from the possessiveness that had bubbled up at the thought of her with some other asshole's hands all over her. Some other asshole's dick where his was right now. He opened his mouth to say something...what, he had no clue. Something to reassure her.

He never imagined she'd be the one to reassure him. "Baby, come here," she said, disobeying his unspoken request and holding her arms out to him. He'd have been the dumbest son of a bitch alive not to go into them.

It wasn't too hard, in that moment, to almost understand where Brian was coming from now in his need to stake a claim with his woman, to make her his and his alone. Truth of the matter was, though, that it made no difference how much you gave her, or how many rings you put on her finger; there was always a motherfucker around the corner just waiting to try to entice her with a better deal. Didn't he fucking know it.

Even as he relaxed into her embrace, despair ate a hole in his gut. It couldn't last. But he couldn't fight it. As much as he liked taking her control away, her arms around him and her soft body welcoming his stole away every last bit of his own. With only a few words, a touch, she'd brought his ragged beast to heel under her own gentle command.

She hadn't come here to fuck him; she'd come here to make love to him. He wasn't ready for that yet.

"It's all going to be okay," she whispered, stroking his back.

He inhaled the overwhelming sweetness of her skin and hair and released his breath on a shudder, trying to get a grip before he just fucking lost it, right here, right now. There was so much, *too much* shit flying around his head...and maybe this had been an epically bad idea to expose her to it.

"Turn over; let me up."

No use arguing with her. He rolled, pulling her with him. Maybe she wouldn't look at his face too much. God only knew what she'd see.

Planting little kisses along his jaw, she lifted her hips, letting him slide out to just the last half-inch. He groaned, clenching his hands on her ass in an effort not to shove her back down. Slowly, so damn slowly it curled his toes, she sank again. Inch by inch until she'd taken him all and he'd broken out in a sweat.

"Oh God," she gasped. Her warm palms captured his face, and her lips melted over his. Then, as she lifted and sank again, she pulled her head back and stared right at him, lips parted, eyes glazed with pleasure. "*Oh.*"

"Macy..." Heaven. She was a little piece of heaven wrapped around him to offset the hell in his head. Her body moved with fluid grace as she began to love him...it was the only word for what she did. Every withdrawal brought her lips back to his. Her scents—like cupcakes and sex—swirled in his head, and he could drown in the dark luxury of her heavy silken hair falling around him.

A little faster now, but still gently, she rode him, seeking the angle that told him she was reaching her peak and needed to fly. So much for his hope she wouldn't look at him much, because she stared right in his fucking eyes, hers like burning amber glazed with pleasure and need.

"Fuck, that's good," she said, and it was so unexpected he almost burst out laughing.

"Aren't you glad you didn't run screaming?"

"Wha...? Oh." She gave a breathy laugh, apparently remembering her comment about his piercing. "I am. *So* freaking glad."

"Turn around."

"Huh?"

He urged her up with a gentle push on her hips. "Turn around, cowgirl. You'll see." Curious uncertainty flashing in her eyes, she did as he told her, putting her back to him. He reached between them and positioned himself at her entrance, both of them groaning as she sank back down, swallowing him whole.

"Fuck," he breathed. Running his hand up her sides, he drew her back until she lay atop him, turning her head for a kiss as he caressed her belly and breasts. It was a welcome break from her probing gaze, and, given her whimpers and the minute gyrations of her hips on him as he lay perfectly still, he knew his piercing was resting at her sweet spot.

"Seth," she moaned against his mouth. "I need..." Her pussy pulsed around him, involuntary spasms that were going to drive him out of his mind.

God, yes, she needed, and he wanted to be the one overseeing the fulfillment of those needs from now on. He took one of her hands and slid it down over her belly. "Play with your clit, Macy."

The disadvantage was that he couldn't see as she obeyed. He felt her hand leave his, heard the tiny, moist sound of her fingers finding their target and her answering sigh. In little increments, he began to move. It was all she needed—for him to work the very spot he was at. Her fingers explored lower and touched his dick where it disappeared inside her, and the shock of it jolted up his spine, made him growl, made him tighten his arm around her waist.

"I need you to come, baby, before I blow," he said in a rush at her ear. "Need to feel you squeeze me while I'm hard and deep."

"Yes." The brush of her fingers left him and returned to working the little bud he couldn't wait to kiss and tongue and suck later until she screamed. He told her all about those plans while she sighed and moaned, trembled and jerked, until finally she broke over him. Her body undulated in waves while he left control in the dust and took her in long strokes that sent her cries higher and milked his own release from him in great heaving spasms that took all the stress and heartache with them—at least for the moment. Her weight collapsed onto him just as the last shudder rent him.

But she didn't stay. She slid off him and curled at his side, her body still shaking so violently he was compelled to turn and wrap her in his arms.

"Are you okay?"

She only nodded, clinging to him. He didn't push. It had been fucking intense for him, too, and he couldn't have articulated it, so there was no reason to make her attempt to do so.

As quickly as he was able, he took care of the condom. Then, reaching over her, he pulled the lower half of the bedspread away from the mattress and tossed it over both of them, snuggling her closer into his chest. Just in case her shivering wasn't only emotional in nature.

And if it was? If she was as affected by what was happening here as he seemed to be?

He gripped her tighter. Her smooth leg slid over his, and her arm went around his waist, her head nestling under his chin. Warm breath gusted against his shoulder. So much for his grand, smart plans to keep her at a distance. Here in this little cocoon, the world didn't matter, and seemingly anything he'd ever thought or felt before didn't matter either. He would fucking die for this girl.

"You're too good for me," he whispered. Not really what he wanted to spout at the moment, but it was what came out.

"Don't say that." Her voice was still small, husky, breathless.

"I know. It's lame."

Her head lifted, and clear hazel eyes met his gaze. "I want you. And I'm an uptight bitch, remember? I don't tend to want things that aren't good enough for me."

"An uptight bitch? Who the hell ever told you that?"

"No one ever had to tell me that."

"For an uptight bitch, you're pretty damn selfless."

A grin teased at the corner of her lips. "You think I don't have my own selfish reasons for being here?"

"Well, so did I, for that matter. So, how about admitting neither of us is perfect and getting on with life."

"You brought it up."

"It was an observation. Correct but irrelevant."

"*Not* correct and irrelevant."

He laughed, sinking his hand into her hair to cup her neck and guide her lips back to his. "All right," he told her between mouthfuls of her sweetness. "I give in."

"That's the way it should be." She slid her body over his, a devilish glint in her eyes. "You giving in."

"Is it now?"

"Mm-hmm." Her thighs eased open around his hips, and her mouth trailed down to his right nipple ring. When her tongue flicked it, his breath caught. Damn if his cock wasn't already swelling hard against the softness of her belly. "So do these really heighten sensitivity?"

He lifted his hips, pressing his erection into her. "What do you think?"

As she chuckled, a burst of her breath cooled the wetness she'd left at his nipple and he groaned. "I think I could *look* at you and get that reaction."

233

She might just be right about that. "You interested?"

Her incredulous gaze lifted to his. "In *nipple* rings? Oh, *hell* no."

A gasp escaped her as he flipped her under him, the movement causing the blanket to slip off their bodies. "I don't pierce, anyway."

"You don't?"

"Nope. Purely interested in the ink." Her skin was a delicious mix of sweet and salty as he licked the delicate curve where her neck met her shoulder. He knew from experience that flavor only intensified between her legs. "There's so much I want to do with you."

"As long as it doesn't involve needles."

"Noted." He drew one pert nipple into his mouth, sucked it slowly as he skimmed his fingers down her belly. Her hips tilted upward in sweet invitation, and he accepted, sliding two fingertips on either side of her clit but not touching it directly. She gave a little mewl of distress...and then the words that stopped the world's turning.

"Other than that, you can...do anything you want to me."

The building could've caught fire, a tornado siren could've blared, or a fucking wrecking ball could've crashed through the wall, and he wouldn't have noticed at the moment. But those words brought his head up.

"What do you want?"

He could practically see the blush rising in her cheeks. "I thought we were talking about what *you* want."

"No, this is all you. I'd like to push you, but only to places where I'm pretty certain you'd like to go. I'm not going to cross any lines you may have all for the sake of getting myself off. So if there's something you're curious about, or you think you want to try, then you need to tell me."

She averted her gaze from his, studying the portion of the ceiling just over his right shoulder. "I just keep thinking about what you said about your ex, about you staying around because she was crazy in bed. It was the first thing you mentioned when I asked why you were with someone like that for so long."

"And if I'd used my brain, I would never have told you that, especially if I thought it would eat at you. Hey." Gently, he stroked the hair from her forehead, drawing her attention again. "It might've kept me for a while, but it didn't keep me forever, did it?"

"I don't like the thought that I'm not the best you've ever had." Wow. The fierce intensity of that statement took him by surprise, and for a moment, he wondered if he'd just gotten a glimpse of the pre-accident, always-gotta-win Macy everyone talked about. Also...what the *hell?*

"Now I fucking did *not* mean to give you that impression. Jesus, girl." He sat up on his knees, rubbing a hand over his head. She followed, modestly holding the bedspread to the swell of her breasts. "I wish I could even describe to you how I felt that first night we were together. I can't, though, because the only words going through my mind were *holy fucking shit.* That's it. Over and over. That you had even looked my way once, that you agreed to meet up, that you actually pulled the first move and didn't tease or stop me—my life could've ended that night, Macy, and I'd have considered it complete. You *are* the best I've ever had. If all we do from now on is straight missionary sex at eight p.m. on Tuesday nights of months that start with J, you'll still be the best I've ever had."

If he'd expected her to look happy about all of that, he was disappointed. She lowered her head, still clutching that ridiculous blanket as if he hadn't just had her nipple in his mouth. "Then I had to go and mess everything up," she said at last, sounding small and dejected.

"Don't beat yourself up. You explained. It's forgiven. Come here." Scooting to her on his knees, he wrapped her in his arms. Thank God, she finally dropped the blanket, going skin-to-skin with him, burying her face in his shoulder and squeezing him tight. "I'm the luckiest son of a bitch alive to be here right now," he whispered. "Don't ever think I don't know it."

"I'm pretty lucky, myself."

Chapter Twenty

They'd gone out for sushi when the texts started. And then the calls.

Jared was *pissed* that she'd blown him off. She felt bad about that, having called him earlier and broken the news to his voice mail—honestly, in all her excitement, she'd damn near forgotten all about it—but he was overreacting. Apparently, he'd gone by her apartment because he wanted to know where she was. As if she had to answer to him.

When Seth asked her who the hell was trying to get in touch with her, she waved off his questions and silenced her phone. Dammit. She should've told him from the start that her own psycho ex might be hatching right before her very eyes. Ugh. Jared had never struck her as that type. Then again, Jared had never seen her getting seriously involved with someone else.

"Are you sure everything's all right?" Seth asked, startling her out of her thoughts. They'd been lingering over their finished food for a while now. And still basking in the afterglow of everything they'd done just before coming here—or at least, she was. She quickly took a drink of her water.

"Oh, sure."

"If something's going on back home—"

"No, nothing like that. I do need to make a call though. Is that okay?"

"Sure."

"Be right back." She slid out of her seat and headed for the ladies' room, jaw tight with all the words she wanted to fling. The simplest solution would be to turn her phone completely off, but he'd already pissed her off.

The restroom was empty, thank goodness, and hopefully

she could make this brief. Jared answered right away.

"Macy?"

"What is your deal, Jared?"

"Why didn't you come today?"

"I told you. I'm sorry, but something came up. End of story. Now *stop this*. Right now."

"I don't appreciate getting ditched at the last minute. This isn't like you. What's happened to you?"

Despite the flare in her outrage, his words stung. "I think you had it built up in your mind as more than what it was. It wasn't a date. It wasn't a door opening to you and me getting back together someday, no matter what you might have deluded yourself into believing. The more I thought about it, the more it all seemed like a bad idea, anyway."

"I guess you're off fucking *him* again. Blowing off the people who really care about you for that trash. I never thought I'd see you come to this, but now that you have, maybe you deserve each other."

Silent, shaking fury ravaged her, stealing all ability to speak, and she hated that, she *hated* it. Tears burned her eyes. The only thought that could squeeze itself in among the tumult in her head was, *What would Seth say?* The answer came quite readily—at least, part of it did.

"Jared? Fuck right off. I can only hope to deserve him." She couldn't jab the red End button fast enough. Then she did what she should have done from the start: turn the damn thing off. As she slammed her way out of the restroom, she almost ran into some poor lady who was coming in and muttered an apology before skirting past and stalking blindly back toward their table.

Big mistake, she realized as she sat. She should've taken a minute to compose herself. Seth's dark eyebrows dipped as he looked at her. "What the hell happened?"

"Nothing." She strove for nonchalance as she collected her purse and her coat, but didn't think she quite achieved it, so she gave up. "I don't want to talk about it."

"Jesus, you *need* to talk about it. Your face is the color of your sweater." Which was fuchsia. "Looks like you're about to combust. C'mon, babe. Whose ass do I need to kick?"

Oh, she could think of one right off. How *dare* Jared say that about him? About her? Had he always been that big an asshole, or had she just not paid attention in her naive youth? "It's nothing. Can we go back to the room now?"

The shift in his demeanor was apparent without him saying a word. His dark eyes narrowed almost imperceptibly, and there was no mistaking the tightening of his jaw. "Macy. Who was on the fucking phone."

Shit. If she told him, she had to tell him everything. And he might very well do what he threatened. "It's just someone I know being an idiot. It's nothing you need to worry about, okay? Let's just go back and not let it ruin the night. I'll cool off, I promise."

His gaze bore into hers a few seconds longer before he cursed and snatched his wallet from his back pocket, slinging a few bills on the table before standing and shoving it back in its place. He wouldn't look at her.

"Hey," she said gently, standing up beside him. "It's not—"

He walked away from her. Actually freaking *turned his back* and left her standing there.

Well. Looked as if acting like an asshole was catching. She followed him, struggling into the coat he was usually all too happy to help her into. "*Seth.*"

At least he held the restaurant door for her, but he didn't answer, and he didn't meet her eyes. And if she was being deliberately ignored, damn if she was going to beg for his attention. She surged ahead of him and snatched open the passenger door of his car before he could touch it. If he'd even been inclined. The force she used to close it after she flung herself inside probably clued him in a bit to how his behavior was affecting her already shitty mood.

What the hell? *Damn* Jared Stanton. In the momentary silence while Seth walked around to the driver's side, she watched the headlights on the interstate blur, then clenched her eyes shut. All that accomplished was squeezing the tears out. She wiped her cheeks as he dropped into his seat.

"Tell me what the fuck is going on."

"Why the damn inquisition?"

"Because you're keeping something from me, and I don't like it."

"So my life's an open book when I'm with you? I have to clear every phone call with you and relay all my personal conversations for your approval?"

"Where is *this* shit coming from? I only asked for details on the *one* phone call that had you looking like you want to tear someone's head off. If someone's fucking with you, Macy, I want to know about it."

"Well, I don't want you to know about it."

The silence that descended was terrible and absolute. Then his leather jacket creaked as he turned away from her and cranked the car, grumbling something that sounded like, "Crazy ass fucking females." He backed out of the parking spot and peeled out so fast she was scrabbling for a handhold. But at least he didn't drive crazy once they reached the interstate; her heart was in her throat enough as it was.

"I thought we'd turned a corner, you know," he said as he violently shifted gears. "And I always thought you trusted me more than this."

"It's not that I don't, it's just... Shit. I'm mad at a friend. So what. Why are you making it such a big deal?"

"Why are *you?* It's only a big deal because you're shutting me out. I doubt you're this mad at Candace. Or Sam."

"No," she said cautiously.

"A friend, huh."

She clamped her mouth shut.

"Has this *friend* at any point stuck his dick in you?"

Her vision practically went black. "You did not just say that to me."

"Yeah, I did."

"Then I think you need to shut your mouth before you say something else you're going to regret later."

"I won't regret shit, except maybe that I set myself up for

this to start with. Thanks for your lack of denial, by the way. Tells me all I need to know."

"God! You're being so unreasonable. I realize you've been burned and all, but don't project that onto me. I won't tolerate that."

He was quiet for a long time, too long. "There's a lot I won't tolerate, Macy. I have a line. Once it's crossed, that's it. Secrets, sneaking around, other motherfuckers sniffing around while you pretend like it's no big deal. Been there. These are major fuckin' issues for me. You should *know* that."

Macy scoffed, trying to hold on to anger that was fast morphing into heartbreak. "Poor you. Get over it. I don't think I'd be too out of line in suggesting that you're just looking for some reason to believe the line has been crossed when it hasn't. I haven't done anything. I've explained to you that I don't lay my drama out for everyone to see. You want everything up front, and that's a major friggin' issue for *me*."

"You brought your drama to the fucking table back there. You had your drama written all over your face. What am I supposed to think?"

"Fine, Seth. The *friend* I was talking to is Jared Stanton. You saw him at the bar on Valentine's night. I've known him for as long as I can remember. We dated from the time I was fourteen years old until I had my accident. After that, he knocked up some other girl, got married, had twins, got divorced. I give his daughters horse riding lessons because he works a lot, and he knows I'm damn good at it. And yes, he wants me back. I saw him at my parents' house last weekend. He wanted me to come to a roping today. I agreed to go for old time's sake, but *I blew him off to see you.* And he's pissed, and he said some really shitty things just now. End of story. Satisfied?"

"All this has been going on since you've been seeing me?"

"Yes."

"*Fuck.*"

And that was that. He completely shut down. Maybe she

deserved it; maybe—no, definitely, she supposed, considering his reaction—she should've been up front with him about it all. She really hadn't considered it that big a deal. Because it *wasn't* one, at least in her mind.

Then again, she'd never been the one left behind before. She'd always been the one who did the leaving.

Jesus. Who'd have thought being the type of person who liked to keep your mouth *shut* instead of flapping a hundred miles a minute would blow up so spectacularly in your face? Wasn't it usually the other way around?

"Look, I'm sorry," she said, hating the pleading undertone in her voice. "None of this is as bad as it sounds. I've been telling him and telling him I'm not getting back together with him. He knows about you. It's not like I'm keeping us a secret."

"Just keeping him a secret from me." He braked so hard in the parking lot of their hotel that if she hadn't been wearing her seat belt, she might've been thrown into the dashboard.

"For good reason, apparently!" she snapped, unbuckling and flinging the belt off. Once she'd gotten out of the car, she noticed he made no move to do the same. He didn't even kill the engine. Holding on to the door, she leaned in to look at him, her pulse in her ears. "Are you *leaving?*"

His face was in shadow, but given the ice in his voice, that was probably a good thing. "Shut the door."

Oh God, there had to be something she could say to make this better. Some magic phrase that would let him know he had no reason to be jealous or threatened. None whatsoever. But if this was his reaction whenever she received the least amount of attention from the opposite sex, did she really want any part of it?

If this was how he wanted it, then this was how it was going to be. She slammed the door and didn't wait around to watch him leave.

Which he did.

Oh, *hell* no.

Thank God they'd each taken a key card. She let herself into the room and gave her purse a fling in the darkness, hearing the contents scatter wherever it landed. The first thing to draw her gaze as she flipped on the light was his overnight bag on the dresser. She hoped there were no prized possessions of his in there, because she damn sure wasn't going to take it back to him. He was lucky she didn't burn it on sight.

"Crazy fucking females my *ass*," she muttered into the silence of the room. Men were the insane ones. Did he think just because she'd allowed him into her vagina a few times that he owned her? Did Jared think the same thing? She had bad news for him especially. She hadn't exactly been celibate since their breakup, even before Seth. There hadn't been many, but there'd been a few.

Her phone had landed at the foot of the bed. She scooped it up, sighing and switching it on as she dropped heavily onto the unkempt bed, exhausted. Jared had apparently followed her earlier suggestion. No messages from him. Candace had left her a voice mail. Just wanted to chat. Well, she wasn't in the chatting mood.

What the hell was happening? Was he just heading back to Oklahoma without a word? Was he going somewhere to cool off until they could talk rationally? She'd never seen him enraged. She didn't know him like that. Probably a good thing she had gotten a glimpse before this went any further.

Whatever, she thought, dragging herself up from the bed. She'd figured she'd sleep naked in his arms tonight, so she hadn't packed PJs. Bad idea. As she stripped to her underwear, she eyed his bag. Surely he'd have a T-shirt in there; he lived in them. The one she pulled out was black (shocker) and read Cannibal Corpse in dripping red letters. Lovely. But as she pulled it over her head and freed her hair from the collar, his vaguely citrusy scent enveloped her, and the last of her anger dissipated.

She'd get some sleep, go home and try to forget the past few weeks had ever happened.

She jolted awake to a mouth at her neck, wet and hot and

sucking.

Lust crashed over her like a tidal wave, sweeping any grogginess right out of her head and kicking her pulse into double time. With a little gasp, she grasped the sides of his face and pulled his mouth to hers, drinking in warm whiskey-drenched breath—he must have just taken a hit of it, because his flavor made her instantly drunk. His tongue tangled with hers, and she sucked on it, rejoicing in the tormented groan the action pulled from his throat.

Searching her heart for any remnants of her earlier anger and finding it still burning, she knew she should stop him. His hot hand slid under her T-shirt—his T-shirt—traveling all the way up to her breast, and the notion flew out of her head. He kneaded it roughly, tugging on her nipple until it stood at aching attention. She wanted his mouth there. She wanted it everywhere. Her own hand slipped between them, and she practically growled in frustration at finding his jeans still on. But there was nothing frustrating about the thick ridge pressing against his fly. A surge of answering wetness saturated her, and she worked at freeing his cock from his jeans.

An unpleasant thought teased at the edges of her consciousness, and she didn't want to let it take hold, but little by little it grew until it permeated even the need pooled hotly between her legs. What if he was so drunk he didn't know what he was doing? Had he driven like this? Turning her head as his mouth burned down her throat, she saw the squat bottle of amber liquid on the nightstand. Maybe he'd just brought it back and drank here. The TV was on but muted, its light flickering against the ceiling. What if he'd just awakened with a hard-on and—surprise!—there was a warm, willing female body within arm's length?

"Say my name," she whispered against his lips as her fingers completed their task and his heavy length filled her eager hands.

"Macy," he breathed. His arm wound around her, pulling her closer. His other hand abandoned its place on her breast and slid down her stomach into her damp panties. "Macy..."

She spread her legs, moving against his hand. His fingers stroked her, strummed her, wreaked exquisite havoc on her slick, sensitive flesh.

"Fuck me, Seth," she gasped into his mouth. "Please. I only want you. I've always only wanted you."

Tension swept through the body against her, and she prayed the reminder of their earlier words wouldn't douse his ardor. His hand grasped her panties and wrenched them down and off. So much for that fear.

He rolled her beneath him as she fought to shove his jeans down farther. He shifted, positioning himself—not easy since she couldn't stop squirming under him. Then the broad head of his cock breached her, and she threw her head back with a guttural cry, sinking her fingernails into the firm flesh of his ass. Urging him on, begging him for more.

He gave it. Hard, fast, showing no mercy, he shoved his entire length into her, sending shockwaves through her body. If she weren't so wet, so hot, so desperate for him, she might have cried out for him to stop, go slower. She wondered if he even would have listened. "Fuck," he growled as he went so deep she could hardly breathe. "*Fuck.*"

Her own mind couldn't do much better at describing it. One word whirled at the forefront of her thoughts: *yes.* Yes. This was right, this was where she belonged. He pulled out, leaving her whimpering in distress, her pussy clenching against the sudden emptiness he left. Her body ignited when he thrust back in. Starbursts exploded in front of her closed eyelids—and in the depths he reached inside her. Oh God, two strokes and she was ready to come.

That was way less than he had to give her. She tumbled into ecstasy even before the headboard began banging the wall with the ferocity of his passion. And again before he shoved her legs back until her feet were on his shoulders. Then his piercing hit her G-spot with devastating precision, and she came twice more, sobbing his name. She'd lost count by the time he flipped her over and took her from behind. By then, she was raw, boneless, shameless, his to mold and shape like putty. Her T-shirt had disappeared at some point. Patches of skin itched and ached from where he'd sucked on them. There wasn't an orgasm left in her body to wring out...or so she thought.

Chanting his name and loving how it sounded on her tongue, she rippled and constricted around him again. His fingers dented into her flesh hard enough to bruise as he jerked her against him one final time...and left her. Cool air circulated over her overheated flesh in his absence. He growled several curses as he came on her back. Exhausted, whimpering, she collapsed fully to the mattress. He followed, seemingly mindless of the mess between them, and she welcomed his weight on her. His breath gusted against her ear. His heart galloped against her back, and he trembled as hard as she did.

She didn't think she ever wanted to move again. Mmm, yes, she could stay like this from now on.

"You're just going to leave me too," he said, the words practically a hiss in her ear, but laced with so much despair that shock reverberated through her.

"Seth, I'm not—" He rolled off her and left the bed. Somehow she found the strength to lift her head and watch him stalk toward the bathroom, hitching up his jeans as he went. "*Listen* to me."

He didn't. Any further words tangled in her throat and ice settled where the ashes of her heart had been as he slammed the door.

Bastard. Dirty effing unbelievable *bastard.*

Fucking stupid, *stupid.* Ghost was even more pissed at his wayward dick than the woman out there in the bed. Goddamn, his head hurt, and the bathroom light was like a knife slicing deeper into his brain with every thought. He didn't know how he'd had enough blood in his nether regions to sustain wood; every drop seemed to be converged right behind his eyes. It throbbed with every beat of his heart, which had yet to slow. But instead of exertion, it now pounded in fury. At himself. At everything.

A glance at the mirror revealed he looked like hammered shit. Macy hadn't really been able to see what she was fucking or she might have shoved him off. He looked wasted. He guessed he still was. Staring at his reflection, he wanted to put a fist through it, watch his own face shatter like everything else in his fucking life.

Sighing, he spared the mirror and his knuckles, splashed cold water on his face and contemplated a shower. Her warm, sugary vanilla scent was still all over him, and if he didn't get it off, he might tear into that room and have a repeat. Shit. He'd gone raw in her too. Fucking drunken sex-fogged brain. At least he'd had the presence of mind to pull out; now he'd just hope to hell it was enough. He wasn't worried about diseases—she took care of herself and so did he—but after the catastrophe with Raina, he'd vowed never to let that sneak up on him again.

Macy had felt so good the mere thought of her wrapped around him was enough to stir interest despite everything they'd just done. So wet, so soft, so perfect.

He really needed to get out of here before he made a colossal ass of himself, even more so than he had already. He'd been an idiot for coming back and not going somewhere else to get trashed. Now he was trapped in the bathroom with no escape that didn't involve facing her down.

Smooth move, asshole. Now what?

That shower might be a good stalling technique. Cold. He'd never have thought he would need a cold shower after such furious sex. After that display, he needed an ice pack. He was sore, raw. Any other time, he'd be damn proud of himself.

Discarding his jeans, he realized his cell phone was in the pocket. The time read 5:07 a.m. Brian had tried to call once and had texted only a couple hours ago. Yeah, he'd unloaded on Brian right after the fight; he'd had so much furious energy he hadn't known where to channel it. *Dude, Candace didn't know anything about this, either. I think you're overreacting. Call if you need me, I don't care what time.*

Ghost smirked as he left the phone on the counter and cranked on the water in the shower. Brian always texted with perfect grammar. What would his best friend think if he told him he'd just had the best bang of his life, and he was hiding out in the bathroom like a virgin on prom night?

And maybe he was overreacting, but hell. Jared fucking Stanton sounded like a prize catch for someone like her. She should go ride off into the sunset with her cowboy and forget all about him. Here he'd been trying to urge her back into racing...and he'd only pushed her toward her waiting ex. *Yeah, you're welcome, asshole.* He vaguely remembered getting a look at the guy's face, seeing and hearing enough to know he was a cocky prick.

She might've blown the guy off this time, but there was always next time.

Clear your head. That was all he needed to do. He'd woken up with anger and grief warring inside his fuzzy head and an intense hard-on...and Macy's soft, sweet body nestled beside him. A catastrophic combination. For the first few minutes, he'd thought he was having the hottest damn wet dream of his life.

In the end, it didn't matter whether he was overreacting or not. This was only proof that he needed to quit thinking with his dick, get his ass back to Oklahoma and keep it there as long as he needed to. Get her out of his head.

The shower spray hit him, but it didn't bring clarity. It didn't make the decision he'd just come to any easier to swallow. He stood with his hands braced against the wall, letting the water stream down his back. When the shower curtain flung open, he really wasn't surprised—what did shock the hell out of him was the lack of a verbal lashing from the fuming girl on the other side. Macy stepped into the tub with him without a single word, her hair pinned sloppily atop her head, her face and chest flushed blotchy red.

He moved out of her way. Without meeting his eyes, without behaving as if he were there at all, she soaped up and rinsed, while he clenched both fists, repressing the need to put her against the wall and get some words out of that delectable mouth. Even something Raina-esque, like *I hate you, you vile motherfucker* would have made him feel better than her icy silence. But he didn't deserve to feel better.

She slapped him in the chest with her washcloth and stepped out.

Oh, fuck this. He opened his mouth to speak, to call her back, to get her to curse his name, anything…and his phone buzzed to ringing life on the counter. Macy walked out, shutting the door behind her as he damn near broke his neck getting to his phone.

Stephanie. God knew the last time he'd gotten a call from her at this hour, it hadn't been good news.

"Steph?" he answered—more like croaked.

The briefest silence…and then his sister's sniveling voice. "Where are you?"

"I'm—fuck, Stephanie, what is it?"

"The hospital just called. Nana had another stroke." She took a shuddering breath. "Seth…we lost her."

Chapter Twenty-One

"Macy? Are you all right?"

Macy snapped to attention, realizing she'd been staring blindly at her keyboard for the past several minutes. If she didn't stop slacking off at work, her own parents were going to fire her.

She looked up and smiled at Carla, who stood in the doorway of her office. "Fine, thanks. Just a little preoccupied. Come in."

Carla went over inventory with her, all business as usual, but she kept giving her odd looks. Damn. She had to snap out of this funk. It had been three weeks already since her and Seth's disastrous getaway, three weeks since he'd emerged from the bathroom, told her in a shaking voice his grandmother was gone...and then pretty much ignored all her consolation efforts as he shoved clothes in his bag and stalked out.

Now she guessed his not being there when it happened was her fault too. Candace and Brian had driven up for the funeral. Macy hadn't dared, hadn't thought she was wanted. They'd told her it was a nightmare; Seth and his brother had exchanged words after the service, and Brian had to come between them once. Nothing like a funeral to bring all the family drama to the forefront.

She should've been able to be there for him through all that. She would've been, if he'd let her. He was still in Oklahoma, helping to pack up his grandmother's house.

After work, she couldn't face the idea of staring mindlessly at the wall or the TV. Her life had become like a country song— now all those mournful lyrics made more sense than ever before. She found herself driving to Dermamania, where at least her best friend would be there to cheer her up. Maybe Candace could leave early, they could collect Sam and have a girls' pity-party night.

A chorus of greetings went up as she walked in, and she tried not to let her eyes be instantly drawn to Seth's sadly empty station. Candace came forward and gave her the usual hug, holding on a little longer than she normally did.

"How's it going?" Brian asked, tilting his chin up at her from behind the counter. They seemed to be having a lull in business, but then, it was Monday night. Probably not the most hopping night of the week at a tattoo parlor. Starla had a client she was chattering with as she inked the girl's shoulder blade, but that was it.

"Fine," Macy said, hearing the lie in that one word. "Can I talk to you guys for a minute?"

"Sure." Brian motioned her back. Macy and Candace followed him to his office. He closed the door behind them and leaned back against his desk, crossing his arms and sharing a little grin with Candace.

Wow, flashback. Only, when the three of them had come to this very room to discuss what Macy knew about the parlor's vandalism almost a year ago, Candace and Brian had been the heartbroken ones staring sorrowfully at each other.

Macy hadn't wanted to fix that, not really. She'd thought they were no good together, that her best friend was really screwing up by getting mixed up with this guy. She and Seth had hung out one time at that point, shared some laughs, but she'd generally had the same feeling about him, despite her raging hormones. She'd thought he was much like Brian: hot, funny, very bad news.

Showed how adept she was at standing by her convictions.

"How is he?" she blurted, interrupting the minor flirtation going on before her eyes and knowing she didn't need to identify who she meant.

"He's in pretty bad shape," Brian said, face going solemn. "But the stupid son of a bitch is driving down to Austin tonight to play his band's gig."

Was he *insane?* "What—are you serious? What is he

thinking?"

"I tried my damnedest to talk him out of it. In fact, I was thinking of driving over myself, just to make sure he's all right."

Candace suddenly sat ramrod straight in her chair, looking earnestly into Macy's eyes. "Go with him."

"Oh, I couldn't. I have work tomorrow."

"Hey, that's the perk of being the boss, right?" Brian grinned at her. "Really, I hadn't made up my mind whether to go or not. But I will if you want to."

Her stomach practically churned with indecision. After the way he'd behaved, she shouldn't give a crap what happened to him. The fact remained that she did, though, and she couldn't deny it.

First instincts were usually correct, right? Her first instinct was screaming at her to go. "It would probably be a wasted trip. I doubt he wants to see me."

"I kinda swore this was off the record at the time of disclosure, but...I can pretty much guarantee that he does. He knows he was out of line."

Well, that was the first step. Candace was grinning like a goon. "What about you?" Macy asked her. "You'd be coming too, right?"

"Can't. I have an exam tomorrow. A sadistic one."

Brian scoffed. "You know you'll ace it."

"Yeah, but it's an eight a.m. class. What the hell was I thinking taking an eight a.m. class?"

"I asked you that when you signed up," he chided.

"Oh well, it's almost over anyway. But if not for that, I'd go."

Macy shifted from one foot to the other. God, would the craziness and the drama and the road trips ever stop? "Are you really okay with this?" she asked her friend.

"With you gallivanting off with my boyfriend?" Candace laughed. "I know I don't have anything to worry about." She shared a sickeningly loving stare with said boyfriend. Macy was getting ready to step between them when Brian finally tore his gaze away and checked his watch.

"We'd better jet, then. I doubt we'll even catch the set at this point."

"I don't...I don't even know what to say. To him *or* you guys."

"Aw, we love you, Macy, and we love him too," Candace said. "You both are miserable. We've got to give it one more shot."

"I don't know when he's coming back," Brian put in. "This might be your only chance to catch him for who knows how long, unless you want to drive to Oklahoma again."

"He was...so mad at me, and I don't think he had a good reason to be. I mean, I should never speak to him again after...well, some really ugly things happened that I don't feel like I deserved."

"Hey, it's up to you," Brian said. "The offer's there if you want it. If not, then I'll go out front and get back to work."

"Come on, Macy," Candace urged, practically bouncing.

Maybe he would talk to her now; maybe he would *listen.* That's all tonight would be about. They'd each get their grievances out there, and see where it went. She had a lot to say to him; the heaviness of those words had sat in her chest for weeks and more were added every day as she turned the situation over in her mind. If nothing else, she would be able to get them out, even if he stood there like a brick wall while she flung them.

She looked up at Brian. "Okay. Let's do it."

"You look like shit, bro!"

The shout rang out the moment Ghost trudged into the back hallway of Crossbones, and he shot Gus the finger for being so kind as to point it out. Yeah, that was the way everyone wanted to be greeted. "Look like shit, feel like shit, in a world of shit," he grumbled.

Gus grinned. "I've got something for that."

"Naw, man. Where's my guitar?"

"C'mon, I'll show ya. Gotta get warmed up myself."

"Thanks for bringing it." He always felt like a fucking giant walking next to the much-shorter Gus.

"No problem." As the other guitarist prattled on about the drama going on in his life—and never once addressed the drama and loss overshadowing Ghost's—there was a moment when he wanted to turn on his heel and go the hell back to where he'd come from. But what for? Nana's business was handled, and he'd been a leech on Stephanie for long enough, even though she swore she loved him being there.

So he'd packed all his shit into his car before leaving the Oklahoma City suburb, resolving to go back home after tonight. Brian needed him. Of course, helping Brian carried a high probability of coming face-to-face with Macy at some point, and wasn't that a grand clusterfuck. But it was one that needed to be sorted out, for his own sanity, if nothing else.

Even through all the grief over his grandmother, there had been no clearing his head of that girl. She was fully entrenched, and he'd come to terms with that.

Gus was in the middle of a cuss-binge about his ex-girlfriend when the unmistakable sound of Raina's warm-up growls reached Ghost from some indeterminable point up ahead, stopping him in his tracks. Gus looked at him, cocking an eyebrow.

"What is it, man?"

"What the *hell* is she doing here?"

The other guy shrugged. "Mark told her to come."

He was going to knock the son of a bitch out.

"Come on, dude. What's the big deal? She's just going to do a few songs with us."

"It's the fact that she's here at all. I don't want to be dodging her crazy ass all night."

Gus scoffed. "So don't. Maybe if you hit that a couple times for old times' sake, you'd feel better. Hell, I would."

"Shit, no." On top of everything else, he didn't need Raina in his face. He looked longingly back at the exit, sighed and ran a hand over his head. There was only one thing that would make this night tolerable. Oblivion. And knocking Mark out. "I changed my mind. Point me to the Jäger. And what else have you got?"

A grin lit up his so-called friend's face. It wasn't a pretty sight, more like the way the serpent might have smiled when Eve bit the apple. "Follow me."

Hauling ass toward Austin for a heavy metal gig with her best friend's boyfriend. While this was a place Macy could honestly say she never thought she'd be, it was every bit as awkward as she would've imagined.

"I can't believe I'm doing this," she said at last, realizing she had almost chewed her thumbnail to the quick.

"The things we do for love, right?" Brian said.

If only she knew that's what this was. She knew how *she* felt, but she wasn't foolish enough anymore to call it love when she had no idea if it was reciprocated. "I wonder if maybe I should've thought this out a little more."

"Sometimes the spontaneous decision is the right one."

"I guess so. He really wants to see me, then? You didn't just say that?"

He cut her a glance beneath his black ball cap. "Like I'd let you walk into that. Come on. He's more worried that you'll never want to see him again."

"I never meant to drag you and Candace into this. That was exactly what I *didn't* want." And one of the reasons she hadn't wanted to get into this whole thing to start with. No matter, though. She was in it. She was in it up to her eyeballs.

"Don't worry about it."

"He doesn't know we're coming?"

"Not at the moment. Do you want him to?"

She remembered that night at his house, staying awake until the sun came up, talking and laughing and arguing and having earth-shattering sex. How earnestly he'd talked about his music and how much she could tell he would've liked her to be there for his show. Brian had said they would probably be too late to catch the set, but if Seth still wanted her, she'd come to every damn gig he had from now on to make up for it.

"No," she said, allowing a little smile at the thought of his face when he saw her there. "Let's surprise him."

"Cool."

"So when are you going to marry my best friend?"

He laughed in surprise, suddenly looking adorably embarrassed as perfect dimples appeared on his cheeks. If it weren't dark already, she would swear he was blushing. "You're all right with that, huh?"

"Well, not that you need *my* permission or anything, but yes, I'd be very all right with it."

"I appreciate that. Never really thought you were crazy about the idea."

"I'm sorry if I ever gave you that impression. To be honest, yeah, I didn't know about you at first. But that was strictly me being a shallow bitch."

"No, that was you looking out for your friend. Which is admirable."

"I'm really glad she has you."

He smirked. "Think you could talk her parents into feeling the same way?"

"Oh, don't worry about them. Either they'll come around or they won't, and if they don't, they're fools. You never answered the question, by the way."

"Mace, I'd marry her tomorrow if I could. But we want to do everything right, not rush into anything. Be carefree and spontaneous and without responsibility for a while."

It was a foreign concept to her, a future she'd never envisioned for herself, and not even for Candace when the two of them would sit up late at night and romanticize about their dashing future husbands and their three to four perfect kids. Candace had more or less abandoned the fantasy with ease. Macy didn't know if she could do the same. She'd always been about responsibility and drive and her life clicking along at the perfect pace, the next logical step being finding someone with equal drive and determination to settle down with.

If the past few weeks had shown her anything, it was that

there would be no settling down with Seth Warren for a long time, if ever. He was a whirlwind. There would be no domesticating that one.

But here she was, chasing him like a lovesick fool. At least tonight would probably let her know if there might be a future with him at all, whatever it entailed.

Dammit, she'd gone from gnawing her thumbnail to her index finger now. She was going to ruin her entire manicure before they got there.

How Ghost made it through the show without bashing his guitar upside Mark's head would be a mystery to ponder until the day he died. The answer probably lay in the mass quantities roaring through his bloodstream, and the fact that he spent most of his time onstage avoiding Raina, who kept coming too fucking close to him, wanting to sing into his mic on their shared vocals.

At the end of it, he made his feelings on the entire situation clear by bashing his guitar against the drum platform a dozen times instead, not caring which direction the shrapnel flew. He thought he'd caught a piece above his eye, but who the fuck cared. He took great satisfaction in feeling the stunned aftermath as he stormed off the stage.

Now. Get somewhere before you pass the fuck out. Damn good thing he'd decided in the end not to swallow the shit Gus had slipped him earlier; he'd probably be dead. He staggered down a short, too-bright hallway and veered into the first open door he saw with darkness beyond. Immediately he slammed his shin on something and nearly toppled over. *"Shit!"*

His hands met cushions as he caught himself and, realizing the offending object was a couch, he groaned and plopped down on it, stretching out along the length and burying his face in the back cushions. Darkness. Yes. No telling what past transgressions had transpired on the slightly foul-smelling piece of furniture, but at the moment he couldn't give less of a shit. It was soft and horizontal. That was all he required.

When the door clicked shut behind him, he said a silent thank you to the considerate fucker who had bathed him in blessed darkness, and contemplated unconsciousness.

A hand, small and gentle, slid down his sweat-slick arm. Beyond the fingertips he felt the hardness of long nails. A grunt left him, and he jerked away. *Leave me the fuck alone.*

"Are you okay?" a soft voice asked. He didn't know if he heard it or dreamed it, hovering in the gray between awake and oblivion.

"Go away," he said all the same. His voice sounded like his throat was made of gravel.

It didn't go away. That soothing hand kept right on rubbing, exploring his back, just barely squeezing his arm, his neck, moving downward until it grazed his bare side where his shirt had ridden up a bit. It slipped under to score his flesh lightly with those nails. Something strangely familiar about that. Familiar and...oh yeah, fucking hot. His dick twitched and swelled. He groaned. He thought of Macy. Her soft hair. Her smell. Sinking into her wet heat. Vanilla filled his head, almost as if she were here with him.

Strong, sure fingers rubbed his erection through his jeans, and he lost his breath, grinding into the touch. A sigh escaped from somewhere behind him. It turned into words. "I missed this so much."

He missed her. Oh fuck, he missed her. Even through the dense fog in his head, he saw her face. He couldn't even drink enough to make her go away. What kind of hell was that to be in? What the fuck did he ever do to deserve to go there?

Soft, cool lips brushed his neck. Warm breath tickled his ear. He thrust hard against the hand rubbing his now rock-hard cock, and before he knew it, those deft fingers had freed him.

Whoa, fuck, what was happening? Jerked out of his funk, he jacked up off the couch and grabbed whoever-it-was by her arms. Yes, definitely female. A surprised gasp sounded. He'd heard it a thousand times before, when he sucked on her nipple rings or her pierced clit or thrust hard into her always-willing pussy.

Raina. Motherfucking *Raina* with her hands on him.

It was no wonder all his thoughts were sex-oriented; he was so hard it hurt. But it wasn't because of her crazy ass.

"What in the fuck are you doing?" he demanded. She wrenched her shoulders out of his grip and tried to push him back down. He wasn't going—or so he thought. His uncoordinated muscles said otherwise, and she managed to get him halfway reclined again and her fishnet-covered leg swung over his hips. Her splayed hands slid up his chest.

"Fuck me, Ghost. Oh, God, I'm so wet for you. You remember how it was, don't you, baby? No way that piece of rich-bitch pussy gets you off like mine did."

Oh, shit, she did feel good smearing against him. It would be so easy, and who the hell was there to care? He grabbed her wrists and wrenched them behind her back, capturing them both in one hand. A strangled growl tore from her throat; she loved that.

"Yes! Baby...oh, please. *Please.* Come into me." He stared up at her shadowed, frantic form as she tried to squirm into position without the use of her arms. "I love you so much. Let me love you."

He believed her. Putting pressure on the small of her back, he brought her down over him. Her hot, wet mouth fastened to the side of his neck. He growled, waiting...she was a biter. And a scratcher, and a slapper when she really got carried away. Yeah, she'd whacked him more than once in their wilder, rougher escapades. There was a reason he'd had a thing about pinning Macy's hands down. Not that she would ever do that, it had sort of just become his thing. Especially with her.

Macy.

Raina's teeth scraped at his skin, but only for a moment. Her throaty voice poured seductively into his ear, raising gooseflesh on his arms. "I haven't been with anyone since you. I'm only yours. This is only yours." Her wetness slicked over him...she'd already lost her panties before she'd climbed on top of him, if she'd been wearing any to start with. "Only yours.

Take it."

"Raina..."

Just his utterance of her name seemed to set her off again. Her wrists tugged sharply against his hold, but he tightened it, and she wasn't going anywhere. "Let me touch you. I'm here, baby, you know I'm the only one who's always here for you. Right? Don't you know that?"

"I do know that."

"God, I fucking missed you." It was said in a rush against his lips. "You don't know how much."

"I know you did." He slid his free hand up her side. She gasped and tried to insinuate her breast into it, but he eluded her and placed his palm flat to her chest. "Raina?"

"Yes, baby?"

"Get. The fuck. *Off me.*" And he shoved her upward, getting her mouth off him but making *damn* sure he kept his grip on her hands.

She thrashed and cursed, and he thought she tried once to headbutt him. The struggle continued until finally he managed to leverage himself off the couch, dumping her ass-first onto the floor. Disadvantage being, he no longer had a grip on her, and he couldn't see. For all he knew, a lamp might fly at his skull any second now.

"You bastard!" she screeched.

"That's right, I'm a bastard. But I'm a bastard who could've fucked you just now and gone back to ignoring you tomorrow. Would that make you feel better? Because that's all anything between you and me would ever be."

"She doesn't love you like I do. She won't. No one ever will. She'll fuck you over and fucking walk away like that other cunt did. *Why can't you see that?*"

"I already see that. It doesn't make any difference."

"No. You love me. You have to." Tears in her voice now. Shit. "You *have* to. What we had..."

"What we had was something you could go out and have with any motherfucker in this building. Fighting and sex and more fighting. Maybe you need that toxicity to be fulfilled, but I don't. It wasn't love, Raina; it never was. It was something else. It was ugly."

"That *is* what you need," she said, voice seething in the dark. Her hands found his thighs—she must be up on her knees—and he was so off-balance he almost fell back on the couch. Fuck, he had to get out the door. "Not these squeaky-clean sunshiney bitches you and Brian have. You *need* ugly. No one else will understand that about you."

"Then I guess I'll be alone." He shook her off, stepping back out of her reach and just then realizing he needed to stuff himself back in his pants in a big friggin' hurry, before she got to him again and he did something stupid.

"Seth...?"

"What."

"I can't live without you."

Amazing, that the angry little she-devil on stage, the unhinged banshee every guy in the crowd would've killed to take home and have her violate him twenty different ways, was reduced to this weak, sniveling, disjointed plea in the dark. Over *him*. He wanted to stay angry at her, but all he could muster at the moment was pity. And sadness, that he could understand. Hell. He'd been there.

He was there now.

"Here's a thought, Raina. *Try*."

He was zipping up his fly when the door flew open.

Chapter Twenty-Two

It was amazing. Brian seemed to know every person in this building. At least ten of them stopped him to ask about ink. Most of them he indulged for a minute or two, ever edging toward the back. Always, the questions involved some variation of, "When are you gonna leave that one-horse fuckhole and set up shop here, man?" Perish the thought that he and Candace should leave. At least he always replied with, "I'm needed there way more than I am here," which was comforting.

A few girls stopped him too, of course. Macy stuck close by his side, earning more than a few weird or outright hostile looks. Brian commented to her that he couldn't wait to see how many texts Candace received alerting her that he was here with some other chick. When they reached a door to the side of the stage, a huge, black-clad bouncer who looked like someone from pro wrestling cut a glance their way. Great. This was probably going to be trouble.

She should've known better. Brian's clout wouldn't be denied. Grinning, the guy put out his hand, and Brian grasped it, engaging in those quick back-slapping half-hugs guys did. They exchanged obscenity-laced small talk for a minute while Macy shifted her weight back and forth, impatience eating at her. At last, Brian asked, "Ghost back there, man?"

"Haven't seen him come out. He all right?"

"I think his head's a little fucked up."

"I think more than his head is fucked up."

"Why do you say that?"

"Were you fuckin' here just now?"

"Actually, no, we were late."

"He demolished his fuckin' guitar, bro. I mean, that shit goes down on a regular basis around here, but it's not like him.

Great show, though. Sucks you missed it." The guy looked at her, doing a quick once-over, then raised his pierced eyebrow at Brian. "Where's the Candy girl?"

"Back home. This is her friend. She's the one needing to talk to Ghost."

The big guy scoffed and shook his head. "Somebody needs to do something with him."

"Can we get back there? We'll take care of him."

"Sure thing." He winked at Macy and jerked his head toward the door. "Go on back, sweetheart."

"Thanks," she said, knowing she wasn't heard over the rambunctious crowd. Brian preceded her through, and she crossed her arms, wrinkling her nose at the smell. Pure alcohol and enough weed that she would probably flunk a drug test tomorrow. But at least there were fewer people. Her head was beginning to pound.

Brian had apparently been back here before too; he checked a few different places, asked a few people they ran into. No one had seen Seth since he left the stage. At last they encountered a short guy with a Mohawk making out in a hallway with a purple-haired girl even shorter than him. He held a bottle of Jack Daniel's, and when he broke away from his giggling partner, he took a swig that probably drained half the bottle. Spying Brian and Macy coming toward them, he held it out in greeting.

"Ross! You catch our set?"

"Missed it. I just need Ghost. Where is he?"

"Probably passed out." This time he held his bottle toward a closed door at the other end of the hall. "I saw him go in there. No, wait." He grinned. "I saw Raina go in there too. So he probably *ain't* passed out. I'd leave him alone all the same."

Macy's heart all but stopped. Brian echoed the words that exploded in her mind, in exactly the tone she thought them.

"*Raina?* What the fuck is she even doing here?"

Mohawk's make-out partner kept trying to kiss him, tugging his face toward hers. He let her for a second, and just as Macy was ready to step between them and pry them apart, he broke away. "Mark had her come."

"I'm sure he didn't check with Ghost about that."

"All the same, she's here. And in there. With him."

Macy's entire universe had focused on that door. The two guys went on talking, but she wasn't aware of anything but *that freaking door*. And what might be going on behind it. Her head rushed with blood; she trembled all over.

"...the fuck did you give him, Gus? Are you out of your mind?"

"Hey, he *asked* me— Dude, I'd grab her if I were you!"

The last was said as her mind finally snapped and she stalked toward that door, every step seeming to make it farther away rather than closer. She hoped she never reached it, even as she knew she had to.

"Macy, wait!" Brian caught her arm, and she yanked it from his grasp, the tears already building.

"*Stop* it."

She reached for the knob; he grabbed her again and planted her back to the wall, inches away from her intended destination. "No, babe, I'm not going through this shit. I'm getting you outta here."

"He wouldn't...*be* with her, would he?" How humiliating, how *fucking* mortifying, that Brian, that *anyone* would see her like this. For that, she hated Seth Warren right then. Hated him and hoped she never saw him again—except to open that door and scream at him what an idiot he was for getting back with that...that...whatever she was.

She's someone who knows him better than you, looks like he wants, acts like he wants, almost had his child, for God's sake. And what are you? Someone he thinks will break his heart someday. While she might be off her damn rocker, she's someone who would never *do that. And he knows it.*

"Macy, he's drunk. And possibly on something else, according to Gus. Even if he is with her...he's not in his right mind."

"I can't know this and not confront him."

"*I* can't be a part of it. The guy just lost his grandmother.

He just lost *you.* For weeks now, he's had to deal with Brooke and his fucking brother. My advice, Macy, is to go back home and hash it all out once he's back and coherent. This isn't the way."

The tears spilled, and all of her hatred wasn't reserved for Seth right then; a little of it was for herself, for letting herself be so upset. For letting herself be affected. Brian, tight-jawed and angry, didn't let his burning blue gaze leave hers for a moment. Probably trying to reassure himself she wasn't going to snap and start screaming. "All right?" he finally said. "I'll take you to get a hotel room. Then I'll come back and take care of him, whoop his ass, whatever you need me to do. But I need to make sure he sobers up."

"He makes a habit of this, does he?" she said bitterly.

His eyes narrowed, and she knew all of his anger wasn't at Seth, either. "No. Not really. But I can distinctly recall one other time."

"Are you trying to put the blame for this on me? Because that's bullshit, Brian. I know that's your 'boy' and all, but if he's in there screwing her, it's because either he wants to be, or he was stupid enough to get hammered with an unstable ex floating around. Grief is no excuse. He shouldn't be here in the first place."

"I know it's his fault, all right? But I'm not letting you go in there all the same."

The hell you aren't. "Fine," she huffed, crossing her arms and staring at some blurred fixed point to the right of Brian's head. Hesitantly, he let her go, first one hand and then the other falling away. She did her best to look whipped and miserable—hell, that wasn't a stretch.

"Look, I'm sorry." He gave her a gentle nudge toward the direction they'd come from. Mohawk and the object of his affections had moved on to a more private locale, at least. She let herself be led away. "We'll get you settled, and then you can call Candace, and you girls can rage all night about what slimy pigs we are."

"Sounds good," she said, giving a sad little chuckle. "You're not a slimy pig, though, Brian."

"I had my moments before Candace came along. Don't write him off yet, Mace. Give him a chance to explain."

"I intend to." She cast a sideways glance at Brian. He'd gone off alert.

I intend to...right fucking now.

Whirling, she sprinted back toward the door, reaching it and flinging it open almost before she even registered Brian's exasperated, "Aw, *damn.*"

A swath of light cut through the otherwise dark room and lit up everything she never wanted to see: Seth fastening his jeans, Raina on her knees in front of him. Both of them winced from the sudden illumination, Seth cursing as Raina leaped to her feet. He looked ready to fall off his.

"What the hell is going...?" His voice drowned away as recognition filtered through his eyes. "Macy? Oh, fuck— *Macy!*"

That expression, that dawning devastation on his face, was damn sure not what she'd hoped to see as she and Brian made the drive over. She turned and darted away. Brian was leaning back against the wall, arms crossed, head lowered. He looked up and only watched her race past. But she heard him intercept his friend.

"Leave it alone, man."

"Get the fuck off me. Macy!"

"Goddammit, you're not gonna get shit accomplished right now. Don't make me slam you."

She didn't know where she was going. Where could she go? She was here with Brian—which had been Huge Colossal Mistake #1. He was her only way home, and now he had his hands full. A sob escaped her, and she rubbed hard at her face, rapid steps grinding to a halt. She'd opened that door because she wanted to confront him, and here she was, running away in typical Macy fashion.

"Macy, *please.*"

A glance back showed Brian to be doing an effective job holding Seth at bay...hell, with his bloodshot eyes and slurred voice, it was a wonder he'd even got it up for that bitch. The bitch who took that particular moment to saunter out of the room and directly toward Macy. She nearly jumped back. Raina wore white-out contacts and her eyes were liberally smeared with black, and she looked like something out of Macy's worst nightmare. But the worst thing, the thing she'd see in her head from now on, actually wasn't the makeup, the clothes, or the dead eyes. The worst thing was the tiny, smug grin of triumph curving her black-lined lips. The worst thing was the little exaggerated show she made of wiping the side of her mouth with one tattered black sleeve as she swayed past.

This was what he wanted.

This was what he could damn well have.

Her heart raced like a fleeing rabbit. Seth had managed to wrench himself from Brian's grasp and stalked toward her.

"I'm sick of trying to talk sense into you fuckers!" Brian threw his hands up. "Be dumbasses, then. I don't care."

"*Macy.*"

She fell back a step as he advanced, and then another. He looked as terrible as Raina, except the black under his eyes wasn't synthetic. A fresh well of tears pooled in her eyes.

"Please, baby, that wasn't what it looked like."

A laugh burst from her, loud and horrible. "I'd hoped for something a little more original from you. Maybe then I might actually believe you at least *give a shit.*"

"She came on to *me*, all right? I didn't fucking *do* anything. I thought about it, I'll admit that, but it didn't happen. Nothing happened!"

"So I'm supposed to believe she was down on her knees...doing what, Seth? What could you even possibly supply right there? That she was looking for a lost contact? She had both of those freaking things in, so no go. I'd have to be the biggest moron on the face of the earth to believe any spin you try to put on that scenario. If the next words out of your mouth are anything *other* than 'I let her suck my dick,' then I'll know what you think of my intelligence."

He shook his head. "That's not how it was. I was half passed out. She opened my pants before I managed to push her off, and she landed on the floor. Then I got up, and you came in, and I *swear to Christ*, baby, that's all that happened."

It wasn't the most implausible thing she'd ever heard, and she could believe it of Raina, but...oh, God. She dropped her head in her hands, then shoved her hair back, blinking tears away as she stared up into the harsh overhead lighting. She found it increasingly harder to look him in the eye the longer they stood here. "I just...I have to get out of here."

Brian ambled up behind Seth. "Finally, someone speaks sense. You should have decided that about five minutes ago."

Seth ignored him. "Let me take you somewhere and we can talk—"

"*No.* You're drunk. Or high, or whatever the hell. I'm not going anywhere with you." It was then, as he tried to reach for her and she stepped back, that she noticed the reddish-purple patch of skin on his neck just at the edge of his collar. "Oh, God, Seth. Apparently you lay there and liked it long enough for her to give you *that*." She shoved him hard in the area with one finger.

"Dude has lost his fucking mind," Brian muttered, rubbing a hand back and forth across his brow.

"Shut up, man. Macy...you just have to believe me."

"Oh, I *have* to? Why? You didn't believe me."

"Or don't believe me. What-the-fuck-ever."

"Excuse me," Brian cut in, "but I liked her idea. Let's get out of here before this turns wicked."

Before it turned wicked? Was it not already? "Yes, please," she told Brian, hating how small she sounded. "Get me out of here."

Seth stared at her for one seemingly endless moment, nostrils flaring, and, given the visible tension racking him, she had the terrible thought he might hit something. His only options were Brian, the wall, or her.

Brian noticed. "Hey," he said, taking his arm. "Take it down a notch, bro."

Seth only yanked himself out of Brian's grasp and then shoved past him, muttering curses until he turned the hallway up ahead.

Macy kept her hotel room pitch-dark so she wouldn't have to watch the incessant blurring of the ceiling through her tears, which wouldn't stop.

Why hadn't she calmed down and listened to Brian? That hadn't been the time to cause drama, no matter what had been going on in that room. Seth wasn't even hers; she had no right to mark him as her exclusive territory. To make a scene like that in front of his friends when he was already hurting? If she hadn't been so blinded, so out of her head with jealousy, she would've seen it.

Stupid, stupid. Thinking about what might have happened in that dark room was futile. Only two people knew, and both had good reason to lie about it. Mulling it over, she realized she could believe both sides equally. The only solution was to get one of them to fess up.

Why did she care? The whole ugly scene played out again against the back of her closed eyelids. His face when he'd recognized her. The wreckage there. Tears pooled again and squeezed out and spilled over each side of her face. She didn't try to stop them anymore, but flopped over on one side and sobbed into her pillow. There wouldn't be any sleep tonight. Her heart lay in bloody pieces.

Her cell phone chimed and she almost didn't bother to reach for it. Despite Brian's suggestion that she call Candace and vent, she hadn't wanted to talk to anyone. Brian had dropped her off and she'd hardly even flipped on a light before slipping out of her clothes and under the sheets, letting the hum of the air conditioner lull her.

Nevertheless, she reached for it and sat up straight when she saw Seth's name. *Im at ur hotel. Plz talk 2 me.*

God, she couldn't. Could she? She was weak right now, so weak and desperate to believe him that she might fall for something stupid.

But her need to see him apparently made her stupider. She

texted him her room number, then collapsed back and cursed herself, rubbing her still-pounding forehead hard with the heels of both hands.

By the time he knocked, she'd gotten up and slipped into a T-shirt and boxers. The sound, though expected, sent her heart slamming in her chest. She let him in without looking at him, knowing if she did, she might be well and truly screwed. In more ways than one.

"Are you okay?" he asked, shutting the door as she sat on the bed and glanced at the clock. It was almost two. She wondered if he'd had a chance to sober up much yet; somehow, it seemed like it.

"I'm fine."

"You've been crying."

"So I have."

He cursed under his breath, rubbing a hand over his head. "Baby, I know what you said is true. Nothing I can say will make what you saw look any better." He took a seat at the little desk along the wall opposite her, straddling the chair backward, putting himself in her line of sight. Close enough to touch, but he didn't, and she appreciated that. "Really, you don't have any reason to believe me. But you don't have any reason to believe her, either. She's the one who put her own spin on that scenario. Not me."

"I was just lying here thinking about that," she said. "How either one of you has as much reason to lie as the other."

"I have more to lose," he said softly. "I admit that. I have *way* more to lose."

"That doesn't really speak in your favor."

"I know. But it's the truth."

"Seth...I'm so sorry about your grandmother. I haven't been able to talk to you to tell you and...I'm sorry about that scene tonight. Whatever was going on, it wasn't right of me to do that. I never thought I'd be reduced to...that."

"You weren't the only one who was reduced. When I saw you..."

"I know."

269

"I'm going to fix this, Macy. I don't care if we have to start all over again. I'll put the work in to rebuild it all." A weak smile flickered across his features, at odds with the passionate way he spoke. "It's what I do, you know. I get rusted-out old heaps of junk back on the road, I turn scars into art. Maybe I get once-broken cowgirls back on the horse. I'll do the same for us, if you'll let me."

She wanted so much to believe him, to put all her trust back in him. Silence descended, one she didn't know how to fill, or even if she should. Her anger had burnt itself out, leaving her empty. Tired but with no hope of any rest.

Some things even he couldn't fix. But if he kept saying things like that, she might be inclined to let him try and...it wasn't for the best.

"I think we're no good for each other, Seth. I've said it before, but I think we both know how this will end. We're from different worlds. I saw tonight how much yours can hurt me."

He gripped the chair back so hard his knuckles paled. "But you've also seen how good we are together. How well we bridge the gap when it's just us, and that's all that matters, isn't it? Because in the end, that's all it'll be. Just you and me."

"It's looking more and more like it would always be you and me and *Raina.*"

A helpless look crossed his face, and that was when she realized something. He really was helpless when it came to Raina, and honestly, what could he do? A restraining order? What a joke. How the hell *did* you get rid of someone who simply wouldn't let go?

"I need some time," she said. "That's all I can give you right now." Another silence fell. "You have a room?" she asked finally.

"Yeah. I guess you're saying I should get to it?"

"I'm exhausted, and this was a bad idea."

He made a move to stand but didn't quite make it. Renewed agitation hit him, and he sat again, rubbing his face hard with his hands. "Shit, Macy, I can't walk out the door if I think it'll be the last time. Always wondering if there's something else I could've said to—" He broke off, seeming to get a grip on the emotion strangling his voice, his hand scrubbing his chest as if trying to assuage some phantom ache there. "The fact you even came here to see me... And then for you to see what you did...fuck. I can't live with myself. I just want to rip off my fucking skin, I feel so foul. I should've dumped her ass off me the minute I realized who she was but I just needed...to hurt somebody. The way I hurt. Since I lost Nana, since I pushed you away."

At least he admitted it. "Did it make you feel better?"

"Hell no. Worse. It was wrong. I know that. I told her what she and I had was never love; it was ugly. That's how we were to each other all the time. It was like we took out our anger at the world on each other. She was an easy target at the right moment."

"Sounds meant to be." There was no mistaking the bitterness in her voice, and she didn't even try to suppress it.

"I also told her I don't want that in my life anymore. I'm done with it all. I want what I have with you. I want the way we laugh together. I could never see us turning into anything like that."

"We did, though, Seth. That night in Fort Worth...that wasn't right. After we were done and you said I would only leave you, you made me feel pretty foul myself. You turned your back on me when I tried to be there for you. You threw a bunch of accusations in my face and found a reason to run."

"I did. And I won't ever do it again. Because as scared as I was of having someone like you—and I was pretty damned scared—I see now that I'm far more freaked out about not having you."

Maybe she was stronger than she thought. While she did want to believe him—God, more than anything, she wanted to—not only about what had happened with Raina but about how things would be from now on, she kept firm guard around her heart. She hadn't exactly been forthcoming with him either.

"I need to explain something about me."

His brows dipped lower over his eyes, a crease appearing between them. "Okay."

"I really was miserable on Valentine's night. I mean...yeah. You called that one, I was in the dumps, and not just about differences between me and my friends. I was lonely. I had been for a while, but that night was, like, the culmination."

"I knew that from the moment I saw you. I made up my mind to do something about it."

A few more hot tears slipped out, but she forced a smile for him. "Well, you did. But the thing is...you told me once I didn't seem like a girl who was looking for commitment, but I am. I'm ready to have what my friends have, and more. I want marriage, and I want kids. I'm not saying I want it all tomorrow, or even next year or the year after that. I only have to know...that I'm with someone who can see those things in his future too. If you can't, then I'll ask that you not waste my time."

He blew out a breath, not looking at her but at her hands resting in her lap. She'd just about twisted her own fingers into knots during that speech. "Wow."

"I know that was blunt, but now's a good time to get it all out there, right? I think we started out with some preconceived notions about each other. If we know from the start we'll never give each other what we need, why go on? Relationships that drag on for years and finally break up because of indecision on the part of one or the other...I don't want that. That seems like such a waste to me."

"Marriages do the same thing. The vows aren't the finish line. How many married couples do you know who are miserable, and you look at them and think, 'Damn, just get divorced already'? Because I know quite a few. I think you're limiting yourself. Even if I can't see those things in my future now, maybe I will after a year. Or two. Maybe something will happen in your life, and you *won't* see those things anymore. People evolve."

"I guess I'm not that cynical yet. I'm still convinced when it happens to me, it'll be happily ever after."

"Well...sure, you deserve that."

Silence again, so heavy with unspoken words. Like he said, she deserved it; maybe everyone did, but could he give it to her?

Could *she* give up everything she'd ever dreamed of and believed in to be with him? To be a couple of feathers floating in the wind together with no foreseeable destination...

She looked at him, allowing herself to stare for probably the first time since he came in. Grief etched heavy lines around his mouth. He looked older, a little gaunt, and his all-black attire only lent to the shadows under his eyes. She missed his devil-may-care grin. She missed everything about him.

"You should get to your room and try to sleep," she said softly. "Don't think about me right now. We'll both step back. You're still grieving."

Staring at the floor, he nodded and stood. He didn't look in her eyes as he leaned over and brushed a kiss across her forehead, lingering an endless moment before pulling away. "Without you, I'm grieving over two instead of one."

As she watched him walk out the door, it was all she could do not to run after him.

Chapter Twenty-Three

"Do you think I'm doing the right thing?"

Brian glanced over at her, then returned his gaze to the road. Despite the late night, he'd been ready to go bright and early, meeting her in the hotel parking lot a little before eight. He looked as if *he'd* slept fine.

What a bust this had been.

"Taking a break? I think so. I mean, it hurts, I can attest to that. But it's necessary sometimes. You either realize that you can't live without them or that you were fucking crazy for ever trying to live with them."

"Do you believe him? Honestly. Forget the guy-code BS and tell me if what he said made any sense."

"We're talking about Raina here. Yes. It made perfect sense."

She laughed without mirth. "I guess so. Did you talk to him this morning?"

"No. I did late last night. He was going to sleep it off and head for home later today."

"He'll be okay, right?"

"He'll be fine. He's been through worse."

"I don't doubt it. You'll look out for him?"

He nodded once and tugged his cap lower over his eyes. "Always."

"Good."

"Candace said you never called her last night."

Sighing, she rubbed at the headache that had never quite left her overnight. "I couldn't. There was no way I could've talked about it, even with her."

"Just so you know, I didn't tell her anything. She asked how it went, and I only said it didn't go so well, and you were upset. You can tell her what you want."

"Keeping it in your vault, huh?"

He made a motion as if he were flicking a key away from his lips. "In the vault."

"Thank you, Brian. And I'm sorry more than ever now that you got dragged into this."

"Hey, I hope it works out for you guys. I really do."

She watched as the green landscape rolled past outside her window. Spring was everywhere, it seemed, except inside her soul. Winter still festered there, bleak and unrelenting. "I'm sure it will." But she didn't hear a single note of confidence in her voice. She couldn't even muster a fake one.

Days went by. He didn't call. Even if it was the very thing she'd asked for, it weighed on her heart to think of him alone in the house where he had memories of his parents and his grandmother, all of them gone now. Memories of a sister who wasn't around for him, and a brother who'd ripped his heart out and apparently still didn't give a damn about it.

So many times she found herself driving by his house like a psycho stalker. Like Raina, she often thought with a smirk. But where Raina was probably building shrines and doing voodoo love spells or something, Macy was just trying to work up the courage to stop. To get out, to walk up and ring his doorbell. To put her arms around him. She never could quite muster it.

For all she knew, her speech about needing a family someday had scared him away more than anything else. It wasn't exactly what a girl should spout when she was trying to snag a man, and she still wondered what possessed her to do it. Just a burning need to lay her soul out there for him, to let him make a decision about her, knowing everything he *thought* he knew about her was wrong.

She had some decisions to make herself. Like if she believed him about Raina.

If it even freaking *mattered* about Raina. Somehow, the anger at him wasn't there anymore. It was all at that girl. At that annoying little pest who would probably always be lurking around, waiting for her chance to resurface with a new strike against them. Macy could just see it now. Nuclear war, and all that would be left were cockroaches and Raina.

She couldn't go to Dermamania anymore, either. Every time she thought of stopping by to visit Candace, Seth was there. Even the convenient excuse to go in and see him wasn't empowering enough. She was terrified to face him. What if he acted like nothing had ever happened between them? What if she was only kidding herself?

And why did she miss that damn place so much now that it was off-limits to her?

"Macy, just come by and talk to him!" Candace pleaded with her almost two weeks after the blow up in Austin. She'd never admitted to her friend what had really happened. In fact, she hadn't let herself talk about Seth with Candace at all, mainly to avoid hearing those very words come out of Candace's mouth. But Macy's own vault had been getting full enough to burst; she'd had to ease the pressure.

"Maybe. Not anytime soon."

"You know how you always like to tell me when I'm doing something stupid?"

"Yes. But I don't need to hear—"

"Nuh-uh. You don't get off that easy. You're being stupid."

"The thing is I was always wrong in your case."

"Look, I've been where you are. So *please* take it from me how bad you're screwing up right now."

Her heart fell. "Why? He's not...like, starting to see someone else, is he?"

"Seriously? *No*, dummy. But he needs you. He quit the band."

Her fallen heart flopped around sickly for a second or two. "What did he do that for?"

"He's pissed at them for bringing Raina to Austin without him knowing, apparently. Said it was the last straw."

"He just...quit?"

"Is she causing you guys that much trouble? Is that what this is about? God, I can't stand that bitch."

"*Candace*. He *quit*?"

"Oh my God, are you listening to me right now? He *quit*. It was ugly. He's been fighting with Mark for days; even Brian has had words with Mark—that's the lead singer, in case you didn't know. It's been drama central up in here. You're missing it."

"I've had enough drama to last me a good long time."

"So has he. Macy, I didn't want to be the one to tell you this, but he's seriously talking about moving to Oklahoma. Brian is beside himself."

Macy's eyes filled with tears. Instantly, just like that, the thought of those weeks without him turning into something permanent released the flood she'd been holding back ever since getting home from Austin. She sat in silence for so long trying to find her voice that Candace said, "Hello? Mace?"

"I'm here," she whispered. It was all she could manage.

"Oh God. I'm sorry. But do you see? You've got to talk to him."

"What do I do? Keep him from going? As much as we hate it, what if that's the best thing for him? All I've been thinking about is how lonely he must be. He doesn't have anyone here." She knew her friend could hear the sobs threatening to overtake the words.

"He has us! He could have you too, if you weren't so fucking stubborn. Do you love him, Macy?"

"I do."

"Then *tell* him."

What if he didn't love her back?

It was the thought that kept her awake, burning in her brain as if it had been branded to the inside of her skull. And she cried. She cried for days, cried rivers, found all the emotions she'd tamped down and buried and never wanted to face again after her accident. If she'd had something to hit in her apartment, she'd have pummeled it.

Jared tried to call her; she told him to leave her alone. He wasn't really guilty of anything except trying to get her back, but his trying had caused all this shit in the first place. She told him she was in love, and even if it didn't work out, there would be no going back for them. His anger at her probably meant she'd never get to teach his adorable little girls to ride again, but it wasn't her place to worry about them. They would find someone else.

But she found herself hanging out at her parents' place a lot more than usual, enduring Mom's concerned frown and her dad's jovial obliviousness. It was the latter she gravitated toward, hoping to work up the courage to ask his advice. While her love life had never been a hot topic between them—she actually shuddered to think of talking to him about that—if there was a person in her life who would give it to her straight, it was good old Dad. He might love Jared, but he loved her more. He wouldn't push her in that direction if she didn't want to go, she was sure of it. Now Mom, on the other hand...

Late March was beautiful at the ranch, and she'd just gone out to feed the ducks and enjoy the mild evening air—really missing Ashley and Mia, who loved to help her do this—when her dad yelled at her from the arena.

"Macy-girl! Want to give Pixie a run?"

Grinning, she wiped her hands on her jeans and strolled over. "Sure."

"I can set up the barrels for you." His graying eyebrows waggled under his John Deere cap, which he'd taken to wearing constantly now that he was losing his hair. It was a taboo subject around their house.

Her heart leaped into her throat as she stepped through the fence. "Oh..."

"No push," he said, shrugging as if he didn't care one way or the other. Dammit, he knew how to get to her.

Mouth dry, she looked toward the barn. The rush of blood in her veins was almost audible as she considered. Her dad's hand came down gently on her shoulder.

"I'll just say this. I know how you are. I know the main

thing holding you up right now is fear, but it's not fear of what might happen but that you think you might not be perfect. It's been years, Mace. Give yourself permission to not be perfect. Life's too short, but you're still young. Give up that iron-knuckle grip you have on excellence and just...have fun. For a change."

Her gaze swung up to meet his. "You always know the right thing to say, Dad."

He grinned the grin her mom professed still made her heart go pitter-pat. "Could be. Or it could be that I have a stubborn mule of a daughter who takes after her old man."

It was so much like old times, she could almost imagine her gaggle of rodeo friends hanging out around the fence. Country music blaring from Jared's truck. Jared beaming at her, cheering her on. He'd usually been the one timing her. Now it was just her and her dad, and there was no admiring crowd. It was somehow far sweeter this way, and she knew she would remember it forever.

She only wished Seth could see her. Wondered if he'd be proud, or if he'd even care.

Pixie, her palomino quarter horse, pranced underneath her, and Macy gave her a consolatory pat. "I know how you feel, girl."

"Ready?" Her dad didn't have a stopwatch; he'd told her to take it easy to start, no serious speed. Good advice. Having been out of the game for years, she wasn't conditioned. Yes, true to her dad's earlier speech, that irritated the hell out of her, and she vowed to start working on that as soon as she could. At least Pixie could bail her out a bit. The horse's previous owner had been a racer, and Macy's dad had bought her only a few months ago. So she knew the cloverleaf pattern well, and Macy had already walked her through it a few times.

Inhale. Blow out slowly. Her horse wasn't the only thing about to be galloping; her heart was too. She narrowed her gaze on the barrel to her right, her first target. There were no traumatic memories of the event to assail her, at least. As she'd told Seth, she didn't remember a thing. No flying through the air, no bone-crunching impact. Her dad probably had worse images in his head right now than she did. If he could face those head-on like this, so could she.

"Remember, take her easy, now."

"Yes, sir."

"Go!"

She almost didn't. Almost dismounted and said, "Some other time." Knowing she'd be proving right everyone in her life was all that made her shoot ahead. Seth telling her she was afraid. Dad telling her she was too much of a perfectionist. Candace telling her she was a control freak.

She rounded the first barrel. *That one's for you, Candace, you freaking little free spirit, I guess you were right after all.*

Then the second, her dad hollering at her to swing a little wider. She made the turn, careful to follow his instruction lest she knock it over. Something she'd done before, because she didn't like to listen. *See, Dad, I'm not that stubborn, not anymore.*

She knew the third was where she'd lost it before. Apparently a video existed of the whole thing, but she'd never allowed herself to watch it. Probably for the best. As Pixie kicked up dust whipping her big body around the last barrel, Macy couldn't help but grin. Her favorite part was the mad dash to the finish. Maybe the anticipation of it had made her sloppy and that was how she'd ended up eating dirt and flirting with lifelong paralysis.

The wind in her face, Pixie's frantic hoofbeats jarring her bones...it was cleansing. The guilt over what had happened to her beloved Sugar had weighed on her for years, another reason she'd never thought she would race again. But Pixie was bred to do this, trained to do it. After going through it with her, Macy couldn't wait to unleash her full potential. The horse overcompensated for her name in size, but she could damn sure fly. She rode like a dream.

When she pulled back on the reins and wheeled Pixie around, grinning at her dad, she felt reborn. All from running a pattern so familiar it was practically ingrained in her. She'd missed it. God, she'd known that she missed it, but she hadn't even realized how much until that moment.

Her dad didn't make a big deal about it. No running up and hugging or fawning all over her. His cool acceptance told her he'd always known this day would come. Congratulations weren't necessary, because she should have taken this step as soon as the doctor gave her the okay to return to riding with his one simple admonishment: *"If it hurts, stop."*

It hadn't hurt. It had felt damn spectacular, and she was damn lucky. She would take advantage of that, not live a sham of a life.

"Thanks, Dad," she said later as she helped him with brushing. He glanced at her over Pixie's golden back, his expression as unreadable as usual. It was only because she knew him so well that she knew he had something to say.

He shrugged. "I didn't do anything."

"Well, you might think you didn't, but you did. Thanks for, you know, my life, for everything. After what happened, you probably thought I was ungrateful for all the things you've done for me, but I never was."

"I never thought that." He gave Pixie a pat. "You know, when I saw the way you hit the ground...I almost hit the ground too. And all I could think about was holding you on Prancer for the first time when you were barely big enough to walk, how your eyes lit up. I thought of that a lot in the weeks afterward. You always had that spark. After your accident, though, it went out."

"I know," she said quietly.

"But I never had any regrets, Macy, and I wouldn't have, no matter what that doctor said when he first came out of your operating room. Because that spark was beautiful and something a lot of people never have no matter how long they live or how many miles they walk."

"I'm sorry if I let you down."

"Let me down? Not at all. I don't think I was ever prouder of you for the way you fought your way back. Hell, if you never wanted to *look* at another horse again, I wouldn't have blamed you. I might not have liked it, but I would've understood."

He probably didn't realize how close she'd been to that extreme at first. She'd practically forced herself back in the saddle. Little by little, it had gotten better. Baby steps, she realized. She'd been taking them even back then. She'd only thought she'd toddled as far as she could. No more of that. She was ready to get up and walk boldly. No, run.

"You've got it back, you know," her dad said, gesturing at her without really looking up from his task.

"What?"

"You're lit up."

"I don't feel very lit up," she laughed, though for some reason his words made her beam. Hell, maybe he was right.

"Not just today, either. Yeah, you've been kind of grumping around the place for a few days, but overall something has brightened you up. Is it Jared?"

All at once, her bright shiny mood shifted dangerously toward crashing. "No, Dad. It's not Jared. I hate to burst your bubble, but it won't ever be Jared."

"Well, then, I figure it must be someone. So out with it."

"I'm in love."

"No shit."

"Dad! I just...I don't know."

"You just said you were in love. So what the hell is there not to know?"

"I'm going to go ahead and risk your coronary and get it over with. You know the comedic trope where the well-to-do daughter gets mad at her parents for one reason or another and hires a guy totally inappropriate for her to bring home and pose as her serious boyfriend or fiancé to get back at them?"

"I'm somewhat familiar."

"Let's just say if you meet him, you'll probably be asking yourself what you've ever done to me. He's Brian Ross's best friend, if that tells you anything. They work together."

"Tattoo artist, huh? You've said Brian is a good guy, right?"

"He is. He's great."

"Well, look, kid. I know you have a good head on your shoulders. I know you wouldn't do anything stupid, and you wouldn't settle for some idiot punk. I trust your judgment."

"Thanks, Daddy. I guess after everything Candace went through—"

"Candace's parents are assholes. They're worried about who's good enough for their little princess. But I trust that I raised a strong enough woman to know who's worthy of her and who isn't. If this guy is good enough for you, and he's the one who has you floating around on cloud nine and giving you back your spark, you can be damn sure he's good enough for me."

Idly, Macy ran the brush over Pixie's coat, her mind miles away.

"And someone worth keeping around," her dad added. "Just in case a certain stubborn mule-headed woman keeps pushing the poor guy away."

"Oh, *Dad.*"

"Am I wrong?"

"You're not wrong. You just don't know everything about the situation."

"I don't have to." He stood up straight, his gaze direct and steady on her. "Whatever's wrong, you know if it's worth fixing or not. If it is, then fix it. If not, leave it alone and move on. If I raised you to be strong, then that means I didn't teach you to sit around and wait on life and happiness to happen to you. You *go after* it, Macy."

And if something is standing in your way, you go through *it.*

Right. You go through it. Her dad didn't say the words, but he had before. Many, many times.

She wondered how this man had allowed her to lie down for so long. Maybe it was only because he knew this was a point she needed to get back to mostly by herself. Maybe he knew her well enough to realize all she needed to get back to her fighting spirit was something worth fighting for. "You know, it's good to get your speeches again."

He grinned. "For such a long time, you didn't want to hear 'em anymore. I'm afraid your break's over, though. We've got work to do."

In more ways than one. "I'm ready."

Chapter Twenty-Four

Mezzanine Music wasn't a place Macy ever had reason to visit. Hopefully that would never change, because after today, she might be banned for life.

"What does she drive?" she asked Candace over the phone, staring at the building as she sat in her Acadia and mustered her nerve.

"Actually, I don't know."

No way of determining if Raina was working today, then, without going in to find out. Cornering the girl at her job wasn't the smartest way to handle this; she knew that. But there weren't any other options. She didn't know where she lived, and neither did Candace without asking someone and blowing the whistle on Macy's plan. Besides, any meeting with this girl needed to be at least somewhat public so Macy didn't end up decapitated in a ditch somewhere.

She smirked at the thought, absently surveying the large windows of the music shop. No sign of multicolored hair in there. "There's a big Dermamania flyer in the window."

"Yeah, Brian and the owner are friends. We trade advertising. He got Raina the job there when she first moved to town."

"Is there anyone Brian isn't friends with?"

"My parents?"

"Right."

"Are you sure about this?"

"No, but what else am I going to do? I'm hanging up now."

"Good luck. If I don't ever hear from you again, I love ya."

"Tell the detectives who I was meeting."

"Got it."

Well, here goes nothing. She left the safety of her car, unwilling to sit there long enough to see if the girl ever ventured outside for a break or a smoke or something. If she was even working.

And she was. As Macy pulled open the front door to a pleasant-sounding chime, Raina glanced over from the counter at the end of the large room, and Macy had the intense satisfaction of seeing her expression deflate a split second before the accustomed sneer appeared. It really was an unattractive look for such a pretty girl, but she didn't give a shit. She would feel sorry for Seth, but it was his own fault for putting up with it as long as he had.

"What do you want?" Raina's whiplash question turned the heads of a couple of guys checking out the guitars hanging on the wall.

"I'd like to have a word with you."

Raina extended her arms to indicate their surroundings, giving Macy the "He*llo*?" voice as she said, "I'm at *work* right now?"

"I realize that. So let's set up a time and place for later—public, please—and I'll leave."

"No. I don't have anything to say to you."

Macy crossed her arms. "That may be, but I have plenty to say to you. I can say it here and now, if you like. I bet I can say an awful lot before I get thrown out, and probably things you don't want anyone to hear."

A long-haired guy stuck his head out the door behind the counter, frowning at Raina and looking Macy up and down. "Is there a problem?"

Must be Brian's friend. But she wouldn't name-drop; she'd reserve that in case Raina said there was a big freaking problem and to throw Macy out on her ear. Surprisingly, she didn't do that, blowing out a gusty sigh instead. "I need a few minutes, Dave. Is that all right?"

"Take it outside."

Raina made barely an effort to walk around Macy as she headed for the front door, knocking into her shoulder. Such class. But she *had* accosted her at work, so maybe she wasn't much better. And she'd told Seth she had left the fighting-over-a-guy thing behind in middle school. Ha.

Granted, she hadn't been around Raina many times, but she struck her as the kind of girl who had a constant air of exasperation about her, as if the world and its annoyances were exhausting. Now was no different, as she walked to the edge of the building and turned to face Macy. "All right. Talk."

"You're going to tell me what happened in that room. The truth."

"Oh, really. Hearing the gory details about me sucking off your man turns you on or something?" Her lips curled in a catlike smile. "Mmm. It does me, just thinking about it."

"See, here's the thing. I don't believe you. So unless you convince me otherwise right now, I really have no choice but to go with what he says. He says you're a liar."

"Yeah, he would, wouldn't he? And you're full of shit, because you know I'm right. It's like I told you. He's got a hard-on for girls like you, maybe, but he knows where to come when he wants to get *fucked*. Do you need another demonstration?"

"If you're so convinced it's you he wants to spend the rest of his life with, then where is he, Raina? Why isn't he with you? And if by another demonstration, you mean you're going to try again to practically sexually assault someone who's half unconscious, then no, I'm sure none of us need to see that again. It's kind of illegal, you know."

Raina's jaw clenched, her lips trembling. Whether she was about to leap for Macy's throat or burst into tears, she couldn't tell. But that look told her everything she needed to know. "That's not how it was."

"Wasn't it? Look," Macy went on, "I want you to know that I realize you and he went through some really emotional stuff together, all right? I'm not unsympathetic to that. I can see where it would be hard to let go, but—"

"It's none of your fucking business."

"*He's* my business. He's no longer your business. It would tickle me pink if you would go back to where you came from, but since you're not smart enough to know when you're not wanted, I'm telling you straight, and in language you can understand." She stepped closer, almost nose to nose with the other girl. "Stay. The fuck. Away from—"

Raina's arm jerked up. Macy was ready for even that lightning-quick move, knocking her hand aside before it could connect with her cheek, keeping a tight hold on Raina's narrow wrist. "—him," she finished. "I might look like a wimpy rich bitch, Raina, but I only look that way. I know people. I've wrestled animals bigger than you. And I can shoot."

Raina fumed, her breathing fast and shallow, her pulse racing under Macy's gripping fingers. But Macy didn't think she was mistaking the surprise and the hint of fear in her eyes. "Oh, threatening me now?" She didn't sound nearly as tough as she had moments ago.

"Nope. Not at all. Just advising against any *Fatal Attraction*-type retaliation measures you might be considering. Seth always said you're more bark than bite, so I'm hoping we won't have to deal with any of that. Because I'm telling you, if you come near him like that again, I will go straight country bitch on you."

When Raina jerked her hand away, Macy let her, still not dropping her guard. But the other girl only lowered her head and crossed her arms over her chest, looking small and suddenly vulnerable. Her big hair only made her seem that much tinier. *Here comes the sob story.*

But it didn't come. When Raina lifted her head, her eyes were wet, but all the fight seemed to have gone out of her. "I want you to leave."

"I want you to move. And I don't mean from this spot. I mean far away from us. Go back to where you came from."

"Are you out of your mind?"

"I know you were only staying here for him, but you don't have him, and you never will. There's nothing for you here but a lot more heartache than you already have."

"What-fucking-ever. Can I get back to work now?"

Macy scoffed, thinking that maybe making the girl lose her

job so she'd be forced to go back to whatever she had in Austin wasn't such a bad idea. But she hadn't sunk that low. Yet. "As long as we have an understanding?"

Raina's eyes narrowed. They were some indistinguishable color Macy pondered over for a second before deciding they were simply gunmetal gray. Then the mouth below them twisted. "For as long as he keeps you around, anyway."

She supposed it was as good an acknowledgement as she was going to get. Nodding, she stepped aside and let Raina walk past her. No way would she turn her back on her at this point. Raina didn't shoulder-check her this time. Maybe it was a good sign.

She watched until the other girl disappeared around the corner of the building...and finally allowed herself to breathe again.

Now for the hard part.

"That movie fucking sucked, dude."

"Your face fucking sucks."

"That was seriously the worst acting I've ever seen in a movie that didn't show tits during the opening credits."

Brian had to lift his needle to laugh at Ghost's assessment or risk maiming his client. Ghost grinned, keeping his own focus on coloring inside the line. And off Macy.

He'd been through this shit before; he knew it would get better with time. But at least back then he'd had the luxury of Brooke being *gone*. As it was, every time the door chimed as someone came in, he dreaded looking up, knowing he was about to suffer stomach-crushing disappointment when it wasn't Macy, or the utter devastation of seeing her face. His fear of seeing indifference there when the time came—and he couldn't avoid her forever—kept him awake at night.

Oh, he could function. He kept up appearances; he wore the mask. Only Brian and Candace were privy to the fact something wasn't right...well, hell, for all he knew, everyone was by now. If they were, they didn't say anything.

He didn't know how much longer he could keep it up before he packed everything he could haul in his backseat and lit out of town in the middle of the night. Before he said *fuck it*, fuck it all. He'd start over somewhere else, away from Macy, away from Raina's fucking insanity. Not a day went by that Raina didn't text or try to call, leaving voice mails pleading for him to meet up with her. He'd change his number if he wasn't afraid that Macy might try to call him.

Not that he believed in miracles or anything.

"Come on, it wasn't that bad," Brian said, still hung up on the crap movie.

"Then I'd hate to see what you consider bad."

And on it went, the parlor chatter shifting from bad movies to commentary on the complaint someone had made about the music. Which led to observations about the different genres of metal and Brian's usual declaration. "Death growls mostly bore me. Who wants to hear the Cookie Monster? *Sing* your fucking lyrics. Put some emotion behind it."

And Ghost's usual retaliation. "Aw, I'm sorry. Do you need a hug, emo boy? You know, you might want to cross your legs. Your vagina is showing."

"Suck my dick."

"I know you'd like that, but Candace would have to return it first."

"Burn!" someone proclaimed, and even Brian laughed.

"Look, he doesn't even deny it."

Yep, business as usual. He hadn't lost his snap, but underneath, exhaustion ate at him. That happened when you felt like you had to consciously tell your lungs to keep expanding with air, your heart to keep pumping. Showing a crack in his exterior would be a good way to get eaten alive by this crew, though. When Brian had been torn up over Candace, at least he'd had the luxury of being the boss. No one had fucked with him; they simply avoided him. Ghost didn't have that protection.

He finished up with his client, forgoing the aftercare instructions because the dude was one of his regulars; he knew the drill. The guy was heading toward the door when it opened and a girl breezed in. Ghost saw her from the corner of his eye, but even before he looked up and verified that it was *her*, all the oxygen left the room. Turning immediately away and putting on the show of straightening his station, he tried to drag in what breath he could.

"S'up, Macy?" Brian said.

Her purposeful steps were coming closer. Shit.

"I just need him," she said.

Him? As in...me?

He couldn't help it. He turned to face her, preparing himself for the shock of seeing her again, but it wasn't possible. That damn sure wasn't indifference on her face. She looked at him, only at him, like she wanted to crawl inside him—or maybe that was damn wishful thinking on his part. But the spark in her eyes and the color in her cheeks... He knew that look. He'd given it to her before himself.

"Do you have a minute?" she asked as she reached him, small voice at odds with the purpose etched on her delicate features. He wanted to take that face in his hands, kiss those lips until they were plump and red, but he had to keep his cool. Fuck, the whole place was watching. Candace had even ventured out from the back and moved to Brian's side, the two of them exchanging little secretive smiles.

"Sure," he said with a shrug. "Come on."

He led her back to the room where she'd asked him to take her on their first date, flipping on the light and closing the door. "What's up?"

She didn't answer right away, fingering a lock of her hair and looking at him so closely he shifted uncomfortably under the weight of the stare. Something was...different about her. He couldn't put his finger on it.

"Heard you quit your band."

That wasn't what he'd expected. "Yeah."

"Thought you told me you'd never let anything make you quit doing what you love."

"Guess I didn't love it that much anymore."

"Is that really the reason?"

"Yes, Macy, it is." God, she looked beautiful. And smelled beautiful. Shit, she'd never looked or smelled more beautiful. He took a deep breath, hoping it would bring some fucking clarity. It only brought more of her scent. "It wasn't so much the band or the experience as the people. They were starting to be a drain on me. And the Raina thing...it wasn't cool."

"Then I'm glad you cut it loose," she said simply.

"Okay. Are we done catching up on me now?" He edged toward the door. If he didn't get away from her soon, he couldn't be held accountable for what he was about to do—which was shove her against the wall and kiss her for the next few hours. Days. Whatever. He wasn't sure yet that was what she was here for.

"I went to see her. Raina."

Thoughts, meet brick wall. He froze. "You... Come again?"

"I went to her job." She smirked. "Thought I was going to get thrown out, but...we talked. We cleared some things up."

"You. Talked to Raina."

"I did."

"And there was no bloodshed, flying fur, ER visits...?"

She crossed her arms. "I resent the implication that I can't conduct myself in a civil manner."

"I'm implying that *Raina* can't conduct herself—"

"Oh, she took a swing, I threatened to shoot her...typical girl stuff."

"Holy shit." He stared at her in absolute awe. "You gotta be fucking with me."

She put her hands on her hips. "Well, that's what it was going to take, right? *You* couldn't very well rough her up or threaten her—that would be frowned upon. Me, however... I will make her spit teeth, and I doubt many people would blame me."

He'd jumped the gun earlier. *Now* she was more beautiful than he'd ever seen her. That's what was different about her. She looked *ferocious,* still riding her adrenaline high. "So...don't think I'm not impressed, but...what did you do that for, exactly?"

"Isn't it obvious?"

"With you? Babe, nothing with you is obvious." He wondered if she remembered those words from Valentine's night, saw as she smiled that she did.

"I seem to remember someone lecturing me about fear holding me back. I guess it stuck." She shook her long, ferocious hair back. "So. Are *you* scared?"

"A little bit, yeah."

"Good. Let me scare this into you. You have about as much to worry about from my stupid ex as I have to worry about from yours. Which is zilch. I see that now. So can we both vow to let that rest?"

"Baby, I'll vow anything you want me to right now." Where he'd been inching toward escape earlier, he was now crowding her into the corner of the room with his feverish gaze locked on her lips. But her palm came up flat against his chest

"No, wait. Before all the blood drains south of your brain. I mean it. I *won't* have jealous outbursts like that."

"I told you that wouldn't happen anymore."

"Just so we're clear. But other than that, I'm not putting any stipulations on you. I told you what I want out of life, but I want you too." Her gaze flickered over his face. "However I can have you."

His heart did flip-flops and sang hallelujah. Maybe they'd continue on like this for years. Maybe, after a few months of her, he'd be like Brian wanting to tear the walls down to marry the woman he loved. Even the thought of an accidental kid or two didn't induce the panic attack it had with Raina. If ever he were going to reproduce, he couldn't pick a better person to do it with. "Macy, I can tell you with absolute certainty that no matter how or where you and I end up, you will not have considered it a waste of your time."

Before he knew it, she'd maneuvered him around and into her former position. Backed in the corner. Her palms met the walls on either side of his shoulders. She looked into his eyes with a directness that murdered any will to resist that might still be cowering in the corner of his brain. And oh, Christ, his cock was already threatening to bust through his fly.

"Promise me that."

"I should have promised you that the other night. I was just—all fucked up." He took a shaky breath. "Yeah. I promise."

"I get it. And I'm sorry. I should have listened to you."

"A lot of people probably don't want us together, you know? I didn't realize it, or I didn't give a fuck before. But now I see, and I don't care what anyone thinks, but are you sure you—"

She grasped his chin, and his entire mental process shut down. The girl had strong fingers. He couldn't wait to feel them wrapped around—

"Ghost?"

She fucking called me Ghost.

"Huh?"

"Shut up."

And finally, miraculously, she kissed him.

They went to her place because it was closer. Brian had taken one look at them as they emerged from the back, smirked at Ghost's beseeching "Dude?" and told them to get outta there with a gesture at the door. Candace had grinned from ear to ear.

It almost turned into another frenzied bout of vehicular sex, but somehow they refrained. It was still broad daylight, after all.

As they toppled onto her bed at last, he couldn't stop smiling as he kissed her.

"What?" she asked when he must've begun to look like a psycho.

"I'm happy," he murmured, pulling up her shirt and gliding his mouth down her body to nip and lick at her midriff. "For the first time in...forever, it seems. I feel lighter."

Macy sighed, drawing her knees up and bowing her lithe body toward him. "I'm glad."

It was true. All the pain over his grandmother, it was still there, and he would always miss her. But he also knew he was right where she would want him to be, right where his parents would want him to be, and there was comfort in that.

And perhaps most importantly, for one of the few times in his life, he was right where *he* wanted to be.

"So you're not moving away from me?" Macy asked, her voice soft and breathless.

He could almost laugh at the timing of that question. Lifting his head, he let his gaze tangle with hers. "Are you nuts?"

"Well, Candace said…"

"Candace and Brian have listened to me run my mouth a lot lately. And yes, I've thought about it. But my life is here. *You* are here."

He couldn't get undressed fast enough, couldn't get *her* undressed fast enough. But the moment he slid into her clenching, needy pussy, he dragged out his strokes, unwilling for this to be over too quickly. Making love to her like she'd obviously wanted on their disastrous rendezvous in Fort Worth—he was ready for it now. Macy's sighs and whimpers filled his head, clearing out the chaotic thoughts of the last few weeks, bringing a calm and a rightness he'd never known nor anticipated ever knowing. And when she gently brought his head down and kissed him, her tongue swirling around his in the same perfect rhythm her hips tilted to receive him, shit, he was in heaven.

Something was still different, though. *She* was different. He couldn't pinpoint why; he just trusted the bond they shared enough to know there was something going on in her head despite what was happening with their bodies.

He smeared his lips across her cheek and whispered in her ear. "Are you okay, baby?"

She nodded in her stoic way. But he couldn't let her shut him out right now, not when she was so open and beautiful and vulnerable. Not when it was so obvious in her kiss that she was yearning for something, yearning hard for it.

"If I could give you anything, what would you ask me for?"

"I…don't…"

"You know. Look at me. What would you ask me for?"

Her beautiful eyes opened, her gaze meeting his directly.

The words came, the ones he wanted to hear, and he knew they were true. "Your love."

"Hey, that's easy. Don't you know you already have it? So it's all good. Right?"

The little throaty sound of relief that escaped her as he spoke was the sexiest thing he'd ever heard. Her fingers clenched tighter around the back of his neck, and he dropped his forehead to hers. "I do love you, Macy. I love you." His lips captured hers. "I love you."

"I love you too."

Given the tears that slipped from her eyes then, he wondered if maybe those words had been a burden on her for a long time. He'd been such a fucking idiot. But whatever else happened, those little words would keep him going forever. Whatever else happened, for at least one moment in his life, Macy had loved him. But he would do his damnedest to turn the moment into a lifetime. He smiled down at her. "Well, don't cry about it."

Chapter Twenty-Five

"Are you okay?"

"Why wouldn't I be?"

"Well...you know." Macy watched him as he flipped on the blinker to turn into her parents' driveway. The desire to touch him, squeeze his hand, reassure him in some way, was overwhelming. She rubbed her damp palms on her skirt instead. What was *she* so nervous for? It was just her parents. He was the one under the gun. But...still. Oh God. She hoped this went well. This *had* to go well.

Not because she was eager to please her folks. Not because if they didn't like him, she would have to give him up. Never in a million years. They weren't like that, anyway, despite what stupid Jared might think.

What she wanted—the ridiculously sappy daydream she'd allowed to play in her head over and over the past few weeks— was for them to welcome him in, love him, be as close as possible to the parents he'd lost all those years ago. Her mom had the capacity to mother anyone, really, but her dad, despite his words the other day, might be a harder sale.

"I'm fine. Any last-minute tips for me?" he asked, and she wondered if his barely creeping up the long driveway was just a method to put off the inevitable. "I've never, like, met the parents before."

If he was nervous at all, he really didn't show it. She was more nervous than he was. And the most common thing to say in these situations was probably, *Oh, just be yourself,* but she wasn't sure that was exactly the best advice, at least not for the first meeting. Maybe for, oh, the twenty-seventh or so. *She* loved him the way he was, but...

Giving in, she reached over to put her hand on his. "As far

as my dad, he'll talk your ear off, and all you need to do is give an enthusiastic grunt every now and then. Mom's a little harder. She'll ask a million questions. I already gave her the primer, though."

"Cool. Wow," he added as he steered around a curve and her parents' rambling house came into view. "Nice spread."

"If you keep on going instead of taking the circular, you'll end up at the barn. I'll have to show you later. You can meet my horses."

"As long as—"

"You don't have to get on one, I know," she finished for him, laughing. He pulled into the circular driveway, whistling at the sight of the large fountain in the center of the greenery. Macy tried to imagine seeing all of this for the first time. She'd grown up here, so it was simply home to her, but yes, it was quite beautiful. The yellow jessamine was blooming on the archway leading to the garden, and the Chinese fringe shrubs were an explosion of fuchsia.

"Ready?" she asked as he braked. The front door of the house opened, and her mom stepped out, smiling. She must be too excited to wait.

Here we go.

They might be put off a little at first, but eventually, they *would* love him.

"As I'll ever be. Don't touch the door."

She'd been about to do just that. "Oh, going in for the kill," she kidded.

"I always open your doors, killjoy." He winked at her, and she melted. She'd been doing a lot of that lately. From his touch. From the way he looked at her. As he popped open his door to get out, she grasped his arm, stopping him.

"What is it?"

"I want you to know none of this matters. My parents or what they think...what anyone thinks. You started to ask me about it the other day, and I meant to tell you. I *don't* care. So you don't even have to worry about it." Shit, she was about to say it. And mean it, even. "Just be yourself."

His gorgeous mouth curved at the corners, and he reached up to caress her cheek. "Babe, I don't know any other way to be."

With that, he got out and trotted around to her door. As he opened it, she heard her mother happily exclaim about what a gentleman he was. Macy hid a smirk as she took his offered hand and stood from her seat, tugging down at the hem of her skirt. Gentleman, right. She would make sure to keep a little distance between them at the dinner table, so his wandering hands wouldn't get any bright ideas.

His gaze devoured her just as it had when he first picked her up earlier this evening. Just as it had when he'd backed her straight into her bedroom and toppled her on the bed. And during the rough and wild sex that followed. She'd had to redo her hair and most of her makeup afterward.

Okay. Maybe she'd keep a *lot* of distance between them.

God, she was blushing bright red right in front of her mother, who'd just descended the front steps. Her dad was at her mom's heels now. He wolf-whistled as he spied Seth's car.

"That's a sweet ride you have there, son."

"Thank you, sir."

Leave it to her dad to address the car before any introductions had been made. "Um, Mom, Dad...*Dad*"—she insisted when he couldn't tear his eyes away from the GTO—"this is Seth Warren. Seth, Jennifer and Daryl Rodgers."

Her mom greeted him warmly and even gave him a quick cheek-to-cheek, but her dad was still in muscle-car heaven. "I had a Goat *just like* this when I was sixteen," he said proudly. Macy rolled her eyes, but at least he managed to stick his hand out, even if he didn't actually look at his guest. Seth shook.

"Pleasure to meet you," Seth said.

He might as well not have spoken. "Remember, Jen? I took you on our first date in that car. It could be the same damn one."

"Oh, wow, you're right!"

"Maybe it is the same one," Seth said. "Weirder sh—stuff has happened."

"Wouldn't that be something?" He laughed. "You did all the restoration yourself?"

"That I did." He launched into specs that were like Greek to her, because though her dad had insisted she be able drive older cars, she damn sure didn't know what was going on under the hood of one.

I bet I'll learn, though, hanging out with him. She smiled, watching her dad listen to Seth in rapt attention. He prowled around the GTO like he was considering jumping behind the wheel and speeding off down the driveway.

"Amazing," he proclaimed at last.

Yep. Everything was going to be fine.

"But I do have one more question," Dad said. He waited until the suspense built for a minute. "What the hell happened to your hair, son?"

Oh. No. He. Did. Not.

Seth passed a hand over his head and grinned, unfazed. "I did this deliberately, sir." He gestured at her dad's shiny dome. "What's your excuse?"

Freaking. *Hell.*

Macy's heart dropped. She closed her eyes, waiting for the fallout. One second ticked by. Two. A lifetime. Surely Dad could be civil this one—

Her dad's laughter rang out suddenly, shocking her eyes open as he hugged her to his side and gave her a peck on the temple.

"Finally got yourself a straight shooter, Macy. I like him already."

She blew out her held breath, so full of relief that it shuddered as it left her. He was so going to get it later for giving her that mini heart attack, but for now, she grinned across at the guy who'd given her so much more. Herself.

"I kinda like him too."

About the Author

Cherrie Lynn has been a CPS caseworker and a juvenile probation officer, but now that she has come to her senses, she writes contemporary and paranormal romance on the steamy side. It's much more fun. She's also an unabashed rock music enthusiast, and loves letting her passion for romance and metal collide on the page.

When she's not writing, you can find her reading, listening to music or playing with her favorite gadget of the moment. She's also fond of hitting the road with her husband to catch their favorite bands live.

Cherrie lives in East Texas with said husband and their two kids, all of whom are the source of much merriment, mischief and mayhem. You can find her at http://www.cherrielynn.com, at the various social networking sites, or email her at cherrie@cherrielynn.com. She loves hearing from readers!

Loving him couldn't be worse than losing him... Could it?

Rock Me
© 2010 Cherrie Lynn

Candace Andrews has had enough of pleasing others. In an act of birthday rebellion, she sets out to please herself—by walking into the tattoo parlor owned by her cousin's ex-boyfriend. All she wants is a little ink, and Brian's just the guy to give it to her.

As soon as she submits to his masterful hands, though, the forbidden attraction she's always felt for him resurfaces...and she realizes the devilishly sexy artist could give her so much more.

Sweet, innocent Candace is the last person Brian expected to see again. She's everything he's not, and her family despises him. He doesn't need the hassle, but he needs *her*, and this time no one is taking her away. Not even those who threaten to make his life a living hell.

Backed into a corner, Candace faces the worst kind of choice. Cave in to those who think Brian is a living nightmare...or hold her ground and risk it all for the one man who rocks her world.

Warning: This book contains explicit sex, naughty language, tattoos aplenty, family drama, a hot rock concert...and a bad boy hero who's pierced in all the right places.

Available now in ebook and print from Samhain Publishing.

SAMHAIN
PUBLISHING

It's all about the story...

Romance

HORROR

www.samhainpublishing.com